The Blue River Valley

THE BLUE RIVER VALLEY

James Howerton

iUniverse, Inc.
New York   Bloomington

THE BLUE RIVER VALLEY

Copyright © 2010 by James Howerton

All rights reserved. No part of this book may be used or reproduced by any means, graphic, electronic, or mechanical, including photocopying, recording, taping or by any information storage retrieval system without the written permission of the publisher except in the case of brief quotations embodied in critical articles and reviews.

This is a work of fiction. All of the characters, names, incidents, organizations, and dialogue in this novel are either the products of the author's imagination or are used fictitiously.

iUniverse books may be ordered through booksellers or by contacting:

iUniverse
1663 Liberty Drive
Bloomington, IN 47403
www.iuniverse.com
1-800-Authors (1-800-288-4677)

Because of the dynamic nature of the Internet, any Web addresses or links contained in this book may have changed since publication and may no longer be valid. The views expressed in this work are solely those of the author and do not necessarily reflect the views of the publisher, and the publisher hereby disclaims any responsibility for them.

ISBN: 978-1-4401-8319-5 (sc)
ISBN: 978-1-4401-8317-1 (dj)
ISBN: 978-1-4401-8318-8 (ebk)

Printed in the United States of America

iUniverse rev. date: 2/8/2010

(For Madison Sophia)

"Nothing that is should not be."
--Choe Kwang-su

Prologue....

The craft shot out of the Spaceway and decelerated as it approached the station orbiting Planet Mara.

It was a Directorate ship, very official, and only visible at first as a line of sharp sparkles in the reflected planet-light; Kosan, the Maran diplomat, wondered at its speed in getting here. He frowned out of the transparent plexium dome that floated in black space. His closest friend and colleague, Relomar, was on that ship. The Directorate had sent him, but they gave no reason why. What clues Kosan could piece together told him that it wouldn't be pleasant.

Planet Mara glowed like a green-and-white droplet in the distance, her twin moons just particles of blue. Kosan stared off into the galaxy as possibilities ran through his mind. He had been a diplomat far too long to ignore the warnings of his instincts: something was wrong, but what could it be?

As a senior diplomat, Kosan was himself a member of the Directorate, where secrecy was more than a rule, it was an environment. There was a secret here, of course, and he feared being kept out of it.

They have assembled and conducted a quick meeting without informing me, he thought. Why? And why is Relomar speeding to me afterwards?

The brain on the dome's console suddenly glowed lavender, and the circular console screen indicated the approaching ship.

"Representative Relomar sends you greetings," the brain said. "And asks to meet with you immediately and in private."

"Direct him up here. Seal the dome and block all signals."

Kosan stood at the dome and stared into the vast theatre of stars. He prepared himself for some unpleasant news, and put on his gravest "intimidation face". He was taller than most Marans, and his face was generally grave anyway, two qualities he had used to his advantage many times in the treacherous game of galactic diplomacy.

Why do I now have to use them on my oldest friend?

The floor dilated, and Relomar rose silently into the room, his flowing yellow hair and pale blue robes making him appear for the moment almost phantomlike.

"Kos, old friend," Relomar said. He sounded tired. "It's been too long."

Relomar, a master diplomat, had a face that could not be read, even by Kosan. But he was upset. He didn't try to hide that.

Kosan moved forward and hugged Relomar. "It has been too long."

"Sit down. We need to talk."

Frowning, Kosan sat down, a bluish cloud immediately enfolding him, so that he seemed to be floating on a sparkling mist. He studied his friend and felt a tingle of fear. "Aren't you going to sit down?" he asked.

"No, I don't think so." Relomar cast a worried look out at space, then at his friend. "I'll stand."

"You won't get any advantage standing while I'm sitting," Kosan said. "Surely you can't believe diplomatic tricks will work on me; I'll only be more comfortable than you."

"No tricks. Something terrible is about to happen—to you personally."

"What?"

"The Bhutaran have requested a Paj from the Gathered."

Kosan frowned. "I see." *Against me?* What for? That at least explains why the Directorate chose to excuse me from their emergency meeting. "What are they accusing me of this time?"

"Not you, Kos—your son."

Kosan stared at him. "Against Donis? What kind of madness—"

"There isn't much time," Relomar interrupted. "From the moment we got word from the Gathered we've been scrambling to get this under control. The Bhutaran, in the meantime, are scrambling to destroy Donis."

"Rel…"

"They have requested and been granted a *Death Paj.*"

"What! What is this?"

Obviously Relomar was uncomfortable with whatever it was. He stared into the galaxy beyond the dome. *Kosan truly does not know,* he thought.

"You know where Donis is," he said.

"Yes. He's been doing research on Earth."

"For a good long time. He has been far too long in the field. That was probably why the Bhutaran began watching him."

"The Bhutaran have been watching Donis? Why?"

- 6 -

"To get to you, of course. If they can destroy your son, maybe it will also destroy you. Do I need to tell you how the Bhutaran play the game?"

"How can they destroy Donis?"

Relomar was still reluctant to get to the point, as if the path wasn't quite paved.

"How long since you've seen him?"

"My son?" Kosan frowned. "A long time, I'm sorry to say. He has his research on Earth, and I have my duties here. Now tell me."

"According to the Bhutaran, he has been doing more than research."

"What law are they accusing him of violating?"

"They're accusing him of Hybridism."

Kosan stared at his friend. No diplomatic face could cover his shock. "That isn't possible, not Donis."

"It certainly wouldn't be the first time it has happened."

"Not Donis. You can't believe that, can you? Donis would mate with an animal?"

Relomar looked away. "He has been in the field a long time. These things are known to happen."

Kosan felt repulsion; shame--burning rage. They dare accuse my son Donis of mating with an animal? Few crimes were worse than Hybridism. If proven to be true, it automatically warranted a Death Paj.

"Donis is fascinated with the life forms of Earth," Kosan heard himself saying. "He maybe went a little native…that only makes him a good scientist. But my son would never jeopardize his life by allowing a hybrid--"

"I am afraid that he did exactly that," Relomar cut him off coldly. "The Directorate has investigated, we sent our own people to Earth. They couldn't find Donis, he seems to have tried to make himself vanish—another violation, if you want to add them up—but it appears to be true. It seems your son mated with an Earth woman, and a hybrid was born."

"Ah!" Kosan shuddered in disbelief. He could not imagine his son… ."Not Donis. I can't believe….he would make a monster?"

"Kos…."

He stared over at his friend, who was studying him in that sad judgmental way only an old friend could.

"Why do I say these things?" Kosan admitted to him. He turned his sad gaze to the galaxy beyond the dome. "I don't know my son. I was always busy. I was….in truth, I know nothing of him."

"It's almost certainly true," Relomar said softly.

"Why do you tell me this thing!" Kosan roared out. "Why doesn't the Directorate arrest him, destroy the Earth female and the hybrid, and bring him back for trial?"

"As I said, he's disappeared. Also, of course, there are difficulties involved. The Bhutaran are already searching Earth for them, and they won't bother to arrest him if they find him. They have the right of death in their brown claws. I speak for the Directorate: We tell you this for two reasons. One is noble, the other expedient. We are more than your colleagues, we are your friends, and we want to help you save your son. We also want to finish this before the Bhutaran do. If you can get to Donis first, you can maybe save your son. Politically, I'm saddened to say, it would signal that we can solve our own problems. We have decided that you should handle this, and that you attempt to make it so that it never happened."

"To avoid scandal."

"To avoid giving the Bhutaran a bad scandal, yes; but more important, to save Donis."

"I see…"

Despite the terrible shock, Kosan's mind immediately knew the situation: this is my mess; the Maran Directorate doesn't want to involve itself. They want me to go to Earth, use my Kin-field to find Donis, then…

"Capture my son, destroy all evidence and get him back to Mara before the Bhutaran kill him," he voiced the last of the thought.

Rel frowned and nodded

"Even so," Kosan went on. "The Directorate will impose the Death Paj."

"It is not yet proven that Donis committed any crime beyond breaking contact with his university," Relomar said quietly. "He would have to answer for that, of course. As for the crime of Hybridism—if you can reach him before the Bhutaran do and make it all vanish…"

"I understand." Kosan stared out the dome. "How could he do such a thing? How could he throw away his life like this; how could my son create a monster?"

"Humans are seductive creatures. Donis probably developed a dangerous fascination with one of them. He fell in love with humans, and finally wanted to be one of them; an occupational hazard with many researchers and explorers. He hardly invented the crime."

"How close are the Bhutaran to finding him?"

"We can't say. They have a head start, and they know you can find him with your Kin-Field, so they're scrambling to find him first and of course to kill him. They presented evidence compelling enough to convince the Gathered to issue a Death Paj. It is likely that a hybrid exists on Earth. But if it disappears, likely is not certainty."

"What about the Gathered?"

"You know their policy: What is not known is not known."

Kosan frowned bitterly, and then in rage. "My own son opens the door to attack by doing this unforgivable thing? And the Bhutaran rush right in."

"The time for diplomacy and all the other is over. Go and save your son, no matter his sins; that's all that should matter to you."

Kosan gave his old friend a guilty look. "I once wrote that Diplomacy is neither good nor evil, and that makes it worse than both."

"I read it," Relomar said, looking away.

"Destroy the female who made Donis commit this crime—"

"And most important, destroy the hybrid. That is what truly matters."

"Destroy the hybrid." Kosan frowned at his oldest friend. "Tell the Directorate that I will do what I have to do."

Donis jumped awake and stared across the bed. Cynthia lay sleeping beside him, burrowed under the coarse blanket of the motel bed. Ariel lay in her crib making tiny snores.

Donis slipped out of bed and padded over to the motel window. Something had shocked him from sleep. Kin Field? Is it finally you, Father? I failed you—so kill me. Kill me, as the Bhutaran will. I feel your angry Kin Field. And I feel the Bhutaran close by. And what others are now hunting us to death?

Their room was on the second storey of the Hudson Inn, room 212. He stared out at the moving lights of the interstate and the stationary lights of this civilization, the frantic, oxygen-charged motion of life on this world.

The great *wanting* they have, these people. My people.

He stared at the glittering Earth city, Gainesville, Florida, under the wet black sky.

You knew this paradise could not last, he reminded himself.

His home world, Mara, was a desert land where Marans had learned before any time to shatter rocks and see tools, or die. Earth was a lazy and luscious place composed almost entirely of water. A dream world of things all spinning and soaring and making noises at existence; a garden too rich to worry about evolving quickly.

Few lives had ever grown on Mara—as against this world, where trillions of crazy things had sprouted and crawled over the face of time, all of them grabbing at abundance: warm water worlds like Earth had evolved slowly—sensuous and dreaming, not needing or wanting to squirm up out of animalhood…a long ago quote from a Maran professor?

Animalhood.

- 9 -

You went back, he accused himself. You went back to animalhood.

There, he felt it again, the electric scamper. Father, you're using your Kin-Field to find me. They know; the Directorate, the Bhutaran Council, the Ty-Cees, the Gathered. All of them must know by now, this soon.

What Donis had dreaded was coming to pass, as he knew it must. But he had wanted more time. He wanted more of what he had found on this child-world: love; the great, terrible drug the humans called love. He looked at the human girl, Cynthia, sleeping on the motel bed. He looked at their baby Ariel, asleep in her crib. I only wanted more time...

What will happen now, Father?

He stared out at the dank Florida night. Everything came to him suddenly in a nightmare, what he had done with Cynthia, how he had gone love-mad and thrown lives away making a wrong life. And what was out there to punish the crime.

The all seeing gods.

He looked again behind him at his love, Cynthia, sleeping in the bed; then he looked at his little black-maned baby in her crib. Ariel's green Maran eyes were closed, but they moved in sleep.

Terrifying love. To be only a human and to be no more.

— too much to ask; isn't it, Father?

Yes.

Donis stared back out the window, feeling the Kin-Field in his spine, the blood force trained on him. Family power, the shared Mist, the electricity that leads you to me. The ghost of judgment.

Do you plan to kill me, Father, as the Bhutaran will? No, you'll destroy evidence, take me back to Mara and hold me before the Directorate. And you will trade your shame for my life, as a good father would. Better to die running, to escape as long as possible. I don't want to live if Cyndi and Ariel can't. I will not live beyond their lives; I love them to all our deaths. You understand so much, Father—then understand that.

Suddenly he spied something down there--someone, a figure in the shadows beyond the motel lights. The figure stood so still that he at first wasn't sure—but yes, it was someone. Father?

Or worse.

Terror crept into him as he stared down out of the window. A second figure had joined the other, the two of them just beyond the fringe of the light; squat, waddling shadows that seemed to huff at the humid air.

Bhutaran hunters.

He turned and went to the bed and softly woke Cynthia.

"What?" She sputtered awake, and stared up at him. His face told her there was danger. "Donis—what?"

"We have to leave now," he said, trying to keep his voice from betraying panic. "You get Ariel ready and I'll gather up our things."

Cynthia seemed unable to move for a moment. Donis had explained to her many times that this would happen, must happen, but in the back of her mind she never truly believed it. Then the weeks of moving from place to place; she was certain that no one could track them down. They never used credit cards, they never...

"Cyndi, listen to me! We have to go now!"

"Is it them?" she asked. "The ones—"

"I don't know. It may be my father. For you and Ariel, it doesn't matter."

The look he gave her broke the shock, and she got out of bed and quickly tried to get dressed. Her hands were shaking so that she could barely operate.

"I'll go down the back way and bring the car. You wrap up the baby and meet me down there. Don't go near the window."

Donis slipped quickly out of the room with their backpacks, and Cynthia gathered up the baby. She stared over at the window, the glittering night. She looked at the clock on the motel wall: 3:05 a.m.

What was out there? And how did it find them?

His father?

She had awakened the baby, and she whispered to Ariel to keep her quiet as she slipped down the stairs and exited the back door of the motel, as they had talked about and rehearsed if this should happen. And it could never happen. But now, now...

Donis waited just outside the glass door, the Toyota Celica purring. He quickly got Cyndi and the baby loaded into the car; then drove out of the motel parking lot. They had heard and seen him by now. Now he must put as much distance between them as possible.

Turning onto the Interstate ramp, he glanced behind him at the motel and watched the black SUV wheeling out of the parking lot. He stepped on it, and the Celica raced down onto the Interstate.

Get far enough ahead that I can turn off a ramp before they see me do it. Get out of sight, get off the Interstate.

He watched in the rearview mirror the headlights roaring down the Interstate ramp a half mile or so back there. At this hour, with so few vehicles moving, he would be easy to keep track of.

The baby began crying, and Cyndi took her and held her, murmuring "Oh, Ariel, don't cry. Don't cry little baby. Yeah, yeah, my little baby."

She stared behind at the headlights still a ways behind them. She looked at Donis, the tight worry in his face. She had never really believed it was true, even after all the things he had shown her and told her.

- 11 -

Donis raced the Toyota up past ninety, and finally the headlights of the SUV disappeared from view. He took the opportunity to fish-tail onto an exit ramp and race south. Cresting a hill on this new highway, he slammed on the brakes, shut off the car and the headlights.

He rolled down the window, and dense humid air flowed into the car. They listened to the quiet Interstate. The jungles around them chirped and twittered and whispered in the heavy darkness. A river ran parallel to this highway. Here beyond the city the night was very dark and close.

He stared into the rearview mirror, saw the glaring headlights. His face fell. "It didn't work."

He turned on the car, stepped on the gas, and the Toyota roared south down the highway, the baby squalling again. Cyndi looked behind her at the headlights climbing up over the hill behind them, the big SUV. She held her daughter close and tried to keep her mind from panicking.

A tube of blue neon shot out of the SUV. She screamed, and Donis jerked the wheel of the car. The blue ray grazed the Toyota, and Cyndi felt an intense heat and smelled roasted metal.

"Donis!" She screamed. "What!"

The ground in front of the car burst into flames as the blue light struck it. Cyndi felt her mind going into shock. "What?" she heard her voice ask.

"Melt," he said to her, his voice scared.

She screamed and clutched her baby as Donis spun off the concrete and onto a gravel road that went toward the dark of the river. Cyndi felt a madness coming into her mind, and she heard her own voice speaking from far away: "Don't cry, Ariel. Don't cry, my baby…"

Eric Holmes taught General Science at Lakeview High School in Gainesville. He was 26, a tall preoccupied young man who preferred solitude to company, study to fun. He had done his share of drinking and carousing in his college years, and now, with the responsibilities of a new career and a certain respect from the community he enjoyed being by himself and having the time to study his passion, Astronomy.

What had brought him out to this buggy, humid field near the river, the darkest spot he could find, was a meteor shower; and it had been a good one tonight. He had spotted twelve of them in the last three hours, and the event had fallen conveniently on a Saturday, so he could sleep in tomorrow.

It was a night crawling with bugs and lizards. He could hear hundreds of croaks and cheeps and whirs around him. This place was submerged in life of every imaginable form, a scientist's delight. Some things, however, he was to find were truly not imaginable.

It was four a.m., time to go home to bed. A satisfying night; a meteor shower and no moon, and on a Saturday night no less. Better, really, than slobbering drunk over a bar pick-up in her apartment bedroom. He was proud of himself and content.

Yawning widely, he gathered up his telescope and high-speed camera and loaded up his Honda Civic. He drove out onto the gravel road that crossed the river five miles north of the highway.

Suddenly he saw light ahead, a dancing fire. Driving over the hill, Eric gasped: a car was in the ditch engulfed in flames.

Oh God, a wreck! At this hour. He stared at the blazing car. Another vehicle, a big SUV with blazing spotlights had pulled over to the wreck, and Eric sped his little Civic ahead.

Nobody's going to live through that ball of fire, he thought in horror.

Then in his headlights he saw the figures running toward him. He slammed on the brakes.

At this point in his life, Eric Holmes had made two critical mistakes (he didn't know it, of course), which would spectacularly alter and define his future. His first mistake was being proud and content, wanting to lead a calm and orderly life, to be free to do as he pleased, to study science in peace and solitude.

What he loved about science, you see, was its quiet devotion to study, its wonderful way of drawing you into a life of endless fascination. A life you could get blissfully and safely lost in. Science had promised him a safe and rewarding life...

That was all beside the point now, because his second mistake was, of course, being on this road at this place and time.

He stared at the two figures running toward him. A man and woman, only the woman ran strangely burdened. She was holding a baby.

They stopped before his car, and the man said something to the woman, then he broke away suddenly and sprinted like a madman off the road and into the field. Suddenly out of the darkness came a blinding blue light. It shot out from near the wrecked and burning car. It struck the man, blowing him apart in flames.

Eric stared in disbelief. What! Oh, my God, what! Some terrorist attack...

He saw the dark figures up ahead, where the burning wreck was, where that plasmatic beam had shot out. They moved like strange, dwarf things, not like people. He stared at the woman who came running up to the passenger side of the Civic.

- 13 -

"What…!" He stared at her.

The woman yanked the passenger door open. Her face was white with terror. She laid the baby she was carrying on the passenger seat next to Eric.

"What!" He stared at the swaddling child. "Ma'am—what!"

"Go now!" she yelled at him. "Go now! Get out of here!!!!"

"What! Ma'am—ma'am, get in the car, I'll take you—"

"No!" she said. "You don't understand."

"What was that—"

"Take my baby and go!" she yelled. "Please take my baby. If I survive, I'll come for her."

"What! If you-- No! Ma'am, you're—"

"Drive away now or you'll die," she said.

The woman slammed shut the door and took off running across the field next to the road. The dark forms scrambled up there on the hill, and again a blinding blue ray shot out, striking the woman and blowing her into flaming particles.

Eric Holmes spun the civic around and gunned the engine, the headlights bouncing at the river up ahead.

This is a dream this is a dream this is—my God!

He glanced down at the baby on the passenger seat. He tried to understand what—but this is a dream. This can't be real.

He saw the headlights in the rearview mirror, the big SUV speeding behind him. Oh God Oh God Oh God…those things. That blast of blue energy. This is a sci-fi dream.

Wake up, he told himself. Wake up from this. This is not real. This can't be. What is this?

The baby began crying as the car bounced madly toward the river, the headlights of their pursuers gaining in the rearview mirror. What does the baby in this dream mean? Symbolic—I was never out here watching the sky, this is a dream.

He thought of the man and woman, the blue ray that had blown them to flame. A *fear* dream—I'm being chased. Come on, wake up! WAKE UP!

He saw the river and the bridge ahead; he slowed the car before coming up onto the bridge. At that moment the supernatural blue light burst in his rearview mirror. He begged himself to wake up.

The car exploded around him, flipped eight feet into the air, grazed the bridge railing with raging sparks, then smashed down the river bank, rolling and crashing into the water. He knew he was dreaming now, because he was not part of it, what he saw around him, the roar of the crash, and going round and round in the rolling car, and down the steep river bank. He saw it, but he was not part of it. He seemed to float in a strange opaqueness, a calm equilibrium, as if he and the baby were suspended in a liquid drop of some sort. They seemed to float in *otherness* as the car rolled down, flames bursting out of the engine, and splashed dramatically into the river.

Come on, wake up.

He hadn't felt himself rolling with the car, he hadn't felt the jolt of the explosion. It was as if he were the center of a gyroscope, where all around him the world twisted and turned; yet he floated, some force lightly adjusting him level. Something compelled him to glance down at the baby. It too floated in this liquid dream. When I wake up, I have to remember this one.

Now the car was in the river, and the current swept it down away from the bridge. Eric saw headlights back there, approaching the bridge; then the Honda Civic swept around a bend and now only darkness as the nose of the car dived under the current and the fires hissed out.

Oh, My God—no! This is your death! Wake up! Wake Up!

Eric saw water crawl quickly up the windshield. He felt the car slide under the current. He scooped the baby off the passenger seat. Holding her tight to his chest, he leaned back and kicked open the car door. Water roared in, washing him and the baby into a whirlpool. He pushed out from the passenger door, swam to the window and holding onto the baby, clawed out of the sinking car.

They were free of the car, but the current caught them and swept them away, then they snagged on a tree branch, and suddenly the current dragged them straight under. Eric clutched the baby and tried frantically to swim against the river, but they were under now, and he fought his last breath against it and prepared to die—or wake up.

Then suddenly he was beyond it again, in that droplet, a safe place that merely showed reality as a movie. A dream, a dream. I will remember this. I must wake up, though—I must wake up from this. Wake up now. This is horrifying—how can I know that I'm dreaming while I'm dreaming? But I'm drowning, and I know that I'm drowning. You won't remember anything when you wake up, you won't remember this strange liquid egg you're floating in, with this strange black-haired baby.

Eric felt the membrane moving down the river.

Not an egg, more like a rubbery bubble, and the bubble finally rose, bobbing out of the river. Eric saw the river surging around them, black as oil. He kicked lightly at the fabric of the bubble, and managed to nudge it toward shore. There was the slow-motion warping of time that betrays a dream. As they drifted downstream, he kept kicking at the wall of the invisible rubber until they bumped the riverbank. He reached out, and suddenly the bubble popped. He found himself sloshing in the shallows, trying to drag his feet out of the muddy current. Clutching the baby, he grabbed at a tree root and crawled out of the mud and water. He managed to get them to his feet; then he climbed painfully out of the river and up to the still, buggy night.

His heart kept slugging his ribs—come on, wake up! His breath was so ragged that he had to stop and rest. The baby had started crying again. He laid her on the ground and flopped out on his back, dripping wet, panting; he stared in shock at the night sky. *Wake up!*

A burning car, a man and woman killed like that; a baby. Dark things, not human, moving in the light of the flames. A river. That blistering blue ray that shot out. What does this mean? What are these dream symbols? Am I dreaming? Yes! I'm dreaming—of course, you dumb ass! I know that I'm dreaming!

Why can't I wake up?

He sat up, took a deep breath and looked down at the squalling baby, the little thing drenched and dripping with the river mudge and slosh; an elfin thing, with startling black hair for a baby. Strange green eyes. What does this baby symbolize in this dream?

They were in a field of some sort, alfalfa maybe. Eric stared up at the stars. What does this mean? Why can't I wake up?

The baby was crying at him, her face miserable and scared. It was a terrifying sound, the baby's cries echoing in the dense night. A dream symbol—what does the baby symbolize?

Eric's face was sweating relentlessly; damp river slime trickled down his face and burned his eyes. He wiped his face, slinging away the sweat. Can you sweat in a dream?

Then he glanced up and saw the figure approaching them, a tall shadow walking across the field toward them. He froze in terror. This is not real, not real! Wake up, damn you!

He stared at the man who walked out of the tropical night. Not like the other shadows, the troll things. This was a tall, wizard-looking thing. This dream, this—

The man came up to them. He was dressed like a normal man, but Eric sensed right away that he wasn't. There was the quality of a spirit about him. It was not a good spirit.

The wizard man stared at Eric, his face grim. Then he stared down for a long time at the baby on the ground. Eric couldn't find his voice. A dream, a nightmare, a dream, a nightmare…

The spirit-man looked back at Eric. "Who are you?" he asked.

He stared at the question. "I—there was a car wreck—things—I was out watching the meteor shower, then—this woman put the baby into my car—and these blue rays, they killed the man and the woman, and—

"The man was my son," the spirit said.

- 16 -

Eric stared at him, a terrible image. Not real, not real.

"Why? Why—what—" he tried to blurt out.

"Because of this," the wizard said. He looked down at the baby on the ground.

"What? This baby! My God, this is a dream. This has got to be a dream."

"No, I'm afraid not."

The wizard stared at him for a long time, and Eric felt crawly with fear. He had never been so afraid in his life, not in the deepest nightmares—never.

"Tell me who you are," the wizard said.

"Me—I'm—my name is Eric Holmes. I'm—I'm a science teacher, Lakeview High School—"

"Science teacher," said the wizard.

How absurd telling this to a dream. But dreams *are* absurd, they are lessons in the absurd…why can't I wake up from this?

"Science." The wizard frowned away. Then he looked back down at the baby. A frightening hatred darkened his face. "You are not dreaming, human," the wizard said. "You are just very unlucky."

"I—I don't know, I don't know, I don't know," Eric stammered out. "I was out watching the meteor shower, getting some photos—I don't know, I don't know…a woman put this baby in my car—these blue rays shot out… My car! It's at the bottom of the river. And swimming out of that water—I don't know. I just want to wake up."

"It is owed to you in the last moments of your life, Teacher, to know why you have to die. If the Marans have any religion, it is that you owe something to what you have to kill."

"Have to kill—what? I don't—"

"No, you don't understand, and you can't. This is real, it is not a dream. You have proven yourself to be the unluckiest human."

"What, you want to kill me?" Eric gasped. "Why?"

"Because of this." The wizard looked down at the baby. "Because of what you have seen."

"I—this is a dream—a dream—Oh Lord, Oh God Almighty—this—is—a—dream…"

The strange apparition stared at him for a long time; then let out a weary sigh. "Teacher, you have stubbed your toe not on dream, but reality. This is a tragic night for both of us." The wizard looked at the dark river. "My son is dead, the Bhutaran have killed my son—you, of course, understand nothing of what I say."

"I'm sorry you lost your son," Eric said desperately.

Kosan stared at the human, a science teacher, an Earth human sorry that I lost my son. Was it possible to spare him, to send him out babbling all of this to Earth? No; not even if they considered him a madman. The Bhutaran would use him as evidence. The tragedy must be wiped clean from this planet.

"I'm dreaming—a nightmare—come, wake up, wake up!" Eric muttered at himself.

Kosan ignored him. He stared for a long time at the squalling baby on the ground. He sensed the bluish energy around it.

It can generate Mist, he thought. So it has to be destroyed.

He stared round at the tropical woods surrounding this place, the swamplands of primitive Earth. The Bhutaran were out there, panting at the dense air, but still hunting. They murdered my son, he thought. They killed my son.

"A dream a dream a dream," the human was muttering. "I'm going to wake up—"

"Be quiet, Teacher!" Kosan hissed at him. "Death is out there listening. But no matter for you: you are going to die very soon anyway. I give you this knowledge as the only gift I can give you."

"What? What! Why?"

"Because you are a science teacher, that's why the last gift will be given to you—the gift of terrible knowledge."

The wizard glared down at the baby and again his face twisted in hatred. "And you have to die because of this. My son died because of this."

"What—a baby? This baby?"

"This hybrid," the wizard said. He looked back at Eric. "You are spiritual creatures, you human primates. You have rituals. Perform what rituals you need to, Teacher, in order to prepare for your death. There is little time for you."

Eric stared at him. Some vision, some mythological form. Not real, not real. This is a dream, and I must act my part.

"I'm not going to let you kill this baby," he said. "I'm sorry, that's not going to happen."

Kosan stared at the Human. "What?"

"You're not going to hurt this baby."

"All of this must be destroyed," the form said. "I wish that it were not so."

Eric gave him a horrified stare. "What! Kill this baby! No—what? No! If you have to kill me, then kill me! But leave the baby alone."

"This is a hybrid," Kosan said. He looked at Eric. "Why do you care if this is destroyed?"

"Why do I care!—Jesus, this is a baby! What, are you insane?"

Kosan glared at the human. "I am the father of the father of this thing."

"The—" Eric blinked his eyes at the demon. "You're this baby's grandfather?"

"Yes."

"You're this baby's grandfather, and you want to kill her?"

"Her." Kosan frowned down at the child.

"A female, the woman said 'her'. Your daughter-in-law called it her."

"My what?"

"Daughter-in-law. Your son's wife, the woman those things killed. They killed her—some blue ray—Jesus, why can't I wake up?"

Kosan stared round at the dense woods surrounding this field. He sensed the Bhutaran hunters out there, just beyond this field, slow and suffering in this atmosphere, but waddling toward duty nonetheless.

Why are you hesitating? Why can't you act, and make this thing a blasted spot of nothing? That was your pledge to the Directorate.

But now Donis is dead. My son is dead. Why did he die, my son? Did this planet make him destroy himself, or did I?

Kosan breathed the rich air of this Earth night. Why, Donis?

"I have to wake up from this," Eric Holmes, the science teacher, was muttering. "Wake up, damn you...."

"Teacher, prepare for death," Kosan said, trying to prevail. But his voice had lost all conviction. "This is the only gift..." His voice made a fatal sigh.

"You want to kill your own grand-daughter?" Eric stared at him. "What kind of demon are you?"

"It is a hybrid, a monster." Kosan did not look at it. "It is beyond your imagination, Teacher. Teacher of science; Earth thing. You must prepare for your death, and I will show you how."

Eric stared him down. "I'm not going to let you kill this baby—"

"This is not an Earth baby, science teacher. It could be beyond what anyone can know."

Eric tried to act, but suddenly he was again in that slow-motion droplet, everything bulbous and wavy and unreal. A dream-goo. A dream, that has to be it. And you must remember everything about this dream....

He saw the world as a movie. This evil wizard thing—will murder his own grand-daughter? I—can't—stop—him. Nightmare—nightmare—

Why can't I wake up?

Kosan at last stared down at the hybrid. He displayed his tal, his glittering diamond of death, waving death before the baby, the Maran/Human spawn, the monster his son had left him with—a crime against the galaxy. What my son threw his life away for—this! A spawn, a wrong thing...

He steeled himself to destroy it, and be done with the tragedy; then to erase the human, the science teacher. This is what must be done! He stared down at the hybrid.

Suddenly it performed a terrible act—it cried at him. He stared down at its face and saw Donis there, his son. He stared at the girl baby's crying face, seeing the eyes and mouth of his son, and the long black hair he used to tousle when Donis was a child.

Donis, destroyed by the Bhutaran; Donis dead in the jungles of Earth...

He studied the Maran/Human thing, the black liquid hair and aqua eyes. His heart fell, and he shook his head and stared at the night. He fought the water and the weakness that suddenly came into his eyes.

The Bhutaran...

Eric Holmes was staring at him, the luckless human science teacher unable to comprehend any of this.

Am I now going to become a criminal, like my son?

The Bhutaran. They murdered Donis. Legal, practical, even necessary. But they murdered my son. This terrible monster is all that remains of my son. Why?

Kosan looked away from the science teacher. He heard the baby, the hybrid, crying, the strange infant noise echoing in the night. A line had suddenly been crossed. Kosan, the hard, fatalistic master of Galactic *Realpolitic*, died in a moment. He truly felt his self, his old self, vanish from his body. He crossed the line, as his son had, into crime and shame and destruction.

He hadn't the courage to kill this hybrid that bore so much the face of his son. To exterminate this thing and the human science teacher would be right and proper and compulsory under every law of the galaxy...yet somewhere beyond that it was not right.

I am no longer a Galactic Diplomat, Kosan thought with a heavy sigh. My life is over. He traded faces with the terrified science teacher, Eric Holmes. Now I become a criminal.

He stared down at the baby. He knew that she had Mist around her, that wrong things had been allowed.

As he looked into her green eyes, the baby crinkled up her face and pouted at him and let out a startling bawl. She was squalling at him. The line was passed, it was broken. Now move on, even into madness...

Kosan looked at the teacher. "Gather her up and follow me," he said. "And keep this baby quiet! No, say nothing, Teacher! Be very quiet. Gather up the hybrid and follow me. You might manage to keep your life. You might be lucky after all."

"I don't understand," Eric said.

"No. At this moment, I don't either."

"You're a wizard?" Eric blurted out. "A demon, a spirit, something in my nightmare—this nightmare I'm having?"

"Teacher," Kosan said with a heavy sigh. "I am going to explain something to you, and you must grasp it quickly, or your life will be over. You love the science of Astronomy? You love this galaxy?"

Eric stared at the dream creature. "Yes," he said.

"Then understand, Earth human, that I am about to commit a crime against the very galaxy you love." Kosan stared down at the hybrid. She pouted up at him and went to bawling again. The Mist sparkled faintly about her.

Donis, how could you do this?

"Don't kill this baby," Eric said to the wizard. "Kill me and maybe I'll wake up—but don't kill this baby, this innocent baby."

Kosan stared at the human. "There is little time," he said. "I will tell you what you must do in order to survive. I will tell you what to do in order that this survives. If you do not do what I tell you to, you will both die."

"This is a dream—"

"No, Teacher! This is not a dream! I risk everything for this madness. I see it now, that I will follow my son to a dishonorable death, that I will allow a crime to be committed against the galaxy, the place beyond your dreams. That is what I risk, at this time in this place, Teacher: to commit a terrible crime."

"What am I supposed to do?" Eric whined. "I was out here to observe and film a meteor shower, I got ready to go, and—"

"Teacher, be quiet," Kosan said. "Hunters are out there in the dark, and they are hunting this hybrid. They are hunting you as well, and will kill you in an instant. You can be spared from death only if you do what I tell you to do."

Eric stared at the wizard. "This is a dream," he said, "some extremely weird dream."

"No, it is not." Kosan frowned at the human, the primate stupidity that could not *see* what was real, the human thing that naturally believes reality is the dream and the dream reality. "Get rid of the idea that this is a dream, Teacher, because this is not a dream. You must do what I tell you to do, or you and this will die."

"This baby." Eric looked at the wizard. "Your grand-daughter. Why can't you take your own grand-daughter, your son's daughter—why can't you just take her? Take this baby and I'll be on my way..."

"No, Teacher. This is yours. There is no time to explain what you could not understand. This is no dream. If you want to survive, you must understand that you are not dreaming. There are killers out there hunting this child. We must find a safe place and make a plan. A line has been crossed."

"A line?" Eric said. "What line?"

"When I saw my son in its face," Kosan said at the hybrid. "There are many things now that you will need to understand if you do not want to die. You are a science teacher, and maybe you will understand, at least what you must do."

"What I must do." Eric looked at the wizard.

"Exactly what I tell you to do," Kosan said. "Or you will die. And this child will die."

Eric looked at the baby on the ground. She was sopping wet, and she stared up at him and pouted and squalled at him. This can't be real, he thought. This all—no!

He stared at the baby squalling at him, her strange face and flourescent green eyes...

"I don't know anything about—babies, or raising a baby—"

"Teacher..." Kosan frowned. "Teacher, don't vex me. A line has been crossed, I have crossed a line! I follow my son into crime. You can't understand."

"I'm sorry you lost your son," Eric said.

Kosan looked at the primate. How seductive they are, these warm-world creatures, these Earth humans, and their primitive—

Kill it now! And kill this human who saw!

Love...

He stared down at the hybrid. It looked up at him, its face miserable. It wanted love, it demanded love, the baby face pouting at him. He saw Donis in its strange face, demanding love, squalling out for love--that I never gave to him? Is that why you did this?

To give me this half human thing? This warm-world monster...I failed to be a father, and this is all that my son leaves to me?

Kosan sighed at the hot, humid darkness.

"Do you want to live?" he asked the human.

Eric looked at him. "Yes!"

Kosan studied the dark woods along the river.

"Then we must move quickly. Take your daughter."

Eric looked at the baby. "She's your grand—"

"No!" Kosan snarled. "That is impossible. She is your daughter. From this time on, she is your daughter. And if you do not protect her, Teacher, then she will be destroyed, and so will you."

"I'm dreaming," Eric Holmes said.

"Follow me, Teacher," Kosan said with a grim look at the night. "I will try to make you understand." He gave the human one last ominous look. "Don't expect to wake up from this."

Kosan was summoned before the Maran Directorate, as he knew he would be, but it was a formality more than anything else. These were all Marans, wrinkled colleagues, many of them his oldest friends. They comforted him and mourned the death of his son, and most of them condemned the Bhutaran. Hybridism was a terrible and unnatural crime, of course; it was uncertain what sort of creatures would result if species from different worlds were to procreate, what manner of anomaly or plague might be unleashed upon a planet such as Earth. But remember, it was not Kosan who had been charged with the crime.

He lied to them with practiced skill, in bitter, dramatic cries of outrage, denying every bit of Donis's guilt; and if any member of the Directorate suspected him of lying (they all did), no one made a challenge to his testimony. If there had ever been a Maran/Human child, Kosan had made it disappear, rendered it no longer in existence. That was enough, and if the incident made the Bhutaran howl in protest, so much the better. Enough that the beasts had carried out their Death Paj with the usual and efficient barbarian measures, had destroyed Kosan's son and an Earth female. But at the end of the day, the Bhutaran had no categorical proof that the crime of Hybridism had been committed.

Being Marans, they were gracefully practical creatures, and as anxious as Kosan to put the tragedy behind them.

The Gathered had been a more traumatic ordeal. Following a decent interval to allow him to mourn his son, they summoned Kosan to Planet Phelod (as he knew they would), where he would have to face all the galactic representatives, the Bhutaran included. Relomar accompanied him to the giant brown-and-white planet of forever that made a nearly circular orbit around her pale star. A seasonless world older than any memory.

He stood in the great crystalline amphitheatre and told his lies to the skeptical representatives of the many advanced worlds. They all knew he was lying; they wouldn't have issued a Death Paj if the Bhutaran had not provided compelling evidence against Donis. The crime was true, but Kosan did not have the luxury of admitting that it was true. Not here, not to these beings of such power.

The Bhutaran delegates pounded him with the evidence, and even outright accused him of sneaking to Earth to erase the monster. The Bhutaran delegate Autha stood like a wrinkled hump, his pink eyes addressing the Gathered, his form ridiculous in the extreme. Autha described a dread mooncalf unleashed upon this child-planet, a disease of Maran and Human blood. He painted a chilling picture of the crime. How the Flux could be violently shaken, and disease unleashed.

But Relomar had done much snooping on Kosan's behalf, and had assured him that the Bhutaran had found nothing to successfully prove that a hybrid had ever existed.

In the end the Gathered grew tired of the insignificant affair and shelved it, grateful themselves to be on to other matters. Every creature at the Gathered had made sins go away. Kosan had sped the resolution along by threatening to file charges of murder against the Bhutaran. No one really wanted that. This had dragged on far too long. Kosan had lost his son—leave it so.

Finally, all but the Ministers of Bhutar and Ty-Cee voted the ugly incident over with, and it was the unspoken census that if a "hybrid problem" had at one time existed on Planet Earth, someone had managed to erase it, and all was back to normal.

Kosan left Planet Phelod shaken and depressed. He had escaped their judgment, but he had fooled none of them. Relomar tried to cheer him up by mentioning that every representative at the inquiry would have handled the problem as he had.

"Respect is only given under pressure," he reminded his friend.

Kosan refused to be comforted, because there was a greater crime here than any of them imagined. He had stood before the Gathered and lied successfully—difficult, given the fact that they all knew he was lying. He had spent his credibility in the galactic community in the shoddiest way; he had felt the disrespect and condemnation, and of course sweet malice, pouring down out of the amphitheatre onto him.

And the great crime remains. The baby, the child…

My son is dead, disgraced, and now I've disgraced myself, with lies and hypocrisy and crime. My son is dead, murdered by my enemies. Now I've disgraced myself, wrecked my career…

"Careers can be rebuilt," Relomar assured him. "You did what you had to do, Kos."

"Now I am Kosan the Liar, the Criminal," he said bitterly. "My son is dead, a criminal hunted down in a Death Paj. How could he have—"

"It's over. Mourn your son and move on. Careers can be rebuilt. The Gathered have respect for you. Be grateful that it's over."

But Kosan was hardly that. How could it be over when a greater crime had been committed than any of them would believe, including the Bhutaran? Including me?

"There never was a hybrid," Relomar said quietly. "It never existed."

The tone of his voice caused Kosan to glance over at his friend. Relomar's eyes betrayed nothing, but he had been the one sent down to do the follow-up investigation for the Directorate, to ensure there were no loose ends, no evidence; to double-check, to tidy up, if necessary.

He knows, Kosan thought with a chill. And he did what I failed to do?

"If there were ever such a thing on Earth," he said. "Would it probably be dead by now?"

Relomar shrugged. "That's a strange question."

"Well, I've always thought you strange."

Relomar laughed. "It could not be dead, because it never existed."

"And if you discovered such a thing, during your investigation," Kosan said. "The hybrid and all traces of it would certainly be gone now. That would be your duty, to destroy it."

"I see dread in your eyes, old friend; I see fear."

"To not perform your duty would be to commit a crime!"

"You lost your son. Now you must have a time of peace and healing. The terrible thing is over. Take some time to mourn your son."

"A time for peace and healing; I'm showing weakness, you're saying."

"Maybe. Or strength. Anyway, it's over, and we never need speak of it again."

Kosan looked at him. "It's over? Such a thing as that could never be allowed to live. My son created a monster, a possible catastrophe. No need to be coy, you know that. It is a relief that it's dead. You have to agree."

Relomar smiled. "Don't be afraid, old friend, it is not dead."

"Not dead." Kosan stared at him. "The thing is not dead?"

"Now you have more fear than before, I don't know why. You can't kill something that never existed. You're afraid that it's dead and you're afraid that it's alive. But it never was, so stop worrying."

"Rel, you saw it, I know you did. I've lied to everyone else, now I'm tired of lying. You saw it, why couldn't you destroy it?"

"Maybe I'm as weak as you are, or as strong. Things are never certain."

"It's a crime! Something terrible could be unleashed."

"Or not," Relomar said.

"A monster, a crime: something that could cause terrible—"

"Something that never existed." Relomar gave him a gentle look. "A myth, that's all. A monster that never was."

O N E ...

▼

FIVE YEARS LATER...

"Look, Daddy! Look at me!"

The five year old girl ran bouncing across the lawn and startled her father by doing a perfect front flip, landing on the run and making that fierce impish face of hers. Her five month old Saint Bernard puppy, Woodrow, bounded after her, barking enthusiastically. Cathy bent down to give the big puppy a hug.

Eric Holmes frowned. "That's good, Cathy! That's very good—but, Cathy!"

"Now watch this, Daddy!"

"Cathy, settle down now—Cathy! Come on, that's enough."

He watched her do a series of alarming back handsprings, a bouncing sprite in shorts and pink tennis shoes and a pink Barbie tee shirt. Her chipmunk face was beating red, and her long, liquid black hair whipped and rolled in the wind. Those pale aqua eyes burned with a fierce intensity and intelligence, and he often fought dread when he watched her. But not that she would be hurt; the Mist always protected her.

He was afraid of what she would become. Five years, and he had still not wrapped his mind around this. His very life had become a lesson in manageable insanity. He stared around at the secluded farm, the quiet Nebraska valley, the place where things could be hidden.

"All right, Cathy!" he barked out. "Time to come in and get cleaned up. Grandpa will be here soon. Cathy, listen to me!"

She was giving the puppy another hug and kissing him on the head. "I will, Daddy; just a minute."

She looked no more unique than any other precocious little girl, really. You could detect nothing more than an energetic little elf who reads too

28   The Blue River Valley

much. Anyway, everybody loved Cathy. No one who met her would ever believe she was only half…

Half human, he thought. My God.

He stared at the late afternoon sun as it flashed through the great cottonwood trees that stood beyond the yard; one star among inconceivable trillions.

Eric had always pictured his life teaching at a major university in a progressive and cosmopolitan city, wine and cheese parties with brilliant peers, neon and vibrant urban motion outside his windows. Not the empty and forgotten prairie.

Now he watched Cathy dancing on the lawn, she was singing some hit song and dancing to it, her elvin face pouting out the lyrics, Woodrow howling along with her.

He felt pure love come over him. My daughter, my little girl, what a miracle she is. Cathy. The incredible dream I never woke up from. He shook the strangeness out of his head, a habit by now.

I haven't awakened yet, he reminded himself. And I'm a father.

"Now, Cathy!" he called to her. "Come on, play time's over."

She crinkled her face at him. "One more flip, Daddy!"

"No. No more flips. Young lady, Grandpa is coming today to see you, and you need to get in there and into the bathtub and then put on a clean dress."

"One more flip, Daddy. Please?"

"Cathy, if I let you—no! No more flips! March in there right now, Catherine, and take a bath, then put on your dress. Grandpa's very formal. Come on, let's go."

She pouted at him. "I won't get hurt, Daddy. You know I never get hurt."

"I know you won't….but Cathy—"

"One more flip, Daddy. *Please!*"

"No! Then you'll want one more. Catherine, I'm not going to tell you again!" Eric tried to yell. "Grandpa's coming, and he doesn't like you doing all those flips and showing off."

"He does too!"

"Cathy—Christ! All right! One More Flip—no more! Then you'll get your tail into the house, young lady."

She grinned at him and gave him a spoiled chipmunk giggle. "Now watch me, Daddy!"

Crinkling her face into seriousness, she sprinted across the lawn, launched her rubbery little body into the air, and performed a double somersault, landing magically, bowing at Woodrow and putting on her elf grin.

She was the most beautiful thing he had ever seen: my daughter, my little girl. But she had just done something that probably no 5 year old human girl could do.

He conjured up the grim visage of Kosan, the tall dream-man, the alien being:

(She must not draw attention to herself, Teacher)

Eric heard those cold words in his head.

(She must appear Normal; your lives depend on that)

Normal. He studied her. It worried him that she was other-worldly, that there was too fascinating a quality about her. But who would suspect?

"Okay, that was wonderful, Cathy!" he called to her. "Now let's get ready for Grandpa."

"Grandpa's coming!" she cried. "Isn't that great, Daddy? Grandpa's coming to see me!"

Eric tried a weak smile. "Yes, Cathy, that's—that's good."

T W O ...

▼

Kosan's small craft shot out of the Spaceway and into the atmosphere of Earth. As always, he read the detectors before coordinating his landing.

No one out there had detected his arrival. He had no worries about any Earth sensors, his craft was invisible to them. On this water world, still fuddling and struggling, only the insane believed they were being visited from beyond, studied, evaluated, being experimented on; they still clutched importance and godhood beyond all evidence to the contrary. Maran philosophy suggested that all living organisms have gods and dreams and importance and delusions. Are the gods of microbes less powerful than the gods of gods? Are they the same?

The invisible craft shot down into the center of the North American continent, the region called Nebraska, the great zone of agriculture. Kosan landed near the farmhouse, descended from the ship, then stepped out of the invisibility— now he was a form, a tall imposing Maran in the confining and uncomfortable human clothes, striding across the grass face of Planet Earth.

Why?

He had been tempted to end this madness many times in the past 5 years, to simply destroy the hybrid and the teacher, Eric Holmes; to end this crime and bury it forever.

But now the crime was too late, he was caught in it as Donis had been. He stared around at this world. Be here too long and you will get seduced by its beauty, the fantastic lushness, the dream of life that had so retarded the development of humans, a world that welcomed fantasy and superstition and fierce murderous passions over nonsense, the aching call of the animal that dies in the ocean of evolution. It was too late for justice; Kosan had fallen under the spell, the plump primitive dream of this place. The Flux goes where it will, you can only ride along, there is nothing more.

As he strode up to the farmhouse a curtain fluttered in one of the windows. The door burst open and the hybrid came running out of the house screaming, "Grandpa! Hi, Grandpa! Hi!"

Kosan was startled to see a large brownish puppy follow Cathy out of the house, yipping excitedly and stumbling in her wake. He stared at the baby animal.

Cathy ran up to him grinning widely, and he bent down to hug her, embarrassed and heart-broken at the same time. He petted her long black waterfall of hair.

"Cathy," he said, holding her out before him. "Let me look at you. You are growing." He looked at the yipping puppy that danced around her. "What is this?" he asked.

"This is Woodrow!" Cathy squatted down to hug the puppy. "Daddy got him for my birthday."

"Did he."

"He's a purebred Saint Bunnard."

"Is he."

"Woodrow's quite smart, and he's going to get gigantic, Daddy says, when he grows up." Cathy frowned problematically at the puppy. "He still pees on the floor, though."

"Does he. Woodrow, eh? A dog."

"Of course he's a dog, Grandpa." She grinned at him, and he saw Donis in her face. A face that was plainly both human and Maran; the wispy, ethereal beauty of his own people mixed with the dense, amphibious beauty of a human. Does she appear so different? Is she happy? She seems happy.

"Did you bring me a present, Grandpa?" she said, still grinning at him.

A hybrid, he thought, staring down at her: a crime, an abomination, a disease...the most beautiful thing he had ever seen in his life.

"Of course I did," he said. "I brought you the gyroscope you asked for."

"Wow!" she shrieked. "Grandpa, I told you I wanted one. I know all about equal-bums!"

He smiled. "I believe your word is 'equilibrium'."

"Grandpa, I can do flips!" she said. "Want to see?"

"Flips?"

"Watch me, Grandpa! Now don't get in the way, Woodrow. Watch me, Grandpa!"

32   The Blue River Valley

The teacher, Eric Holmes had appeared on the porch. He stood looking at Kosan with his usual caution and dread, that sick half-smile on his face.

"Watch me, Grandpa! Watch me!"

"Cathy!" Eric Holmes called to her. "Not in your good dress, Honey! Catherine!"

It was too late. Cathy ran into the yard, her little yellow dress fluttering over the pink tennis shoes and white socks and Teenage Mutant Turtles panties, the brown puppy waddling obediently after her.

Kosan watched her perform a series of startling gymnastics, and he frowned. The human was letting her become a show-off, he was raising the child recklessly.

But his face couldn't defeat a smile: "Cathy, that is very good!" he called out.

"Now that's enough, young lady!" Eric Holmes yelled at her. "You put on your dress so you could invite Grandpa to your tea party, remember?"

"We're going to have a tea party, Grandpa," Cathy said. "You and me and all my friends."

Kosan was startled. "Your friends?"

"Don't worry," the teacher said to him. "You'll understand when you meet her *friends*."

Cathy took her grandfather's hand and led the tall Maran diplomat into the backyard, where a folding table had been set up. A toy plastic tea kettle was on the table, and plastic tea cups. Seated at the table were a stuffed animal (a bear, Kosan thought), a plastic replica of an adult earth female, and a strange doll man of wood. Cathy led him by the hand, and they took their seats at the table. The puppy Woodrow waddled all over the yard, sniffing and slobbering, and learning to urinate on leafage.

"This is my tea party, Grandpa," Cathy said very formally. "And these are my friends. This is Mr. Bear, this is Barbie and this is Pinocchio. You guys, this is my grandpa."

Kosan nodded solemnly at the toys. "A pleasure to meet you all," he said in a low diplomatic voice, wondering what Relomar would think about this.

Cathy giggled. "Now that the inductions are over, I shall serve the tea."

"I don't see any tea, Cathy," Kosan said.

"You have to pretend, Grandpa! You have to pretend."

"I see." Kosan looked at the toy bear. "I will pretend: How are you doing today, Sir?" he asked the stuffed animal.

Cathy giggled. "Mr. Bear says he's doing all right. And thank you for asking. Now, how do you like your tea, Grandpa? Mr. Bear likes it strong, and Barbie likes it weak, and Pinocchio likes his in between."

"I'll have my tea in between," Kosan said. "Pinocchio seems trustworthy."

Kosan looked at the doll puppet, a wooden man with no life--but with life.

"No, he's not." Cathy grinned at him. "Everybody knows Pinocchio tells fibs." Cathy frowned at the man of wood.

Kosan took the tea cup with the imaginary tea in it, and pretended to sip. "Excellent!" he said. "Just right! Pinocchio did not fib this time. This is the best tea I have ever tasted!" He toasted the wooden puppet.

Cathy giggled. "I love you, Grandpa!"

He swallowed hard at his throat, his eyes made sudden tears.

(If Relomar should see me like this, the great Ambassador Kosan)...

"I love you too, Cathy," he said, smiling in his heart at these imaginary things. "Now this is a tea party—where are the biscuits?"

Later, when the planet had moved away from its star and the child was asleep with the big puppy in her bed and all was dark, Kosan walked with Eric Holmes into the farm yard. The dog was an unexpected addition, but he knew humans liked to live with dogs; a primitive but touching desire. This puppy Woodrow would maybe save Cathy from being lonely.

Kosan gazed at the wide empty land around them, a farming community, dull and unpopulated, asleep in green.

"You have chosen a good place," he said. "Isolated, normal, almost hidden."

"The human word is *boring*," Eric said. "I can't help but feel we could hide out better in a large city, blend in with the faceless multitudes?"

"No," Kosan said. "She would find too much stimulation in a city. I'm afraid she would draw attention to herself. The fewer humans she comes into contact with the better. Besides, if the Bhutaran are still looking, they will look in the large population centers."

Eric remembered those dark dwarf things that night 5 years ago--and the plasmatic blue beam that had shot out from them, blowing Cathy's parents to ash. It was called Melt, Kosan had explained to him, the blue death beams. Melt. A weapon that shot out something like focused gamma rays. He shuddered for the millionth time and tried to push it from his mind.

"Anyway," Kosan went on. "She seems to behave as a normal human female child. She looks exotic, but not so much, do you think, that any human would suspect?"

34   The Blue River Valley

"No, I don't think so," Eric said.

"She must be a normal human child." Kosan gave him those golden eyes.

"She's a child with a force field around her!"

"In time she will learn to control the Mist. But what is this about the behavior?"

"About a month ago." Eric shuddered at the memory. "You told me to inform you if she began acting strangely. Well, one night I heard Woodrow whining, and I went to check on her and she wasn't in bed. I ran around the house like a maniac looking for her, calling out; then I spotted her out here about where we're standing right now. She was staring up at the stars, and she seemed to be in some sort of a trance. It scared me to death. She didn't seem to be aware of me at all, and when I reached out to touch her I got about a one hundred and ten volt shock. It was like touching a live electrical wire. I saw these silvery crackles coming off her head, and the shock almost knocked my brain away. And Cathy didn't even notice; she just stood there staring up in that trance. There, is that strange enough for you?"

Kosan frowned at the human. He still had not calmed himself to the insolence of this Earth teacher, as if the man didn't know he was a primate speaking to a Maran.

"She was signaling," Kosan said. "All Maran children begin signaling at about her age." He frowned. "This is worrisome, Teacher."

"Signaling," Eric said. "What exactly is that?"

"Cathy is beginning to detect the Flux in the Foam, as we call it. Your term is Space-time."

"Spacetime; as in Einstein? The Spacetime continuum?"

"She is beginning to detect it. And you must leave her alone when she is signaling."

"Signaling to whom?"

"To no one thing. These concepts are beyond your understanding, but as you are her father, you should know as much as I can explain to you. At about the age of five or six, Maran children begin to detect the Foam and the Flux, the folds and particles of matter and energy fields. Humans can detect very little when they gaze into space."

"I see stars and blackness, pretty much," Eric said.

"That is because you've not evolved enough. Humans haven't gone beyond the basic primate senses and abilities. But Cathy is beginning to see the sky much differently than you can. She is seeing a sort of moving terrain."

"A terrain that I can't see."

"Leave her alone when she is signaling." Kosan frowned. "Another power she has to conceal."

"Another power?" Eric asked. "What other powers does she have?"

"I think few five year old human girls could perform those acrobatics. Few five year old girls read—what is your knowledge book again?"

"The Encyclopedia." Eric shrugged. "She's a gifted little girl."

"A gifted little girl who *cannot* draw attention to herself."

"I'm doing the best I can," Eric said. "I don't even know anything about raising a *normal* little girl."

"You spoil her, let her always get her way," Kosan accused. "You encourage her to believe she is special, she's better."

"So do you."

Kosan's eyes flared at the human's tone. He was about to lash out, then caught himself. Truth is truth. His diplomatic instincts told him that he must get used to the arrogance of these creatures.

"With me, it is not the same," he said weakly. "You are her father."

"I was kidnapped into being her father," Eric said. "And not because I was expected to be any good at it."

"You need to rein her in, show some discipline. Punish her if you have to."

"I tried to spank her once." Eric let out a crazed laugh. "It was like spanking water, I never touched her. She looked up at me as if I were crazy."

"The Mist will not allow her to be injured by anything on this planet," Kosan said. "The Mist protects her from danger on Earth, but it is no protection against the Bhutaran, or anything else out there. It is no protection from Melt. She *must not* show her power to this world!"

"Out there."

Eric stared up at the night sky and felt that ice demon that had become his companion these last five years. What is out there—surely beyond the mind. That's pretty certain by now. If you haven't awakened from a dream in five years, you're either in a coma or it's true.

Often Eric thought he was in a coma. If that night in Florida he had wrecked the Honda Civic and hit his head and had fallen into a coma; and this was the long dream part of it. If that was the case, then he never wanted to wake up. He would rather be a skeleton dreaming in a coma than lose his little girl. He would rather be dead than lose Cathy.

"You need to do a better job, Teacher," the Maran said to him.

Eric scowled at the disdainful, superior face.

"I'm tired of being commanded by you," he said. "You've already kidnapped my life. I can't get married, you command. I have to live out in the windblown middle of nowhere—you command! I can't have close friends, I can't date women; I can't have any social life. I'm to keep myself and Cathy isolated on a farm--"

"Teacher, I would tone down the insolence if I were you," Kosan said. "I don't appreciate it. You should be grateful that you are alive, and that you can have a daughter like Cathy. I am grateful that I have found something on this world and in that child that has changed me, and allowed me to understand what my son gave his life for. Beyond that, it is a matter of holding what we have, because it might be gone in an instant." Kosan's golden eyes burned into him like the sun.

Eric let out an exasperated sigh. "I don't know what I can do. Everybody who sees Cathy thinks she's adorable. Everybody loves her; nobody's going to think there's anything wrong with her. Folks wonder why I don't start letting her do things, join things, the Bluebirds—"

"Bluebirds?"

"Never mind," Eric said. "I'm doing my best with this—arrangement. But there are things that really scare me. She's beginning to experiment; she's beginning to realize that she has powers no one else has. She was out there today doing double back flips. Cathy swan-dives out of trees when she thinks I'm not watching, because she knows she can't get hurt. She's playing with her power, like she does with Woodrow and her toys. She Knows! She is aware that nothing can hurt her."

"She would be wrong about that," Kosan said.

"What other powers are you going to *command* that I try to cover up?"

Kosan frowned at his tone. "No one can be sure. That is why beings like Cathy have never been allowed to exist. If she is detected and discovered by any of the advanced worlds, they will eradicate her immediately, without hesitation, and no one on this planet will know; a necessary precaution to avoid any possible contagion."

"Like killing a virus," Eric said.

"Yes, Teacher! Like killing a virus."

"And we're supposed to be the primitive ones."

"She must not be detected," Kosan said. "Beyond all your self-pity and incompetence, only one thing is important: If you want to go on living, and if you want Cathy to go on living, then she must not be detected. No one—not even Cathy—can discover what she is. How can I put it to you more simply?"

"I can't keep forcing her to pretend to be average; she'll wind up hating me and resenting me. She's already starting to! She's already starting to demand why I won't let her do all those—super-human things."

"I cannot present reality to you in any starker terms, Teacher," Kosan said. "You may bemoan your fate and your task all you want, but only one thing is important, that you keep the child from being detected."

"Why not just end it then?" Eric asked. "I'm sure you could do it in a heart beat; clean and painless."

"What?"

"Isn't that what the superior space-beings demand? Isn't that the Galactic Law? If Cathy is so dangerous and criminal, then why not just get rid of her—eradicate her, I think that was the term you used before. Why take the chance?"

The question was fair, and that irritated Kosan. "I don't have to explain my motives to you, Teacher," he said. "You have been given your life when it should have been gone, you have been given a daughter, you have been given knowledge that no other human has ever been given, you have learned secrets you were never supposed to learn—you of all Earth primates!--and yet you still complain and cry at reality. Like all humans, you never seem to see what you have been given."

Eric stared at him. "At some point, Cathy is going to have to know the truth."

"No. That would be too dangerous."

"If she doesn't learn the truth," Eric said. "Then one day she's going to go her own way and I won't be able to stop her. That's the way human children work. And in Cathy's case, you can multiply that by at least a hundred."

"She must not know the truth," Kosan said. "How much more simple can it be?"

"For such Advanced Beings," Eric said. "You Marans seem awfully loose with the truth."

Kosan smiled in spite of himself. "I'm afraid, Teacher, that you know nothing of the truth. The primate brain does not, and probably never will, stretch to the truth."

"Well, the truth is getting pretty dicey. You saw her doing those acrobatics. You've sat there and listened to her recite the encyclopedia."

"I know that she is growing out of your control, Teacher. She is growing out of control because you are *letting* her. You're spoiling her, encouraging her to show off. Every time she shows off you reward her with praise."

"And so do you," Eric said.

"Your own human pride is to blame." Kosan frowned at him. "Cathy shows off for you and you hug her and tell her how proud of her you are. Proud! Proud! Don't you see, Teacher, that pride is the most dangerous mistake? No, you are human, you can't see that. You're nurturing her pride, and all because it nurtures your own human pride."

"I'm doing my best. But you're keeping secrets not only from Cathy, but me—the dumb primate."

"Secrets?"

"Why didn't you tell me about her uncle?"

Kosan stared at him in shock. "Her—what?"

"Uncle Rel? I hope to hell you know him, because he's supposed to be your brother; and he's a Maran like you."

Kosan stared at him in disbelief. "Relomar has...."

"He showed up one day and scared the hell out of me. Since then, he's come to visit a couple more times. I figure he's not going to *eradicate* us, because he hasn't yet. And forgive me for being insolent, but he's a hell of a lot more laid back than you are."

"Relomar." Kosan stared into the darkness, the dark valley of Earth. "Relomar has visited Cathy?"

"Your brother Rel; you didn't know?"

Kosan swallowed the fact. "Well, surely Relomar is strict with her."

"No. He spoils her worse than I do. He gets on the ground and wrestles with her!"

Kosan frowned in amazement.

The Human, Eric Holmes, was studying him. "Is that a problem?" he asked. "Surely you knew her Uncle Relomar had come to visit."

"Of course I did. But that is not the problem. The problem is that Cathy is being spoiled. She wants to draw attention to herself, and she will develop powers that ensure that. Attention is the most dangerous enemy of all. And Cathy seeks that most of all."

"What can I do now?"

"I don't know. When I saw her as a newborn and knew she could generate Mist, I should have ended all of this. I made the fatal mistake of looking into her eyes."

"It was a mistake that you couldn't bring yourself to murder your own grand-daughter. And we're primitive."

"The laws against Hybridism are necessary in order to avoid contagion. They have been in effect long before you stubbed your toes falling out of the trees. Cathy is a beautiful little girl, in love with life and in love with herself and full of excitement. But she is also a creature who was never meant to be."

"Those dark things out there, the Bhutaran," Eric said. "Kosan, I have nightmares about them. Every damn night for the last five years I have had nightmares about the blue rays and your son and his wife getting blown to pieces."

Kosan frowned. "The Bhutaran believe Cathy was destroyed five years ago. The Bhutaran are on to other schemes. They have bigger and more dangerous games to play. No one is searching for you, and no one suspects you."

(Except *Uncle* Rel)

Kosan gazed round at the squirming, intoxicating night of Earth. The atmosphere never quiet, never still, always moving; this air a melted thing to his intricate senses, a membranous substance that bred such a multitude of insects and mammals and amphibians. Even here, in the dry prairie, he sensed life swarming all around him. This farmhouse Eric Holmes had purchased lay in a river valley. Pregnant farmlands folded away into the distance. The nearest other humans were over a mile away down a long forgotten dirt road. The teacher had done well, actually. Cathy had a puppy to keep her company. Eric Holmes had secured a respectable job teaching Physics at a small college near the largest town in the area, Mars City. Cathy was due to start her education in the autumn, at a tiny one-room schoolhouse in the nearby village of Chamberton.

That prospect, of course, was worrisome.

"I've researched human education to some extent," Kosan said. "It is legal to teach your child at home."

"No." Eric frowned. "I knew you would come up with that, and I don't think that would be a good idea."

"You are already a qualified teacher."

"We can't keep her away from other people, other children. She needs companionship. She's getting to the age where she needs friends and schoolmates."

"The instructor of her class will notice that she is different."

"Gifted maybe," Eric said. "But I can't keep her stuffed away by herself. Human children need friends. She's been asking me why she can't have a real live friend like the kids on t.v."

"She has a baby dog." Kosan frowned. He lowered his voice to a vicious whisper: "We don't know what she will become, Teacher."

Eric stared at the night, at the terror that had touched his shoulder years ago.

"It would probably attract more attention keeping her *out* of school and away from people." Eric stared at the night. It had broken his heart when she asked him why she couldn't have a friend. "I don't want her to grow up lonely," he said to the night.

"Things become complicated," Kosan said. "Dangerous."

"I'll coach her, make her understand how important it is that she not act unusual, that she not do things other kids can't do. Your brother tells me I worry too much."

"My brother?"

"Relomar."

(Relomar. Why did you--?)

40   The Blue River Valley

"Her teacher will know," Kosan said. "The Earth children will know."

"They won't. I'll let her kindergarten teacher know that she's gifted, and what to expect. She'll be just another little girl. I'll make her understand how important that is."

"She will be just another girl for now, maybe."

"I'll teach her not to be different; I'll make her stop playing with her powers. But I can't let her stay lonely," Eric said.

Kosan stared into the murky night. Less than a mile away was a river, the Blue River. He could smell the rich odor of it. Insects blinked tiny lights in the trees and bushes—lightning bugs, the teacher called them.

Kosan tried to imagine Relomar down on the ground wrestling with the hybrid. Did I draw you into crime and danger, Rel, or did she?

Loneliness covered this land, Nebraska. This is good, or is it? I don't want her to grow up lonely.

"What powers is she going to have?" Eric finally asked.

Kosan studied him. How fond you grow of even the most irritating humans. How you fall strangely and gratefully under their spell, and under the spell of this green-smelling land. I understand, Donis. I understand, Rel.

"Nothing is certain," he quoted his friend.

T H R E E ...

▼

TEN YEARS LATER....

Sherwood North sat in American History class and stared at the back of her head, at the long black hair that made oil rainbows under the fluorescent lights. Outside the classroom Mars City droned about its slow farmy day. Mr. Miller's voice murmured his lecture about the great revolutionary war general that may have saved the new nation at the Battle of Saratoga, Benedict Arnold. A bitter poet, Sherwood appreciated the irony.

Cathy Holmes's hair was mint-scented, perfectly straight and black, with bangs that framed her face. He glanced around, angry at himself, in order to see her face, the fascinating witchling that had ruined his mind the instant he had ever laid eyes on her.

Then he took a deep breath and lay back against his school desk and tried to ignore her, the self-absorbed, phony...

Benedict Arnold's crimes echoed dramatically in the classroom. Sherwood waited for her to maybe tilt her head backward, so that the black hair would spill across his desk; and to look at him upside down out of those pale aqua eyes. One of her many weird games, and she would always say something snotty and sarcastic at him, knowing he was gritting his teeth in love. And who on God's planet wasn't in love with her?

Sometimes she would flip her hair back on his desk, often she ignored him completely.

Sherwood tapped his pen on the desk, despising his own weakness—trying to get the attention of the most thoroughly stuck-up, wicked girl in their sophomore class. Cathy Holmes, the beloved super-girl of Mars High.

He had confided this lack of control to the only one who could maybe understand, Choe Kwang-su, his martial arts instructor, who had taught him

42 The Blue River Valley

every lesson in control and perspective: to esteem modesty and humility above all else. Cathy Holmes had neither modesty nor any other good qualities, unless you counted a savage intelligence, which she would probably wind up wasting…

"Choe, why would such a phony as her make me lose control?" he had asked his teacher. "Why would I care about someone so phony and self-centered?"

"Love?" Choe guessed. He had shrugged at Sherwood. "You say this girl is everything you despise and nothing you respect. Maybe that is what attracts you."

Not the most hopeful answer. Now here he was, staring at the back of her head, tapping the pen on his desk…when suddenly she startled him by hissing behind her,

"Stop doing that!"

"Wha--?"

"Quit tapping your pen like that, it's irritating."

He took a careful breath. The witch! She's talking to me.

"Good," he said. "It makes my day that you're irritated." He stopped tapping the pen. "How surprising; Miss Holmes finds something that irritates her. What else is new?"

"You're very irritating, Sherwood."

"Good, I'm glad. I'm glad you're irritated, Miss—"

"Stop calling me that! You need to grow up."

He laughed. "Oh that's good—Cathy Holmes telling me to grow up. Good punch line."

Cathy Holmes went silent, and now Sherwood was dismissed. She sat toying with her black mane of hair, self-absorbed, precisely as a clueless Valley Girl would do.

Sherwood chewed at the anger, enraged at himself for not being able to simply ignore her, for wanting her attention, for letting her torment him. The thought came to him as always, in a wash of anger and despair: you would never stand a chance with her anyway, never in a thousand years.

Cathy Holmes, only 15; already wearing the senior quarterback's ring like a trophy. The girlfriend of the great Kyle Kuzma. The only sophomore chick in the history of Mars High to be voted onto the First String Cheerleader Squad. Fifteen, and a star cheerleader who performed Olympics-level flips and spins.

Let's have some music!

Fifteen and already a high school goddess; the smartest, the cutest, the best at everything, the center of the universe. The polar opposite of everything Sherwood wanted in a girl.

A wicked little witch who flirts just to be mean, for no other reason.

"You know," he said to the back of her head. "I wish you'd quit twirling your hair like that, it's very irritating."

It worked. Her head flopped back, the black hair washed suddenly across his desk in an oil spill, and he found himself looking into her beautiful upside down face. The black hair fell shimmering onto his desk, and he reached out to touch it.

Not even beautiful, not in any classical sense, damn it. Cute, no more than that; adorably cute, maybe, but not beautiful.

She liked doing this, the head flop in the middle of class, the upside-down stare, knowing it startled him and then tortured him.

She gave him a study with those cat-green eyes, as if he were some annoying child. He sensed the malice in her upside-down face; that she knew full well what she was doing to him, and that it somewhat eased her boredom.

His eyes crawled weakly down to the cleavage in her sweater, tiny young breasts that Cathy tried to enlarge with a push-up bra.

Shallow, phony, self-absorbed, arrogant—hateful; he rattled off every outrage in his mind. Not even a good body; an elf body, all muscle and bone. Kyle Kuzma the great senior quarterback would get bored with that, look for bigger boobs, a rounder…

He offered her a bitter smile. "Hello," he said at her.

She gave him that upside down grin. "Hi, Creep. Sherwood Von Creepaloid."

"Clueless Cathy," he said back at her. "We're both sounding mature, aren't we?"

She sniffed. "I can do things you can't imagine."

"So can I," Sherwood said. "The only difference is I don't wallow in it."

"What? Shut up, I don't wallow." Cathy Holmes raised her head and the soft black hair drifted off his desk. Her cleavage disappeared from sight as she sat up; he felt an aching despair.

"You need to grow up and stop acting like a soph," her voice said behind her.

"I am a soph. So are you."

"At least I don't act like one."

"No, you act like a phony celebrity wannabe."

Some strands of her black hair still moved on his desk. His hand reached out and touched the hair. He felt the hopeless, stupid love boiling inside him.

Now, shut up, he said to himself. Control, that is the order—say nothing to her—ignore her, that's the one thing she can't stand. Dismiss her as she

44   The Blue River Valley

does you. How to beat a snot like Cathy Holmes? Ignore the crap out of her. Control your passion; that is the key, Choe Kwang-su had taught him: the terrible passion to want to use your power. Control it, or it will control you. Control madness or it will control you.

She sat playing with her black hair, those green eyes mildly bored. He stared at the back of her hair, a bitter smile on his face.

Stupid falling in love with someone you don't have a snowball's chance with. Who would make your life utter hell even if you did—and you couldn't, because she's already hobnobbing with the senior high school royalty, the beautiful little sister to all the other cheerleaders, the little *wunderkind* sophomore who had caught the great Kyle Kuzma, the god of quarterbacks. What the hell is she going to be when she's a senior, queen of the world?

Little did she know that they secretly hated her, those glittering senior babes who let her hang out with them, sit with them at lunch. She was vastly smarter than them, more athletic, younger, by far more captivating. She had effortlessly performed the catch of the day, Kyle Kuzma, who would get a scholarship to play at some--college. Cathy Holmes, not even 16 yet, and going steady with the guy they all coveted, the quarterback god. First string cheerleader at the age of 15, a sophomore. The girl who flipped and spun and performed miracles of cheerleading and took all attention away from them. How they must despise her. She deserves every bit of it.

When the big handsome senior graduates, he thought at the back of her head. He's going to go away and forget all about you. You'll have to give back that big gold ring, boo hoo. Then you'll find another star pretty-boy athlete and we'll be juniors, and none of it matters, because I don't stand a snowball's…

Hey, you call me a creep, he thought at the back of her head. But I'm better than you, and you know it. You know it because you're wickedly intelligent. That's what ticks me off. You're smart enough to know better, and you hang out with phony idiots and go steady with a clod-headed football player that your dog doesn't even like. You don't see Woodrow barking at me—you know better. Your dad's a physics professor and you're in the Astronomy Club! That's why I can't—get you…

His stomach cramped in frustration. What are you doing? She doesn't give a rat's backside if you get her or not. She's going to tug at her hair and stare into space and ignore your existence. But you know, Cathy—you know I'm better than those phony a-holes. If you don't like me, that's good; because I might love you, but I damn sure don't like you.

"Phony," he muttered at his desk.

A long pause; God help him, he glanced around at her.

"What did you say?"

Her voice; she was aware again that he existed. Her eyes looked slightly back, bland, milky turquoise. It disgusted him, how grateful he was for her voice.

"I said a word. I was talking to myself."

"What word?"

He smiled. His scheme worked; ignoring her was the perfect weapon. Ignore her and she will cave. A snotty, stuck-up cheerleader cannot stand to be ignored.

"I said the word phony." He smiled at the back of her head.

It worked. To his shameful, aching gratitude, Cathy Holmes flopped her head back and the black hair splashed once again onto his desk. His mind uttered a dismal prayer of thanks. He stared into her upside down elf face, the green penetrating eyes. He was hopelessly and fatally in love with this girl.

Why?

He was handsome, in a sort of intense, beat-poet way. Plenty of good looking girls wanted to go out with him. He had never had a problem getting girls to fall in love with him. He was confident around girls, and could have plenty of dates. He wasn't on any of the high school teams; he didn't play basketball or football or any of that. But he was what none of them knew, a master fighter. It always gave him a secret pride that none of them knew his fighting skills—but he wanted this snotty, no-good girl to know what he could do. That's why he couldn't let her know, of course. That would spoil it, make it a worthless game of showing off.

You have no clue, you witch, he thought, smiling at her.

She stared at him out of the neutral upside down eyes. Eyes that denied his pride, poked at the quiet confidence he had managed to build round himself. "You're the phony," she said to him, "pretending to be some outcast Dylan Thomas or something."

"I'm phony," he laughed. "Come on, even a ditz like you couldn't believe that."

"I'm a ditz like you're a cow pie." She made an upside-down grin at him, and it was like a terrible sword thrust into his eyes. "Sherwood…that's a nerdy name."

"My mother was a fan of Sherwood Anderson. The writer?"

"I know who he was," Cathy said. "He wrote Winesburg, Ohio."

"Catherine is a pretty squirrely name," he said. "Sounds like an overweight aunt who never got married."

"My name is normal," her upside down mouth said. "Sherwood North is ultimately a very nerdy name."

"But it's not boring," he said. "Catherine—that's boring."

"What's your middle name, Sherwood—is it Creep?"

"My God, it is! How did you guess?"

"What's your middle name?" her upside down face demanded.

Sherwood's fingers crawled over the desk and touched the magic hair. His brain cringed. He was so in love with this girl that he hated himself for it.

"It *is* Creep—it really is," he said. "You got it right the first time; must be because you're smarter than everybody else."

"I'm smarter than you." She smiled at him, and he fell deeper into it. Circe, the being who captures you, smiles at your weakness, tortures you, and then lets you die; that heart-breaking upside down smile. She irritates you with those weary aqua eyes and suddenly she makes a cruel smile at you, knowing what it does.

"What's your middle name, Cathy?"

"I'm not ashamed to tell it. Ann."

He laughed. "Ann, that's good. Catherine Ann. Now the spinster aunt has warts."

"Sherwood North is by far the stupidest name—"

"Miss Holmes!" Mr. Miller's voice suddenly echoed out. The grinning moment was gone.

The black waterfall of hair swept off his desk; her face, her tiny breasts, folded up and away. Sherwood stared at the teacher, then around the classroom. Everybody was looking at them.

"Sir?" Cathy was suddenly all innocence.

"Miss Holmes," Mr. Miller said. "Can you tell me what I just said about Benedict Arnold, or were you too busy talking to Mr. North?"

"Yes, I can, Mr. Miller."

"What did I just say?"

"You just said that General Arnold's anger at congress—not his infatuation with Peggy Shippen, a Loyalist—was what pushed him into becoming a traitor."

Mr. Miller's face reddened. Laughter rippled over the classroom.

"Very good, Miss Holmes, as usual; you can obviously chat with Mr. North and listen at the same time. Mr. North?"

"Yes?"

"Why was General Arnold angry at the United States Congress?"

"I blame it all on Peggy Shippen," Sherwood said.

The class laughed, even Mr. Miller laughed. Cathy Holmes laughed. It was like sweet poison.

She laughed.

And if I were foolish enough to tell her that I love her she would stab that laugh straight into my soul. This damn fairy girl who gets off on—hey, Cathy, he thought at the back of her head. You hate your cheerleader friends too—just as they hate you.

"Please save your personal conversations for later," Mr. Miller said to the both of them.

The class tittered, and Sherwood saw her face turn red. He looked around at his classmates. Now he was going to have to deal with a pissed-off Kyle Kuzma, when word got out.

She talked to me, pal, I didn't talk to her.

She tilted back her head, studmeister, and your girlfriend's black hair did spill over my desk. Twice she tilted her head back onto my desk. She was flirting with me and I was minding my own business. She's your girlfriend, Bluto, not mine. And good luck with that.

Now it was gone, and he felt a terrible emptiness. He thought of Meteor Night, two weeks away, the night when the Astronomy Club met at Cathy Holmes's house and Dr. Holmes set up his telescopes and cameras. The wonderful nerd party at Dr. Holmes's farm. How it felt to be in the dark and almost camping out with Cathy.

How he ached for those nights, when it felt like he was…what?

Nothing. Waiting for meteorites while Cathy was berating him—or worse—ignoring him.

My God, Choe, he thought. You prepared me for life; you taught me how to live. How could you not have taught me this?

This poison and misery.

FOUR ...

Eric Holmes tapped lightly at her bedroom door.

"Come in, Daddy," she called.

Entering Cathy's room was entering a very crammed and stunning personal museum, the largest room in the house next to the living room. One corner occupied her collection of stuffed dinosaurs, another her library of books of every imaginable sort, still another the myriad academic and executive toys her grandfather and uncle always had to give her, a microscope, an ant farm, one of those frames of hanging stainless steel balls that demonstrate energy transfer, all manner of science kits, nautical instruments, gyroscopes, Rubik's cubes, and robotic--things. An advanced chemistry kit, globes of the earth and all the planets, a mini recording studio, a rack of CDs that represented an almost schizophrenic range of music. Suspended from the ceiling by wires were model airplanes and helicopters and rocket ships. Her walls held not a single movie star; every square inch of them was dedicated to maps and charts of every kind: charts of dog breeds, cat breeds, horses, automobiles, guitars, ancient ruins, tractors and farming machines, a table of the elements; posters of music, charts of insects and lizards and even firearms. It always gave Eric a jolt seeing her Hubble posters of galaxies and pulsars and nebulae, and knowing it was more than any madman could believe.

An expensive computer and all the technological trimmings (compliments of Grandpa Kosan), stood next to her guitar and keyboards, violin, saxophone and microphone. She seemed to have a fascination with everything, and he should be proud. Shouldn't a dad be proud of a genius daughter? It had been more than fifteen years, and he had earned the right to be proud of her.

So why always dread entering her room, her Maran/Human domain?

He traded stares with a sad-eyed Woodrow, all 170 pounds of him, who lay like a continent next to Cathy on her bed. The giant Saint Bernard thumped his tail lazily.

Cathy was stretched out in bed writing in her diary. She wore her flannel Albert Einstein pajamas, and he frowned worriedly at the distortion of Einstein's face, where a warping of the space-time continuum indicated that his daughter was developing noticeable breasts. My God, he thought, she's only 15.

Woodrow crawled off the bed and lumbered his heavy frame over to Eric. He bent over to scratch the dog's back and rub his face.

"Hi, Daddy," Cathy said, looking up from her tight, precise handwriting. "What's up?"

"Not much. Are you looking forward to Meteor Night?"

Her nose crinkled. "I guess. It's supposed to be a good shower."

For ten years Eric had hosted an Astronomy Club that had grown close to twenty students. On Meteor Night, a night of an exceptionally good shower or some other event in the heavens, he invited all the members out to his farm where it was very dark and they could see and film falling stars; kind of a nerd party, with pop and pizza and nachos and wings and microwave popcorn. Most of the members were his students, some of whom would become astronomers. Professor Kellogg usually showed up, always drunk. Eric's colleague at Midland College and the closest thing he had to a friend... until—maybe-- now...

Cathy closed up her diary and focused her sharp green eyes at him. "I invited Kyle, but he said he wouldn't come unless we had beer."

Eric frowned at her. "I don't like that kind of an attitude."

"Oh, he was just kidding, Daddy."

"Well, if I find out he's been getting you to drink beer, young lady, I'm going to the police. He's a senior, Cathy, and I don't think it's a good idea for you to get all ga-ga over him."

"I'm not doing anything wrong with him, Daddy, if that's what you're trying to say."

He stared at her in horror. "I'm trying to say, that if you *do*, Catherine, I will tear that boy's throat from his body!"

"Daddy, he's a star athlete, he's the first-string quarterback."

"Then I'll use a chainsaw. You're only fifteen, Cathy!"

She gave him a poutful look, her face framed in that startling long black hair. "I'll be sixteen in 6 months."

"And he'll have graduated and"—(thank God)—"be gone. You're not at an age yet when you should be going ga-ga over some older boy. I know what boys his age want."

50   The Blue River Valley

He tried to ignore the distorted picture of Einstein that indicated her imminent womanhood.

Her eyes narrowed in suspicion. "Why do I think that's not what you want to talk to me about?"

"No, it's not. But it's nothing, really." He avoided her eyes. "I suppose I should tell you, Cathy, that I invited your English teacher to Meteor Night."

Cathy gave him a flabbergasted look. "Miss Mason? You invited Miss Mason over here."

"Yes." He put on a defensive face. "Why are you looking at me like that?"

"Daddy, she's one of my teachers."

"I know that. So?"

"So it's bad enough that Sherwood North has to come over—but my English teacher?"

"Sherwood's going to be an excellent science teacher one day, or a writer maybe," Eric said. "If you have to have a boyfriend, he'd be a better choice than the senior."

"Brruuuggghhh!" Cathy pretended to vomit all over her bed.

"He's a member of the Astronomy Club," Eric said. "He makes that fantastic salsa dip—I'm not going to exclude him just because you don't like him."

"He thinks he's smarter than everybody else. Mr. Sarcastic, wry poet. He's an intellectual show off."

"I see." Eric had to bite his tongue. "Well, I like him, even if you don't. It couldn't hurt you to date a boy with brains, could it?"

"His attitude is going to get his butt kicked," Cathy said. "He's always being sarcastic, and one of these days Kyle is going to stomp all over him."

Eric frowned. "Well, I like the boy; the boy Sherwood."

"But you don't like Kyle."

"I don't even know Kyle. I'm sure he's a nice boy—no, I don't like him."

"Well, he's a varsity athlete. Everybody else likes him."

"I agree to like him if you agree not to, how's that?"

Cathy grinned at him. "You like Miss Mason."

"I don't know her well enough—yes, I like her, why wouldn't I? She's a very nice lady."

"She's pretty—for her age," Cathy said thoughtfully. "A lot of the immature soph boys are in love with her."

"Well, she expressed an interest in Astronomy, and so I thought she might...why are you looking at me like that?"

Cathy was studying him, her face partly disgusted and at the same time darkly amused. "Is this a date or something?"

"Not that it's any of your business, Cathy—no, it's not a date. She has an interest in Astronomy, and—"

"I'll bet," Cathy laughed.

"Hey, I'm not inviting her to a kegger. This is Meteor Night, and anyone who wants to view the meteor shower is welcome to join us."

"She coaches Girls Gymnastics," Cathy mentioned.

"I know she does. And?"

"And maybe if you fall in love with her she'll talk you into letting me join." Cathy let out her chipmunk giggle.

"No. I'm sorry, Catherine, that's a no."

"I don't know why. You never let me do anything."

"You have too much on your plate already," Eric said. "Academics before sports, that's the rule. I let you join that cheerleader squad, which I never should have. I let you go to a movie with that—senior boy."

"His name's Kyle. Kyle Kuzma."

"And he's too old for you. I shouldn't have let you join that cheerleader squad, it all led up to this."

"Oh, big wow, cheerleader squad. Miss Mason said I could probably win state if I joined the gymnastic team."

"Miss Mason should concentrate on teaching English Literature." Eric looked at his daughter, still so strangely elfin, mythological. "What are you smiling at?" he asked her.

"It wouldn't bother me to have Miss Mason as a step-mom. I like her."

"Very funny. She likes you too."

"So where did you meet her, Parent-Teacher Conference?"

"Yes."

"And you like her." Cathy broke out laughing again.

"Yes! She seems like a very nice lady. I don't understand what's so funny about inviting one of your teachers over."

Cathy gave him that adorable elf grin, her pale aqua eyes sparkling. It horrified him that he had entrusted her to some horny senior football player, even though the 'movie date' she had tormented him into letting her go on was in a group of three couples—all of them seniors--to his horror--except her.

He traded stares with Woodrow, who seemed to understand, who thumped his tail sadly on the floor. My God, Eric thought. She's no longer a little pixie, she's a young lady. Where did the years go? She's a young lady, Woodrow.

52   The Blue River Valley

"I talked to her at the teachers' conference," he explained. "And we discussed your progress in class, and she happened to mention that she loves to star gaze—what? Why are you being such a giggle-butt?"

"You and Miss Mason star-gazing together! My dad and my English teacher!"

"Ha ha. She happened to mention, by the way, that you tend to be disruptive in class. You talk a lot when you should be listening."

"Is that why I'm getting an A Plus in her class?"

"Don't get smart. She said you were making fun of Shakespeare."

"Because he was a boring crybaby," Cathy said. "Very over-rated."

"She praised your work," Eric said. "But I read between the lines—you're sometimes being a show off."

"Just because she worships Shakespeare and I made fun of him."

"Sometimes, like I suspect—all the time."

"Well, I like her," Cathy said, derailing the lecture. "You let me go on a date with Kyle, I guess I have to let you go on a date with Miss Mason. You'd better not kiss her and hug her around everybody, though." She started to laugh, but then she read his face.

"Ha ha. That's beside the point." Eric frowned at his daughter. "Miss Mason also happened to mention that at school you wear some kind of class ring? You don't have a class ring, Cathy."

Cathy's eyes got big. Her face crinkled, tried to smile but frowned. The aqua eyes became suddenly evasive.

"So?" she said.

"So—you're wearing that senior football player's ring—aren't you!"

"His name is Kyle! And Kyle asked me to go steady with him. Geez, Daddy, it's nobody's business but mine."

"Wrong," he said. "Like hell, Cathy! No. No no no no no. You give him back that ring."

"We're going steady."

"No—Catherine, you're too young for that kind of thing. You're only 15 years old. And this quarterback is what, 18?"

"Actually he just turned 19."

"Oh great, so he was held back a year," Eric said. "How much worse can this get?"

"It's no big deal," she said, scowling at him. "I love Kyle, and he loves me."

He felt a jolt of fear. It could indeed get worse. He stared into her defiant green eyes. A new kind of terror was invading his life, as if all the monsters with their death rays weren't enough.

. "Cathy," he heard himself saying. "You're too young—"

"I'm not too young."

"You're too young to—"

"Daddy, I'm not too young! We love each other."

"I'm not going to allow this19 year old *Man* to seduce and molest my 15 year old daughter! It's that simple. I'll call the cops, young lady! You are going to give the ring back to—Kyle—and inform him that you're not old enough to go steady with him; your father will not allow it. That is what is going to happen, or I go straight to the police."

"You sound like Grandpa," she said. "Like I can't have my own life."

Like Grandpa. Eric shook his head at that one. "Cathy, you—"

"We're in love," she said. "I'm not telling you to Not invite Miss Mason on a date, am I? You can fall in love with her if you want."

"That's because I'm an adult, and you're not. It's different, Catherine, and you know it. Give him that ring back!"

"I love him! I love him, and he loves me."

"Give that class ring back to him, or you will be quitting the cheerleader squad."

"I love him."

Oh, God, this is a dream, Eric thought. A dream or a coma. It's been fifteen years. What's the record for being in a coma? He was beginning to understand that it was neither a dream nor a coma. If it had all been real, this life so far, then only parts of it seemed unreal.

Cathy is a normal girl, after all, and normal girls have crushes. No, she is far from normal. Oh God, oh God…

He sensed it, all the things about her that terrified him and fascinated him at the same time. Often he found himself guiltily studying her, as a scientist would study a phenomenon, studying the Maran presence. He knew that when she would slip away into the woods behind the house, Woodrow clumping at her side, that she was out there playing with her powers, climbing the eighty-foot cottonwood trees and diving into the air, drunk on the magic of her invincibility. Reveling in powers that no one else had.

How many zillions of things to fear in that impossible distance? We all gaze at the stars and we see beauty and harmony and love and God. We are too awestruck to see the terrible truth. What monsters, what Nazis or Mongol ogres, so far beyond us that we are bacteria? We see God in space, why can't we see the monsters? We see beauty and serenity in the sky, but like the happy rabbit grazing under the shadow of the wolf, we can't see the danger: Things beyond our understanding that hold no concept of mercy or right and wrong; that operate as exterminators merely eliminating bacteria.

And I fear an empty-headed boy who can throw a football.

Well, thank God he'll be gone in the spring, off to play football or work at some mill. Eric looked at his daughter. He could sense the Mist surrounding her. It was perceptible whenever her emotions heated up.

Susan Mason had commented on Cathy's genius. She had alarmed Eric by asking why he didn't allow Cathy more opportunities to show her talents. She had spoken to him in baffled tones, as if he, a college physics professor, wasn't aware of his own daughter's remarkable powers. Beyond all that, Susan Mason was very attractive, with a bright smile and warm attitude... the attraction he felt for her—well, never mind. She was 35, never married... she had long, ash-blond hair, and her eyes were very large and intelligent and fetchingly sad somehow. A very pretty face, and Eric had wondered why she had never been...

Cathy was studying him with her cat-green eyes.

"Why are you giving me that look?" he demanded. He gave back to Cathy as angry a face as he could bring up at the moment. "Give the ring back, Catherine, or you'll have to quit the cheerleader squad. That's my final word."

"What? No!"

"Yes! That's what started all this, that damned show-off cheerleading. That's my final say."

Eric's timing had improved over the years, and before she could throw a mega-fit he turned and marched out of her room. What does an angry, frustrated, fearful Dad do? He marches. That had not gone well, he thought with a frown. If only Woodrow would attack and kill the star quarterback...

He made sure his feet pounded the floor, another father's duty he hoped...

"Night, Daddy!" she called to him.

He stopped in his tracks. His heart ached, and he smiled. Maybe it had.

"Night, Cathy. I love you."

"I love you too."

F I V E ...

▼

Cathy was dressed in her scarlet and white cheerleader outfit, the pleated skirt bouncing excitedly. She reminded Kosan of a dancing flower.

"Finally you're coming to one of our games, Grandpa," she said to him. "And you look like you're going to a funeral."

Kosan smiled at her. "I am looking forward to it."

"Good. You'll get to watch Kyle kick the crap out of the Mulligan Knights."

"Cathy, watch the language," Eric said.

"Kyle," Kosan studied her. "Your...boyfriend."

"He's the coolest guy in school, Grandpa. He's the starting quarterback and he's my boyfriend."

"Yes, I've spoken to your father about this boy." Kosan traded looks with Eric Holmes. "The boy who is going to drive you to the game; the boy you seem to have feelings for."

"We were going steady before Daddy ruined everything for me." She gave her father a dark, rotten look.

"Well, I agree with your father," Kosan said. "If this—quarterback—has feelings for you, then he will understand. You're too young, Cathy, to be..."

She grinned at him, knowing it would curtail the lecture. "I love you, Grandpa."

Kosan swallowed at his throat. "I love you too, Cathy."

"Finally you'll get to watch me cheerlead. This'll be a great night. You're going to have fun."

"Yes, I will," Kosan said. "I plan to."

"And Grandpa expects that you will act like a young lady tonight," Eric said to her. "While you're cheerleading."

Cathy scowled at him. "You sound like I'm still ten years old."

56   The Blue River Valley

"And that you will not show off, and you'll be home by—"

"Daddy," she said. "Grandpa finally gets to see me cheerlead. Please do not spoil it for me."

"--no later than ten."

"I'm not a baby anymore."

On that dire note, a sinister black pickup truck pulled into the drive and beeped its horn. They all looked out the window.

"Oh, that's Kyle," Cathy said. "I gotta go."

Cathy bounded up and raced out of the farm house before Eric could even mutter his anger. Kosan saw her run over and jump into this boy's vehicle, a big gleaming black pickup truck. Kosan took the color black to be an omen. He frowned at the teacher. "This is unacceptable, Teacher. Does she plan to mate with this Earth boy?"

Eric looked at him in horror. "What!! Not on God's green earth," he said. "Not if I have another breath in my body."

Kosan watched the truck tear out of the drive and onto the gravel road. "Why didn't this boy approach the house?"

"Because he knows that I don't like him," Eric said. "And I think he's afraid of Woodrow."

"Then why do you let Cathy drive away with him?"

Eric sighed. "It's not easy to explain. It's probably harder to explain than the Theory of Relativity. The important thing is she will not mate with this boy as long as I'm still breathing; I promise you that."

"You have promised so many things in the past," Kosan said.

The drive to Mars City was uncomfortable, of course: as always, Eric only felt mildly terrorized and never at ease in the presence of the Maran. He could only put the impossibilities out of his mind when he was squeezing scientific information out of him, when they spoke of—impersonal things.

"This is the way human girls grow up," he said. "Miss Mason explained to me that this—phase—that Cathy is in is normal. You want her to act normal."

"This Miss Mason may become problematic," Kosan said, staring out the car window at the Nebraska countryside, fields of yellowing corn and acres of green soybean plants. "She may suspect one day that Cathy is not completely human."

"I doubt that. Girls Cathy's age don't want to be different, and she's always known she's different, and she's been—reasonably good at covering it up." Eric frowned. "It won't be a problem. Anyway, maybe what Cathy really needs is a mother."

Kosan looked at him. "You remember what happened to her, Teacher."

Better get off this subject. "Let's talk Science; it's a hell of a lot easier."

Kosan sighed. "You want answers again. You have questions again. You always want to squeeze things out of me that you shouldn't know."

"Yes."

"All right, what now do you want to know?"

"Okay, since we're making small talk, can you tell me how many light years away Mara is?" Eric asked. "Or am I not allowed that far into the 'Advanced' Club?"

Kosan frowned at the sarcasm. "Light years?" he questioned grumpily.

"How distant is Mara from Earth?"

Kosan looked at him for a moment; then frowned out the car window at the passing landscape, now brown, folded hills and a ragged green valley that held a wide stream. The Nebraskan air was cool and dry and, as always, restless: soft wind blew out of the northwest, smelling of grass and ripened grain.

"The concept of Distance is a human illusion, as so much of what you perceive is. Distance does not in fact exist. Time? Another illusion. Time does not exist."

"Time does not exist?"

"Not truly. Time functions as your measure of change, but it does not really exist. Or rather, I should say it exists as simply another disturbance of the Foam."

"A disturbance; what you call the Flux."

"That's correct."

"So all these separate forces, waves and radiations, particles, matter and phenomena—all just particular warps in Space-time?"

"There are no separate forces," Kosan said. "It is the same force acting differently. All dimensions, forces, energies, forms of matter, are simply different expressions of the Foam. You are an organic being, and so is the dog Woodrow. You have the same biological needs, but you behave in different ways. Yet at what you would call the sub-atomic level you are exactly the same. So it is with a rock or an automobile or an ice cream cone or a star."

"We've nibbled about the edges of that idea," Eric said. "We're not complete idiots." He frowned at the haughty wizard-wise face, grateful that Marans couldn't read thoughts. He was a Physics teacher with an I.Q. of over one-twenty, and didn't appreciate being lectured at like a simpleton, let alone compared to a dog.

58   The Blue River Valley

"Quantum Mechanics," he said. "Unified Field theories, String Theory, all are trying to bring the forces into one mathematical equation."

"That will not be accomplished, because what you call forces are not forces at all, they are only disturbances in the Foam. They are Flux. If there is such a thing as reality, then you can describe it that way. You think in terms of fabric, Space-time, you think of warps and worm-holes, all concepts born of your immaturity. You humans think in terms of your own microscopic existence, your own personal geometry, and say that geometry can only obey certain predictable rules. Out there, Geometry obeys no rules. How do you warp Foam? How do you fold it? Only the Flux can do that. Reality is the great unknowable moving of the Foam. You are a movement, as am I. You are a particular vibration, as am I, and everything else."

"That's String Theory," Eric said. "21st Century physics has pointed to nothing but that likelihood. It provides possible answers to some questions."

"One day you will discover that the magic number of the universe and your gods is not six or seven or eleven or twelve, it is two."

"Two," Eric said. "A binary system."

"That's a reasonably good human explanation."

"So the universe operates on a binary code of some sort."

"The magic number of the universe, so far as we have perceived it, is two. That is because on its most basic level, it is the only number the universe recognizes. Your electric brains operate on a binary communication system."

"Our computers, yes."

"Yes—or no. Everything operates on the same simple number two. Call it cause and effect, call it yes or no, call it on and off or call it the Flux and the Foam: all the same."

"Believe it or not," Eric said, "we're pretty close to understanding that."

"You maybe; But you and less than one percent of the population of your world, only because you have managed to shed your superstitions; but most of your world is imprisoned in superstition, and it is more primitive than even you realize. I know this primate world, as I have known many like her. Few humans have the courage or even the ability to look beyond their superstitions. Superstitions and ghost-rituals are drilled into your children at a very early age, and your children become not only terrorized by the superstitions, but mentally crippled--what you would call brain-washed. And when you become brain-washed, there is only one thing you cannot be made to believe—that you are brain-washed."

"You're saying—again--that there's not much hope for us."

Kosan gazed at the passing farmland. "One day Earth humans, if they fail to destroy themselves, will succeed in truly understanding. For now, you are going through a painful birth. With the left hand you clutch the safe and simple illusions, the superstitions and gods, the spiritual, the magical and fantastical—the left hand wants desperately to hold onto what cannot be true. And with your right hand, you touch what *must* be true, and it is like touching a quiet, but savage animal. You reach out and suddenly you touch the truth. You are terrified, yet you reach out and touch it, and when it doesn't turn and attack you, you venture to stroke its dangerous fur. You humans are only now beginning to stroke the terrible animal of truth, and one day you'll understand how tragic it all really is."

Eric stared out at the farms and cropland. It was a minty September evening, the wind dry and sweet. He remembered years ago feeling guilty because he hadn't given Cathy any spiritual education growing up; and when he finally took her at the age of seven to one Sunday school class at the Mars Presbyterian church Cathy wound up arguing with the Sunday school teacher about the impossibility of Noah getting every species on Planet Earth into the Ark--including her favorites, the dinosaurs--according to the measurements in the Bible. How she effortlessly befuddled the teacher with her calculations. And how Eric Holmes was asked gently not to let her upset the class again, which meant not to show up again.

Well, that was the end of that. My God, she squeezed Santa Claus out of me at the age of four. How long before she finds the truth of what she is?

Kosan is right, I don't want to know. I want this: a crisp, gorgeous autumn evening, a football night in autumn and seeing Cathy having fun and especially seeing Susan Mason. I only want this. He's right; I don't want the truth, not if it interferes with this, the supernatural.

At the same time….

"When will we find out about—the others, up there?" he asked.

"Who can say?" Kosan looked at him. "A year? A million years? Earth still sleeps and dreams; it has no concept of what is out there. You are a species that has evolved slowly. All water worlds evolve slowly, because water, contrary to your teachings, slows evolution down. An abundance of water and what you call oxygen and carbon dioxide means too much abundance, and with too much abundance species have no reason to evolve quickly. Call it Evolutionary Laziness. Almost all of your history was dominated by huge, slow fat lizards with no brains to speak of."

"The Spaceway," Eric said. "Is like the theoretical wormhole in space—in the Foam?"

"That is too simplistic," Kosan said. "The Spaceway is only another movement of the Foam—only another Flux; a disturbance of reality."

"You mean a disturbance of Space-time."

60   The Blue River Valley

"No, I mean a disturbance of reality itself. It is not a hole or tunnel, as you would probably picture it—that is why the Maran word for it means Foam. When you move through a tunnel you can only follow the tunnel. The Spaceway is a movement *in* the Foam, like swimming in water, and you can go in any direction or any—what you call distance—by moving the Foam."

"So you find where the Foam—"

"No, you move the Foam yourself; rather the control brain on your ship does it. Please don't ask me to explain much of this to you."

"Okay. One last question: what causes the Foam to move? I know, the Flux does, but what is the Flux?"

"What you would call gravity," Kosan said. "In the very simplest terms."

"I understand—some. Matter creates a warp in Space-time. That's Physics 101 now days."

"And in the case of what you call Black Holes, the Foam is swirled with such intensity that it creates a drain."

"A Black Hole is—"

"A drain," Kosan said.

"And it drains--?"

"It drains gravity, of course. I would have thought that was Physics 101 by now. What you call gravity, that which causes the movement of the Foam, which causes everything, is constantly being drained out of the galaxy. That is why it has such a powerful effect in some ways—as holding onto orbiting worlds—and yet why it is weak enough to allow Cathy to do her flips. It is a great deal like water. Water is so weak you can splash your face with it, and yet so strong that it can destroy one of your cities. So it is with the Flux."

"Black holes drain the force of gravity out of the galaxy," Eric said.

"What you call gravity is not a force, it is a condition. If it were not being constantly drained from the galaxy, you would not be able to move. You would be a stain of protoplasm on the floor. We are approaching the village and the football game," Kosan said with weary sigh. "No more questions."

"One more," Eric said. "Just one more. You compare me to a dog, then protoplasm; you owe me one more: If the gravity is being drained, where does it go?"

Kosan smiled at him. "Even we don't know that."

"So, the Spaceway—"

"I am not a scientist, I'm an Ambassador. I have only a vague understanding of how the Spaceway works."

"So can you travel to other galaxies?"

"Not yet. Beyond our galaxy the Foam becomes far too thin and weak. Without matter, which is the fundamental Flux, everything is too fragile. Most of the Foam never moves at all, and no one has yet to find a way beyond this galaxy."

"Maybe you can't," Eric said, with a smidge of triumph in his voice. He stared out at the beautiful September evening and felt one of his *coma* moments. His mind, supposedly hardened by science, was unable to fully believe that even this conversation was real. And yet it was what science had always predicted.

"The nearest galaxy, Andromeda—"

"No, Teacher, please, enough questions. Build your temples while you can, and believe in your mythologies while you can. Be ignorant and happy while you can. Pray on your knees while you can, and don't be in any hurry to learn the galaxy. You believe that if there are advanced civilizations beyond your star system that they will have moved beyond pettiness and violence and all the other terrible evils. Keep your illusions as long as you can, because you learn the truth at the price of happiness. It may be that the Foam lets you create your own reality, no one can be sure. I have seen on this world the possibility of that. But we are now approaching a football game, an event that Cathy is participating in. Maybe it is best that we suspend reality for now and try to have what you call fun."

"Forgive me, Kosan," Eric said. "But it's hard for me to imagine you having fun."

"It will be easier if they serve ice cream cones at the event."

Eric laughed. That seemed to be the Maran's newest 'Earth craze'.

"No," he said. "Hot dogs, popcorn and peanuts. And pop."

Kosan nodded. "A good combination. Let us hope there are no football fans out there." He glanced at the darkening sky.

Frowning, Eric pulled into the Mars High football field and parked just behind the old wooden bleachers. "This is only eight-man football," he said to Kosan. "See, I can explain things to you too."

Kosan smiled and studied the grass field, the benches on primitive scaffolds of wood; humans arriving to witness this ritual. Across the field was the rival tribe, their combatants, dressed in plastic armor, preparing for the battle; their cheerleaders, in purple and gold, fiercely dancing, causing the rival tribe to yell.

On this side the red-and-white Mars High School band was playing a war song, and the Mars High cheerleaders were doing their own primitive dance and creating a tribal roar.

62   The Blue River Valley

The Human and the Maran bought hot dogs and sacks of popcorn and bags of peanuts and two large Cokes. Kosan followed the professor and they awkwardly climbed the squawky wooden bleachers with their snacks.

Cathy, down on the sidelines, grinned up at them and yelled, "Hi, Daddy! Hi, Grandpa!"

Kosan, burdened with his snacks, could only smile and nod at his granddaughter. She was becoming a beautiful young woman, quite popular it seemed; but not shockingly different in appearance than her peers, was she? It was a relief that Marans were very similar to humans in appearance. Kosan himself, dressed in Earth apparel, only received a few blinking stares from the humans around him.

He heard the crowd yell as their football team raced onto the field. A born diplomat, Kosan didn't approve of barbarous competitions; yet they were conducted enthusiastically throughout the galaxy, even by the Marans themselves. Organic life requires competition, another sad Flux.

As Kosan smiled down at her, Cathy astounded the crowd by sprinting suddenly then launching her body into the air and performing a flawless double-flip, her red-and-white skirt fluttering wildly about her legs. The primitive bleachers erupted into cheers of amazement, Cathy grinning at everyone out of her long mane of black hair. She was, for the moment, star of the show, and Kosan knew that many humans came to these games just to see the dark-haired girl perform.

He snuffed his disapproval. "You let her become a dangerous show off," he muttered, biting into the hotdog.

Eric kept silent. He traded faces with Susan Mason, who was down on the sidelines with the cheerleaders. She gave him a sardonic smile and an open-handed gesture, as if to say, 'See what she can do'!

Kosan was watching him. "That woman down there," he said. "She is the one you've been—interested in?"

"Yes." Eric reddened: "Cathy's English teacher. She also coaches gymnastics and the cheerleading squad. Susan Mason."

"And she is developing a dangerous understanding of Cathy's powers."

"Gifts," Eric said. "A lot of kids are gifted."

Kosan bit into the mustard-tart hotdog. All Earth food was primitive and unhealthy, and therefore delicious; another base seduction of this world, their food. The iced cream in particular. Even Relomar had mentioned becoming addicted to the Valentino's pizza.

The crowd roared again as Cathy went through a series of back handsprings and suddenly launched into a spectacular double back-flip, her red and white pleated skirt flying up, exposing her brown legs and shorts.

Eric frowned. She wore regular white summer shorts under the red and white skirt, but that didn't seem to make her antics any less—inappropriate. Even worse was how she let the red sweater climb up, exposing her tummy. He gave the grinning Miss Mason a dark look.

"She must not draw attention to herself," Kosan whispered out his weary mantra, echoing Eric's dread. The Maran diplomat chewed at his hotdog. The sack of popcorn sat warm and salty in his lap. How dangerously seductive this all is. "Tell me how many times I have tried to make you understand this."

Eric was relieved when the football players ran onto the field, and attention shifted to the game. How to explain the degree of pouting and crying and screaming and blaming she had made him endure before he relented and let her do this terrible cheerleading thing?

He shook his head at Susan Mason, and she gave him a questioning look and again opened her hands at him. Explain to her, one teacher to the next, that this sweater-exposed-tummy thing was not acceptable: this whole cheerleading thing—unacceptable.

"You're right," he said to Kosan. "I'm going to have to put a stop to this, to her parading and showing off."

"It is a matter of controlling your child before it is too late," Kosan said.

"Did you control your child before it was too late?" Eric blurted out. "I'm sorry. I didn't mean to say that. That was a rotten thing to say."

Kosan smiled sadly. "Rotten, but maybe necessary." The Maran looked down at Cathy. "No, I did not."

"I'm sorry."

"No need to be sorry when you speak the truth." Kosan popped the last stub of bun and relish and mustard and hot dog into his mouth, mildly ashamed, after sipping his Coke, that now he turned his attention to the popcorn and roasted peanuts. "I have come to terms with that long ago. What is gone is gone. What is here is here."

"The Flux in the Foam."

"The sadness that makes happiness," Kosan said. "A Maran saying. But know this: there is a—Confederation—called the Gathered. It tries to regulate the galaxy, as much as can be regulated. In their strict galactic rulebook Cathy is a very serious crime. She has powers that could wreak havoc on a planet like Earth if she grows out of control. It has happened before. She is a hybrid, and they are considered too dangerous to be allowed to live."

Eric felt the familiar cold shudder at the back of his neck. "Cathy has never caused any danger to anybody."

64 The Blue River Valley

"The danger is in the unknowable. The Gathered fear above all the unknowable. But leave the future to itself. We are here to enjoy a football game."

He smiled down at the native spectacle, this tribal celebration and competition, the males butting heads against the males in order to impress the females: the ritualized, the ugly, true and grand war that is nature. These Earth humans, they send spacecraft into the galaxy. They have learned to capture atomic energy. They grunt and bellow and butt heads to declare dominance and to impress the females.

Cathy, in her red and white skirt and red sweater, grinned up at him.

"Hi, Grandpa!" she yelled, waving her tiny hand.

"Hi, Cathy!" he yelled back, spilling a bit of popcorn.

"I love you, Grandpa!"

Eric smiled at the Maran. Then he looked down at Susan Mason and shook his head at her.

Some of the farm folks in the bleachers were smiling over at them. A middle-aged lady sitting near Kosan said over to him, "Is that your little grand daughter? She's a sweetie."

Kosan looked at the Earth female with a bit of alarm. "Yes, she is."

"That's amazing she can do those flips and things," the lady said. "I've never seen anything like it."

"She is—gifted," Kosan said uncomfortably. He chewed the wonderful, salted popcorn.

"My grandson is a pretty gifted boy. He's on the football team."

"Oh?"

"He's not first string, but he's doing pretty good. See, that's him, number 27?"

"Yes, I see him," Kosan said.

"He plays second string wide receiver," the lady said. "He's very fast on his feet."

"Oh, I see."

"Is your wife here tonight?" the lady asked.

"My wife? No, she—she is not here."

"I lost my husband just two years ago," the lady said, adding darkly: "Cancer."

"I'm sorry to hear that," Kosan said.

"You have a very interesting accent. It's not Nebraskan."

"Minnesota," Kosan said. "The upper part."

"I was going to say Minnesota, or North Dakota, maybe. It's very Scandinavian. My late husband always told me I have a good ear for accents. Upper Minnesota. It's cold up there, I'll bet."

"It's very cold," Kosan said.

Eric smiled. The Foam moves in unknown directions, following Heisenburg's unrule--or maybe there is no such thing as direction either, maybe we all just float like sponges to where it takes us, where the mysterious Flux moves us. In the midst of unimaginable alien civilizations, the Spaceway, the powers and forces out there, the melting of reality itself, here was a Maran, an advanced alien being from space, from another planet, getting hit on by an Earth lady who had lost her husband and was lonely. Maybe reality is truly what the Foam is at this moment--and nothing more? Is this even reality? How can it be?

He looked down on the sidelines at his daughter, so at ease among the older senior girls, the grown-up girls, the girls who had fully developed and were voluptuous young women; young women who'd grown out of Cathy's elf-girl stage. She looked like a strange little sister among them, such a tiny thing. She looked so delicate, yet she had the power, among others, of invincibility. A greater power than any on Earth. But powers beyond the cosmos and beyond the imagination would hunt her and kill her, and there would be no way to stop them.

My Cathy: a Maran/Human hybrid. His mind couldn't accept it, even after so many years. Nothing of her is me, really, he thought with a sad blink of his eyes. I call her my daughter and she believes she is my daughter, but there will come a time when she'll know the truth.

Together, Kosan, Eric and Relomar had drawn up a conspiracy against Cathy. Somehow the Marans had managed to procure photographs of Cathy's real mother, and the pictures smiled from tables and walls in the farmhouse: the mysterious woman smiling from several pictures in Cathy's room. Cynthia was her name. A great and beautiful lie had grown up around Cynthia.

She had been Kosan's daughter, they had decided; tragically killed in a car wreck when Cathy was less than a year old.

She is gone, Cathy, and there is no need to go back to the past, Grandpa would say to her.

But when she was little, Cathy often asked her father questions about her mom. He and the Maran had coordinated their lies well, and in the end he could always derail her by saying her mother would have been very proud of her.

Eric remembered Cynthia's face that night. A few seconds worth of shock, that's all I knew of your mom, as she yanked open the car door and put you on the car seat, then slammed the door.

Stunned as he was, he remembered the last look she had given him when she said, "Drive away now or you'll die."

The image had haunted him all these years, and he felt that Cynthia must have been a strong woman. And the look on her face seemed to tell him that she knew the truth, that Donis had revealed it to her as his father has revealed it to me. This woman, Cynthia, knew the secret, and she knew she was going to die for it, and she passed the secret onto me in order that her daughter could live.

Not my wife, but maybe someone more profound. The long ago words of the Maran Kosan chilled him: "When she passed the child onto you, Teacher, she may have passed on the beginning of a catastrophic virus."

Cathy. One day she'll know. She's too smart for lies, and one day will she figure it out.

Will she hate me for it?

Susan Mason was smiling up at him, and Eric felt warmth in his face. You know that you are not allowed to fall in love and marry. And then the Foam takes a wrong turn and the Flux gets frisky and you wind up falling in love and not able to get a woman's face out of your mind. The gods of the galaxy commanded that he not fall in love and risk destruction. But he smiled back at her, the familiar thought dashing into his brain that Cathy needed a mother.

"Maybe what she needs is a mother," Eric muttered to Kosan.

The Maran frowned over at him, mouth full of popcorn.

"You think dangerous thoughts."

S I X ...

▼

Sherwood North was weaving his way down the hall at Mars High when up ahead he saw probable trouble.

Kyle Kuzma, the senior quarterback, was leaning against a locker, his arm casually (yet with a sense of ownership), around Cathy Holmes.

You can have her, stud.

Feeling that this was inevitable, and he had provoked it himself, Sherwood felt a sense of relief. This would at last be his trial of humility. Sherwood kept his gaze on Cathy Holmes, but her green eyes only touched his, then she looked away and whispered something to Kyle.

More problematic was the human side of beef, Randy Lynch, hulking next to Kyle: a gross and ugly sidekick. Kyle Kuzma was only a little brighter than a clump of mud, but he was a genius compared to his pal and football mate. Even so, Randy Lynch, 280 pounds of flab (an offensive lineman, Sherwood thought), always seemed to be able to goad Kyle into showing his manhood in some ridiculous way.

How intense was the need to stomp them both in a spectacular show for Cathy Ann Holmes, one that would send a legend down the crowded hallways of Mars High like chain lightning. And how delicious it was to deny the need, to embrace and understand shame.

I understand, Choe. Will this be my first and hardest test?

As Sherwood approached the two senior men, he kept his eyes on Cathy, knowing it would provoke Kyle, sensing the guy's face darkening. She refused to look into his eyes, a weakness she'd never shown before.

I could astound you, Miss Holmes, and wipe away that snotty, superior attitude of yours for good. But you're not worth it. This test is far more important than a self-centered little fairy princess. This is my test, and you're

68   The Blue River Valley

no part of it, he thought: The first lesson, the hardest lesson and the most important lesson.

The two senior football players glared at him as he approached, Randy Lynch's little pig eyes boring into him. He would actually be the easier of the two, Sherwood estimated, although he out-weighed Kyle by a good 80 pounds. One savage kick into the belly and all of that bumpkin flesh would collapse, and Randy would be hurling his monstrous lunch at the floor. How simple it would be if it were not simple.

He kept his eyes on Cathy Holmes, and finally she glanced at him, her face darkening with dread, and shook her raven head at him.

He smiled at her. This is my test, elf-girl, at last. This is my first and greatest test. This is the first step toward burning your wicked face out of my mind for good.

"Hey, Kyle," he said, smiling at the star quarterback. Sherwood was tall for his age, six feet, and he was almost eye-to-eye with the quarterback, albeit only coming in at 160 pounds to Kyle's 200 or so. "Hi, Randy," he smiled. "Hello, Miss Holmes."

Randy Lynch surprised him by attacking first, and without a stupid comment. The beef-boy lurched out, and it was all Sherwood could do to keep from reacting. He readied himself, and felt Lynch's chubby elbow plow into his shoulder, knocking his books to the floor.

"Stop it!" Cathy cried out. "Come on, you guys, knock it off. He's just a soph, Randy!"

Sherwood stared at Randy Lynch. The moment was fascinating. "What did I say?" he asked the red-faced troll. "I said Hi."

"You're looking to get your ass kicked, Punk," Randy Lynch said.

"Oh."

True power can only be forged in shame, Choe had taught him. A crappy but important lesson.

Students passing by stared down at him on the hallway floor gathering his spilled books. Sherwood heard scattered laughter. This reminded Randy Lynch to laugh.

Sherwood felt the shame wash over him, and he tried not to smile. I understand, Choe. I understand why I have to go through this. You have no right to use your powers until you can deny them, until you can overcome them by refusing to use them. You can only earn power by earning shame.

"He's been bothering your girlfriend, Kyle," he heard Lynch say. "He's been hitting on Cee-cee."

Sherwood gathered up his books and stood up, then suddenly Kyle Kuzma was in his face, and Cathy was trying to grab his arm. Must be a tag-team thing, Sherwood thought. All this over a little dark-haired, stuck-up--

Kyle grabbed a fistful of Sherwood's sweater, spun him around and slammed him into the lockers. You would go for this one's face, Sherwood had the weird thought. Pretty boy, handsome, he would fear an attack to the face.

"Kyle, leave him alone!" Cathy said. "Let's get this over with!"

Get this over with?

He glanced at Cathy; then he looked into Kyle's face and tried not to smile. Shame is not so hard to beat, Choe. It's like an out-of-body experience, that's all. I am being attacked not by bullies, but pride; and I must let shame and humility and cowardice wash over me. I can do that.

Only don't spoil it by smiling.

"You want your ass kicked, Punk?" Kyle spit at him.

Sherwood looked over at Cathy Holmes, then back at Kyle. He couldn't resist: "That's kind of a rhetorical question, isn't it?" he said.

Kyle slapped him hard across the face, and Sherwood growled and chewed his teeth holding onto the lesson, the ordeal of shame.

"Kyle, stop it!" Cathy said. "Just leave him alone."

A crowd had gathered to watch him get pimped around, and he looked at Cathy Holmes. She is afraid for me, he thought. I could show you, Cathy, at this *Moment*!!! I could cripple your jock boyfriend at this…

But I would fail the test.

"I'm sorry," Sherwood heard himself saying at Kyle Kuzma. "I don't want any trouble. What did I do?"

Still gripping Sherwood's sweater, Kyle spun him around and he was facing Cathy Holmes. Sherwood tried to find her pale green eyes, but they danced away from him.

"My girlfriend has something to say to you, Poetry Punk," Kyle said.

"She does?" Sherwood feigned surprise. He stared at Cathy until her evasive, pouty face started to turn red. "I don't understand."

"Tell this soph punk," Kyle said to her. "Go on, tell him, Cee."

Her eyes studied the floor as she gave her recital: "I don't want you to be talking to me anymore," she said. "I don't want to have anything to do with you, Soph. So stop talking to me and quit bothering me!"

Finally the green eyes glanced savagely up at him, then away as she read the calm disgust on his face.

"Leave me alone, Soph!" she said.

"What do you guys talk about?" he asked her. "Football?"

"Hey, Punk." Kyle again slapped his face. "You're a little pervert punk, and she's telling you to leave her the hell alone!"

"So get the hell out of here," Randy Lynch added.

70   The Blue River Valley

Kyle shoved him away, and Sherwood stumbled back into the crowd of laughing students: Derision, shame, that awful car-wreck moment when a skinny sophomore is being made a pussy in front of everybody. Sherwood looked at the cruel, delighted high school faces. I don't need your respect, because now I respect myself.

I understand, Choe, Sherwood thought.

Cathy stood humiliated by the scene, ashamed of all this. He tried to find her green eyes, but they were lost, maybe forever. The phantasy is over, Sherwood said to himself. He heard the sounds around him, high school sheep kids whispering, giggling, *bawwwwwwing* at his shame: Punk sophomore, pussy, coward...

Cathy, angry red, startled him by suddenly glaring into his face, her eyes glowing.

"Leave me alone, Punk!"

The crowd laughed, everybody laughed, Randy Lynch laughed at him. Kyle Kuzma put his arm around her and laughed. Then at last, Cathy laughed.

He stared into her wicked face, the face of the beautiful demon.

I was wrong, Choe. Sherwood's heart sank. It was a harder lesson than you told me. You said the hardest part is enduring the shame. That's not the hardest part, not even.

S E V E N ...

▼

"Do you hate the bag so much that you would kill it, Sherwood?" Choe Kwang-su's voice echoed in the training room.

Sherwood stopped attacking the bag and turned, bowing to his teacher. "Just practicing my kicks."

"So I see."

Choe came into the room and sat down cross-legged on the mat, groaning and frowning. "It is said that a life of yoga and meditation will save you from pain and stiffness and arthritis in your old age. It's a lie. It probably makes it worse."

Choe Kwang-Su was a short, stocky man of seventy, with a bald head and a wide yellow face that reminded you of a man-in-the-moon. He had been born in Korea, but that was about all Sherwood knew of his past. Choe's tiny martial arts school was wedged between the dime store and a dentist's office, a narrow room well-lighted but not well-furnished. Sherwood could only try and imagine the bizarre events that could have landed a Korean martial arts teacher in the town of Mars City, Nebraska. But Choe Kwang-su had been here many years and was a respected native.

"I think you are doing more than practicing," Choe said. "You seem to be relieving yourself of some sort of ugly rage. I can't imagine why, you aced the test."

"Yes I did and yes I am," Sherwood admitted. "I passed the test; I gave away my pride in order to keep from fighting. There, I did it, I backed down; I let the pricks slap me and pimp me around. I gave myself up to humiliation; I refused to fight even though everything in my mind and body screamed out to fight. I should feel liberated—aren't I supposed to?--but I just feel like everything was ruined. It all just sucked."

72   The Blue River Valley

"It sucked." Choe nodded. "That's normal after a test like that. A young man of your age cares what others think, that's normal; some bully wants to push you around and every atom in your body wants to kick his ass, to show him your power. And that was why the first test had to be to overcome that. By the time you get to be my age, you won't give a rat's behind what people think of you. But you're not there yet, and shouldn't be. You have tasted humiliation, Sherwood. If I remember correctly, the taste is like a fish that has lain in the sun too long and gone bad—and I hope that taste stays in your mouth. Look at it this way, next time you can take your pride back. Now you've earned that right."

"There may not be a next time."

"Oh, there will be. Anyway, are these enemies so important that you would spend your life in a rage at them, at their weakness?"

"The problem is--it's not them." Sherwood gave his mentor a disgusted look. "It's the girl; Cathy Holmes."

"The girl." Choe stared at him in surprise. Then his eyes narrowed. "It was that girl who started this?"

"In a general way, yes."

"Ahh, her again." Choe stared away. "Show me your kicks."

He watched his young student somersault off the mat and perform a series of savage body and head kicks to the bag. Sherwood was tall and slender, a living whip. He was the fastest fighter Choe had ever taught, and the youngest to have mastered the mental and the emotional discipline-- somewhat, maybe--a little anyway—no, not at all....

Choe smiled. The girl, the *witch* who teased him: what amount of mental discipline can overcome that? One thing worrisome, though: Sherwood North was a darkly emotional lad, too cynical for his age by far; too young to deserve to be bitter at life; too passionate inside.

He keeps his passion in a cage. Add love to that, and serious fighting skills, and you add danger.

Choe remembered all the way back through the strange years his own teacher, the Beloved Tran Lee, reminding him: If you choose to teach someone only how to fight, you are teaching nothing, you are only forging another sword. The most important lesson, and the hardest, is to teach someone how *not* to fight.

Good luck with that, Choe thought, watching Sherwood savage the bag.

"All right, all right," he called out. "Now take a break and come sit down."

Sherwood delivered one last hateful foot to the bag, then came over and sat down cross-legged on the mat. "I don't really want to talk about it," he muttered.

"Then we'll talk about the weather." Choe studied his hak-saeng fondly. "Tell me what you think and feel, Sherwood."

"About?"

"About the weather; it's going to get colder, we're going into another son-of-a-bitching Nebraska winter, and my joints are going to ache until June. Why I'm not in Miami, or better still Hawaii, is some madness or other. Explain to me, Sherwood, why I'm in Nebraska and not in Hawaii?"

Sherwood smiled. "Then you'd never appreciate June."

Choe nodded his head with a smile. A good one, Sherwood North. Talented and focused; a joy to teach and to learn from; but also a brooding, dangerous one. A boy in love with a girl who torments him...

They sat without talking. Choe stared out of the front of his school, at Mars City, the town square and county courthouse, the maple trees leafless now, Nebraska drifting toward her stark, wailing winter.

"You taught me to appreciate what's worth fighting for and what's not!" Sherwood blurted out at last: "To make that most important distinction. Believe me, Cathy Ann Holmes is not worth fighting for, not even close. She's the opposite of what's worth fighting for."

"I know, you've told me that before. But you didn't fight for her. So?"

"No, I didn't."

"But you wanted to. You're infatuated, and next time you will."

"And that's insane, that's madness. She's shallow and phony, she's cruel and vicious."

"What did she do to you this time?"

He glanced at his teacher. "She was there, at my test. She took part in it."

"Ouch."

"And at the end of it, she *laughed.*" Sherwood shook his head. "What she did, Choe—it was with her eyes. She kept making me think with her eyes that she cared about me, and wanted to protect me, that she didn't want it to happen, that at least I might still be her friend. She did it with her eyes. She controls people with her eyes. Now I'm wondering if she was acting, and she engineered the whole thing, if she purposely flirted with me so that Kyle'd get jealous and I'd get pimped around."

"A disturbing way of flirting," Choe agreed. "But common."

"But seeing her laugh with all the rest, and her evil little face—it ruined everything. And maybe it solved everything. It made all I'd built up about her and all my stupid dreams about her sour and rotten. I looked into her eyes and saw how empty they are. And I think that's what I needed in order to forget about her, to break the spell. I saw her for what she is. Finally. She turned into just another sheep in the flock. I always thought there was something different about her, that she wasn't—that she would—there *is* something very strange about her, Choe!"

"Strange, but not different."

"Unique, I don't know....maybe the best thing I got from this lesson is not humility, it was seeing her for what she is and finally, finally getting free of her."

"Yes, I can see that you're free of her."

"As far as having these delusions, yeah. I needed to see how cruel and hateful she is, and how she likes to play with people like toys. I needed something to break me out of the phantasies. Now, I don't care. I don't care anymore."

"And of course now you want to take revenge by beating up Kyle Kuzma in front of her."

"That goes against every lesson you ever taught me."

"I don't know about that, Sherwood. I don't remember ever giving you a lesson about girls," Choe said. "But I was young once, and I fought over a girl."

"You're kidding. Why?"

Choe shrugged. "I was in love with her. Every young man in the village was in love with her. You haven't invented the disease."

"You did win the fight."

"Yes, I did. My rival wasn't much of a fighter, just a big fisherman, strong and handsome and over-confident. I took care not to hurt him too much, and I went to great lengths to not take his dignity away from him. But it was difficult, because a madness came into my brain, and my body's instinct was to beat him to death. When I first made a dodge and struck the big fisherman in the face, I knew from his stunned eyes that I had power over him and could destroy him. I knew then, and I wanted to unleash that power and skill. I beat him to the ground, but I went no farther, because the Beloved Tran Lee had taught me that true power is not dominance but humility."

Sherwood smiled. "That's the first time you've ever said anything to me about your past."

"Well, before you ask, no I didn't end up with the girl. She loved the fisherman even more seeing him beaten on the ground. She nursed him and wept at his pain. She despised me for what I had done."

"I'm not going to end up with the girl either," Sherwood said. "Not even close. And that's the truth of it. I'm wasting away obsessed with her, writing stupid poems about her, and there ain't no damn way in Hell or Havana that she would even consider—and I Know it. And if some miracle that impossible ever came about, she'd make my life miserable. She would be the girlfriend from the black tarpit of Satan's Hell. So why would I get obsessed, Choe?—there's something about her that I can't understand; something bewitching. It's almost like she's some underage evil sorceress or something. I'm not a dummy about girls. But she has—she seems to have weird powers!"

"And her father, Dr. Holmes: you probably haven't spoken your feelings to him about this."

"Oh, my god, are you kidding? It doesn't matter; Cathy Holmes has no feelings for me, why should I talk to Dr. Holmes about it?"

"You're wrong, Sherwood."

"What do you mean?"

"Well, if she went to all the trouble to make sure her boyfriend terrorized you, she must have some feelings."

"Yeah, she has two feelings for me: malice and spite."

"Well, you might find your next test to be as hard as the last," Choe said. "But I've taught you all you need to know about it."

Sherwood looked at him. "You have; when?"

"Only a moment ago, when I told you that I didn't hurt the fisherman badly and I did not take away his dignity."

"I understand."

"Do you? Then understand this," Choe said: "All those years ago in the fishing village, when I fought I gained nothing and lost everything."

E I G H T ...

▼

October was kind to Nebraska. The night of the meteor shower (a Friday by luck), was a balmy 75 degrees. A warm autumn wind blew out of the west.

It was finally Meteor Night.

Big deal.

Sherwood rode his motorcycle down the long rock drive to the Holmes house, a grim light in his eyes. If he had thrown away his pride and dignity on the Mars High stage, it was returning with a vengeance and he kept his mind cold, anticipating his strategy—to ignore Cathy Ann Holmes and her damned existence, to give her a disgusted smile each time she began to flirt and sneer and ridicule him—if she even would...to smile and nod at her immature face and say absolutely nothing to her, and to show her what she really was, nothing; just another baw-sheep in the flock. Leave me alone, soph—na-na-na-na-na. Okay, believe me I can do that.

After I beat the crap out of your boyfriend—soph.

Act like a baw-sheep, be treated like a baw-baw sheep.

She had at last made plain how it was, and that was that. She hates me; okay, I'm fine with that; I'm more than fine. It's the best thing that ever happened that she hates me; otherwise I'd be a seriously flawed person. She only likes what everybody else likes, and does what everybody else does, and believes what—Oh, screw it. She's another sheep. She has no identity beyond the high school flock and her cute pleated cheerleader skirt, and the red planet Mars sweater. All these are trivial high school yearbook things that will be divided, years later, into only two camps: I hated high school—I loved high school.

I'm here as a member of the Astronomy Club, *sheepgirl*. But I'm Dr. Holmes' guest, not yours. You showed yourself to be one of the sheep, and thank God that broke the spell.

He actually smelled the air of freedom, and he could feel the poison draining out of him, evaporating in this perfect wind. Sherwood breathed deep of the wind; he smelled the alfalfa and prairie grass and the almost hidden scent of the Blue River, not two miles away. It was a giddy feeling, knowing the spell had dissolved, the high fever of Cathy Ann Holmes had broken, and he was free, and he saw her at last in all her wicked ugliness, as someone he would look back years later on, seeing her wretched unhappiness, and wonder why he had ever even *liked* her. Now he was free of her, and the world had never smelled so sweet.

He grinned into the grass-dry Nebraska wind. Dr. Holmes' farmhouse was ablaze with lights, and a dozen cars and pickups were parked under the tall yard-light. As he pulled his bike into the yard, Sherwood saw through the big picture window all the astronomy geeks gathered inside munching on snacks and discussing the heavens. He saw Professor Kellogg in the shadows of the back yard, relieving himself of several beers against a tall ash tree.

Woodrow, alert to the sound of Sherwood's bike, came slow and painful down from the porch to greet him. Sherwood smiled.

All's right with the world now, Woodrow, he thought. Your little Cathy Witch, the dark one from hell, is finally out of me, and it feels good. I'm not even going to try and care about her or what she does. It's all over and done with; I might even thank her for making my phantasy so stupid and painless and simple and forgotten, like a crushed bug on the sidewalk.

He got off his bike and squatted down to pet the giant dog. "Woodrow! Come on, let's do the butt scratch."

Woodrow thumped his massive tail and lapped tiredly at Sherwood's face. Sherwood had the sad thought that Woodrow was already old for a huge dog and, like Choe, was beginning to show signs of arthritis.

"You're a good old dog," he hugged the Saint Bernard. "You're one of the good ones."

Woodrow sighed at him, then suddenly glanced up and barked at the porch as the door squeaked open. Sherwood looked behind him and was shocked to see Cathy Holmes emerge from the house. She wasn't wasting time. Sherwood controlled his face and prepared himself. Ignore her; don't say a word. Let her spend her cruel wit on nothing.

But the look on her face stunned him, and he found himself instead gaping at her. She was crying. Still squatted down petting her dog, Sherwood watched her step off the porch. She wore her huge white Husker sweatshirt, jeans and tennis shoes. Her face was crinkled in misery, and she was shamelessly bawling.

What in God's--?

He stared up at her, unable to speak.

She stood above him, wiping away tears; she reached down and petted Woodrow. Then she astounded Sherwood by taking his hand. He stood up, stared at her hand in his.

"What's wrong?"

"Will you take a walk with me, Sherwood?" she asked. "I want to say something."

This was unreal, a cruel video game? Sherwood couldn't believe—what wicked thing is she pulling now?

They walked hand in hand away from the yard light and into the darkness of the cottonwood trees that towered over the farm, into the woods and down to Cedar Creek. Sherwood couldn't believe this was happening. When they were in the deep-shadowed woods, she let go of his hand, and he felt a sudden despair.

"I'm sorry, Sherwood!" she cried. "That was such a terrible thing I did! I'm so sorry! I'm sorry! I'm so sorry! Please forgive me, Sherwood! I'm sorry!"

He stared at her crying face. His own suddenly burned red. "No need to be sorry for me," he heard himself saying. His hand remembered hers. "Now you better start worrying about Kyle."

"I feel awful." Cathy looked away and pouted and cried at the darkness. Even when she cried there was something not quite normal. The black cascade of hair blended so strangely with the night that her face seemed to float in the platinum yard light. Never before had she appeared so otherworldly, her feline eyes burning liquid green in the night. How fast and effortless she wrapped the spell back around him.

Woodrow had followed them, and Sherwood reached down to pet him. Sherwood stared at Cathy. He felt a weird emptiness. The desire to touch her hand, her hair, to hold her and kiss her was maddening. He thought of his relief, not twenty minutes ago, to have her out of his mind.

So much for that plan.

"It's okay, Cathy," he said. "I forgive you."

"I'm not evil," she said. "What I did was evil, but I'm not evil." She broke out crying again. "I don't want to be evil, Sherwood!"

"It was Kyle who did it," he said. "Kyle and Randy."

"I laughed," she said, crying and pouting at the night. "I'm sorry!"

He swallowed hard, took a breath and tried to regain control. "Well, let's put it behind us and forget about it, okay?" He shook his head at the dark wind-blown cottonwood trees. "We're going to see some great meteors tonight, and I'm hungry. Did you make your chicken wings?"

"I'm sorry, Sherwood. I didn't mean to laugh--"

"Cathy, for the love of God! Did you make your chicken wings? With the Ranch, not the bleu cheese?"

She wiped her tears away and smiled at him. "Yes, I did."

"Okay, that's paradise for the time being. Let's munch out and then enjoy the sky show."

"Just so you know, Sherwood, I don't want Kyle to wind up—picking on you again. I don't want to see you beat up, so please don't be sarcastic around him or any of that. Please don't give him any reason to go after you."

He smiled. "You're worrying about the wrong guy, Cathy," he said.

"I don't know what you mean."

"You have secret powers and I have secret powers. But I promise," he said. "I'll leave you alone, and I'll leave him alone."

She started crying again. "I'm sorry!"

"It's okay. Let's forget about it." He almost reached out to touch her; but he knew it would just be another heart-breaking slap across the face. He felt a terrible sadness that was already hardening to dread. He realized that it was worse now. He could have overcome her when she was an evil grinning witchling.

Now it was going to be a lot worse.

It was a fair night, and they counted 14 meteors in all. Jupiter was bright, and they all took turns oohing and ahhing into Dr. Holmes' telescope. Sherwood and Cathy avoided each other all evening, and Sherwood was relieved to keep his distance, although his eyes couldn't stay away from her. He kept feeling her hand in his when they had walked into the woods…

Dr. Kellogg leaned over him, drunk, and told a dirty joke about why so many astronomers go blind. Woodrow clumped about, mooching pets and scratches and hugs and food treats. Graduate students bent their skinny frames over telescopes, and stood in the moonlit yard like the silhouettes of old hand pumps. Beyond that, it was anything but the normal Meteor Night.

First of all, Sherwood had been startled to see Miss Mason, one of the Mars High teachers, here tonight, being cozy with Dr. Holmes. They were enjoying one another, and Cathy would stare over at them in disbelief.

No less startling was another new face, Cathy's strange uncle Rel, a tall albino man with a gentle smile and a strange floating appearance, a guy who looked almost mythological. That's what side of the family Cathy got her strange looks from.

80   The Blue River Valley

All through the evening Sherwood had an oddness in his stomach, as if the world tonight wasn't real—as if things that can't be maybe *can* be. This night, what had happened with Cathy...

Why?

He had to walk into the trees and away from everyone to try and shake away the weirdness of the night. He stood among the giant cottonwoods and stared at the dark prairie beyond. Magic is not real, you idiot.

Then love made his head turn, and he stared through the trees at her, the magic elf wearing the long shimmery black hair that bounced against the white sweatshirt, her face grinning and laughing with the drunken Dr. Kellogg.

"She's exasperating, isn't she?" a voice said behind him.

Sherwood flinched, spun around. Cathy's strange Uncle Rel was standing before him, a blond wizard in the trees. Sherwood felt a jump in the gut.

"Sir?" he said.

"Cathy," Rel said. "She's exasperating, isn't she?"

He stared at this presence, standing below the dark cottonwoods: "Well, she can be, if you let her." Sherwood looked at her through the trees, remembering her crying face, remembering her hand. He looked back at Uncle Rel and had the sudden irrational feeling that the man wasn't quite human. Aside from his vampiric appearance, there was...

"You find yourself in a painful dilemma, Sherwood," Rel said, startling him.

"A--dilemma?"

"I think that's the word. You love Cathy, but you don't like her."

Sherwood stared at the man and laughed. "She can be pretty unlikeable sometimes, not to criticize your niece. You probably know about her mean streak."

Rel chuckled. "She doesn't use it on me. She tells her Uncle Rel everything."

"Everything."

"We have long conversations. She can tell me things she can't tell her father or grandfather. We call it the 'Uncle's Code'." He studied Sherwood with his pearl eyes. They were strangely *lighted* eyes, like his niece's, only these were pale blue.

"I know why she was crying so much tonight," the man said to him.

"Oh, she told you about—about me getting pimped. And her getting off on it and laughing with the others. And now she feels guilty."

"Yes. I know about Kyle and I know about her friends on the cheerleading squad, and I know about you."

Sherwood stared at him. "So she probably got a big laugh out of telling you I'm in love with her or something. That's a delusion of hers, Sir. She wishes. She doesn't have any interest in me; she's in love with the senior quarterback of the Mars High Martians. And I don't have any interest in her. I'm in her father's Astronomy club, that's the only contact I ever have with her."

Relomar nodded and gazed away at the night. So beautiful this desperate world; you fall into a story when you come here. So wonderful somehow—that human word that tells the story of Earth: wonderful. He knew of this young man's ordeal, what this 16 year old human, Sherwood North, had endured. He knew that the young human didn't have to endure it, but he had. He had defeated the need to show his powers.

How wonderful this place, Earth; how mournful and beautiful a story...

"So she talks about me sometimes," Sherwood said at last. "I can't really imagine why."

Relomar shrugged. "She's a young girl, she talks about boys."

"I'll bet she does. She's Miss Mega-Popular, you know. She's the star cheerleader in high school, and she's not even 16 yet."

"I know." Relomar sighed again. "She's very talented and she loves to show off."

"That's a great understatement, Sir."

Uncle Rel chuckled. They stood silent for a strange long time.

"Such a beautiful night," Relomar said at last, staring into the dark emptiness of the prairie. "That wind, that sweet wind."

Sherwood tried not to stare at Cathy's Uncle Rel. But there was something about this man that reminded him of Choe, though in appearance they couldn't have been more Mutt and Jeff; a quality of calmness and serenity, wisdom, a sort of world-weariness and untold secrets.

"I don't know why she would talk about me," Sherwood said. "What does she have to say about me?"

"I think at this point in her life, Cathy looks upon you as being what you would call a 'best friend'."

Sherwood looked at the man. He tried to peel the joy off his face. "She sure has a funny way of showing it."

Best friend. Not bad for the time being. He could barely resist a savage grin.

"Yes, she does."

Sherwood glanced at her through the trees. He had the sensation of falling. "Best friend?" he questioned.

"Cathy grew up with very few friends," Relomar explained. "She is popular, even loved by her peers. But she is different, and so she is lonely."

Sherwood swallowed at his throat. "Different? Not meaning any disrespect, Sir--but she's the same. Lonely? Not to be disrespectful, but I don't think so."

The strange phantom man, Uncle Rel, smiled at him; then startled him by saying, "I know that you could have defeated Kyle and Randy, one at a time or both together. But you didn't. I know that you have fighting skills beyond them. You chose not to use those skills."

Sherwood stared at him, wondering if this was real. "My test," his voice said at this man. "Why are you telling me this?"

"Because Cathy is different," Relomar said. "She has powers. And because you are different, Sherwood, and you have powers."

"There's one!" Eric Holmes pointed at the quick streak of light in the west. "Did you see it?"

"I saw it!" Susan Mason squeezed his shoulder, and Eric smiled.

"That might have even made it down."

"That one had a strange angle."

"Depending on how they enter Earth's atmosphere, they can fly almost horizontally!" he said.

"What a beautiful night," Susan murmered against him. "You have a nice place here, Eric. I love this place you've built."

"A good place to star gaze." He stood against her soft body; the wind blew her auburn hair across his chest. He glanced over at Cathy, who was giving him a yuck face, but he wasn't going to let her spoil this night, it was too good—it was too damn good standing with Susan in the darkness, the Astronomy club gathered round. He was even beginning to accept that a Maran was among them. He would often catch 'Uncle Rel' studying him in mild amusement. This Maran had at least been much easier to deal with than his brother Kosan.

My God, Eric thought, watching the Astronomy Club wander the yard, studying the heavens. If any of them knew or even suspected they would forget all about a few stupid meteors. Well, there's nothing wrong with reality that a little denial can't fix. It is enough to be alive--or imagine being alive--on a night like this, to be standing with a beautiful woman, to have friends and students out sharing the heavens.

If this long coma had taught him anything, it was never to take anything for granted. Worlds are out there, civilizations beyond understanding. One day we will see the true mirror of the universe and microbes will be looking back at us. We grow up on Earth, and so there is nothing but Earth; just as, for a million years, there was nothing beyond the village, the mountains, beyond the seas. My God, my God, is this night real? Will we ever be able to grasp the concept that what is real is only what we *think* is real?

Eric touched Susan on the back and made his plunge: "Would you— Susan-- maybe care to have dinner with me some night?" he asked. "A movie?"

She turned and smiled. "Yes, I'd like that, Eric."

He grinned like a geek. "Great. Susan. Tomorrow's Saturday, do you have any plans for tomorrow night?"

"No, tomorrow night would be great."

"I'll pick you up at six, how's that?"

"All right."

They traded nervous smiles; then Susan Mason looked away, excited but embarrassed. "How will Cathy react if we..."

"What do you mean?"

"I *am* her teacher. And we both know she has no problem speaking her mind."

"She likes you," Eric said. "She likes you a lot. I think Cathy even loves you."

Susan Mason smiled; a beautiful and sad auburn smile. "Maybe because I see what a marvel she could be."

"She's gifted." Eric nodded at the night. He looked over at the Maran Relomar, who was studying him.

"She's more than just gifted, Eric. I've had gifted students before. Cathy is far beyond that."

Eric nodded, frowning. "I don't like her showing off."

"You can't keep her from showing what she can do, Eric. My god!" Susan shook her head. "I'm sorry, maybe it's none of my business, but I'm her teacher. Do you realize what your daughter can do?"

"Yes, I know. She's gifted. Don't worry about Cathy; it's for the most part none of her business who I ask to a film. Let's—Susan--well, I read in the paper that a pretty good Sci-Fi movie is showing at the Grand. Asimov's *I Robot*?"

Susan smiled at him. "I pegged you for a Sci-Fi fan."

"And the Blue River Inn makes a pretty good steak." He smiled back at her.

84   The Blue River Valley

There was a Maran among them. It was ridiculous believing that a space alien was here among them, among the students in the very Astronomy Club. I am in a coma, Eric thought. A wonderful, soft coma; and all this, all these years have been floating in a dream—and it is what it is, and it is...

He stared over at Relomar, and the tall blond Maran smiled and nodded to him.

...something beyond human.

What Cathy needs is a mother, Eric thought; I've known that for years. A stable, understanding mother to keep her from going wild with cheerleading and dating football players and—she needs—

Eric touched Susan Mason's arm, and she turned and smiled at him. Over her shoulder he saw that Cathy was training a suspicious look at them. Eric smiled and gazed up at the stars. If you haven't awakened in 15 years, you no longer want to wake up.

You would rather die than wake up. You would rather it be true and die in one of those blue stabs of Melt than wake up from this.

NINE ...

▼

It was dark and quiet, only the wind blowing through Mars City. Choe Kwang-su was just closing up when the tall yellow-haired man drifted into his school. Choe gave the figure a startled look. He felt a jolt of strangeness, he didn't know why.

What! This was not a man. What was this...a spirit?

"Yes?" he said in disbelief.

The strange spirit floated into the room, smiled at him. "You're the teacher of Sherwood North?" he asked.

Choe nodded with caution. "Yes."

"I know Sherwood," the spirit said. "We both have an interest in Astronomy."

"I see." Choe tried not to stare at the man. He detected--a cloud?--a blue cloud surrounding this being. Can this be real? Too many corn chips and salsa—I'm dreaming.

"Who are you?" he blurted out.

The spirit smiled. "I am Uncle Rel. I'm the uncle of Cathy Holmes."

"Yes, all right. Sherwood's--girl." Choe stared at this—what?

"I am Uncle Relomar."

"Sherwood—the girl he—"

"Yes. You've heard of her, and you know she has powers."

Choe breathed deep. This was not a human, this was a spirit? My people said there were spirits of the ancestors, they swore there were spirits of the ancestors—but I never believed that nonsense. What is this if not a spirit?

"Sherwood has told me that this Cathy is special," he said to the mat on the floor.

"Sherwood was picked on by bullies at the high school," Relomar said.

86   The Blue River Valley

Choe stared up at the statement. This is a dream, he thought. Some dream, some dream is speaking to me.

"Yes," he said.

"And he can defeat those at his school who want to bully him?"

"Yes."

"But he didn't. Why? He could have shown off, made himself respected. When males in a tribe fight, it is for dominance in the tribe, is it not? Why didn't Sherwood fight? Why didn't he become the dominant male?"

Males in a tribe?

Choe tried not to stare into the luminous eyes of this man. My own eyes are failing, I must be going senile—I imagine crazy things. This is a strange fellow, nothing more.

"He had not earned the right to" Choe said. "First he had to go through the trial of humility. You can't embrace power until you've embraced humility, otherwise power will destroy you. All of your life you will forget power, but you will never forget humility. You have no right to do battle until you've learned how Not to do battle." He looked at the man. "Martial Arts 101," he couldn't resist. "It all has to do with an ancient story about an old warrior who left a young warrior on a river bank."

"One day you can tell me this story." The spirit smiled at Choe. "Power can destroy you." The spirit looked out the windows of the school at Mars City, at the dark windy autumn night. "A good lesson."

Choe stared at him. The man had a gentle face, but Choe couldn't stop seeing the blue neon that clothed him. But this was no man, was it? This was not a human being, this was—what does it want from me...

"Your—niece, Cathy Holmes?" he ventured.

"Yes," said the spirit. "I want you to teach her."

"I see."

"I'll pay you what you want," said the spirit. "Money is nothing."

"I don't..."

Choe stared at the man. That was a conversation stopper, money is nothing.

"Sherwood says that she is—unusual."

"She needs to learn what you can teach her," Relomar said. "What I hope you can teach her."

"I might teach her what I can. But why do you want me to?"

The spirit stared away for a long time. In the midst of this insane encounter, Choe did remember hearing that money was nothing.

A strange looking fellow, that's all. You imagine things, old man. If this niece is what Sherwood said she is, Cathy Holmes would be taught at a high price. But there is something here beyond price? What is this man, clothed in blue electricity?

"I'll teach her if I can," Choe repeated to the spirit.

The being kept staring away, and Choe tried to get the sizzling blue of him out of his eyes. You're getting old, that's all. When you get old you imagine many things. Why do I fear that a secret is coming?

"She is gifted," the spirit muttered. "That could be a danger to her. We worry about her always showing off."

"Gifted in what way?"

Uncle Rel studied him. "What gifts did Sherwood say she has?"

Choe frowned. "I've heard of her gymnastics at the football games. And according to Sherwood, she has the gifts of vanity and cruelty. And that she enjoys tormenting him."

"I'm afraid she's more than that," Relomar said. "I'll send her to you, and you can decide if she can be taught—or not."

"I'll teach her what I can," Choe said. "But I can only teach those who want to learn."

"You taught the boy Sherwood," Relomar said. "Try and teach Cathy the same way. Teach her to not show off. Money is nothing."

All right, that was the clincher. His own teacher, the Beloved Tran Lee, had warned him against falling in love with money—but advised also: that didn't mean he couldn't like it.

"Well, have her come to me," Choe said uneasily. "I'll do what I can." He stared at the spirit. "Who are you?" he asked. "What are you?"

"I am the uncle of Cathy Holmes."

"Tell me what you are?" Choe asked. "Are you a spirit?"

Relomar gave him an ominous look. "I hope to be a *friend*."

TEN ...

▼

Now, damn the world, and damn humility and wisdom--it was time for payback!

Sherwood North saw Kyle Kuzma down the hall and locked stares with him. Kyle started to grin; then thought better of a frown. He savagely kicked shut his locker door, startling the hallway of students around him. Sherwood approached, staring into the

a--hole's face until Kyle glared back at him in disbelief. Sherwood smiled, his eyes never leaving Kyle's face. Sherwood felt power, something in his body that screamed and clawed to escape. That had earned the right to escape.

As he passed by, Kyle grabbed his sweatshirt and pulled him over, playing to the crowd. "What are you smiling at, Pussy!"

The flock of high school sheep immediately gathered round, sensing another drama, one that they could watch and *baw* at and talk to each other about and not have to be a part of. The safe adventure, like television, of watching and not being. A high school hallway video adventure that was no adventure at all.

"Oh. Hello, Kyle." Sherwood tightened his smile. "How are you today?"

"I heard you were bothering Cathy the other night, Perv, like at your comet crap night. You're just begging to get your little ass kicked, aren't you, Punk Perv? You just gotta like be a smart ass."

"All I said was hello," Sherwood smiled into the darkening, volcanic face.

"You want your ass kicked? Is that it?"

"Not here," Sherwood said, his eyes hardening. "Hageman's Field, after school."

Kyle stared at him. "What? What are you talking about, like Hageman's Field?"

"I don't want to fight you," Sherwood said. "But if we have to fight--and we are going to fight--let's not do it on school grounds and wind up getting expelled."

Kyle let out a laugh. "You fight me? A punk soph wants to fight Me?"

"I don't want to fight You. But we should put an end to this thing; I'm already tired of it. I don't hit on your girlfriend, I have no interest in your girlfriend, I don't *like* your girlfriend. So, meet me after school at Hageman's Field and we'll get this over with."

"Over with. You're calling me out?"

Sherwood shrugged. "I'd rather put an end to this. So, are we agreed?"

"Fight you after school..." Kyle let out an uneasy laugh, glanced round at the gathered sheep. "Cee-cee's right, you won't keep your mouth shut, you want me to kick your ass."

"This has nothing to do with *Cee-cee*. I'll meet you there Hageman's Field. Tell Randy Lynch about it. I'd like at least one witness."

He took Kyle's wrist, pinched the nerve, and the quarterback yelped and let go of his sweatshirt. Kyle grabbed at his hand. "Jesus! You little—"

"See you after school."

Sherwood walked away down the hall. He had seen pain and disbelief in Kyle's face, and the flicker of fear. He walked through the whispering and parting of the sheep.

Later in the day he approached Randy Lynch as the beast was on his way to the gym.

"Could I talk to you for a second?" Sherwood asked.

The beef boy grinned tomato-red, his eyes glinting. "You're going to get your sorry little ass kicked, soph. You are so stupid! You are like one retard."

"Yeah, I am. Anyway, I want to talk to you about that. I want you to try and talk Kyle out of this fight."

Lynch snorted out a laugh. "Too late, you're toast, soph. You got some kind of retarded mental illness. And pretty soon you're going to be having like brain damage."

Let the fisherman keep his dignity...

"Kyle wants to finish out the season, doesn't he?" Sherwood asked. "If he gets injured, he might not be able to play. If he fights me, he'll be risking injury, and maybe even putting his football scholarship in—"

"Are you a total retard?" Randy Lynch gawked at him. "You're going to like injure Kyle? Wait'll I tell him that, it's funny. And you're retarded, man.

If you like show up at Hageman's, your ass is like..." Randy's vocabulary seemed to run out.

Sherwood nodded sadly, although he was more relieved than sad; to at last get this madness out of his body and over with forever. If Kyle was so determined to get his ass kicked, and Cathy was so determined to watch it happen, then let it be so; let her see true bloody reality for once. And damn every sheep at Mars High School, Sherwood vowed to make bloody reality.

"All right, I tried." He gave the whale a parting stare: "But I want you to remember that I tried to stop this."

The last schoolbell of the day blared out of the speakers; students wandered out of the old brick building. The sky was overcast; gray clouds spooked the late afternoon. Sherwood rode his motorcycle away from Mars High. Darker purple clouds had gathered in the west; it would probably start raining in an hour or two.

Hageman's Field, famous in Mars High School lore, was an overgrown plot of weeds on the outskirts of town. Old man Hageman didn't hay it or garden on the land, he only mowed it; and it seemed to have no other purpose than to host legendary high school fistfights. How many teenage bumpkins had squared off there over the years, going all the way back to barefoot brutes in overalls?

Sherwood wasn't surprised to see all the cars parked at the field. So there would be a crowd. Mars High, where if you let out a sneeze there would be a crowd. A better word was *Flock*, he thought. He saw Cathy Holmes standing in the gloom with Kyle and Randy. They were all staring at him as he pulled his bike into the field. The flock, twenty or thirty strong, all stared at him, some of them bawwwing in disbelief. No one could believe he was doing this, picking a fist fight with the god quarterback Kyle Kuzma.

It should be his moment of triumph, knowing now that he could finally unleash his power. But it was only grey and overcast and dismal. He should be chuckling inside, but he only felt sad and tired. He wanted it over with; he wanted Cathy Holmes and her little game over with.

Sherwood parked his bike, got off and approached Kyle. The flock of high schoolers formed something of a circle round them. Baw! Baw!

"Sherwood, what are you *doing*!" Cathy cried at him. "Are you *crazy*? Stop this, you two!"

"I want an end to it." Sherwood said. He stared into Kyle's eyes and saw the beginning of dread. *This little punk sophomore showed up here—Randy said he never would—and he's actually going to fight me.*

He's not afraid of me.

"Just leave him alone, Kyle," Cathy said. "He's not worth—"

"Cathy," Sherwood silenced her. "You don't know what I'm worth, so shut up. If we have to fight, it's Kyle who will get hurt. Do you care for your boyfriend? Then stop him before he gets hurt. You want to play football, Kyle? Then don't get hurt doing this stupid thing. I'm willing to walk away right now—"

"Okay, Pussy." Kyle threw off his jacket, getting himself pumped. "Bitch! Come on, Bitch!"

"You're saying those words because you're scared." Sherwood made a cruel smile at him. "I don't want to hurt you, Kyle."

"He just told your girlfriend to shut up!" Randy Lynch bellowed out.

Sherwood heard scattered laughter and tense whispers from the crowd; the bawwwwwwing of the sheep. *This was better than a car wreck. Everything else floated in a kind of muted serenity, a grey weariness. They are nothing, she is nothing. Everything is nothing. This should be my triumph, Choe. But it's nothing.*

"You're risking an injury, Kyle," Sherwood said. "You want to finish out the season, don't you?"

"Kick his ass and get it over with," Randy Lynch said.

"No, Kyle!"

"Let go!" Kyle threw Cathy's hand off his arm and glared at Sherwood. "Come on, Bitch!"

"You say that word because you're afraid."

Sherwood shifted his eyes to Cathy. He gave her a long-remembered smile. He felt the sheep gathering round, their eyes fixed on his calm smile, knowing some bizarre event was about to occur.

He laughed into Cathy's scared eyes, the moment was so intense; he was so rid of her. She stared at him in alarm. *The tension made him feel at peace. He was alive, and he was rid of her at last. Goodbye, little elf princess, goodbye forever. I'm going to smash your fantasy, little elf-girl—and you can despise me or not.*

"Jesus Christ, Kyle," Randy said. "The little turd's disrespecting the shit out of you!"

Sherwood smiled over at Kyle, and saw his face turn into a volcano.

"You little punk ass—"

Now at last it began: Kyle tore into him and Sherwood pivoted like a door, tripped him, and Kyle went splattering elbows cracking to the ground.

A gasp from the sheep, but it was a far away sound now. Sherwood felt himself in the perfect moment that Choe had described, that Choe had warned him against, the pure joy of power: now that he was doing it the sadness vanished. Now intensity made him crazy with joy: the pure shameful joy of this thing, the unleashing of it at last. Get up, Asshole!!!—get up! *Fight me!!*

"Let's not fight, Kyle," he heard himself saying, a mockery to his adrenaline. "You have a scholarship to con—"

"Ahhh!" Kyle's face clenched into a blind hate. He leaped off the ground and charged Sherwood like a bull; and like a bull fighter Sherwood side-stepped at the last second and smashed his forearm into the back of the quarterback's neck.

"Ahhhh!" Kyle staggered and gaped at him in horror, his head twitching at the jolt to his spine, the electric shock shivering down his body.

Sherwood risked a glance at Cathy Holmes. The green eyes were astonished. He looked back at Kyle.

The lesson is that you not take away his dignity. Let the fisherman keep his dignity…

"I don't want to—" he tried to say.

"Jesus, Kyle!" Randy interrupted him. "What the hell you doing? He's making you look like a bitch!"

"I don't want to fight," Sherwood said. "I'll walk away now—"

Kyle let out an animal scream and came at him, fists flying. This time Sherwood stepped into the attack, surprising Kyle, brushed aside his fists and slammed his elbow into Kyle's jaw. He got the ugly crunch of teeth and bone, Kyle went limp and fell wall-eyed to the ground.

Sherwood looked over at Randy Lynch, who returned the look in stupid disbelief. Sherwood stared at him until he saw fear crawl into the piggish face.

Then he looked down at Cathy Holmes, who was kneeling over Kyle, getting him awake, lifting him into her arms.

"He might have a broken jaw," Sherwood heard himself say.

Cathy stared up at him as if he weren't real.

"Was it good?" he asked her.

"What?"

Sherwood looked around at the sheep. They were all stunned to silence.

"Was it good?" he asked them. "Bawww—was it good?"

Cathy cradled her boyfriend in her arms until Kyle came to and stared up at her as if he didn't know where he was, what had happened.

She loved the fisherman more seeing him beaten on the ground. She nursed him and wept over him. She despised me for what I had done…

"Kyle?" she said. "My God, Kyle, are you okay?"

Kyle tried to speak, but only let out a sharp cry and touched his jaw.

Cathy looked up out of the flock of students, but Sherwood North was gone.

E L E V E N ...

The Bhutaran Gota studied the data on the brain-screen, the flowing chart that showed Ambassador Kosan's travels over the years. Most of the expeditions of Kosan were of a diplomatic nature—some clearly were not. It was protocol for an ambassador to screen his ship when he traveled, nothing unusual in that. Kosan traveled invisibly, as all ambassadors do, but there were usually indications of his destination, some conference, some meeting of the Gathered.

Not often, but sometimes, Kosan would travel when there was no obvious destination on his agenda. Where to? To what secret meetings, and with whom?

Now with war against the Marans looming, it was vital to discern secret meetings, deals and alliances. Kosan, as a senior ambassador, naturally worked to avoid conflict; but he knew what was coming, and the Maran Directorate was no doubt preparing for it. Kosan himself had written once, "Peace is the only friend of peace; war is the only friend of war."

The Marans had many tenets and philosophies about war; they were a dreamy race, and in that way weak. Bhutaran scholarship did not include much philosophy, or any other useless musings about metaphysical things. War was fought for gain; there was no more than that.

Gota looked up from the electric brain and stared for a long time out the plexium dome at the terrain of Bhutar, the toothy frozen mountains and the grey sheen of the iron valley below: a cold and colorless planet. There was no Bhutaran word for love, so he did not love his home; but there was one for acceptance—*Thaa-ba*. It meant, specifically, the acceptance of duty and the acceptance of what is. His people had evolved quickly in the few habitable places on this world. Their environment did not allow the Bhutaran the luxury of a long childhood. Unlike the warm, lazy water worlds, the

Bhutaran had discarded any creeds that were spiritual or mystical in favor of only that which was brutally proven to be true. Gods and angels and prophets were early and savage victims to reality. What could not be demonstrated or proven was of no use in the crucible of survival. Survival is war, and war is everything. There is no other truth than war. And nothing is more ideal than war, because in war is great unpredictability and unknown opportunity. Dreams, delusions, high philosophies might bring comfort; but at every moment of its existence a living organism is at war with something.

As it had in most of the ice worlds, utter pragmatism had taken over quickly in the evolution of the Bhutaran, making a dangerous race, technologically advanced, tuned to survival, a race without memory of humor or gayety, dedicated to the uncompromising rules of existence. To duty, even if it is tedious. Planet Bhutar was what the flux had made of it. Gota could not say that it was beautiful, because the Bhutaran had no word for beautiful.

Gota's duty was to study and evaluate the Maran diplomat, Kosan; to find weakness, a way of attack, a way to gain advantage before the certain outbreak of war; a war that would just as certainly spread beyond Bhutar and Mara.

Where does Kosan go?

It was Gota himself who had killed Kosan's son, the Hybridist, long ago, down on the murky swamp of Planet Earth. They had been close to politically destroying the Maran then. And yet the Maran had managed to kill the monster and erase the crime. He had since regained his stature and power in the Gathered, and Gota found himself shoved into a corner, a failure, doomed to study charts.

Still, there is duty.

Gota stood and waddled over to the plexium bubble. He was an average Bhutaran, short and squat, with a bullet-shaped head and a dwarfish appearance, a form heavily furred, evolved to store fat and heat. He placed a wrinkled paw on the plexium dome that shielded him from the ice-wind of his home. In war is great opportunity.

Is he forging secret alliances? Where does he go?

T W E L V E ...

▼

Now there was change, and Sherwood didn't know if it was for the better...
or probably not.

October wind blew into November wind; soft green Nebraska died to
crunching brown. Mr. Miller had moved America into the War of 1812,
his voice droning in the background. Mars City went about its slow rural
drudgery. A quiet, normal day in American History class, except that now
the sheep were giving Sherwood strange looks. Girls were giving him their
eyes. Wow, he's a secret Karate Man.

Sherwood felt that he could ignore her now, and that worried him. He
stared at the back of her head, the long black shimmering hair; he scratched
his fingernail on his desk. He wanted her to hiss back at him to stop doing it,
but somehow he knew she wouldn't, and that comforted him—no, it didn't,
it worried him. She was more than ignoring him, she was avoiding him.

That's fine. I'm avoiding her too, and something's changed? It's all over?
There's a purple elephant in the room now or something...?

She's finally gone from your life—be glad you're rid of her; she never was
anyway.

She loved the fisherman more beaten on the ground...

And then all at once he caught his breath as the silky black hair spilled
over his hand and her head flipped backward. He stared into her upside
down face.

Thank you, God. How good it is to be wrong.

"Just so you know, Sherwood," she said. "You sent Kyle to the hospital."

"I didn't mean to."

"I know you didn't." She studied him, the green eyes searching his, her
tiny nostrils flaring as if they smelled game. Sherwood had the strange sense
of being studied, as a new and surprising insect.

"How did you learn to fight like that?" she demanded.

"None of your business." He gave her a sour smile.

"Why did you back down before? Why didn't you—okay, none of my business."

He looked down Cathy's blouse at the silver lace border of the tiny white bra; breasts as small and hard as apples, as hard and cold and unresponsive as the rest of her. Nothing soft about her; and yet her hand was soft and warm that night he had held it—Meteor Night.

"Is he okay?" Sherwood asked. "Kyle's going to be okay?"

"You broke his jaw," Cathy accused. "He's going to be out for the next game, and maybe the one after that. He lost two teeth. You pretty much ruined his reputation."

"I wish it hadn't happened," he lied.

Those upside down eyes, the black hair spilt over his desk. Her boyish form arched backward, all bone and sinew. Something so scary and powerful, but he didn't understand what it could be. She's clueless—worse, she's one of the sheep. She might be little Miss Princess Sheep, but...

Hard, cold, dinky; nothing warm or feminine about you, Cathy. I always thought I'd fall in love with a soft poetess with large pillowy breasts, a kind of earth mother girl in a dream of candles and incense, someone warm and kind and understanding.

"Where did you learn to fight like that? Tell me, Sherwood."

Her face, impish and demanding, floating in the long inky hair; aqua eyes blinking at him.

"I'll tell you if you admit you're a clueless gwerk."

It worked. She grinned at him, the green eyes sparkling. His heart, so sure and balanced, stumbled and fell into the abyss.

"Okay, I'm a clueless gwerk," she said. "Now where did you learn to fight like that-- Creep?"

He smiled. "Why do you want to know?"

"None of your business."

"None of my business?"

"I want to learn how to fight."

"Why?"

"None of your business, Creepaloid! You said you'd tell me—now tell me!"

That upside down face; mean, threatening. That face that he lived to see like this, in all its elfin power.

"Believe it or not," he laughed at her. "There's a guy here in Mars by the unlikely name of Choe Kwang-su; a Korean/American guy, my best friend, and my wise old grandfather. He teaches martial arts. He has a school downtown next to the dime store, and--"

"I thought so." Her eyes narrowed. "He's the guy Uncle Rel wants me to see."

Sherwood gave her a stunned look. "Choe Kwang-su—what? No way."

"Good, he can teach me how to fight."

He stared at her in disbelief; then gave her a hopeless laugh. "You want to be taught by Choe Kwang-su."

"Why not? He taught you how to fight, and I'm a better athlete than you are."

Her eyes were studying him, and Sherwood felt again that eerie sense of being a specimen.

"You don't know what he teaches, I'm sorry. You'll never be able to learn what he teaches."

"Why not?"

"Because what he teaches is discipline and humility, those kinds of things. He teaches restraint, he teaches wisdom. There's no way in hell he'd ever agree to teach you anything. I'm sorry, Miss Holmes, but I don't think you can learn what he has to teach. In fact, it goes beyond any—fantasy of yours. What he teaches is humility."

"He doesn't have to teach me that," Cathy said. "I just want to know how to fight."

Sherwood laughed and shook his head. "He's not going to teach you how to fight, the first thing you'd do is go out and beat somebody up."

"Like you did."

Sherwood was secretly stroking her hair, making oil paintings of it across his desk. She seemed unaware. Was she?

"What are you talking about?"

"You broke Kyle's jaw, remember? You sent him to the emergency room."

"What I did was wrong."

"It was. You pretty much ruined Kyle's life. I can't believe I cried in front of you."

"Whatever Kyle did, he did to himself," Sherwood said. "He didn't have to fight, I offered to back down. He didn't even *want* to fight; I could see that in his face. But he did it because you sheep made him. He could have ignored the flock, but he didn't. He heard you all go Bawww, and he went stupid. You sheep made him do it. Baw."

"Baw," Cathy said back at him. "What stupid metaphor is that?"

"The sheep metaphor. I know, it's lame and stereotypical. But look around you, Miss Holmes. What is high school but a flock of scared sheep? And remember, I *told* you to stop him."

Cathy studied him so strangely that Sherwood actually began to grow uncomfortable: her bewitching upside down eyes...

"You're right, Sherwood, you did," she surprised him by saying. "And I want Mr. Kwang-su to teach me what he taught you."

"I don't know, Cathy. You, a student of Choe Kwang-su? I can't really imagine anything that strange and ridiculous."

"You can't imagine that I'd be better at it than you—but of course I would. I'm several million times the athlete you are."

"He would try to teach you humility," Sherwood laughed. "I think that's several million times impossible. Anyway, it doesn't matter. He wouldn't accept you as a student if it snowed in Hell."

"Yes he will, because Uncle Rel already signed me up and paid him."

Sherwood stared at her. She gave him a mean grin.

"Well," Sherwood laughed. "When Choe gets a load of you, he's going to dismiss you and give the money back, really fast. You can't even learn what he has to teach, Miss Holmes. I'm sorry, I don't want to sound mean or anything, but—what?"

Her upside down grin vanished at once, and Cathy's eyes took aim at him: "Why didn't you tell anybody you could fight like that?" she demanded.

"See, you've already flunked the first test, by asking that question."

Her face all at once crinkled adorably at him. Sherwood stared down at her boyish cleavage, touched the silky black hair, blinked his eyes in hopeless love. This strange little elf-thing.

"You made Kyle look terrible in front of everybody," she said.

"Did I take away his dignity?" Sherwood asked.

"Yes!"

"I shouldn't have." But tough crap, he thought. "Why do you want to learn how to fight?"

The black hair swept off his desk. Her face, her body disappeared.

"Okay," he said. "None of my business."

THIRTEEN ...

Choe studied this strange girl. He saw right away what had drawn Sherwood into her web: She was other-worldly, a being something like her uncle, the tall phantom. Only this one was a little sprite, with long petroleum hair and a startlingly beautiful face.

This one is not all ghost, he thought. And not all human. Choe had to take a long breath.

This is insane. Senility is creeping over you, old man. I prayed to the spirits when I was a child, but they never came to feed me. How will I teach her if I can't believe she's real?

"Miss Holmes," he nodded formally to her. "It's nice—"

"Cathy," she interrupted him. "Sherwood always calls me Miss Holmes, I know. And it irritates me quite a bit."

Choe blinked his eyes at her. "Cathy. All right. I was going to say it's nice to meet you."

"It's nice to meet you, Mr.—"

"Choe," he interrupted her.

Her face turned red. "My Uncle Rel said I should come over here and see you. He wants you to teach me how to fight."

"No, he doesn't," Choe said. "I've spoken to your Uncle Rel. He wants me to teach you how to stop being a show off."

She glared at him in disbelief. "What did you say?"

"I said what is true. And I can only teach you that, of course, if you want to learn that."

"I can learn *that*," Cathy said back at him. "So?"

Choe gripped his jaws together, tried to take a serene breath.

"So--it may be a harder lesson than you think."

"And maybe not."

Choe couldn't help staring at her, this snotty imp. She was used to being stared at, of course. Surely others stare at her. Sherwood had said she was different, but Choe never imagined…

"I take that back," he said to her. "It *will* be a harder lesson than you think."

"I'm a fast learner," she said.

Suddenly she grinned at him, and Choe was stunned. He blinked his eyes at the grin. Her greatest weapon, Sherwood had said.

He took a breath and smiled into her pixie face. She used the grin to dazzle, to make instant friends, to disarm, to mask her fear. She had learned, of course, that the grin could make people forget that she was different. A brilliant but desperate grin, lonely underneath and begging to belong.

"Your uncle told me that you have—that you are gifted," he said to her.

"I can do things." The grin collapsed, and now her green eyes went to the floor. How quickly her expressions changed, like strange darting fish. "I'm not supposed to," she said.

"Why?"

"I don't know. I can't talk about it."

"Why?"

"I don't know!" She gave him a defiant look. "Daddy doesn't want me to show that I can do things, that's all; or Grandpa."

"Or Uncle Rel." Choe nodded thoughtfully. "But you do feel different."

She studied him for a long time, and Choe felt ice trickle down his back. He sensed a dangerous intelligence in her eyes. He tried not to fall into their green poison. Sherwood said she was a seducer—she was.

The spirits never fed me a crumb, why should they try and seduce me now? What do they want?

"I'm not different," she said. "I'm the same as everybody else."

"That wasn't what I asked you."

"No, I don't *feel* any different than anybody else."

"All right," Choe said. "Then I'm afraid I can't be your teacher."

Her eyes narrowed. "I don't understand. Uncle Rel—"

"Uncle Rel asked me to speak to you and to determine if I could teach you what you need to learn. He emphasized the word 'need'."

"Well?"

"Well, no I can't. If you want to be taught by me, then you have to trust me, and I have to trust you. That's the first step."

"What do you mean?" she asked.

"This isn't like your other schools. You don't begin your first lesson in this school by lying to your teacher."

"I didn't lie to you."

102   The Blue River Valley

"Yes you did. You are different and you feel different. I see that fear in you. Forgive me for sounding like a wise and ancient Asian martial arts guy—but it's pretty damned apparent."

There was a long silence. The imp pouted down at the mat.

"I am different," she admitted finally, and stared up at him. "But I'm not supposed to show it."

"Why is that?"

The pale turquoise eyes went to studying him again; Choe had never felt such a direct stare, and a strangeness that he couldn't understand. *This one is a sorceress. Sherwood, you were right. I didn't believe you, of course, but--*

"I can't be different," Cathy said, breaking the spell. "It's very important, that's all."

"Sherwood also feels different."

She looked at him. "Sherwood can be very irritating. I'm sorry, I know you like him. You're right, though, he's the one who's different."

"He's not the one."

Her face pouted, and she seemed about to cry. He saw fear there, a very deep fear, and a deeper loneliness. Her face grew so sad and tragic that he felt his heart ache.

"They won't let me do anything!" she burst out.

Choe was startled. "You want to show your powers."

"Yes! Why shouldn't I? I can do things that are great...and they won't let me! I can't show my talents, I can't be a star athlete? I can't use my talents... why? Everybody else can."

"I don't know," Choe overcame the outburst. "There must be a reason. If you want to be my student, we can try and figure that out."

Am I falling under a spell, like Sherwood?

"I don't want to be a stupid show off," Cathy Holmes said. "I just want to do what I can do. Is there supposed to be something wrong with that?"

"I don't know," Choe said with a heavy sigh. *The spirits didn't feed me, why should I teach them? Well, an old man can change his mind, what there is left of it.*

"Do you want to learn what I can teach you, Cathy?"

"I don't know."

He blinked his eyes at her. "Impolite honesty. Good, now we're getting somewhere."

"I'm sorry," she said. "I didn't mean—"

"No, no, that's good. I'll teach you everything I can—only if you decide that you want to learn, and that you *will* learn."

"I'll try it out," she said.

He frowned at her insolent, pouty face and felt that clenching of the gut that Sherwood often described. A goddamned little crying snot! My God, how to overcome such arrogance?

"All right; then *try* it," Choe said coldly. "Your uncle has paid for six weeks of lessons, that's five times a week. It's up to you to come here or not. Either way, it's understood that I won't give the money back."

"I'll be your best student," she said. "I'm not the ditz that Sherwood probably says I am. I'm a very brilliant athlete. I'm a greater athlete than anybody knows. You'll find that out. And I'll be the greatest fighter you ever trained."

Choe groaned and shook his head. This one was going to be impossible. He didn't believe in the spirits of the ancestors or the spirits of anything else, but far back in his mind a terrible thought stared out: what powers could she have?

F O U R T E E N ...

"Do you think this teacher of fighting is a good idea?" Kosan asked.

Relomar sighed at him. "Do you think that's even an issue at this time?"

"No," Kosan admitted. "But this man Choe Kwang-su will discover that she is..."

"He teaches humility," Relomar said. "Anyway, it can't be so important at this time. We need to keep our minds on the Bhutaran."

"You're right." Kosan stared out of the plexium station at Mara, floating peacefully in her crib of Flux. "You think there will be war, then."

"I think so. What do you think?"

"Yes." He looked over at Relomar. "The Bhutaran want war because they know that we *don't* want war. It's a matter of opportunity to them. Have you ever detected any subtlety in any Bhutaran?"

"They mistake treachery for subtlety," Relomar said. "We can only hope there's a difference."

Kosan nodded soberly at him. "They reach until their hands are burned, then they withdraw, only to reach again."

"Well, the hands seem to get greedier. They've coveted Celome for a long time. If they decide to go ahead and 'liberate' the Celomese, then it's an invitation to war."

"They probably will," Kosan said. "It would weaken them to back down now. If they show signs of it, I'm afraid it's only to lure us into relief."

"So it's now simply deciding whether Celome is worth unleashing another war over."

"If it's not Celome, it will be someone else in the future. There are plenty of worlds with plexium to 'liberate'. They want those Celomese plexium fields. That would only make them stronger and bolder."

"They want to push us to declare war," Relomar agreed. "But if we declare war over an insignificant world like Celome, it will make a bad taste in the mouths of the Gathered."

"It's not insignificant," Kosan said, staring away at the universe. "The Bhutaran would have an enormous supply of raw plexium. Still, it will be— delicate—presenting our case to the Gathered. Bhutar will claim Proximity, hoping the Gathered will consider it unfortunate for the Celomese to have voracious neighbors, but hardly worth launching another catastrophic war over. Many stand to lose if we start this thing; that's what the Bhutaran are counting on. Many billions of lives could be lost."

Relomar looked at his friend, still staring out the plexium bubble. He sighed. "We face the terrible prospect of galactic war, and yet our minds are both on the lost world of Earth."

Kosan frowned at him. "You bring a teacher of fighting into Cathy's life?" he said. "I understand why, but it's very worrisome."

"He's not a teacher only of fighting. He teaches the two things Cathy may need most: He teaches restraint; he teaches the importance of *not* using your powers, *not* being a show off and a conceit. That lesson is less dangerous, don't you think, than letting her go on drawing attention to herself?"

Kosan nodded. "You're right. And the second thing he teaches?"

"Maybe the more important one," Rel said: "how to fight."

Kosan shifted his eyes back into space. He sensed the struggle beginning out there, thousands of ships flying out of the Spaceway in a wind of needles, blue strobes of Melt blistering ships and stations and cities and farms and beings, blistering to death entire worlds. Long tubes of blue incineration hot enough to boil a star system.

Such would be the fate of Celome if the war began in her halo, to be obliterated in the name of her plexium mines, or to live under the eternal rule of the Bhutaran. War would mean the sacrificing of Celome, extermination of a world for the greater good of the galaxy.

He looked at his friend. "When we present our recommendations to the Directorate there can be no second thoughts. Billions of lives are at stake."

"I agree; but if we don't make a stand in the Halo of Celome, there will be another place in the future, and the enemy will be that much stronger."

"Enemy." A word frowned upon in the galaxy, where the terminology tended toward 'opposition' and 'strategic concerns' and 'realms of influence'. But yes, the Bhutaran were Kosan's sworn enemies, and he hated them more than he would ever admit. They were a race without even the words for good and evil.

"Yes, we should challenge the enemy in the Halo of Celome. If the Bhutaran ever withdraw, they will withdraw there."

"I don't think they will," Rel said. "This armada they're gathering can't be for show, it's costing them too dearly."

"So, we must expect war." Kosan's face darkened. It was a cold and treacherous game, vying for the best interests of Mara; war was always so terrible a gamble. To doom a planet to extinction simply because they have what the Bhutaran want...

"If we let them 'liberate' Celome," he said. "They will work them to death in the mines anyway. They will have the Celomese exterminated in no time."

"Unless the Gathered can be convinced to intervene," Relomar said quietly.

"No," Kosan said. "Too many of them smell blood, too many of them want us to fight Bhutar, to weaken one another. To bring this matter to the Gathered would do no good, and it would send the Bhutaran a dangerous signal. They would take it as a flinch, and it would undermine our resolve. We must instead send the message that this is our concern, and that we will not hesitate to address it."

"So it is your recommendation, that we send the Maran fleet to the Halo of Celome."

"Yes. You also?"

"Yes. War with Bhutar will come, that is certain; better that it come now when Bhutar is at its weakest, and most likely to back down. It's happened before." He stared away into the galaxy. "We have built our reputations on difficult diplomacy."

"There never was diplomacy," Kosan said. "Not with the Bhutaran. They understand nothing of diplomacy; they have no use for it. In that respect, they are more honest than we are."

"Don't start admiring the enemy." Relomar smiled.

"No worry about that. This Choe Kwang-su—he will find out about the Mist. He will find out the secrets of Cathy."

"Probably; but can you tell me Cathy was moving in the right direction?"

"With her flips and cheerleader things? No."

"Well, then."

Kosan made a sad smile at the universe. "Well, then...."

F I F T E E N ...

▼

"You knew that soph had like all those martial arts crap, didn't you?" Kyle accused her.

Cathy stared at him. "No! I had no idea. I didn't want any of this—"

"Bullcrap!" Kyle's jaw was wired up, and it made his voice bitter and slurry and spitty. "Don't play your little innocent game. You like did all this when you started hitting on him. Now, how in hell I'm ever going to go back to school? Jesus, what the hell I'm going to do?"

"Just forget about it, Kyle." Cathy's face crinkled and she started to cry. "I don't care. I don't care about Sherwood North or any of them, I care about you!"

"You ain't the one going to get laughed at and disrespected. You don't know—Jesus, you ain't got the slightest clue. You had to flirt with him, didn't?"

"No! I didn't flirt with him. I love you."

"Now—I can't damn believe it. I let a skinny soph knock me out and send me to the hospital. Like a skinny little poem-writing nerd! Sent me to the freaking hospital! The team's going to be pimping me like a fat ho."

"It's over." Cathy stared out of Kyle's pickup at the cold brown hills. A winter wind came out of the north, sweeping tiny crystals of ice that seemed to hiss against the truck.

"A skinny little soph poetry boy—Jesus!"

"It's over, Kyle." She stared away, crying. "How could you have known that he can fight like that? Nobody did. Just—forget about it."

"Like hell. Forget about it? You don't get it; I got to get my respect back. Don't you like get it, Soph? I got to pound that little punk's face in! I can't let it go like this. He pulled some trick crap on me."

108   The Blue River Valley

"No, Kyle. Why do you care what they say? You're first string quarterback for the Martians. Who cares what anybody says, I love you."

"Right," he said. "If you really loved me, you wouldn't have been flirting with him. You wouldn't invite him over to like watch comets all the time."

"I don't invite him over; my dad invites him over,"

"How I'm ever going to go back to school—Jesus! I have to fight that little turd again and beat him—otherwise I might like just as well drop out. How I'm going to lead the team now?"

"No, Kyle. Please. Just—"

"You had to wiggle your little butt in his face, didn't you?"

She stared at him. "What!"

"I give my ring to a chick, like she belongs to me," Kyle said. "She don't flirt, she don't hang out with other guys, you get it? She don't like flip her head back on some guy's desk and—"

"I wasn't flirting with him!"

"I give my ring to a chick," he explained again. "She belongs to me."

"Why are you—stop doing this."

"Don't tell me what to do. You understand? You wear my ring, and that means you're mine, not like some little ninja nerd's."

"Kyle—please…"

"You knew he was trained in karate or something."

"No I didn't. That's a lie."

"Like bull crap, you little slut."

"Oh--LIKE--kiss my butt!" Cathy snapped.

He lashed out to backhand her, but his hand suddenly smacked—what!—like slapping a waterbed…he pulled his stinging hand back in fear. He looked at it. He hadn't touched her. "What the hell?"

She was staring at him; her green eyes widened. "Kyle…"

"What the hell?"

He stared back at her, and she felt the fear and the familiar heartbreak. How they all stared at you sooner or later, as if you weren't real, as if something was wrong with you. Her eyes wandered out of the pickup at the grey Nebraska clouds, the brittle wind, knowing that something was wrong, terribly wrong. She remembered the nightmares, and how they seemed more than nightmares, how they jolted her out of sleep. Visions of these things, brown trolls that waddled and panted across her mind, and waking up crying and terrified. And then staring at the ceiling of her bedroom trying to calm down, remembering: Nothing can hurt me!

And that there was something very wrong…

"Did you try to hit me?" she said.

"What is--?" He stared down at his hand.

"You tried to slap me."

"I'm sorry. But you were like being…a bitch…" He frowned at her. "What happened?"

"You stopped yourself," Cathy said. "You didn't want to hit me."

"What?"

"You didn't want to hit me, did you?"

He stared at his hand. "I just like lost it for a second. Jesus Christ, Cee-cee, how I'm ever going to face the team? Those guys— Damn It!—freakin' knocked out and sent to the hospital by some nerd soph…thanks a lot."

"I'm sorry," she said.

"Christ. One of your little soph friends like knocked me out in front of the whole school—Jesus! I can't believe it."

"I'm sorry."

"You should be grateful that I even like gave you my damn ring!"

"I am grateful. Kyle, I love you."

"So what do you do? You like give it back to me."

"I'm sorry. I didn't want to. I love you."

"And did you ever prove it by doing me?"

She looked at him: "No, I didn't."

"I gave my ring to a little soph." Kyle laughed bitterly. "And Daddy made her give it back."

She was studying him, crying and pouting like a spoiled brat. What was it he'd slapped? It wasn't her bitchy little girly face. He had slapped something, but it wasn't her face. What the hell?

"That's it. You're too weird for me," he muttered at last. "I don't like need you jamming up my life anymore."

She stared at him. "What are you saying?"

"You've like messed up my life enough already? Like that's what I'm saying?"

"Kyle…?"

Kosan stepped out of the invisibility and strode through the great trees that cast shadows over the farmstead. A cold, windy night. Nebraska, this part of planet Earth, was going into its winter; a clean frost chilled the wind as it sang down from the northern polar ice cap. Dead dry leaves swatted his legs, swept by the sad, lonely air.

He stared out at the dark river valley, and he wondered if this was a dream he would ever see again. They say that to die in a blast of Melt is not

110   The Blue River Valley

so bad a way to go, a sudden not being. But how would they know? A bitter possibility: to die in some cloddish Bhutaran's sights, to vanish in silver mist. To never have this again, the mad dream of animalhood, of sweet and distant memory.

He breathed the cold, spicy wind. This can take you away from the terrible things out there. Why in the old myths is paradise always primitive and hell always civilized? Do all primates instinctively know the future, the coming of the machines? How can this storybook know the truth: worlds beyond its understanding are at war; and war is not an evil to rise above, because it cannot be risen above. It is not something that can be stopped or controlled; it is nature, it is an essence, like the Foam. It becomes more damaging and more colossal and more unthinkable and more antiseptic, but it cannot go away. Primate worlds forever ask, 'Why is there war?'--not conceiving that everything around them is war.

War is what makes the Flux, the Bhutaran believed. Not a part of the process of life, but the process itself. And damn them, they were probably right. An ambassador may grow so cynical that there is nothing left but cynicism. Then you see a place like this.

Suddenly he stared through the trees. He heard a strange wailing sound beyond the wind, and he went in that direction. He first encountered the giant dog, Woodrow, who came growling and thumping and barking out of the darkness until he recognized Kosan, and then began waving his great tail. Cathy said the animal liked being scratched on the rump, and Kosan complied. "Why are you whining, Woodrow?" He rubbed at the animal's silky coat. "What is wrong?"

Why am I asking questions of a dog? But it wasn't the dog. What was that sound?

Then ahead, in a clearing of brown leaves, he saw Cathy sitting on the ground in the darkness, her hands cradling her face.

"Cathy?"

As he ventured into the clearing, she looked up at him crying and sniffling at her nose.

Kosan stopped in his tracks. The dog rubbed at his leg and whimpered, upset. Kosan stared at his grand daughter, crying at the night. His mind shot back to the vision years ago, the black-maned baby bawling up at him, the baby covered in river slime; the baby who looked like Donis, loudly demanding love.

"Cathy," he said quietly. "What is wrong?" Terror shot through him. Was she signaling? Have the Bhutaran—he glanced quickly around at the cold night.

She howled at him suddenly, scaring him to death, her face crinkled and miserable. Then she leaped off the ground and ran up to him and hugged him. "Grandpa!" she cried.

He held her, startled. He hugged her and stroked her long black hair. "Cathy, what's wrong?" he said.

"Grandpa!" she sobbed into his neck. "Kyle broke up with me!"

"What?" He let out a shaky breath of relief.

"He broke up with me and he called me a bitch and he said I was weird!"

Cathy let out a long moan and sobbed into his neck. Ambassador Kosan held her, stroking her hair. "Oh…Cathy…"

"I love him, Grandpa!" she cried. "And he said he doesn't love me anymore!"

"Well, he's—he's an idiot then—I think that's the word," was all Kosan could say. He stared up at the sky and breathed relief: to have this simple and foolish and wonderful heartbreak and not have empiric war. To not have to return to the great galaxy and its tiresome sophistication, its frozen pragmatism, its soul-less automatons, suffocating truths and endless intrigues. All of that is nothing here in this world and her beautiful mythologies…

"He said I was weird, Grandpa. Everybody thinks I'm weird!"

"No…Cathy, you're special. And if this boy doesn't see that—"

"I love him, Grandpa!" she bawled into his neck. "I wanted to marry him, and now he says I'm weird!"

Kosan stroked her hair. "No, Cathy…no."

He patted her lightly on the back, stroked her hair, held her to him, staring over her sobbing head at this Blue River Valley, at the cold Nebraska wind so clean and lonely.

Galactic war with the Bhutaran; trillions of organisms acting out trillions of stories, all moving toward nothing, toward a great timeless drain; all forgotten as if they never were. Is there a difference between a great galactic war and a broken-hearted girl on Earth? Both—all-- race to nothing.

She finally broke away and stood sniffling and gasping at him, her face crinched up so that he was reminded of the dog, Woodrow.

"All right, Cathy," Kosan said. "Enough. Please stop crying. Come now, stop crying; calm down."

"It's Sherwood North's fault," she cried. "And Daddy's fault too." She glared at the farmhouse. "He didn't like Kyle, he didn't even give him a chance."

"No, no. It's the boy's fault. The boy Kyle is stupid if he doesn't want to be your friend. You know that it's his fault, and you know that he is a fool. It's been understood for some time."

She wiped her eyes and laughed. "He's not very intelligent—but, Grandpa, I love him!"

"Yes, but don't start crying again," Kosan said. "The boy who doesn't want to be your friend made a stupid mistake, and he will come to regret it."

"He wants to fight Sherwood again," she sniffed. "I hope they beat each other's brains out."

"You will fall in love again. I know that it works that way—here."

"Not like with Kyle." She pouted at the dark river valley beyond the cottonwood trees. "Now he's going to tell everybody how weird I am."

"No one will care what such a stupid boy thinks, Cathy."

They were content to stand and listen to the brown leaves rustling in the wind. He put his arm around her, and she laid her head against his shoulder. A blanket of dead brown leaves covered this clearing, piled by the wind. Gradually Cathy's eyes dried up and began burning a pale turquoise.

"He's been checking out Kirsten—just watch, Kyle's going to start going out with her. He's going to do it just to hurt my feelings."

"No, Cathy, no more crying, it upsets Grandpa." He patted her back and gave her a puzzled look. "Who is this Kirsten?"

"Kirsten Pavelka. She's a senior. She has big boobs and I don't. Plus, she's blond."

"This is important, this blond?"

"Yes. Kyle wanted me to dye my hair, but Daddy wouldn't let me."

"No, stop crying, Cathy. To change your hair to yellow?"

"To blond. It's no big deal, Grandpa." She scowled at the farmhouse. "Every girl on earth does it. But of course Daddy had one of his mega-fits when I asked him if *I* could."

"Your father has developed some wisdom through the years," Kosan said. "I agree with him completely, you should not change your hair."

"It's just that Kyle said I'd be cuter with blond hair. I knew he was tweaked out when I told him I couldn't."

"Now you can show him that it no longer matters what he thinks," Kosan said. "Did this Kirsten change her hair in order to attract boys?"

"Yes. She's a brunette."

"A--?"

"Her real hair is brown," Cathy said.

"And do you want to be like this brown-haired Kirsten girl?"

"No." Cathy wrinkled her nose in disgust.

"All right, then. Have you talked about this with Miss Mason?"

"Yes. At least she knows. She's a lot more understanding than Daddy ever was."

"What about your new teacher, this Choe Kwang-su?"

"No." Cathy snorted and frowned. "Sherwood North's always hanging out there, and I don't want the two of them gloating. Sherwood probably thinks he's king of the world now that he ruined my life and Kyle's life. Every time he looks at me I can see him gloating, and I want to bash his face in."

"I think he would probably let you do that," Kosan smiled. "Without trying to fight back."

Cathy glanced at him. She blinked her eyes, the green signal that she was going to confide something: "Can't tell anybody," she said to him. "Grandpa's Code."

Kosan frowned soberly at the passwords: "Grandpa's Code," he said.

"Okay. Grandpa, I think Kyle tried to hit me."

The frown turned seismic. "What!"

"I think he tried to slap me. I got mad and told him to stick it up his butt or something, and he lashed out at me. And—you know...."

"This Kyle—he tried to—"

"Don't tell anybody," she said. "Our Code, Grandpa."

"Yes, our Code." He studied her. "Is that why he called you weird? When he tried to hurt you and couldn't?"

"I didn't make any big deal out of it," she said. "I didn't say anything."

"Good. Let this stupid boy think what he pleases."

"But you know, Grandpa." Her green eyes started to glisten with tears again.

"I know that you should forget the stupid boy."

"You know I'm weird, Grandpa. I'm so different..."

"Nonsense. If you let this stupid boy Kyle make you *think* you're weird, then it's your own fault; because you are *not* weird."

"I'm different, Grandpa." Her face pouted at him. "You know...."

Kosan shrugged. "So? I'm different, this Sherwood is different, Miss Mason—everyone is different. We all have to be different, and often it's painful. Now give me a hug, and let's go into the house. It is a cold night. Are you different, Cathy? Yes. So are we all."

"I love you, Grandpa."

"And very soon, this ridiculous Kyle will want to be your friend again." Kosan hugged his grand daughter, his veteran heart aching. This cold black night on Planet Earth, the dead leaves of Nebraska scraping his ankles. Will I ever see it again? Will I ever want anything but this again?

The moon of Earth fell under the sky. It was a sparkling night, and Cathy was asleep upstairs with her giant dog. Kosan stood with the science teacher on the farmhouse porch. The wind had died, and now the loose crust of brown leaves lay still on the ground. It was cold enough that they exhaled thin clouds of steam as they spoke.

"I haven't been able to talk to her about it," Eric said. "She blames me for chasing that Kyle away."

"She is already getting over that," Kosan replied. "We had a good talk. I'm grateful, because I may never see her again."

Eric looked at him. "What are you talking about?"

"When I leave this night, I may never return, Teacher."

"What?"

Kosan smelled the earth night. Winter's cinnamon breath. "There is war out there," he finally said. "A great war is about to begin."

"A war?" Eric stared at the glittering night sky. "How can that be?"

"It is what it has always been. Did you think that as a species evolves and advances into the galaxy that it abandons war? Everything that is alive swims in the wake of war. Long ago on this world, beyond any memory, a microscopic being attacked and ate another microscopic being, to take its life in order to live. Many things have changed since then—that hasn't."

"A war between whom?"

"The Bhutaran and their allies, the Marans and their allies, others beyond your understanding. It could become a great galactic war, a very great twisting of the Foam. So I do not know when I will be able to return, if ever."

Eric's stomach squirmed, remembering the dwarf things in the headlights so long ago, the Bhutaran. After so many years of expecting change, dreading it, now it's suddenly here?

"Why is there war?"

"In this case, the dispute involves a small planet less significant than even Earth; a planet that finds itself in an unfortunate area of the galaxy. I can't explain, Teacher. You know what war is. A million years from now it will be the same. You may not feel it or see it or hear it, but every living second there is war."

"Not like that." Eric found himself gawking at the night sky. Which stars, which--"How will that affect us?"

"It won't," Kosan said. "You won't even know it is happening."

"This war—will it—produce a lot of casualties?"

"What you call death? Yes, probably more death than you could ever conceive."

Eric shuddered. He swallowed at his throat. "You sound so cavalier about it."

"What?"

"So—detached. Death beyond conception?"

"Death is another human illusion," Kosan said. "Humans believe strongly in Death, of course, because Death doesn't exist. Nothing ever dies, it merely changes. When you spray insects and kill thousands of them it means nothing. When thousands of your people die, it means something. But in the end it means nothing."

"I understand that. But still..."

"Yes, I know," Kosan sighed. "It is a terrible act, taking life. The Marans have always believed that. The problem: others do not."

"The Bhutaran. Will this war put Cathy in danger?"

"No. For Cathy and for you it is a fortunate thing. If war breaks out and if it escalates, Earth will be a forgotten memory."

"This war—"

"No, Teacher, you don't need to know anything about it. I have important duties, and I trust you as always to watch after Cathy. I take my leave of you, and hope that I can return some day. If not, then see that my grand-baby is...happy."

"Did you tell her anything?"

"No; only that Grandpa will be busy for awhile, and might have to miss her sixteenth birthday, but that I would see that she gets the birthday present she asked for."

"I hate to imagine."

"What is called a Hummer," Kosan said.

Eric stared at him. "What do you mean, Hummer?"

"That is what she asked of me for her birthday. It is a large driving vehicle. You don't know what it is?"

"Yes, a Hum Vee, which means—I don't know what it means. Cathy asked you for a Hummer?"

"For her birthday, yes. Why do you stare at me? Will this vehicle draw attention to her?"

"Yes!" Eric looked at the sky. " My God, Cathy asked you to buy her a Hum-vee."

"Yes, a Hum-vee Model H3."

"And you said you would."

"Of course. This 16th birthday celebration is very important to her. She will be getting her license to operate vehicles. She told me that she will need a vehicle to drive herself to school."

"Oh, she said that."

116   The Blue River Valley

"I will have the Hummer brought here for her birthday, as I promised. I leave it up to you to teach her how to operate it. I hope to be here, but I may not even *be*." Kosan drew something out of his coat pocket. "Here, Teacher," he said, giving Eric a grim stare. "Against my judgment, and at Relomar's insistence, I give you this."

"What?"

Kosan held up a small, oblong crystal. It had facets, like an elongated gem, and it sparkled red, yellow, green and blue in the yard light.

"A diamond?" Eric took the object. It was strangely light in his hand. He turned it round, watching the flashes of prismatic color. "A crystal?"

"It is a very special form of plexium," Kosan said. "None of this element exists on Earth, or so little as to be undetectable. It is an element that contains great power."

"What is this?"

"This is called a tal; it is an object that you must put away some place safe and leave alone. I give you this because one day you may have to give it to Cathy."

"Why?"

"That I won't tell you, only that each face of the tal is a power, including Melt. If some day you need to give this to Cathy, do so. But only if you must, only if it is a matter of life or death—until then put it away and leave it alone. It is important that Cathy never understand what she is. But if her life depends on it, and if she must know, then give her this."

Eric stared at the crystal. "This is a weapon."

"And other things."

"How will I know when—"

"Maybe you won't," Kosan said. "Maybe you will. That is all I will tell you about this. No! No more talk. The time for talk is over. Put the tal away and leave it alone."

They stood silent for a long time, Kosan staring out at the dark river valley, the final rustle of brown leaves. He took in the cold air of Nebraska. Finally he let out a misty sigh. "It is time for me to go, Teacher. Tell Cathy that Grandpa loves her."

Eric watched the Maran Kosan stride off the porch and away into the trees; then suddenly vanish as if he never was.

Eric stared for a long time at the trees. A star-ship was out there that would soon streak out toward the Spaceway—toward some war—a star ship as invisible and soundless as a radio wave; something that never was…

He looked down at the plexium diamond in his hand. What power was here? What strange twist in this dream that was his life. Galactic war? What did any of this mean?

Only that he always knew things would change, the small dream here in Nebraska would seek the vaster reality and finally discover it.

He stared into the dark trees beyond the porch; only the soft sound of dead leaves, and the spooky hooting of an owl.

Gone as if he never was. As if none of this ever was. The Maran Kosan, a vanished memory? Will Cathy have vanished, and am I finally waking up from this dream?

He rushed into the house and up the stairs to check. Cathy lay sleeping next to Woodrow, her tiny nostrils flaring, her face pouting at some dream she disapproved of.

Oh God—all right, relax. Jesus Christ, Cathy, a Hum Vee?

He left her bedroom and went back downstairs and out to the front porch. He stared at the dark trees, the place where the Maran had stepped into invisibility. He still clutched the plexium diamond in his fist. It hasn't vanished, Cathy hasn't vanished. Those memories over the years—they haven't vanished. It's still true.

Only now the change was coming.

SIXTEEN ...

"Hey, Cath."

Kirsten gave her a sad yet radiant smile; Kirsten Pavelka, bleached blond, full and voluptuous; a grown up woman, Kyle's new rubbery squeeze.

Cathy looked up from tying her tennis shoe. "Hey, Kirsten."

"Like, sorry to hear about you and Kyle."

Cathy stared up at her. Kirsten's radiant smile quickly morphed into a radiant sad-face, her booby chest bounced nervously.

Cathy Holmes had such strange, menacing eyes.

"It's all right." Cathy pinned her green eyes back on the tennis shoe lace.

"If you like need somebody to talk to…"

"No, I'm okay."

"God, I'm sorry to hear about your locker. That was like really bad. Whoever did that—"

"What?" Cathy stared up at her. "My locker."

"You didn't know? Oh, God. Somebody like spray painted your locker."

Cathy frowned. "What?"

"Somebody like spray painted some crap all over your locker. I'm sure it was that dumb ass Randy, or--."

"Who? Kyle? Who—"

"I don't know who did it, but it was like cruel."

Cathy tied her sneakers, leaped up and ran out of the gym and down the hall to her locker. Several students were gathered round it, chuckling.

She stared at her locker. In black jagged paint were the letters—what? B-B-O-B.

Cathy read her locker in puzzlement. B-B-O-B?

She marched back down the hall to the gym, pausing at Kyle's locker long enough to swing her fist savagely into it. The Mist bounced her fist harmlessly away, and she went frowning back into the gym.

"Kirsten," she said. "Did Kyle do that?"

"I don't know." Kirsten looked at her in mild alarm. Everybody knew that she was really weird. "I'm sorry, Cath. It was like probably that fartbag Randy Lynch. I don't think Kyle would do a thing like that. Not even after..."

"It says B-B-O-B," Cathy said. "What's that supposed to mean?"

Kirsten choked back a laugh. "Cath, I'm sorry. It was a cruel thing—"

"What does B-B-O-B mean?"

"It's like some kind of guy thing. It's a stupid thing."

"What?"

"It means like 'two bee-bees on a board'."

Sherwood scratched nervously at his desk. He stared at the back of her head.

Cathy Holmes looked straight ahead at Mr. Miller and sat rigidly listening to the Battle of New Orleans. Her expression was--controlled.

He had read the locker, as had everyone in the entire school: Kyle and his rapier wit. Why is he taking it out on her, why not me? I know why.

So? It's not like the little princess didn't have it coming. You wanted to be one of the sheep, Cathy, he thought at the back of her head. Well, this is what the sheep do to each other. It has been pointed out to you—by an A-- hole, I know—but it has been pointed out to you that you are not perfect, not by everybody's standards. Oh, boo hoo! You have small breasts, and you'll never have big ones unless you go to the plastic surgeon, and you probably will—you undoubtedly will. You'll get your rich grandpa to buy you a boob job, that'll probably be your 16th birthday present. Boo hoo, poor Cathy. Grandpa, the other kids are making fun of me—buy me big boobs for my birthday!

He watched the back of her head, wishing that she would splash her hair back and look at him upside down; but this time--

Okay, just leave her alone, that's what she wants. Let it go, stop being happy that Kyle dumped her and she's miserable. It doesn't matter anymore. There's nothing to be happy about. She hates your ever loving guts now anyway, so leave it. Let it go! I'm *not* sorry you're miserable, Miss Holmes, he

120   The Blue River Valley

thought at the back of her head. And it's *not* my fault, it's yours. I'm not even going to try and be smug about it.

"Baw baw go the sheep," he muttered, making an acid frown.

She didn't even favor him with a flinch. She stared straight ahead, studentish, into the Battle of New Orleans, as if there never was a Sherwood North.

"Bawwww," he whispered, feeling cruel, but unable to stop himself. "Do you finally hear the bawwwwwing of the sheep, Miss Holmes?"

He shut himself up. That was stupid, immature; not even mildly original. She was not amused. He glanced secretly around to glimpse her face: sober and nun-like. "Baw," he whispered.

"Shut up!" she finally hissed at him. "Is that some kind of stupid modern poetry?"

"Kind of," he said. Sherwood scraped a groove in his desk, he was so glad to hear that voice. "What was done to your locker was stupid," he said at last.

"How is it any of your business?" She looked behind her.

"Well, I had a fight with your boyfriend," he said. "That puts me at least in the supporting cast."

She smothered a laugh. Then her nose shot up and she was once again the snotty bitch. "I don't care what you or Kyle or Kirsten or anybody else thinks of me. You're all butts as far as I'm concerned."

"Butts?" He laughed.

"Go ahead and gloat, Sherwood. Now you're the karate man, go ahead. Now the sheep look at you and respect you and they're making fun of Kyle. I don't care if you gloat or not, Sherwood, because you are a butt."

"Is that better than a creep?"

She laughed, and the black hair shimmered purple; then a smeary rainbow suddenly in the fluorescent classroom light.

"I'm going to show Kyle that I'm better than him, and I'm going to show Kirsten that I'm better than her, and I'm going to show Mr. Kwang-su that I'm better than *you*," she said behind her.

"That must have really scared you, what you saw on your locker," Sherwood said.

She stiffened, was silent for awhile. "What?"

"You're too scared to even tilt your head back. Cathy's a chicken."

He folded his hands prayerful on the desk, and the miracle happened. The black hair washed suddenly over his hands, and her impish face appeared, upside down.

"Bite my butt, Sherwood," she said.

He smiled at her. "Is that an invitation?"

"Barf me into infinity." She made a green sneer. "You really ruined Kyle's reputation. He said he's going to come after you when his jaw heals, and I hope he beats your face up. I hope he beats you into creep city."

Sherwood laughed. "I don't think so. Otherwise he wouldn't wait for his jaw to heal. No, Kyle will want to save his pretty face for all those college co-eds next year." He caught himself. "I probably shouldn't have said that."

Her eyes stared into him: "Why did you have to ruin everything?"

He started to speak—her face, pouting, adorable—he felt a strange tragedy that went beyond them, he didn't know what or why. Was he—something was different now?

"I think you know why, Cathy."

"Maybe you like me."

He stared at her in alarm. The sudden upside down grin overwhelmed him. He touched the silken black hair with his hands: something not of this earth...a siren leading him to the sea cliffs.

"Maybe I do," he heard himself saying. "I know—before you say it—but you don't like me. I like you, but you don't like me—so what."

"You ruined everything," she said. The grin dissolved; the warm aqua pools were suddenly two judgmental stones of jade.

How quickly her face changes...Sherwood took a breath and tried to calm his heart. "You don't like me—right? So..."

"That's correct," her beautiful upside down face said. A poison imp, a murderess; the last thing on God's earth he should fall in love with. "But you like me a lot."

"Go ahead and gloat, Miss Holmes. I'm not the one who has the right to gloat, you are."

"You're glad you made Kyle look so bad," she accused. "You're glad he broke up with me."

"I am," Sherwood said. "God help me, I am."

"Why? Just because I *laughed* at you?"

He stared into her beautiful and savage face, the tiny flaring nostrils, the upturned nose, the cute imp, arrogant, hateful, superior, phony, malicious, clueless, flirty, grinning, elf-evil, weird, spiteful...

"You like me a lot," she grinned at him. "That's why."

"God help me," he said. "And you like me."

"No, I don't." Her nose made a green wrinkle. "I don't like you. You and Daddy ruined everything for me, and I don't like either one of you."

He gave her a look. "What?"

"I don't like you, Sherwood Stupid Name North, because frankly, you're unlikeable."

He couldn't believe—

"Unlikeable? Catherine Boring Name Holmes is lecturing me about being unlikeable."

"That's right. You always talk about the sheep and laugh at the sheep—but you're worse, because you think you're better than the sheep. And you're not."

"And you are," he said.

"Anyway, *sheep* is a pretty trite and over-used metaphor. It shows zero creativity."

The black hair swept off his desk, she sat up and it was gone, whatever it was—something...I guess I'm officially dismissed.

He sat and scraped at his desk.

"I love you," his voice said in anger.

"What?"

"Nothing."

SEVENTEEN ...

Sherwood didn't know what he was doing.

Yes, he did. What he was doing was riding his Kawasaki 650 up the rock drive of the Holmes place, the 75 acre farmstead where—something—what?

I know what I'm doing, he thought, but what the hell am I doing? This is really the most desperate, most embarrassment-prone, idiofoolish—My God, Choe, if you talked me into this madness just to put me through more humiliation then rest easy, it's on the way.

Dr. Holmes' Honda Civic was parked in the yard, next to the Toyota Celica that belonged to Miss Mason. Uh oh, company—is that good?

Sherwood parked his 650 in the yard and Woodrow came lumbering off the porch, happy at the sound of the motorcycle.

One thing here is glad to see me anyway. This is a mistake. This is a mistake, Choe.

"Butt scratch!" he said nervously to the Saint Bernard. He squatted down and rubbed Woodrow all over the back, the dog whining and licking at his face. He looked up at the farmhouse. It was a Friday evening. Shadows were just sneaking into the trees, but the yard light hadn't come on yet. A blazing, candy-colored sunset swept the western skies.

God is setting a spectacular stage for this disaster, Sherwood thought. He rubbed the big dog and stared up at the window in the second storey of the house, where he knew her room was.

What am I doing?

Soon enough the door to the house squeaked open and Dr. Holmes came onto the porch. "Sherwood, is that you?"

"It's me, Dr. Holmes."

"We heard your motorbike."

124   The Blue River Valley

"Yeah, I was just passing by and just thought I'd stop in and see how you're all doing." Sherwood gave him a weak smile.

Dr. Holmes nodded. "Cathy's up in her room. Miss Mason is here—visiting."

"Oh. Well, I don't want to intrude or anything. I just wanted to see if Cathy was okay. I heard that some kids at school made fun of her."

"Yes, I know." Dr. Holmes frowned. "Well, she's in her room."

Sherwood looked up at the second-storey window. "I just wanted to say hi to her, see if she's okay and all that..."

"Go on up," Dr. Holmes said. "She'll be glad to see you, I'm sure." He gave Sherwood a tight smile. "I said before—Miss Mason is here? She's one of Cathy's teachers."

"Yes, I know Miss Mason."

"Cathy is sort of blaming me for this quarterback thing." Eric Holmes frowned thoughtfully. "And so I'm—consulting with Miss Mason on the problem. Go on up and say hi, Sherwood. I'm sure Catherine will be pleased to see you."

"Yeah..."

Feeling suddenly *out-of-body*, Sherwood followed the giant Saint Bernard up the porch steps, Dr. Holmes alongside clapping him fondly on the back. They stepped into the house and he said hello to Susan Mason, who smiled up from the couch in the living room. Sherwood was amused to note that they were watching *Sleepless in Seattle*; a strange way of 'consulting'. He glanced up the stairs, where Cathy's bedroom was.

"Go on up," Eric Holmes said. "Her room's at the end of the hall. She'll be glad to see you, Sherwood. But the rule is, keep the door open."

"I will, Sir."

Woodrow, groaning suspiciously, followed him like a tank up the stairs. *An over-protective dog that weighs more than me...hmmm.*

Down the wooden hallway, and here was her room. Here was Cathy Holmes's bedroom. Strangeness flooded his body. He looked down at the Saint Bernard, who thumped his tail encouragingly. Sherwood tapped at her door.

"What, Daddy?" her voice said.

"It's—no, it's Sherwood." He tapped again. "Sherwood North? I'm knocking at your door. Don't tell me you didn't hear my bike."

"What?"

"Sherwood North. Woodrow is out here too. It's—well, it's Sherwood. I think your dog wants in," he added stupidly.

"Come in," she said after a long pause.

Adams apple stuck in his throat, Sherwood entered her room, and was stunned. He stared around at the science instruments, the computer and digital recorder and musical instruments, the globes of Earth and the moon and all the other planets, the models of aircraft hanging from the ceiling, crystalline electric robot toys everywhere, the stuffed dinosaurs in cartoon colors smiling from their corner, the charts on the walls, the photos of Newton and Einstein, Franklin and Edison, and a woman who must have been her mother.

A dense clutter of knowledge and learning and curiosity and fascination. Slides and microscopes and an ant farm; a glowing aquarium where strange fish moved in blue water. The room of a mad scientist, not a spoiled sophomore high school girl.

"Holy—Ca-rap!" he stared around him. "Is this the museum of the Starship Enterprise?"

"What!" Cathy Holmes looked at him over the book she was reading, *Madame Bovary.*

Her face, here in this bedroom—the same face from history class, only now something more. He swallowed his astonishment and managed to smile at her.

"Sorry to spoil the end, but she *does* get busted by her husband," he said. "Emma Bovary…"

"What are you doing here?"

She lay on her bed wearing a black cotton robe decorated with yellow planets and moons, and she automatically covered up her legs. I can die now, Sherwood thought, and it'll be all right. Take me now, God, and I will not bitch.

He tried to be suave: "Strangely enough, I didn't have a date tonight, so I just thought I'd stop by and piss you off," he said. "You have an interesting room here."

"My dad knows you're up here?"

"Yes. He wanted me to come up and check on you, to see if you were all right."

"Why wouldn't I be all right?"

"Because you're a gwerk; and I worry about gwerks. They're never all right."

"That's not even a word," she said. "Writers always think they're clever if they make up new words."

"Blame James Joyce." Sherwood smiled.

Unbelievable seeing her like this, in her bedroom, on her bed, in her night robe. The elf-princess Cathy Holmes.

He expected her to say something outrageously hateful, but she said nothing, just studied him with her oceanic eyes. Woodrow jumped onto the bed with her, causing it to buckle and groan; she absently rubbed at the great dog's slobbery face. "Daddy said you could come up to my bedroom?"

"Yes, he did…but notice I left the door open."

He stared around at the collection of genius things she had crammed into this room. It seemed that every time he saw her, the fascination amped up, and he washed closer to the rocks.

I can't keep falling deeper in love with her, it would be a disaster. I can't let her draw me deeper in, she will destroy me. I will bash against the rocks, and the last thing I hear will be her laughing. This was—as I predicted, Choe—an embarrassing mistake.

Okay, enough of this.

"Well," he said with a gruff sigh. "I just wanted to say hello, see how you're doing and all that. The creep Sherwood will go now, I'll leave you alone."

He got as far as her bedroom door when she trapped him by saying, "No, it's okay. You don't have to go, Sherwood. Daddy's right, I feel like crap."

"I'm—sorry." He turned and smiled at her. He rolled the chair out of her computer desk and sat down, rubbing at his face. "No, that's a lie. I feel pretty good, actually. And I'm not sorry."

"What?"

"I feel good, and I don't give a rat's ass if Big Man Kyle feels bad or not. I don't care what they sprayed on your locker."

"You don't care about anybody but you."

"Wrong. Wrong as usual, Catherine Ann. And you know it. I came here because I like you a lot, that's it."

She studied him, the eyes bewitching his own, glowing beyond earth, this terrible powerful siren…

Then came the grin, and he could have died at that moment. His eyes stared at her grinning face. He was deadly in love, he was deadly in love.

"You came here because you like me a lot."

"That's right. A damned lot."

He looked around him at the museum that was her bedroom. Not a bedroom, but a den of knowledge, a lonely world of the mind. He looked at the Hubble posters of galaxies and nebulae, the strange charts covering the walls of her room.

Her eyes studied him so deeply that he felt unreal for a moment. Choe, you prepared me for everything, how could you not have prepared me for this? Falling into her poison-green eyes…

"Do you want to kiss me, Sherwood?" she startled him.

He stared at her. "Yes, you know that—yes."

"Okay, you can kiss me."

Sherwood tried to swallow at his swollen throat: Cathy Holmes in her black and star-yellow robe on her bed, the beautiful pouty face overwhelming his eyes. God, God, God.

He went to her bed, Woodrow eyeing him and assembling a growl in his throat. Sherwood leaned over toward her, the elfin face moving toward his—

"But not like this," he said.

"What?"

"Here, turn around, Cathy."

"What?"

"Turn your head around. Right; now lift back your head, like you do in class."

She giggled at him. "You are very weird."

"I know. But I'm proud of it."

"Kyle told me I'm weird," her beautiful upside down mouth said. "I suppose everybody thinks I'm weird now."

"I've always thought you were weird," Sherwood said. "That's it. Now turn your head back."

Her upside down face stared at him. The long magical black hair lay across his lap. Her tiny nostrils flared as she looked into his eyes as she never had before. Her robe, the bed...

"Let me kiss you like this," he said.

"Kiss me, Sher-weird," she grinned.

E I G H T E E N ...

▼

Choe Kwang-su wasn't being paid a lot of money to think of spirits and their powers. His mother had many times spoken to what she called the *Si-ryeok*, her sad, weary face aimed at the Korean moon. Choe had never really believed.

This new student, Cathy Holmes—no matter if she is a spirit or not. Who knows these things? Uncle Rel has paid me a great deal of money, and it's understood that money buys discretion. Well enough. I've accepted my life and the money, and I am content to be here, at this time. I will keep the secret and try to teach around what I've seen. If I am not going mad, maybe one day a doctor will explain to me what this is all about. No, I'm not going mad—somehow, it's true.

It was astonishing what she could do with her body. He had seen such mastery in China, where young girls perform breath-taking feats of gymnastics, their bodies like tight live wires. This one was like that, able to fly into spectacular flips and spins and twists, her long black pony tail dancing down her back. Never had Choe witnessed such perfect balance and electric energy in such a controlled form.

But it was something else that he had seen, what pushed it into the supernatural: one day he watched Cathy sprint across the mat to do a double flip, but the mat was wet and her foot slipped. She only managed a flip and a half, and Choe grimaced watching her tumble down.

Then suddenly she lay suspended, as if she were floating, and she fast recovered herself, looking around at him. Something had stopped her fall, something had protected her. Now nothing was the same between them.

"Caught myself on that one, didn't I?" she grinned at him.

"Yes, you did." He couldn't hide the shock, and she read it in his face.

"What's the matter?"

He studied her, his mind trying to make sense of this. Then he stared for a long time out the glass doors of his school at Mars City, the lonely prairie place he had made home. The old wooden houses of Mars City creaking in the wind; the brick buildings of downtown moaning ever in the wind. This is how she can do these things.

How is it possible? Can spirits you deny so long ago find you at last, here in this place, Nebraska? Can the si-ryeok find you here and make you believe?

"Cathy," he said with a heavy sigh. "Come here, sit down on the mat."

She danced over and folded herself down cross-legged on the mat, her green eyes studying him with suspicion; that black-maned face not of this world.

"What is it, Mr. Kwang-su?"

"You are a very good gymnast," he said. "Naturally talented—"

"I told you I was a great athlete."

"Please don't interrupt me. I'm the wise Asian teacher, you are the student. The student doesn't interrupt the wise Asian teacher. Yes, you are a gifted athlete. It will not be difficult to teach you how to fight, I'm sure you'll pick up the techniques quickly enough."

"A lot quicker than Sherwood," she muttered.

"Yes, well...But if I teach you how to fight, there must be no secrets between us."

"I don't know what you mean."

"Yes, you do. I've seen you launch yourself so reckless into the air that I aged ten years and imagined lawsuits, and you in an iron lung. I couldn't believe you could be so fearless—and now I know."

Her eyes grew large. "Know what, Mr. Kwang-su?"

"You're fearless, Cathy, because you have nothing to fear."

"But fear itself." She giggled nervously at him.

"That's right. A wise saying, I wish I'd thought of it." He studied her until she stopped giggling. "You have no fear because something protects you."

They traded stares for a long moment. Her green eyes changed, searching inside his. He sensed danger in the eyes, an intense power--and he had to finally look away, at the sanity of the small Midwestern town outside the school, the safe and changeless moving picture, the stores and rattling pickup trucks, the grey courthouse building. The school, my school; the dream of every teacher, to have his own school, no matter how small, no matter where; then years later to sit back and laugh at the spirits. Those who control our Karma, my mother believed: those things that move our lives. She can't have such a power, it is nonsense—it has to be nonsense. But I saw.

"I can't talk about that," she said at last.

Choe felt his stomach tighten. You're not senile, old man, it *is* true.

"Well, you're going to have to." He swallowed an unknown fear. "As I said before, I can only teach you if there is trust. And there can't be trust with secrets. Not secrets like that, anyway."

"I'm not allowed to talk to anybody about it." Cathy's eyes grew tears, and she stared at him with such a fierce misery that Choe's heart sank.

"It?"

"This thing, *It*; this thing."

"This thing that surrounds you." Choe studied her. "This thing that protects you."

"I can't talk about it!" she said, crying at him. "It's very important."

Choe nodded cautiously at her. "A teacher can only expect trust if the teacher is willing to give trust. What is secret to you is secret to me. Anyway, it's not a secret now. I'm no old fool, Cathy, although I may look like one. Something surrounds you and protects you. That's why you're reckless. That's why you can launch your body into danger without any care."

"I don't want to be different, I can't be!" she said, putting on the pout. "I'm so tired of being different. People always look at me like I'm weird. I can't be different."

"What is this thing, this *it*?"

"I don't know what it is." She stared at the mat. "All I know is I'm not supposed to tell anybody about it, or show it. It's always been on me and I can't get rid of it."

"It gives you incredible power," Choe said. "I could attack you right now with sixty years of martial arts experience and skill, every dirty trick in the book of dirty martial arts tricks, and it would do me no good at all, would it?"

"No."

She put her face into her hands and bawled like a baby, and Choe looked away. Did Sherwood know?

No, he would have really flipped out if he did. What power is greater than this, that nothing can harm you? And what other powers does she have?

"So now there is one less very big secret." Choe gathered himself and smiled at her. "Good. Wipe away your tears, Cathy, and stop feeling sorry for yourself. That will be the theme of today's lesson. The first lesson on the road to wisdom is this: nix all blubbering and sniveling. What my beloved mother called accepting Karma, before she slapped me upside the head. Self pity is not in the curriculum of this school. What this is—'it', we'll just have to work around. Your father knows."

"Yes."

"Your grandfather; and of course Uncle Rel."

"And nobody else. Well, now you!" She bawled relentlessly into her hands, her black shimmering hair veiling her face. "No one can know!" she sobbed.

"No one will know. Now stop crying, Cathy. I'll talk to no one about this. This is a dead secret. Quit bawling, it gives the school a bad name. A martial arts school doesn't like a lot of crying and whining. It turns away customers."

She cried and sniffed out of her hair and rubbed at her eyes. "I don't know what it is, but I don't like it. It's terrible."

"Power can be terrible," Choe agreed. He looked at her. "Sherwood doesn't know."

"No. Sherwood can be a very irritating butt sometimes—excuse me, Mr. Kwang-su--and he doesn't need to know anything about me."

"But he wants to. Sherwood—the butt—is in love with you."

Her face reddened. She let out a tearful laugh. "He had the nerve to come over to my house and kiss me the other night, the dork."

Choe smiled. Finally Sherwood had taken some of his advice. "I'm glad he did."

Cathy stared at him suddenly with such bewitchment that Choe actually drew back: the eyes, those liquid-green magic eyes—the elfin stare.

"No one can know," she said to him.

"I understand," Choe said. "No one will ever know from me. There are secrets, and there are dead secrets. Believe me, this is a dead secret."

Her strange eyes penetrated and examined his own. She was a being of two worlds, he sensed. And there was fear in her eyes, more than being different—some terror that she did not seem to understand.

"No one was ever supposed to find out."

Choe nodded at her. "I see now what your Uncle Rel wants me to teach you, beyond how to fight. He knew I would find out, of course. He wants me to teach you how to conceal this—It...Cathy, what's wrong?"

"I'm scared!" She began to snivel again, the goddess at once a little girl.

"What are you scared of, Cathy?"

"Being so weird!"

She broke out bawling again, and suddenly hugged Choe, and he held her crying against his chest. He felt the blue electricity that enfolded her, like the sparkling needles of strange water. He looked out at the world beyond his school. The cloud-grey autumn, the maple trees swaying in sad wind.

"I have dreams, Mr. Kwang-su. Dreams of monsters."

"So do we all sometimes, Cathy."

"But somehow I think they're more than dreams."

Choe felt himself shudder.

"These monsters in your dreams; are they always the same?"

"Yes. They're like—Morlochs, or Neanderthals or something. Like strange animal-men."

Choe looked away. The spirits were never real; they never came to feed me. Now, an old man, they come wanting to be taught. Sherwood desperately loves this sprite. What does he believe she is when he looks at her?

What is she?

Choe Kwang-su had the strange suspicion that even she didn't know.

And what are they?

NINETEEN ...

▼

Gota stared out of the plexium bubble at the needles swarming away from Bhutar, the warship fleet shooting into the nickel sky. He had no word for joy, only satisfaction—that events were underway at last.

Galactic war, the great enterprise in which all is risked to gain all, where the great Flux moves in tidal waves beyond prediction; the destruction and domination of enemies for gain. It was a self-evident truth, known by all and yet denounced by so many.

Why? Are the Marans not always saying that truth is more beautiful than illusion? And yet they cling to the illusion that there is anything but war. Uncountable illusions flow senselessly across the Foam, but only one truth:

War.

The silver ships of battle flew silent up into the Spaceway. Gota studied the rock valley below the plexium dome.

Warriors fly toward the great battle, and I sit here studying a phantom on a brain screen. What I have done in all these years is nothing now, against the great thing that is about to happen.

Still, there is duty.

Trips to the faraway Spiral Arms, in the direction of Planet Earth? It is maybe more than nothing after all. When the war comes, the Flux will move in unpredictable directions. Things can be gained with remarkable speed in times of war.

He looked around as Ghalla, his Commander, rose out of the floor. Gota bowed respectfully, and Ghalla returned a cold, impatient look.

"So, Clerk Gota? You asked to speak to me?"

"Yes, Commander. I may have found out where the Maran Ambassador Kosan goes when the anomalies occur in his schedule."

Ghalla scowled at him. "So? Where?"

"I believe Planet Earth," Gota said. "Ambassador Relomar also goes there."

"Earth? No, that's nonsense. Why would he waste his time traveling to the Spiral Arms at a time like this?"

"That is where his son created the hybrid."

"Hybrid! Gota, we are on the eve of galactic war. Do you think it matters anyway where some Maran ambassador goes?"

"It may, Commander. Ambassador Relomar also—"

"Goes to Earth? This means nothing, Gota. We are on the eve of a great war, and you speak to me of this?"

"His son created a hybrid long ago," Gota explained. "The ambassador—"

"Enough!" Ghalla frowned. "These things mean nothing. Why do you bother me with nonsense at a time like this?"

"I seek permission to use a few ships to follow—"

"We are on the brink of war, and you want precious ships allocated to—what?"

"It may be important, Commander."

Gota knew that it would come to this, but he needed to try. The opportunities were out there, in the hot theater. Not here at a brain screen, on cold, metal-gray Bhutar. Words would be recorded and analyzed by the Gathered, words that might live on.

"We are at war," Ghalla said to him. "Wherever Kosan or any other Maran goes is of no importance now."

Gota bowed. "Forgive me, Commander."

"You waste my time, Gota." Ghalla dismissed him with a haughty glare.

"I understand. Deepest apologies, Commander..."

Ghalla marched to the floor portal and sank out of the room. Gota stared away at the brutal wreckage that made his home, the yellow sheen of moons on cracked tables of rock. Snow-wind sweeping white mist across ruins of iron and granite and glittering mica; a cold sun that let only the terrible things live. If you want to live, said the sun of Bhutar, you must be terrible.

The behavior of his commander did not affect the clerk. It was the Cult of Arrogance, and Gota practiced it with those below him. It was expected; there would be no discipline and efficiency otherwise than to brutalize those below you.

Yet the Flux may change things with great speed. Commander Ghalla has his duties, I have mine. It is proper that Commander Ghalla chastise me, I have bothered him with nothing.

Gota stared out the dome, his pink eyes squinting. There is duty; and duty can sometimes lead to more than nothing. One can move upward in times of war. Ghalla is a military being, he sees nothing political. But it may be that the political can be the more powerful, and that one day I will frown at Ghalla, and he will fear me and bow to me, and I will dismiss him as nothing.

Kosan and Relomar both visiting Earth, the primitive swamp that hasn't even sensed the galaxy yet. Why? The monster was erased long ago, an old scandal. There is nothing on such a planet to…

Why though?

He stared at the leaden sky, where needles of war had sparkled into the fat clouds. The fleet rockets away toward war, soaring toward death and domination. Here on Bhutar calculations are made.

Gota's gnarled face twitched as he stared away.

Earth is nothing, a swamp in nowhere. Yet he goes there. On the eve of galactic war he goes there, and Relomar too. What can this place in the Spiral Arms mean against what is to come?

TWENTY...

▼

A drear evening, the wind cold out of the north, a muddy Nebraska sky.

Downtown Mars City was almost deserted, her orange streetlights just blooming alive. The maple trees around the county courthouse clattered at Sherwood like skeleton claws come up from the crypt.

Ugly, grey, wind-shattered Nebraska.

Still, no condemned fellow had walked to the gallows with a more hopeful heart.

Make that a really stupid heart, he thought. This dismal November evening tells it all. I can feel her glistening web around me, the harder you fight the more tangled you get.

Maybe there's a poem here.

It would be the bitterest one he ever wrote, and he had written quite a few bitter ones. He remembered the softness of her lips, and he felt an odd terror. How those lips would one day laugh into his face as she destroyed him?

He passed the dime store and peered into the glass window of the school, the only fluorescent life on the block besides the Grand movie theater. Cathy was going through a simple series of punches, Choe Kwang-su holding a punching-pad against her blows, explaining things to her as she jabbed at him. Cathy Holmes wore the stereotypical James Bond white Hollywood karate pajamas that made her look more adorable than dangerous, her long hair in a ponytail; and she had, of course, tied a black belt arrogantly round her waist.

I'll bet Choe was happy to see that.

Watching her, Sherwood was struck by how tiny she was, not more than five foot four and ninety pounds dripping wet.

Okay...

Sherwood entered the school. Choe lowered the pad and smiled at him in relief. "Ah, my assistant has finally arrived."

"Assistant?" Cathy Holmes looked behind her. "What are you doing here, Sherwood? This is my two hours."

"I asked Sherwood to come," Choe said. "He is one of my master students, and I want him to work with you on the things we've gone over so far. I'm too old and tired to be holding this." He tossed the pad like a frisbee to Sherwood. "We're working on punching," he said, with a frown of warning. "Remember, Cathy, no kicking."

"Okay, punching." Sherwood adjusted the pad. He smiled at Cathy in her white karate pajama uniform. "Is this okay with you, Miss Holmes, the ninja warrior?" he asked. "I don't want to irritate you or anything."

"I'm okay, Mr. North, the butt-creep."

Choe let out a groan. Cathy glanced at him; then stared back at Sherwood's face until it burned red. Having broiled him done, she giggled at him, those secret lips he had kissed, like cinnamon and mint. "In two weeks I'll be able to kick your butt all over this mat, Sherwood. I probably can now."

Sherwood traded looks with Choe. The memory of kissing her in her bedroom, and how at that moment all hope had vanished, and he had smashed headlong into the rocks. A terrible dream comes to life. You listened to the siren, but you weren't tied to the mast.

"I'm afraid she's not joking," Choe said.

Sherwood provided himself as a moving punching bag, and even he was astonished at the girl's savagery and speed. He stared in awe at her as she pummeled the pad he was trying to shield himself with, and was soon backing away from her attack.

Choe studied them. How is it she can pummel Sherwood like a bobcat, and yet the floor cannot let her fall? She can do things she wants to do, yet things can't be done to her. The force was for protection only. Sherwood had kissed and hugged her, so it was not something always around her. She can be touched but not harmed.

He watched them going at it, Sherwood desperately dodging and moving and parrying her blows with the pad, backing away, finally out of breath, laughing in admiration.

"Okay okay okay! You hate me that much?"

She stood back and gave him a red elfin sneer. "Why are you panting, Sherwood?" She laughed. "You didn't know I could fight, did you?"

"No, I didn't. Not like that."

"Everybody thinks I'm a little dink," she said. "I can—"

Choe cleared his throat, and she glanced over at him. He frowned at her.

138   The Blue River Valley

"I've learned all the basic punches and defenses and counter punches," she said back at Sherwood. "I figure if you can master it, it can't be all that hard. I can already fight."

"Yes, you can. I can tell by your karate costume and your black belt that you are now a super warrior, better than everybody else."

"Better than you," she sneered. "I'll be able to kick—"

Choe groaned loudly, and she again glanced over at him. He gave her a dyspeptic frown.

"I believe you," Sherwood said. "Someone as perfect and superior and humble as you—"

"All right!" Choe clapped his hands. "Time for a break. Come sit down you two."

Sherwood and Cathy folded themselves down on the mat. Choe stared for a long time out the glass front of the store. Another day darkens sleepy-eyed Nebraska. Strange spirits follow you even to this place. He expelled a long and hopefully wise sigh. He looked at Sherwood. "Tell Cathy why you didn't fight Kyle Kuzma that first time," he said.

Sherwood stared down at the mat for a moment. "I had to taste humility and shame."

"You sure did—"

"Cathy, please shut up," Choe commanded. "Sherwood, why did you have to learn humility and shame?"

"It's the first lesson and the most important lesson."

"Why?"

"It gives you permission to have power."

"Why do you need permission?"

"Otherwise, power will destroy you, and more important, it will destroy others. To learn humility is to learn true power. True power is not pride, but humility." Sherwood looked over at Cathy. "It is to finally have the courage to not care what people say about you or think about you."

"Very good." Choe looked at Cathy, who was studying Sherwood with those cat eyes. "You see, Cathy? The first and most important lesson you can learn is the hardest. If I can't teach you that, I will never be able to teach you anything."

She frowned and pouted down at the mat, and Choe felt his heartburn rise.

"I'm not the show off he probably says I am." She sneered at Sherwood and he angrily stuck his tongue out at her. She stuck out her tongue back at him.

"Well, since we're discussing matters in a mature way," Choe said. "What is it that you earn, Sherwood, by going through the test of humility?"

"Freedom," Sherwood said, regaining his tongue.

Cathy Holmes stared for a long time out the glass front of the store. Sherwood traded looks with Choe, the boy shaking his head and rolling his eyes. Choe smiled, seeing the blood in Sherwood's face, how his eyes couldn't leave her for long.

"Freedom is what you earn only when you embrace humility," Choe said to her.

"I can do that," she said. "I'll pick it up. I'm not as shallow and phony as you guys think."

"No, you're not," Choe agreed.

"But you're really close," Sherwood laughed.

Cathy laughed back at him, and Choe saw Sherwood's face blaze red. Choe clapped his hands ceremoniously. "Break time over," he said. "Now, Cathy, continue to pound Sherwood. Remember to change up your punches, and no kicking—surprise is the greatest weapon, remember that."

"Thanks a lot," Sherwood said, vaulting off the mat.

After her lesson Cathy stood in the wind outside the dime store, wearing the white Cornhusker sweatshirt three times too big for her, the hood a white fold under her long black ponytail, her hands in the sweatshirt pouch. She looked like a tiny cloud.

Waiting for her father to come and pick her up: the white-robed elf princess standing in the prairie night. Choe locked up the school, bowed to his students and puttered away in his vintage 1968 Chevy Camaro. Sherwood walked up and stood with Cathy in the cold wind.

"Daddy's picking me up," she said, glancing at him.

"Yeah, I know. So, is it such a tragedy that I stand and wait with you?"

"Maybe." She grinned at him. "I'm pretty good, aren't I, Sherwood?"

"You're—amazing." He looked down at the sidewalk. Mars City yawned and rolled toward slumber; a car and a truck drifted by under the orange streetlights. The neon stripple of the Grand Theater announced Spiderman Two. He wondered what it would be like sitting with her at a movie, on a date. Stores dark and silent stood around them in the restless wind; a Midwestern town going off to sleep.

Her eyes studied him out of the darkness. Her imp teeth grinned. "I know why you're hanging around," she said at last.

"Why am I?"

"You want to kiss me."

140   The Blue River Valley

He smiled into the wind. "As always, you know everything."
"Well?"
He swallowed at his throat. "Did you learn the lesson tonight?"
"What?"
"The lesson. You only learned it if you can say one thing."
"What's that?"
"That you *want* me to kiss you."
"You couldn't kiss me if I didn't want you to. I wouldn't let you."
"So, you didn't learn the lesson."
"Okay! Since you're following me around and won't leave me alone—"
"Do You Want Me To Kiss You, Miss Holmes?"
"Yes!"

He took her in his arms and kissed her. The tiny elf body pressed into his. It was the wildest dream of joy and the wildest nightmare of terror. He knew this moment would haunt him for the rest of his life. That sky-colored aura glittered around him, sending every sense into a riot. He felt a blue cloud of diamonds enfold him. Her tongue flickered into his mouth, and he felt her lips stretch into a smile against his.

The great crashing into the rocks.

When they came up for air, she said, "I can't believe I'm making out with some weird soph. I must be crazy."

He held her, the electric body, nymphan—and so suddenly surrendering to his touch. He kissed her in the cold November wind, and knew he had died against the rocks.

"You're not the one who's crazy," he said against her lips. "You're the one who's sane."

TWENTY-ONE ...

▼

THE HALO OF CELOME:

"We have time," Kosan said to the brain screen.

The Bhutaran ambassador's simian face nodded at him; the wrinkles of these brutes still mocked him now, all these years later.

We killed your son, and now we will kill all of the Marans.

"We have time, Kosan," Autha said at last. "But will we have a deal?"

Autha's tiny pinken eyes peered at him.

"It would be worth a try," Kosan said. "War will weaken Bhutar and it will weaken Mara. There are many who would like to see that happen. It is no sign of concession that we don't happen to be among them. We hope you aren't either."

Relomar, seated next to Kosan, let out a tired sigh. This was no more than an academic pantomime, an idiocy; there was no diplomacy left. Now it was a last minute effort to place blame for the awful thing that was going to happen.

Kosan understood that he was playing to the crowd, the Gathered who were listening in on this conversation, some of them smiling in satisfaction. He studied the ambassador on the screen. Like all Bhutaran, Autha was squat and heavy with a flat forehead and a skull that had evolved more horizontally than the Maran and human skull. Kosan had read Cathy a bedtime story one night, about magic forests and trolls. Seeing the illustration in the children's book of the troll, Kosan had thought, they must sense the Bhutaran out there, to have invented one.

Ambassador Autha stared at him in dull silence. Kosan chose his words carefully: "If Bhutar believes that trying to avoid this conflict is a sign of fear or weakness, Bhutar is making a mistake. Don't misunderstand us when we say we wish to avoid this conflict. And don't misunderstand us when we say that if the Bhutaran fleet enters the Halo of Celome, we will immediately attack it."

"Celome is nothing," Autha said, playing to a different side of the Gathered. "We never wanted this; we want to avoid this. I have asked you a thousand times, Kosan, and you never answer: why are the Marans so determined to go to war? This affair is between Bhutar and the Celomese. We never spoke of war with Mara. Why does Mara provoke war with us? Has Mara never colonized planets in her proximity?"

Kosan nodded and looked away from the twisted face on the brain screen. The sins of the fathers plague the sons. He had dealt with the Bhutaran long enough to know that you couldn't deal with them. They had to be crushed; it was in their nature to crush or be crushed, nothing else. They had never known fairy tales or imaginary tea parties, or pistachio ice cream; those things would baffle and disgust them, those things that were not composed of pure truth and pure science and pure reality; things that primitive and awe-struck creatures believe. The Bhutaran didn't have the ability to imagine that which isn't real. Their strength, or their weakness? No matter, they are that which has to simply be destroyed, there is no other way around it. Exterminate them as you would a plague, before the plague exterminates you.

He tried to maintain his diplomatic perspective, but the Gathered were all aware that he had a special reason to despise this ugly race.

Relomar made his own point to those listening: "This conflict is about whether the Galaxy will keep balance, or not," he said to Autha.

Autha frowned. "Balance. What concept is that? Mara maintains the right to colonize and exterminate those worlds in her proximity—yet when others do, Mara cries balance! Balance! What exactly is the Maran definition of *balance*?"

"Those things were wrong," Relomar said. "Those things happened long ago."

Kosan sighed and tapped Rel on the leg. He stared out of the warship at the other ships patrolling the Halo, needles that pierced the Foam and sparkled in the dim planet-light of Celome. Weapons ready to strike. Behind them Planet Celome was a brown and green pebble preparing to die; an especially tragic Flux—nothing more?

His mind drifted to primitive Earth, and he smiled at Autha, who showed nothing in return. Why not smile and dream of it? What they were doing here was a hopeless cause.

"You smile at me," Autha said. "Why, Kosan?"

"I can only say that war will weaken us both. There are enemies of Mara and Bhutar who want that."

"The Maran fleet has invaded and is occupying the sovereign Halo of Celome. The Gathered have ruled that this is a violation of Bhutaran Proximity."

"Some of them did," Relomar put in. "Not all."

"You are wrong about war," Autha said, the tiny pink eyes staring out of the screen. "In war, only one side is weakened. The other is strengthened."

"We expected nothing else," Kosan said. "So, war it is."

His mind wandered to the world such an imagination away. He tasted pistachio ice cream in his memory, and he smiled. "Have you ever tasted something called ice cream, Autha?" he asked.

The Bhutaran ambassador frowned his mass of wrinkles. "What?"

"I didn't think so." Kosan smiled into the troll face. "You demand war and so we will give you war. And now, there is nothing more to talk about, is there, but pistachio ice cream?"

Kosan's smile was more than a wistful memory, it was also a last diplomatic move; he had found that the Bhutaran were always taken aback when something smiled at them. If this was a useless exercise, at least try and poke the enemy one last time. The Bhutaran frowned well, and they scowled excellently—but a smile concerned them.

"You make that smile with your face," Autha said. "But this is war we speak of: the destruction of the Maran fleet. Is this primitive world so important that your people would risk war and destruction to conquer it?"

"To protect it," Kosan said. He kept his smile on the brain screen, enjoying the Bhutaran's pink squint, but also mindful that the Gathered were listening. "It is Bhutar's choice to fight or avoid. If your fleet exits the Spaceway, they will be attacked. That is where we are now."

"Is Mara so eager to stir the Foam?"

Kosan looked away from the screen at Relomar. Rel gave him a tired shake of his head. Diplomacy had, of course, died long ago. This was merely a Bhutaran effort to buy time and place blame, to influence the Gathered. Sad to tell, the Gathered would regard the loser of this to be at blame, whichever side it was.

"Is Mara so eager to wage galactic war?" Autha demanded again, his blundering style of diplomacy.

Taking Kosan's cue, Relomar smiled at the brain screen. Was he thinking of the place, Earth, of the Valentino's pizza? Is that why we can smile at war?

"There is little time now," Relomar said to the brain screen. "If Bhutar wishes not to fight, Mara must know immediately."

144   The Blue River Valley

Autha's face frowned at him from the screen. "Mara is eager to go to war, to unleash that Flux against the galaxy. Mara will regret that decision. Bhutar does not want war."

"Then Bhutar must not enter the Halo of Celome," Relomar said.

He traded looks with Kosan, who was gazing off, an almost dreamy look on his face. This was play-acting. There would be war because the Bhutaran wanted it. This was diplomatic nonsense, only performed to convince the Gathered that one side or the other was to blame. It was well past time to avoid war, now it was time to avoid responsibility.

They all understood this: "We state here and now that Planet Mara does not want war," Kosan recited. "If war is forced on us, we will have war—but we do not want it."

"The words of Marans are words," Autha said. "But your actions are not your words. What you say is well and good, but what you *do* is reality."

Kosan was sick of reality. Time was running out. Soon the Bhutaran fleet would swarm out of the Spaceway and there would be the silent and savage destruction. So little time now to think of that place, the sub-atomic particle called Nebraska, the Blue River Valley so far away in the Spiral Arms.

If I die here, in the Halo of Celome, let me die with that in my mind, what I found, what Donis found so long ago. Did my son feel at peace when the Melt tore him away?

To go into dark forests and fight demons: that was the theme of the bedtime stories he had read to Cathy, when she curled her imp feet under the covers, the big dog lodged like a mossy brown-and-white boulder against her, and Cathy gave Grandpa her fascinated green eyes. His diplomatic voice became epic as he read and acted out the parts, the good and evil, the decent heroes and odious beasts; he worshipped every second of the dramatics. To go into the dark forest with a white spear and fight the monsters. Not what you want to do, but what you have to do. The Foam moves that way always: We of the advanced worlds, who unravel and use the power of the Flux, of nature, to survive—we who rule like supermen--must fight monsters, just as bacteria must.

Autha remained silent. It was well beyond negotiation now, of course. The Bhutaran smelled hesitation, and now it was only a matter of buying time.

"Relomar," Kosan turned to his colleague: "Speak for us now, my friend. Speak for Mara."

Rel nodded and stared at the Bhutaran face on the screen. "You want more time, Autha—but time is gone. What we do now and say now is nothing—"

"Because you have already decided on war!" Autha cut him off. "What the Marans say is nothing, what they do is everything."

Relomar started to speak. Then he grunted and looked over at Kosan. Will we ever see that place again? his eyes asked. That made all of this sickening to us?

"You want war," he said. "All of the Gathered know this. And *some* of them want it too—"

"Rel." Kosan cautioned him. The Gathered were listening, and most of them disapproved of assumptions.

Relomar ignored him. "You are simply moving in to steal what belongs to the Celomese," he said defiantly at the pink squinting eyes. "It is that simple. Bhutar wants to *steal* the Celomese plexium mines—nothing more. That is because you are evil."

"Evil!" Autha made wrinkles of his face. "The concept of a primate. You invade and occupy a planet within the legal proximity of Bhutar, you interfere with an affair that does not involve you; Mara goes where she does not belong. This is an alliance between Bhutar and Celome. You have no right to interfere. It is Mara that is deciding on war."

"It's no alliance," Rel said. "It's invasion and slavery. The Celomese brought their vote to the Gathered. We are here because Celome asked for our help—against you."

"It is what we all know it is, Autha," Kosan said quietly. "Diplomacy is over."

He looked over at Relomar. He gave him a sad smile.

"There is no more time," Relomar said to the face on the screen. "We have to report to our Directorate."

"Bhutar requests more time to consider this problem," Autha said.

Relomar nodded. Problem. How so many in the Gathered must be chuckling fatalistically at this moment. It was all a charade, an act. They had known long ago that this was imminent, and they had prepared. Now it was here. War would be fought; eye-burning beams of Melt would stab the Foam and blow apart any matter in their way, including an atmosphere. Death. Napalmic death to billions; the blue death that ruled the galaxy.

"If the fleet of Bhutar enters the Halo of Celome," Kosan said. "They will be attacked. There is no time left, Autha. Will this be war?"

"Bhutar is not anxious for war," Autha said. "We wish to avoid war. Why does Mara insist on it?"

Kosan looked at Relomar. What they knew long ago was here, now. The Flux was moving unimaginable Foam toward their people. Will Mara live through this? Will I live through this and manage to go back there and hug my grand daughter?

146   The Blue River Valley

"I dream of Earth too," Rel whispered, smiling at him. "On the cusp of war and death, I dream I'll go there again."

"I want to see her again," Kosan said. "My grand-baby, Donis's child. Death doesn't worry me; only, I want to see her again."

"I do too. I want to see my niece and her friends."

"Such things are nothing now," Kosan sighed.

"Or everything."

Kosan smiled at the brain screen. Ambassador Autha was staring out of it; arrogant-faced, a wrinkled rock; a being defined by granite brutality. And how sad that this would not even be a war about good and evil, not like in the fables he had read to Cathy. He wondered why Rel had blurted out that about evil. Only the primates believed in good and evil. Neither existed. This war would be fought not for good or evil, but for plexium.

Kosan stared out at the warships glittering in the dull planetlight. If we fight, we are fighting for plexium, nothing more.

"I want her to be happy," Kosan said under his breath to Rel. "I don't want her to be lonely."

"I understand." Rel smiled at the Bhutaran face on the brain screen. "Notice, Autha gets uglier when we smile at him."

"What are you confiding?" Autha said. "What are you whispering of?"

"We are whispering of war," Relomar said to him.

"If the Maran fleet attacks us," Autha said. "The price of this war will be on the heads of the Marans."

"Some of us will not have heads after this day," Kosan said.

Autha was about to speak, but Kosan suddenly ordered the brain screen off and it went dead.

Relomar looked at him in surprise. "An extreme gesture," he said. "Was that necessary?"

"I don't know." Kosan studied the blank screen. "If there is a last hope, then maybe I gave it. If there is no hope, then it doesn't matter."

"Well, I'm afraid it doesn't matter," Relomar said. "Long ago we knew there was no hope."

"I'm afraid too."

"An extreme gesture, and a good one," Relomar decided. "He hated it when we smiled at him, did you see that molten face?"

"I have just ended all negotiations." Kosan looked out at the Maran fleet suspended in blackness. "I can feel the Gathered frowning."

"We both know the Gathered," Rel said. "Some wise, some not--all pragmatists."

"This human teacher." Kosan let out a long sigh. "An instructor of fighting; do you think that's in any way wise?"

"He can possibly teach her to conceal her abilities, as he did with the human boy Sherwood."

"Yes, but a teacher of fighting?"

"She has a dangerous tendency to draw attention to herself."

"Her father told me that this is normal in human girls of her age. The earth woman Susan Mason said that it is normal."

"Well." Relomar smiled at him. "If Uncle Rel has made a mistake, surely it can't matter now. This could be the death of everything we know. I'm horribly glad that Earth is so far away."

Kosan smiled at the galaxy. He stared toward the distant fuzz of the Spiral Arms, where that place lay, where the primates played in the sandbox of childhood—so beautiful and innocent; children carefree and playing in the wind. Children learning but not yet knowing.

"She was never meant to be," he said, staring away.

"I miss her too," Rel smiled. "After the holocaust, we should go there together, Kos, and have the Thanksgiving Dinner they talk about."

"After the *holocaust*; that's a human word, Rel."

"Yes."

"After this, if we survive, we will have a dinner of thanksgiving."

"I vote pizza. The Valentino's, those with the shrimp and the mushrooms and the black olives and the garlic breadsticks besides."

"Agreed," Kosan said, "so long as somewhere along the way there is ice cream."

TWENTY-TWO ...

▼

"Thanksgiving break in one week," Eric Holmes said.

"Won't that be nice."

Susan Mason was peering at the moon through his telescope. Eric rested his hand lightly on her back. He looked cautiously round the yard at the students wandering about, pointing into space and explaining things to one another, some of them bending over telescopes. It was a wintry night, and not many of the astronomy people had shown up, only the die-hard fanatics, most of them his students at Valley College. That was okay, less gossip.

They heard the 650 Kawasaki scrabble off the gravel road and rumble up the long rock drive.

"Sherwood's here," Eric said.

"He said to tell you he'd be late." Susan looked up from the wondrously detailed face of the moon. "I saw him in the hall today."

"Ah."

"Of course you know, he has a huge crush on Cathy," she said.

"Ah, well....what? No."

"Yes. Why should that surprise you?"

Eric sighed at the sky. Nothing should surprise him anymore. He had loved the stars from the first moment he had stared up at them. But he couldn't see them now with such awe-struck innocence. What was up there was down here, there was no mystery at all, not really.

Every piece of scientific information we have, he thought--(and I have some doozies)--only makes us less significant and important. How can you ever get back to the child's delight, knowing they were out there in the ultra-zillions, more life than a word could describe? That this galaxy alone among billions of galaxies is crawling, oozing, swarming, permeated with life. So long we asked: is there life beyond us, or are we special? And how to adjust to

- 148 -

the fact that life is everywhere, and that the bible *was* right—we are all just animated dust.

Kosan out there, involved in some miasmic galactic warfare. How will I explain to Cathy if Grandpa never comes back, if she never sees Uncle Rel again? Life out there, so abundant that a lunatic would gape at it, fear the idea of it. To discover life beyond the earth—our greatest achievement?

No…our greatest disappointment. Then we'll have to go on knowing we're nothing.

Millions on millions on millions on millions of worlds can surf the Milky Way. They are more evolved, more intelligent; they know things and have things that we can't imagine. They are more advanced than us, superior, those things murdering one another out there.

But they aren't any better, maybe that's what takes the mystery away; what will break the hearts of future scientists: they're out there, in freakish multitudes and forms inconceivable--but they're no better than us.

"Eric, are you all right?" Susan asked.

"What?"

"You were staring off so strangely. It's not the end of the world, that a boy has a crush on her. It's normal."

Eric watched Sherwood North roll his motorcycle into the yard. A lingering fear over the years: his daughter would one day fall for a boy who rode motorcycles. He looked around the yard but couldn't find Cathy. She had wandered into the trees with Woodrow.

"No, it's not that. He's a good…are you sure he has a crush on her?"

Susan laughed. "You didn't get very good grades in Biology, did you?"

"I was better at Atronomy," he admitted.

Sherwood North approached them, smiling in his rather fatalistic way. Eric should glare at him in disapproval, but no, that would be stupid. Some boy is going to want to be with her and—do things with her sooner or later. If the disaster has to happen, better it be with Sherwood, who at least has a brain.

"Miss Mason," Sherwood nodded to them. "Dr. Holmes."

"Sherwood." Susan Mason smiled. "Look at the moon."

Sherwood peered into the telescope, his fatal smile turning into a grin. "My God," he said. "The old prize fighter."

"What's that?" Eric said.

Sherwood looked up from the telescope. "I always think of the moon as the old prize fighter. His face has been mashed up so many times he has scars over scars. But he still keeps that lop-sided broken grin."

"You wrote a poem about that," Susan Mason said. "I read it in the school paper."

150   The Blue River Valley

Sherwood looked around, embarrassed, at the quiet farm. "Not many here tonight."

"A good night for the moon," Eric said, "but not much else."

"I think Cathy is down by the creek." Susan smiled at him. "I saw her go down in that direction with Woodrow."

"Ah. Okay, I guess I'll see how she's doing, and all that..."

Sherwood made a quick exit across the yard and into the cottonwood trees, Eric watching him with new eyes. A friend is one thing...

"She'll be glad to see him," Susan said, cuffing him on the shoulder.

Eric looked back at Susan. "I mentioned Thanksgiving Break, didn't I?"

"Yes."

"Do you have plans for Thanksgiving? Any kind of tradition?"

"I usually drive up to my brother and sister-in-law's place, in Grand Island. We have dinner."

"Oh. I was just thinking that—well, I'm inviting you to spend Thanksgiving with us this year, here. I understand if you have other plans."

"No." Susan grinned and kissed him on the cheek. "I'd love to."

Eric smiled round the yard. His students were engrossed in the heavens, their imaginations gone from earth for the time being.

Okay!

He took Susan in his arms suddenly and kissed her, and he felt the longing and desire and terror shudder through him. The years of knowing and hiding and fearing and the God-awful heat of the blue Melt all those years ago, down by a Florida river—Oh my God!

"Whew!" Susan said, finally peeling her lips away. "Dr. Holmes has a passionate side after all."

He smiled, embarrassed. "I'm—sorry...It's that I haven't been with a woman...well, in a long time, I have to confess...it's that—my God! My God!"

She laughed. "Yes, I'd love to spend Thanksgiving with you and Cathy. Do you have a tradition?"

"We eat everything we can get our hands on then we veg out and watch the History Channel and give thanks. Not much of a tradition, I admit. But we do give thanks."

"I make a mean turkey," Susan said. "And my mother's corn-and-mushroom-and-oyster casserole. What do you make, Dr. Holmes?"

"Me? Nothing. Cathy makes Thanksgiving dinner, all of it. I'm afraid I'm not much—or any kind—of a cook. Cathy's made Thanksgiving dinner since she was five."

"Five? She cooked Thanksgiving dinner at the age of five."

"She's a very good cook. She has a good memory for recipes and—things."

"She's the most precocious student I've ever had," Susan said. "I've never seen anything like her, Eric, or even close. You've read some of her writings, I'm sure."

"Of course. Yes. Well, her pumpkin pies are—anyway, we'd love to have you over for Thanksgiving. Cathy will be thrilled."

Susan looked into the dark grove of cottonwood trees that stood along Cedar Creek. "He wrote a poem about her," she said.

"What?"

"Sherwood. He wrote a poem about Cathy."

"A poem—where?"

"Don't worry, it was a poem about a mysterious un-named girl; I know it was her, though."

Eric frowned into the trees. "Are you trying to give me another ulcer?"

She laughed and turned and pressed her body into his. Damn the graduate students, and damn the dignified Marans, Damn the universe!!!

He made out shamelessly with her here under the moon…

Sherwood wandered into the woods toward the stream that ran between Dr. Holmes' property and the alfalfa fields beyond. Dry grass scented the wind. The cottonwood trees whispered. It wasn't long before Woodrow came galloping and growling out of the dark like a mad cave bear, and Sherwood called out, "Woodrow! It's okay, buddy, it's me! It's good old Sherwood, don't kill me."

He bent down and the giant dog snuffled up to him and splashed his face. He rubbed the Saint Bernard on the butt and stared around the trees. "What are you doing out here, old boy?"

Woodrow whined at him, and Sherwood felt a sudden danger. Invisible gnats prickled his spine. What? Some faint electric field—what the hell?

He stood and followed Woodrow through the trees, and at Cedar Creek he saw Cathy standing, staring into the sky. She wore her usual tennis shoes and blue jeans; and her giant white Nebraska sweatshirt that always smelled faintly of chlorine, the hood pressed below the long hair that fell like a veil down her back. The hair was silvery black in the night. The white sweatshirt enveloped her, she seemed a child almost, wearing a grown-up's coat.

152   The Blue River Valley

Sherwood wandered onto the streambank and watched her. Cathy pretended to be unaware that he was here, pretended to be in a trance; pining for Kyle, no doubt.

"Cathy," he said. "What's up?"

His stomach rolled at once. She wasn't pretending; she *was* in some kind of trance. On some kind of drug. Cathy Holmes, on drugs? No…she's playing another one of her mind games on you.

"Planet Earth to Planet Cathy," he said. "I know my cute face paralyzes a lot of girls, but…"

She said nothing. He saw that it was no dumb prank. She didn't know he was here talking to her. Jesus, did she take some overdose or something?

Woodrow whined, startling him. He reached down to pet the dog. "Cathy," he said. "You okay?"

Her green eyes glowed up into space; her face was a wide-eyed mask. He saw a deep and terrible fear, something—

"Cathy!" he said. "Are you okay!" He reached out to touch her and the air spittled, and he got an electric shock. He backed up with a frown. One mean jolt of static electricity.

Cathy closed her eyes suddenly and shuddered. She looked down at the brown stream as if it weren't real.

"Cathy! Sherwood here; are you okay?"

Her eyes flashed open at him. A witch—a green-eyed witch staring dangerously out of the dark. Suddenly she wasn't Cathy Holmes. He could feel Woodrow's fur rise under his fingers as he rubbed at the dog. Sherwood couldn't take his eyes away from her.

"Cathy…what?"

"Something is happening," she said, staring at him with those neon eyes. He realized that she was still in that weird trance.

"What? Happening where?"

"There." She pointed at the night sky. "Something terrible is going to happen."

"Up there?" Sherwood stared up at the stars. "What?"

"I'm scared," she said, her voice suddenly breaking. "I'm scared!"

"What? Cathy, there's nothing to be scared of. Cathy, wake up, what's the matter? Did you take something—pills or something?"

She took deep breaths, let out a shudder, and all at once was back to herself. She stared at him for a long time, breathing painfully, her face assuming the normal pout.

Her luminous eyes cleared, she was Cathy again.

"What are you doing here, Sherwood?"

"I'm studying plant biology at night," he said. "The thing is, what are you doing out here?"

"None of your business."

"You're right. Okay, I'm not out here to study plants, I want to kiss you."

She giggled, but it was a scared trill that was never there before. Sherwood had the strange feeling that he'd stumbled onto some secret, he couldn't imagine what.

"Why should I kiss some soph nerd?" she said, blinking away the last of the trance.

"Because I'm a good kisser."

"No, you're not. You kiss like crap, Sherwood."

"You kiss like a frozen cod fish."

"You kiss like a cockroach."

"How do you know that? No, don't tell me. Anyway, you're lying."

He took her into his arms and kissed her in the dark trees by the stream. The moon grinned down, the old prize fighter.

He held her, not caring about what had happened, that trance, or anything, just grateful for this, so grateful holding her against him. He threw himself against the rocks.

He brushed the black hair from her tiny ear. "I didn't mean that about the cod fish," he said, holding her, kissing the ear. "You're actually a relatively average kisser."

"You're just lucky my dad has a girlfriend, otherwise he'd be out here with a baseball bat."

"I can't really picture your dad swinging—or even *owning*-- a baseball bat." Sherwood smiled, holding her in the winter woods, holding this elf in the bulky, chlorine-clean Husker sweatshirt, the cold wind of Nebraska blowing through the brown trees along the stream. Is she that freaked out about her dad having a girlfriend?

"What did you mean?" he asked her.

"About what?"

"When you said something terrible is going to happen—out there? What did you mean?"

"I don't know." She wrapped herself into him, and Sherwood held her tiny body against his, the too-big cloud of sweatshirt pressing into him. He held her in the cold Nebraska night.

She startled him by crying. Cathy cried against him, and moaned in misery suddenly, and Woodrow, alarmed, started whining and moaning along with her, his tail sweeping the brown leaves.

Sherwood stroked her long catblack hair. He felt a strange, shivery fear.

154   The Blue River Valley

What?

"Cathy," he said, kissing her hair, smelling mint. "What's wrong?"

"I don't know!" She pushed away from him suddenly and looked at him, crying, her face crinkled in misery. "I don't know! Something's wrong out there—I don't know what! Something terrible is going to happen out there!"

Sherwood stared up at the stars. "Whatever it is, I'll always be with you," he said. "Whatever it is, I'll be with you to the end. I'm the one who will never leave you. Not until I die. Then—well, I won't have any choice."

She sobbed into his jacket. He held her, touched the magic black hair. I am holding the elf in my arms. The elf-girl is crying against me, as in the ancient mythologies.

"You don't know!" she cried against him. "None of you know—even Daddy doesn't know!"

"Know that something—"

"I saw terrible things, Sherwood! I saw monsters."

"I don't care what you saw. I don't care. You're a gwerk anyway, so what does it matter?"

She settled down and finally smiled against his chest. She kissed his neck, and Sherwood felt electric tears sparkle down his shirt.

"Be quiet, Woodrow," she said to the dog. "I'm okay now. Stop whining, he's not going to rape me."

"Darn," he said. "I'm not?"

"Quit feeling me up. Stop touching my butt, Sherwood! That's disgusting."

"Good. That's the impression I was trying to give." He kissed her newly pouted lips, forced his tongue into her mouth and tasted her. They melted into one another, swimming in this perfect, rolling kiss. His hands crept slowly down and encircled her butt, he drew her to him.

"I will always be here," he said to her. "I don't care what happens. I'll be the last one to leave."

"Good." She dragged his hands up to her waist. Then she broke away and her green eyes stared up at the moonlit sky. "Because something terrible is going to happen."

TWENTY-THREE ...

▼

THE HALO OF CELOME:

The brain on the console bloomed lavender, the alarm sounded. All eyes shifted to the screen where pixels of sparkling red announced the Bhutaran ships swarming out of the Spaceway.

The Maran admiral Zarya issued orders and the command ship sped into its position in the center of the fleet. He looked at the two ambassadors. "It begins," he said.

Kosan and Relomar traded looks. There was an unspoken regret that they had not been able to prevent this, although it had never been a real possibility. The power of diplomats was illusion (often important illusion to be sure), but the day had always belonged to the warriors.

They stared out of the clear plexium hull of the warship at the universe, sensing the approach of the Bhutaran ships that would soon envelope this space in silent savagery and murder. The Maran fleet waited; a proud triangle of silver needles. Planet Celome lay behind them, brown-and-green in the glow of her yellowish star; a luckless, innocent people, soon to be gone forever.

"Nothing for us now but to sit and watch," Relomar sighed.

Kosan nodded, staring out the dark plexium bubble. He had been in the Maran Spaceforce many years ago, as had Relomar. Both had served on warships and faced death. The very worst part of it was, of course, the waiting.

"Commander Mesto," Zarya calmly addressed the brain screen. "It looks like they'll be coming at your sector. Hold your formation, and don't let them break through. We'll reinforce you if they attack." Zarya stood and gave the universe a thoughtful half-smile that startled both Relomar and Kosan.

156   The Blue River Valley

"It could be a diversion," Commander Pelmar's voice said from the brain screen. "They're confusing my signals."

Zarya stared out of the plexium bubble. How strange that the tedious measures and counter-measures involved in this moment only ensured that he would have to simply try and out-guess the enemy.

Everyone on the control deck of the warship eyed the black beyond. Sparkles on brain screens meant nothing, because they could be lying. This was the moment when cyber-space and reality disengaged. It might even be that Commander Garga, master of the Bhutaran fleet, reserved the plan of attack for the last possible moment. Such latitude was given commanders in the Bhutaran spaceforce.

"We're receiving information," the console said. "That indicates dispersal. It could be a general attack."

"No, it's not, it's a feint." Zarya stared away thoughtfully. "Garga will concentrate on one big blow. He won't throw a thin line against this kind of triangular formation."

"Now some of them are moving toward your sector, Commander Pelmar."

"They're doing a dance," Zarya said. "They've practiced this dance, and only at the moment of attack will Garga say how the dance comes out."

"If their entire fleet attacks one sector," Commander Mesto's voice: "they will probably break through before we can reinforce."

"Exactly," Zarya said. "So it's a simple matter of guessing Garga's target."

"Now they seem to be concentrating on Commander Pelmar."

"I request reinforcements," Pelmar's voice came out of the brain screen.

"There's time yet," Zarya said. He turned to Relomar and Kosan. "Ambassadors, you are experts on the mind of the enemy. You both know Garga."

"I have met him," Kosan said. "He didn't seem rash."

"No, he's a calculator, like all Bhutaran." Zarya stared back out the bubble of plexium. "So put your own calculators together, Ambassadors, and give me an opinion."

Kosan looked over at Relomar. He was amazed at the commander's coolness and control at this time. Very soon a great battle would illuminate that black space.

"Garga will probably do his dance to the last instant," Relomar said. "He will wait for you to make your move."

"And if I don't?"

"Then he will simply attack and hope."

"As always," Zarya agreed. "The important question is where?"

"Two likelihoods," Kosan said. "He will either attack the most obvious place, or the least; probably not in between. Attacking the most obvious place requires the greater risk, and Gorga didn't strike me as a gambler."

"He is a gambler," Zarya said. "At mind he's a calculator, at heart a gambler, a very good one. He wouldn't be where he is if he were not a good gambler."

Again Kosan marveled at Zarya's calmness, when fear tried to rule so much of this place.

"Our fleet is in her trapezoid," Relomar said. "So he will want to concentrate on one flank with as many ships as he can bring to bear."

"Yes," Zarya said. "That means that he'll have to swing round one sector and go in for the thrust. He either pounds his way through, or he gets pounded back. Our goal at this moment must be to ensure that Gorga stabs for flesh and strikes shield. You ambassadors probably know the Bhutaran mind better than any of us. I want a quick opinion."

Kosan glanced at the brain screen, feeling the strange hot mist of impending battle. "He continues his odd dance."

"He wants to make me panic and flinch," Zarya said, staring thoughtfully out at the blackness. "I think I'll comply—but first I need to have a good idea of his target. I think it's time to do a little dance of our own. Commander Seay, move the reserves toward Commander Mesto's sector. We want to look like we're assuming a feint. But be prepared to change course immediately; and I mean immediately." He looked at the ambassadors. "He wants to see us flinch, so we will pretend to flinch; we'll pretend to lunge at the bait." Commander Zarya gave Kosan a cunning smile. "A feint is most effective when it's not a feint."

"So Gorga will try to charge on through."

"We can't know until it happens where he will mount his charge," Zarya said. "This is the moment when we can only guess and hope. But this is also the moment when Gorga can only guess and hope."

"His fleet dances in order to rattle us," Relomar said. "And so we dance to panic him."

"Gorga never feels panic; that is beyond any part of him," Zarya said. "If we can out-guess him and mount a good defense, he will think nothing of throwing his people to death. Make no mistake, Gorga will choose a place and spill his blood there."

"Commander," Kosan said to him. "A quiet word?"

Zarya silenced the brain screen. "It better be good," he said.

"I believe he will attack Commander Pelmar's sector," Kosan said. "Gorga will believe that is the weak point. Obviously you agree."

"And why is that?"

158   The Blue River Valley

"When he asked for reinforcements, Commander Pelmar blinked."

"Yes, I noticed that." Zarya said. Staring out of the plexium windows of the bridge, he could see the enemy ships approaching, like stars closing in from the black distance. "Commander Seay, turn the reinforcements around and form a line behind Commander Pelmar's ships." He looked at the ambassadors. "I agree," he said. "The feint is not a feint. And so now the stand will be made."

Kosan saw the sparkles, the separating glints of enemy warships. He saw the formations swinging round toward Pelmar's flank position. Gorga would hit the shield; good!

"Do you ever wonder, Ambassadors," Zarya said thoughtfully. "That in all the long history of warfare, only one thing has truly changed, and that is sound."

Kosan stared at him. "Sound, Commander?"

"Yes. The only real difference between war on a planet with an atmosphere and war in space, is that out here it is perfectly silent. The warfare makes no sound."

"And does it make the process seem less real?" Relomar asked.

Zarya glanced at him. "It shouldn't, but I think it does, in some ways. All right, Commander Pelmar. I see them coming at you."

The points of light came toward them, some already revealing their needle shapes. How gut-wrenching, Kosan thought; watching enemies charging headlong at you, wanting to destroy you. It had been the same sensation every time he had witnessed it, ships of death that seemed to attack him personally. He thought of Cathy, and the Blue River Valley. You are here, in the hellish Halo of Celome, facing blue death. But you only want to be there, where dreams still rule.

Commander Zarya turned his warship quickly and followed the reinforcements toward Pelmar's sector. Silver needles flowed around them now. Leftward out the plexium window was Planet Celome. Kosan saw the green-brown face of her, the pockets of blue water. What rituals were the Celomese performing at this moment of apocalypse? What mournful incantations from the dawn of their existence?

"Celome," he whispered. "A world gone forever."

"They fight on our side," Relomar reminded him. "They fight the Bhutaran alongside us. They hate nothing more than those gargoyles."

"Yes, so they commit planetary suicide. Why?"

Commander Zarya looked away from the plexium bubble. "No mystery there, Ambassador."

Kosan stared at him, at the sparkling fleet coagulating in the blackness behind him; Zarya, calm and sardonic, seeming to be having a pleasant conversation.

"How do you mean, Commander? A species would *choose* its own extinction?"

"Everything becomes extinct," Zarya said. "The Celomese know that they will either die a quick and glorious extinction fighting, or a slow and shameful one as slaves: to die a warrior, or to die a slave. No mystery why they choose to fight. I only hope they're good at it."

Zarya turned again to the bubble that displayed the great space fleet in a curved theater. He watched the formations gather behind Pelmar's front. "It looks like he means to hit you straight in the face, Pel. That wasn't even a good feint to the left."

"I see that. I'm forming the trapezoid right now."

"Good. Gorga seems too far along now to pull back, so I believe we'll be giving him a bruise." Zarya rubbed thoughtfully at his cheek as he stared out.

Suddenly Kosan could see the far off zaps of blistering blue, the heat-rippled Foam, could see the strange silver puffs of instant dead warships.

Zarya stared at the blue display. Tubes of Melt shot down toward the atmosphere of Celome or ended in the puff of warships. Zarya had the unique ability to put unessential thoughts away at times like this. His men, those who had not managed to pod out, were dead whether he mourned them or not. Warriors signed up to die or survive with pride.

As the command ship approached the battle zone, Zarya could see that he was already winning this thing: Gorga was throwing his ships into slaughter; his spearhead formation was already beginning to disintegrate.

Zarya watched with pride as the Bhutaran attack began to collapse. The command ship was erupting in cheers. Plasmatic blue lighted up space; waves of super-heat churned the Foam and burst to silver sparkles any matter in its way. Bhutaran ships popped silently in silver instants: a great theater of blue and dazzling silver. Zarya was more than a good commander, and he knew it. A good fleet commander is competent, loyal, fearless, cold on his feet, able to make decisions at crucial times, willing to gamble.

But in order to be a *great* commander, you have to love this. You must love war; deep in the most hidden and awful part of your brain you must love it and rejoice in it and live for it. He listened to the triumphant cries of his officers in the command center.

As far as crucial decisions go, there weren't any. Zarya stared thoughtfully out of the command ship. He frowned. This is wrong. Gorga can't be this mad. He's committing suicide. He can't hope to break through now.

160   The Blue River Valley

"All right, Commander Seay, move the reinforcements up and let's plug the holes," he said with some hesitation.

"There aren't many holes."

"No, I see." Zarya stared in concern at the silent particles popping beyond the dome. *What is he doing? This is not Gorga. He's trying to bash his head into a wall. Something can't be right—what?*

Zarya moved quickly over to the brain screen, studied the dots of light (red was Bhutar, green Mara), that indicated the battle. No different than the brain screen games they had played in the Training Academy. This was real, but not different. Starship coordination under battle conditions required great skill, and Zarya had that well enough. But why wasn't Gorga challenging it?

Gorga is being much too foolish.

Kosan stared at Planet Celome, engulfed in the blue and silver incineration. The stray shots of Melt had finally ignited her atmosphere and now her face grew suddenly red and black. The hot colors spread over her surface, and soon she was glowing red like a miniature sun, all things on her gone forever. Kosan could see the dreadful waves of heat flutter off her surface.

"Untold billions," Relomar whispered.

Kosan sighed. "We've seen it happen before. Now is only to destroy the Bhutaran."

"To exterminate them!" Relomar cheered with the rest. "And that's what the great Commander Zarya is now doing."

"Gorga has struck shield," Kosan said with satisfaction.

Zarya heard the comments, but put them in the back of his mind. He no longer listened to his cheering ship-mates. *This is not Gorga. This attack of his—something is wrong.*

"Pel," he said at the brain screen. "How goes it?"

"They seem determined to punch through. We're weakening on the left tangent, but there's no doubt we'll hold."

Zarya nodded. He should be satisfied, elated even. But something was wrong here.

Kosan stared at Planet Celome, a red ember now, to glow until nothing was left to incinerate, then to join the uncountable dead orbs rolling senselessly round their stars; a moment of red-and-black inferno, of eternal water sizzling away; eventually, timeless cold. A rich world blessed with plexium and, in the end, cursed with plexium.

"Something is wrong," Zarya looked up from the screen at Kosan. "Gorga is not this mad."

"We are winning, Commander."

"We are destroying the Bhutaran armada—"

"Yes, I know," Zarya interrupted. "But maybe we are destroying a ruse."

"A ruse, Commander—how can that be?"

Kosan stared into the battle. The silence zaps of blue gave back the darkness, the light show was over. Planet Celome burned red in the background. He looked at the brain screen.

"The Ty-cee!" he breathed.

"Yes, I see them." Zarya studied the battlefield, Commander Mesto's quiet flank, where suddenly swarms of orange particles flew in ambush out of the Spaceway and converged. "The Ty-cee stab our backs," Zarya said in disbelief. "Mesto," he looked sadly at the brain screen.

"Yes, Commander," Mesto's voice came out of the console. "I see them. They're not Bhutaran."

"No, they're Ty-cee."

"Open a channel to the Ty-cee Ambassador," Kosan ordered the brain.

"Channel denied," the brain said.

Kosan looked at Relomar.

"Open a channel to the Ty-cee commander," Relomar ordered.

"Channel denied," said the brain.

"Mesto, prepare for rear-guard action," Zarya ordered. "Can you hold?"

"Doubtful, Commander; they're attacking in force."

"The machines!" Zarya stared at the orange particles forming up to attack his weak tangent; the Bhutaran had sided with those who would make the Bhutaran slaves. "We are going to have to withdraw, Mesto."

"Yes, Commander."

"But slowly and without panic. Lose no more ships than you have to."

"Yes, Commander. Are we leaving the field?"

"We are," Zarya said. "I'm ordering a general retreat to the Spaceway."

"Commander—"

Mesto's voice crackled and died. Zarya stared at the brain screen, at the orange sparkles of the Ty-cee warships. Stabbed in the back. He traded looks with the stunned ambassadors.

"I was told nothing of Ty-cee betrayal!" he roared out at Kosan.

"We knew nothing as well," Kosan said in shock. He watched the rightish flank of the Maran fleet collapse against this new monster from nowhere. The Ty-cee, the machine things, the metal things that couldn't feel, only calculate, who now plowed into Mesto's formation as out of a horror tale, scattering and destroying the Maran ships. Was the destruction of Mara so pathological that Bhutar would enslave herself to such things in order to gain it? And what other beings of the Gathered were involved?

"Withdraw, Pelmar," Zarya said to the brain screen. "Withdraw immediately to the Spaceway. Save every ship you can."

"Commander, we are destroying—"

"Withdraw immediately, Commander!" Zarya's cold voice said. He glared at the two ambassadors. "We were never warned."

"Neither were we," Relomar said.

"Only it was your job to be warned."

"Yes, Commander." Kosan traded frowns with Rel. "It was."

"No matter now. Conditions have made it plain," Zarya said, "that this will not be the main theater of war. Celome is now a dead stone; her plexium mines belong to the enemy. And we have a new enemy. What matters now is Mara."

Kosan felt sick. A wicked scheme unfolded before him, and he saw how stupidly they had wandered into the trap. There had never been any warning that the Bhutaran had conspired with the Ty-cee, but their arrogant confidence should have signaled a danger. The voting patterns in the Gathered should have raised alarm. His mind raced with new and awful implications. Will Mara suffer the same fate as Celome?

"We have to contact the Gathered," Relomar said. "File a formal protest, issue a—"

"Issue what?" Zarya snapped at him. "I'm afraid, Ambassador, that such things are too late." He stared at the destruction of his right flank, and as the command ship raced away he felt a rage that he was barely able to control. Rage was too late as well; now it was only to form up around Planet Mara and save what could be saved. They had concentrated on their sworn enemies, the Bhutaran, never seeing the danger beyond.

Zarya held up the command ship and watched his crippled fleet escape into the Spaceway. The Ty-cee warships swarmed closer, the blue Melt, the heat ripples dying into blackness. Kosan stared at Planet Celome, boiling red. He saw death swarming toward them, the Ty-cee ships; the mechanical things that would aid the Bhutaran then enslave them. What promises, what agreements and alliances with machines had been made that he had never anticipated? I went too many times to Earth, I gave myself to its gardens, I loved it too much, and so with Relomar. We fell into love and happiness: a grand-daughter, a niece, and the Ty-cee representatives must have sensed distraction; those who hadn't the ability to feel and know the weakness of feeling could very well calculate it. What was long ago called evil, and is now the blank law of survival and conquest. Not evil, because the ancient concept of evil *requires* feeling, a warped passion. Maybe Relomar was right, the Bhutaran are evil; but this is beyond evil, it is the mere operation of machinery.

Kosan watched the robot ships approaching. He glanced at Zarya, who was also watching the ships, his face unknowable. This was now more than war with Bhutar, this was war with the metal things that moved on gears and fluids: uninspired, uninquisitive *things* that bled acid and traced their evolution not to organic swamps but melted pools of carbons and alloys. Kosan knew at this moment that a new age had arrived.

At the last possible moment of death, Zarya scowled and ordered the brain: "Enter the Spaceway."

They escaped the final instant, Kosan only getting a last glimpse of the blasted planet and final sparkling *pops* of the Maran rear-guard warships. He stared over at Relomar, who was staring at him. A tragic failure of diplomacy, though the diplomacy of Ty-cee was pure mathematics, nothing more. No subtlety or compromise, nothing beyond numerical probabilities.

"What now?" Rel sighed.

Zarya answered him: "Now we fight for Mara and our own lives. Now we have to fight the gods, or try to."

"It makes no sense," Kosan said, staring away. "Even the Bhutaran know it is suicide to form an alliance with the Ty-cee. They are setting a trap that they themselves are in."

"I think they've already sprung the trap," Zarya said dryly. "And they felt they were in it long ago."

Rel looked at the commander. "Have you ever been to the Spiral Arms, Commander?" he asked.

Zarya looked at him. "Once, long ago, when I was in the Academy; I saw nothing much there. Why do you ask, is it important?"

"No." Relomar looked over at Kosan. "Not important at all."

T W E N T Y - F O U R ...

▼

Cathy heard the familiar sound of the big pickup truck outside, and she looked out her bedroom window. Kyle's truck pulled into the drive and parked under the yard light.

She was surprised, but a veangeful smile crept onto her face anyway. Kyle sat in the truck for a long time, staring tragically up at her bedroom window. She immediately went into her bathroom, sprayed a puff of perfume onto her wrists, popped a spearmint gum into her mouth, brushed her hair and studied herself in the mirror. The smile jumped to a grin.

"Cathy!" her father's voice echoed up the stairs. "Cathy, you'd better come down, your ex—the boy—that Kyle is here!"

"Okay, Daddy," she called, dancing down the stairs and into the living room. Her father looked up from his book. It was Hawking's newest on black holes, and Eric had looked forward to a night of peace and quiet in order to enjoy it. Now, of course, he found himself on the Event Horizon of another kind.

He folded shut the book and intercepted her as she was heading for the front door. He frowned outside at the ominous black pickup parked under the yard light. "I thought you and that boy were broken up," he said. "Remember, you blamed me?"

"We are," she said.

"Then why is he here?"

"I don't know."

"Why is he just sitting parked out there like that? Like some stalker."

"I don't know! I'll go see."

Eric scowled out the window at the senior 'curse' he thought he had been rid of. "Go out and see what he wants, but no going anywhere, Catherine. Don't even think of climbing into that truck."

- 164 -

"I won't."

She scooped her black leather jacket off the peg in the kitchen and slid it on:

Another submission to her whining and pestering, the purchase of a black leather motorcycle jacket.

Fearing that his night of serenity with Hawkings was ruined, Eric watched her flip on the porch light and trot out to the quarterback's truck. Woodrow lumbered into the kitchen and growled through the screen door at the truck in his yard. Eric patted him on the head. "Good boy, Woodrow. If she even thinks about getting in that truck, I'm going to let you out. You hate the quarterback, don't you? You'd like to rip his passing arm off and eat it, eh? Yeah, that's a good dog. He avoids you and he avoids me, and that's good."

The Saint Bernard rumbled deep in his throat watching Cathy out the screen door. She was leaning against the truck, talking to the senior boy. In her dark jeans and black jacket, when she turned her head she almost melted into the night. She would be sixteen soon, and Eric thought of the brand new military vehicle, the Hum-vee H3 that would no doubt arrive on her sixteenth birthday from Grandpa K, and how it would turn his hair completely white, if he was lucky and it didn't just all fall out.

How do you expect her to avoid attention with That, Grandpa, her tooling around the county in a luxury tank?

"I know, Woodrow," he said rubbing the giant dog on the head. "It's okay, you growl as much as you want."

"What are you doing here, Kyle?"

"Hi, Cath." Kyle stared sadly out of the pickup truck. She smelled beer on his breath. "You look good. You look—pretty."

"Thank you."

Kyle let out a long tragic sigh and beer-smell stank out of the truck. "I came over," he whined, "because—well, because like this: I miss you. I like miss you."

"You miss me. Kyle you broke up with me, remember?"

"I know. I just lost it, that's all. I like went crazy after that fight. I blamed you, like an idiot, but it was my fault. It was all my fault and I'm sorry. I'm so sorry."

"So sorry that what?" she asked.

"So sorry that—I'm sorry!"

She studied him. He was very drunk.

166   The Blue River Valley

"What's the matter, did Kirsten break up with you?"

"I don't care about Kirsten. She's nothing compared to you."

Cathy fought a smile. "What about Sherwood North? Are you going to want to fight him again and keep this stupid thing going?"

"No, I'm over that. I don't care about him. He's a soph. I'll leave the Karate Kid alone."

"What about when you graduate and go off to college?"

"I don't know. What's with the questions? Like, I don't know! All I know is that I love you and I miss you. I'm sorry for everything I did, and I'm asking you to take me back."

"Take you back." Her strange green eyes studied him. "You're drunk, Kyle."

"Yeah, because I'm going crazy, that's why. I want to get back with you. We were pretty good together, weren't we? I mean, don't you still have feelings for me?"

"I'm not sure," Cathy said. "But—I don't think so."

"Great. You don't think so, great. But you have feelings for that nerd sophomore? He's not even on Junior Varsity."

"So? Football's a stupid sport anyway."

"What?" Kyle frowned at the blasphemy, coming from a Mars High cheerleader. Then he sighed and put on his most tragic face. "Don't do this to me, come on. You think this is easy for me, driving up here like this? Look, I'm sorry, I like screwed up, I'm asking you to forgive me and to take me back, that's all."

Cathy looked at the house, where her father stood on the porch grimly checking his wristwatch. "I have to go," she said.

Kyle glanced at the nerd father on the porch: Professor Asshole and the monster dog. "Okay. But just think about it, okay? I'm like asking you for a second chance. Okay?"

"I understand. Good night. Watch your driving."

"I love you, Cee."

Cathy turned away from him and trotted back up to the porch and stood with her father as they watched the black pickup roar snaking away, flinging rocks out of the drive.

"He's been drinking hasn't he?"

"What are you doing standing out here, Daddy? I told you I wouldn't get in the truck with him."

"So what was he doing here?"

"He came to say he's sorry for dumping me."

"Christ. You told him, I hope, to stick it up his drunken rear end."

Cathy laughed. "No, I didn't tell him anything. I don't know what to think."

"Think about this, Cathy: he broke your heart once; that means he'll do it again."

"No, it doesn't."

"I thought you were seeing Sherwood."

"No. I'm not seeing anybody. It really is nobody's business anyway."

"Like hell it isn't. If I have to turn this Saint Bernard loose on that senior football player, I won't hesitate. He touches you, it's child molesting."

Cathy squatted down to hug her giant dog. "Oh, Woodrow, you beast. Don't growl; I love you more than any idiot boy in the world. You're my only boyfriend."

"Good," Eric said. "That's the way it should be."

She looked up at him. "You don't understand. What if Miss Mason breaks your heart?"

Eric frowned. "Then I guess I'll just have to lie around and bawl and feel sorry for myself."

"I didn't do that."

"Oh? What? Okay, I'll make a deal with you: if Susan breaks my heart, I'll blame it all on you, how's that?"

Cathy rubbed her dog all about the face and pressed cheeks with him. "Ky-yial-yial—luh-uh-uh-uhves me. He looked so sad with his jaw wired up. Either he dumped Kirsten, or she dumped him. Now he lo-o-o-o-ves me." She giggled into Woodrow's ear.

"Jesus," Eric swore. He instinctively stared out at the black sky, the stars, the impossible Foam, where a silent and invisible war was taking place. This was beneath insignificance, this tiny drama starring an A-hole who wouldn't even get out of his truck. It had, though, ruined Eric's night with the black holes—the gravity drains that led to the unimaginable. Now the damned worry and fear would plague him. He thought of the dreaded Hummer H3 that would arrive, he was sure, for Cathy's sixteenth birthday. And what had she asked the other Maran, Uncle Rel, for? A damned two-seater ultralite aircraft!

Sixteen candles. The foolish song played in his brain, mocking his fear.

"Anyway," Cathy said. "Mr. Kwang-su is teaching me to control my emotions. That's what I plan to do. I'm not going to trust any boy ever again."

"Good," Eric said. "Excellent teaching."

"Mr. Kwang-su has all these philosophical sayings about humility and controlling your emotions and your pride and your ego. He's lived in Mars City for a million years, but there's still a distinctly non-American aspect

168   The Blue River Valley

to his teachings. It's a quiet Asian thing, where you learn mind and body control. It's interesting, but I hope I don't go all weird like Sherwood."

"Mr. Kwang-su is right," Eric said. "Controlling your mind—and your body—that's good teaching, although this martial arts thing is probably a mistake. Fighting is a stupid thing to learn."

"Mr. Kwang-su teaches that too."

"And then he teaches you how to fight, how to hurt people."

"No, weirdly enough, he teaches you how not to. And Uncle Rel is very proud of the progress I've made."

"Well, your Uncle Rel won't be the one who gets the crap kicked out of him when you don't get your way," Eric said. "It'll be me."

Cathy giggled. "No it won't."

Then her green eyes turned fearful all at once. She rubbed at Woodrow, and Eric immediately sensed some disaster. He had wondered where this conversation was going.

"This Mr. Kwang-su: are you afraid he might find out….oh, God!" Eric said. "This martial arts teacher—"

"He knows, Daddy." Cathy gave him a fearful look. "He found out."

"What! Oh, Jesus God…." The old horror came suddenly awake. "It was going to be a good night," he said to his daughter. "I was going to kick back, read a little Stephen Hawkings, enjoy myself. Then the senior boy shows up drunk in his black truck, and now you're telling me that this teacher knows? My God! All I wanted to do was curl up with Stephen Hawkings and his black holes…that's all I wanted."

"Well, things didn't turn out the way *he* wanted either."

"Cathy, you're saying this teacher of yours knows about—it?"

"I didn't tell him. He found out, that's all."

"My God, I have to talk to him." Eric stared into the black heavens.

"I didn't tell him. Well, I did, but only after he found out."

"Oh, God. Does Sherwood know? Does Kyle know?"

"Nobody knows but Mr. Kwang-su."

"I'll have to talk to him."

"Daddy."

She pierced him suddenly with her green eyes. "You know what it is. Stop pretending. I'm grown up now. Tell me what it is!"

"Cathy, you always said you didn't want to know, it would make you feel different."

"I said a lot of things. But now I want to know."

"You're not grown up, you're…." He stared into her burning green eyes, knowing always that this moment would come, that she was going to have to know some day.

"It's called Mist," he heard his voice saying. "It's a powerful field, something along the lines of magnetism....you know, that game we used to play on the kitchen table, Cathy; when you tried to push the positive sides of your magnets together and they repelled one another and scooted one another across the table, and how you giggled?"

She studied him for a long time. "But when we reversed the poles," she said. "It didn't repel. It attracted."

He looked at her, surprised as usual. That she would even think of that at a time like this. "That's all I know about it," he sighed. "It's called Mist."

"Mist." Her green eyes peered at him with such intensity that he drew back.

"Things will be explained to you--but not tonight."

"Am I going to be able to draw things toward me?" she asked.

"I don't know."

"Am I the only one who has this?"

He sighed at the black universe. I don't know what to do; I don't know what to say. I only know that I don't want her to feel lonely.

"No, Cathy," he said. "You're not."

TWENTY-FIVE ...

▼

Kosan rose out of the floor of the Bhutaran ship. He greeted the ambassador Autha with a respectful nod.

The Bhutaran stood but refused to bow. "Kosan, we meet now under different circumstances. The Flux has shifted."

"Yes, it has." Kosan sat down, a cloud enfolding him. "Bhutar has destroyed herself in order to destroy Mara."

Autha's heavy eyebrows rose. "No one has yet been destroyed."

"The Celomese; how many billions of them? They haven't been destroyed?"

"That was always their fate. Now Planet Celome belongs to us. We have begun cooling her surface, and soon we will begin extracting her plexium. There is no more need for war."

"When Planet Celome has cooled," Kosan said. "It will be Bhutaran slaves working the mines for the Ty-cee. Surely you know this."

"If you are to speak of the Ty-cee, then the Ty-cee should be represented here." Autha gave him a burning look. "Yes, I do know; and I accept."

"Agreed," said Kosan. He experienced the irrational thought that he had never seen a Bhutaran that didn't have pink-colored eyes.

He looked back at the entry, and the Ty-cee ambassador 5201 rose out of the floor. Kosan nodded at the machine; then he gave Autha a bland look. If the Bhutaran thought he was going to spring some terrible surprise, he was as unwise as all of his kind. Kosan knew, of course, that the Ty-cee were monitoring and would appear.

"Ambassador 5201," Kosan said to the mechanism. "I'm glad you're here. We were attempting to negotiate an end to this thing before it gets out of control."

"Calculations indicate," the machine replied, "a 68 % probability that the planet Mara will be destroyed if war escalates."

"The Flux cannot be calculated."

The Ty-cee ambassador aimed its glassine face at Kosan. There were no expressions to read, only a flat opaque surface. Its body was a fluid thing of gloss metal; and in motion it was a rippling of aluminum. A lanky, buglike form, spawned and programmed for inter-galactic diplomacy. Its arms were wires attached to a million-use claw that could delicately arrange molecules or crush solid steel. Its legs-- wrapped cables of light-weight alloy—if legs they were--could retract its frame up to three meters or down to one. Its skull was a globe of information and quantum calculations that sheared off to the plane that was its face, like a slab of ice behind which you could see faint sparklings of colored electricity. Its mouth only appeared as a ripple when it spoke. It had no eyes to look into—or rather all of it was eye, the entire flat pane of its face, and all of it ear.

"Why should the Ty-cee want to see Mara destroyed?" he asked, feeling hopeless in the asking.

"Calculations indicate," 5201 said, "that Maran interests in the present galactic plexium availability are hindering Ty-cee interests."

Kosan looked at the Bhutaran ambassador: "Remember, Autha, if we are now, you are later."

Autha looked at the Ty-cee. "The Maran fails to understand."

"Flux calculations indicate," the machine said. "That Planet Mara will have a 75 % probability of ceding her plexium interests. The Bhutaran are to gain 50 %, and the Ty-cee 50 %. Mara will gain the opportunity to survive."

Kosan felt cold chills. I am now obsolete: the age of ambassadors is over. Rel always tried to convince me that we were obsolete long ago. Kosan's mind suddenly wandered to the beautiful child-planet in the Spiral Arms. Cathy, what are you doing at this moment? Are you happy?

"To live as slaves," Kosan said to the machine. Then he looked at Autha: "Bhutar will be next."

Autha peered at him, pink stone eyes in wrinkled fur. "Mara must now either cede her plexium mines, or burn to death as Planet Celome. You were warned to stop provoking war. But warlike Mara, greedy for plexium, did not listen."

"You're not listening now, Autha."

Kosan collected his thoughts, mindful as always that the Gathered were listening, judging. He could only try one last time: "Bhutar has greater enemies than Mara. We can grant one another the right to live; we can learn to understand one another. We can...no matter. I see that these words are signaling weakness to you. With you there can be no compromise. But remember this, Autha: when your time with the Ty-cee arrives, you will get no understanding or negotiating; compromise will then become impossible."

"Marans are crippled by compromise," Autha said. "That is why you lose."

"Yes, often times we may be," Kosan said. "Bhutarans have no emotions, I understand that. But Bhutaran are post-primates, just as Marans are. You are made of soft tissue, as we are. I tell you this, Autha, I tell all of Planet Bhutar this: if the Ty-cee destroy Mara they will calculate against Bhutar next."

"That will not occur," 5201 came alive to say. "Ty-cee demands 50 % of Planet Mara's plexium interests, 0 % more."

How strange that even pure mathematics can lie.

"The machines will come after you next, Autha, and there will be no Mara to stand against them with you." Kosan made a final and futile effort.

"The Ty-cee fulfilled exactly their agreement with us," Autha said. "We judge not by speech, but actions. The Ty-cee act as they speak, the Marans do not."

"It would be better to become a fire-ball than a slave," Kosan said. "The Celomese understood this."

"Calculations indicate," 5201 said, "that the Maran Directorate will disregard your advice and cede her plexium mines."

"So you see," Autha said. "This is not a negotiation."

"No, it's a show for the Gathered, as always. As always, it is a matter of plexium."

Kosan betrayed a sad smile. Relomar was right in his warning. I may not be there for Cathy's sixteenth birthday, and it will break her heart.

He understood why Donis wanted to escape into the paradise of the dream. This mechanism, Ty-cee 5201—how to negotiate with such a thing? A thing risen from molten slops of alloy; a metal insect housing an electric brain that had evolved to so much ability--but not the ability to have a dream.

Kosan gave Autha his sad smile, knowing it would disconcert the Bhutaran, whose race had given up their dreams and smiles long ago…but maybe there were primitive fragments left.

"The machines want the galaxy," he said for the benefit of the Gathered. Those members made of soft organic tissue would maybe heed him. They all feared the metal things and their super calculations.

"The machines want to destroy and enslave everyone, including the Bhutaran: including, some day, the Gathered."

With that one statement he threw away his career for good.

"Incorrect," 5201 said. "Ty-cee demands 50 % of the Maran plexium trade. An agreement will be reached. Mara is to cede her plexium interests or face destruction. Ty-cee ships of war are now converging on your home world."

"This is not a negotiation," Autha said. "You have only now to deliver the news."

"To die in fire or to live as slaves," Kosan said.

"Calculations indicate that the Maran Directorate will choose surrender," the machine said.

Kosan knew that it was true. It was the practical Maran creed: if you are alive, anything is possible. If you are dead, nothing is possible.

And then I will vanish, Kosan thought. Vanish as Relomar already has, into the lush dream of Earth. Better a dream than slavery.

"I speak now to the Gathered," Kosan said, staring out the plexium dome at the ugly grey skies of Bhutar. "And I speak to the Maran Directorate. Last, I speak to the Bhutaran Council: If we do not fight the machines, they will destroy us. Ambassador 5201 has his calculations, but they are all aimed at the eventual enslavement of the galaxy. All forms composed of soft organic tissue will be destroyed if we do not fight."

"You speak nonsense, Kosan!" Autha roared out.

"Maybe so," Kosan admitted. "I speak as a Maran ambassador for the last time: I state now before the Gathered, that if my Directorate agrees to become slaves in order to survive, then I will vanish forever from the galactic stage."

"Dramatic words," Autha said. "And correct: you are no longer a Maran Ambassador. Now you are a messenger, nothing more."

Kosan looked over at the machine, the rippling metal insect. "I have fulfilled my duty, hopeless as it was. I go now to a 16th birthday," he said.

"That is not understood," 5201 replied.

"There are many things the Ty-cee can't understand." Kosan looked over at Autha. "Many things the Bhutaran won't understand. But one day you will."

Gota was listening in, and maybe understood?

Sixteenth birthday. It was close to 16 Earth revolutions ago when the hybrid was destroyed.

174 The Blue River Valley

Gota stared at the brain screen that aired this meeting aboard Ambassador Autha's ship. He wanted war, of course, but it would likely be enslavement. War with machines was suicidal nonsense.

The Bhutaran had only one religion, one that told of a day when gods would come to lead the galaxy—and they would be made of metal.

And Kosan vanishes—to Planet Earth? A coincidence, but even not, what possible gain could be had now? Even if the hybrid still lived (and Gota thought that unlikely), the affair would still not be worth pursuing. Kosan had willfully ceased to have importance, as had for that matter Planet Mara.

Gota shifted his pink eyes out the plexium bubble at Bhutar, the broken iron-and-ice valley. I have no purpose, he thought. It has been sixteen years, Kosan, and you have taken away my purpose. You come here to announce the removal of my purpose. How terribly the Flux shifts. The Ambassador Relomar vanishes, now Ambassador Kosan disappears from the galactic stage. A useless speculation if he goes to Earth or not—what gain from this?

Why, though? Gota could not keep his mind from asking. He remembered that swampy wet place and her black swarming night all those years ago, and how Kosan had snatched away his opportunity at the last moment with his Kin-field.

I killed the son, Gota's mind said. I know the son Donis was destroyed, I know the earth female was destroyed. I do not know that the hybrid was destroyed.

It seemed impossible that Kosan would risk letting it live, when he could have wiped it away forever.

Then to risk all by lying to the Gathered? Why would he do such a thing? It could not be possible.

But I do not know that it was destroyed.

T W E N T Y - S I X ...

▼

Eric Holmes glanced up from his book, sensing a presence on the front porch. He jumped to his feet, marched into the hallway, opened the front door, and there stood Relomar. The tall Maran gave him a sad smile.

Eric felt his stomach ripple.

"Rel?" He stared at the Maran. "My God, what's happened?"

"I don't want to wake Cathy, or Woodrow," Relomar whispered. "Let's go inside, Teacher, I'll tell you only what you need to know."

Feeling the *coma moment* again, Eric stepped aside and followed Relomar into the living room. Rel sat down wearily on the couch. Eric found his reading chair and fumbled himself down into it. He stared at the dark hallway, at the stairs going up to where Cathy lay sleeping with Woodrow. The Maran wore a grim face. Terror seemed to hiss suddenly from the silence. The long-awaited snake of terror.

"The—war?" he asked.

"Did not go well," Relomar said. "Mara is gone. I exile myself to this planet. I live here now, I'm an Earthling."

"Oh God." Eric swallowed at his throat. "Mara is gone; how?"

"Not incinerated, as others were. Maybe worse than incinerated. I can tell you little more. It is now in the past, that's all. It has come, so far, not to galactic war but maybe worse." Relomar stared away: "Another Flux in the Foam."

Eric felt a chill: "Kosan?"

"I'm uncertain; he may be joining us soon. I hope so."

"Cathy will be very glad to see you."

The Maran smiled at him. "Is she falling in love with Sherwood?"

"They're dating—under strict supervision. She's too young for love."

"And are you too old?"

176   The Blue River Valley

"No, maybe not."

"If you don't mate soon with Miss Mason, Cathy's teacher, you may run out of time."

"I—yeah…" Eric stared at him. "Kosan. Did he—"

"Unknown. I knew from the moment of the Ty-cee that it was over, and that I would escape here. Kosan believed to the end that he could change the Flux."

"Kosan might be dead?"

"I don't know," Rel said. "If not, then he will come here, as I did."

"The—what did you say, the moment of the Ty-cee? What does that mean?"

"It means nothing, only that Mara is gone, and I am here. Out there is a great warping of reality, Eric, and I've had enough of it. Here is dream, and this is what I want."

Eric had another out-of-body, out-of-mind sensation. Here in the familiar and comfortable living room with the hardwood floor, dull normal Nebraska beyond the windows, snow fluttering through the cottonwood trees, to be talking about this with a Maran, who had just admitted to him that this was a dream…

"Kosan—you don't know if he's dead?"

"Kosan is a realist; he will be like Commander Zarya and escape at the last possible moment. If they do not kill him, he will be here for Cathy's birthday party. You don't know what I'm talking about, of course."

"Kill him—who, the Bhutaran?"

Rel smiled sadly at him. "I can tell you very little, Eric. You think you want to know, but you don't, and I will spare you with little knowledge; only that you can stop worrying. The Flux has spun wildly out there; here is peace. I hope Kosan finds his way back here; I know that he will try."

"What is the Ty-cee?" Eric asked.

Rel let out a tired, hopeless sigh. "Like Cathy, my niece, you're too inquisitive. Your people learned tools a million years ago. A million years is this." Relomar clapped his hands softly, startling Eric. "A million years is nothing. Planets of a million trillion living things explode and die in an instant, their primates stupified at the long-awaited Death-God of whatever religion they believe. Planets far beyond Earth die in an instant. It happens every time your heart beats. This place has not yet come out of the soft dream. Earth has yet to be born to the terrible galaxy, the endless canyons of time. All I can say is, don't leave the dream. Out there, everything is as cruel as it's always been."

On that happy note, Eric looked out the living room window at the night sky, the soft flutters of northern snow. "She keeps asking me if Grandpa and Uncle Rel are going to make it to her birthday party."

Rel smiled. "I predict that both will. But Kos always told me I was a hopeless optimist."

"And..." Eric looked at him. "The ultralite airplane?"

"Yes, Cathy's birthday present. A very well-engineered craft: a 2-seat Maxair Drifter XP. Cathy will have much fun in it."

"So, the microplane—this isn't a cruel joke—the microplane—"

"Already purchased," Relomar said. "Cathy promised that I would be the first to fly in it with her."

"My God, Rel..." Eric stared out the window. "We never have a problem finding things to talk about. What are the Ty-cee?"

"They are—I suppose what you would call machines."

"Machines. Like robots?"

"No. They were not built, they evolved just as humans and Marans did, only in a different way. On primate worlds, like Earth and Mara and Bhutar, life evolves from electrically-stimulated protoplasm, tissues that will develop bone and shell, but will always remain relatively soft. The Ty-cee evolved from electrically-stimulated metals. Don't ask for any more secrets, Eric. You've been taught that life evolves from certain special elements. But life evolves from all elements. No, please, Eric, no more questions."

"One more, please!" Eric stared at him. "These—metal things, the Ty-cee: they are more dangerous than the Bhutaran?"

"By far," Rel said. "When the Bhutaran tried to destroy you all those years ago you managed to escape them. You would never have escaped the Ty-cee."

"So, these Ty-cee, they go beyond..."

"They are probably the future of the galaxy," Rel said. "An awful thought that I never could make Kos believe. I think they are what nature and the terrible future have in store for organic life in the galaxy. Mara never suspected it could come for her so soon, but there really is no such thing as soon and late. Don't give me that look, I warned you against asking. No, Eric; that is all I'm going to tell you for now." Rel glanced up the stairs. His tired face made a smile. "Cathy's asleep?"

"Yes. I'll wake her up. She'll go nuts when she sees you."

Relomar smiled. "No, let her sleep, I'll see her tomorrow after school."

"She goes to that karate place tomorrow after school. Choe Kwang-su's class."

"Perfect. I'll see her there. Maybe Sherwood North will be there."

"He probably will be. He's been helping that Mr. Kwang-su teach her how to fight. And if it wasn't for all the nightmares you and your brother have given me over the years, I never would have allowed it. But if she's in danger, she probably should at least know how to defend herself." Eric looked at the Maran. "This Choe, her karate teacher—he knows, Rel, he knows about the Mist!"

"Yes, I'm aware of that," Relomar said. "He knows some but not all."

"He wants to meet with me," Eric said. "What am I supposed to tell him?"

"Tell him what you know about the Mist," Rel said. "Nothing more."

"Tell him—my God, no one was ever supposed to know! I don't want to put her in any kind of danger. If this gets out, she'll become a worldwide freak."

"I believe the most important danger has passed," Rel said. "There toward the center of the galaxy, where the stars are dense, where Mara and Bhutar and billions of other worlds exist, a great wave is sweeping the Foam. Earth is not even a distant ripple."

"That's the good news?" Eric asked.

"No more talk of what is out there, good or bad." Rel looked at him. "I'm very tired of what is out there, but happy for what is here."

"I'll get you fixed up in the spare bedroom."

"No, no. I have a room in the motel in Mars City. I need a secluded place to regain my energy. Also, it's just down the street from the Valentino's Pizza Shop."

The Maran rose and walked silently to the door. "Don't tell Cathy, I'd like to surprise her at the karate school. And let's hope that Kosan escaped and appears soon."

"She's going to be asking about him."

"I know." Relomar frowned thoughtfully. "One last thing, Eric—the tal."

"The tal?"

"The device Kosan gave you. The gem of plexium?"

"Oh, the thing, the diamond. I've got it locked up in the safe."

"Just as a precaution I may have to show you what it can do."

TWENTY-SEVEN...

▼

Choe Kwang-su was quietly meditating on the mat when Cathy let out a screech that nearly scared him to death. His eyes burst open, and he glanced round and saw the tall spirit, Uncle Rel, enter the school.

Cathy pattered barefoot off the mat, where she was sparring with Sherwood, ran up and stood on tiptoes to hug the man. "Uncle Rel!" she shrieked.

The spirit bent down, hugging her, smiling, then tousled her long black ponytail. "Surprise!" he said.

"I can't believe you're here!" she said. "Daddy said you wouldn't make it for my birthday, and I knew he was full of it. God, I can't believe you're here!"

The tall Maran smiled over the top of her head. "Hello, Sherwood. Mr. Kwang-su."

Sherwood, holding the punching pad to his stomach, bowed. "Sir, it's good to see you again."

"Yes, it is." Choe also bowed; then traded looks with the uncle. "I'm glad you're here," he said. "You can see what Cathy has learned."

"I'm kicking the living crap out of Sherwood, Uncle Rel." she said.

Sherwood reddened. "I'm afraid that's true, Sir."

"Well, before that," Rel said. "I have another surprise for you."

Cathy looked behind him and let out another bone-chilling screech. A second spirit appeared at the door of the school, smiling his way inside. Choe stared at this second one, not as tall, less strange looking than the uncle; older, with very light golden eyes; but also with that unmistakable bluish nebula surrounding him. Am I the only one who has this in his eyes?

180   The Blue River Valley

"Grandpa!" Cathy ran and hugged the tall Maran as he entered the school. "Grandpa, I knew you'd come! Oh, my God! You guys came!" Sherwood thought she would hyper-ventilate she was so excited. "Oh, my God!"

The tall spirit hugged her and stroked her hair, Sherwood smiling on. Choe couldn't shake the visions from his head. So this is the legendary grandfather. He would say these were only interesting people, a wealthy and eccentric and bizarre family, nothing more; and the sense of spirits and ghosts was no more than an old man going senile. But he had seen too much, he knew about *it*. And he knew that his senses were in some way—although what possible way?--correct.

His blood cooled when the grandfather looked at him with those golden eyes and nodded, getting acquainted. Choe nodded, tried a smile. This one had a very Socratic face; and like the others, penetrating eyes that set you on edge. This was the fabulous grandfather Cathy always boasted about.

The eyes let him go suddenly and shifted over to the lad who was watching him.

"Hello, Sherwood," the grandfather smiled. "It is good to see you again."

"Good to see you again, Sir." Sherwood grinned at Cathy, who was hugging the stoic gentleman, making him embarrassed.

"Did you say?" Rel asked Choe. "That Cathy and Sherwood were pretending to fight?"

"Yes, exactly that," Choe said.

"You guys can see me kick the butt of Sherwood all over this mat!" she said, grinning red, biting at her lip. Sherwood saw that scary halo of energy around her, she was so excited. "I knew you'd come! I knew you'd both come!"

They all laughed. Choe traded looks with Sherwood. The boy has no idea?

Yet he always told me of her strangeness. The tired old saying must be true, love is blind, and it is also deaf and incredibly stupid. Well, if strange spirits have come to test me, I'll do my best.

"We should sit down," he said formally, now a host. "I regret, though, that there is only one chair in the room. In the land where I was born it is the custom to sit on the floor; maybe because chairs were too expensive."

"Then we'll sit on the floor!" Kosan cried, his arms around Cathy. He barked out a startling laugh of delight, causing everyone to look at him; then he smothered it with a frown. "Rel, let's sit on the floor with Mr. Kwang-su and see what Cathy has learned."

"No," Choe said. "First we must *all* sit on the floor."

The grandfather gave him a curious look. "Why is that?"

"She can't show you what she's learned until she tells you what she's learned." Choe gave Cathy a menacing look. She started to pout, bowed her head humbly then jumped up and down, her tiny bare feet popping on the mat. "Grandpa, in two weeks I'm going to be sixteen!"

"Yes! Sixteen years old!" The grandfather spirit looked at Choe. "Now, we must do as the Teacher says. We'll sit down and hear what you've learned."

She took her uncle in one hand and her grandfather in the other and led them over to the mat, where they all sat down cross-legged. Like gods and mortals beginning a ritual?

Sherwood kept blinking his eyes as if this were not happening.

Surely, my brilliant student, cross-legged in this coven, you must feel the presence of something not of the normal world; maybe not of the world at all. Otherwise, I am going mad.

Cathy was red-faced, excited, and tried to control her giggling. She sat proudly between her grandfather and uncle, two stern pillars with strange and imperial bearing, both of them smiling, only in a very controlled way. Choe could not help but study the grandfather Kosan's face. The smile seemed almost to give him a wonderful pain. Maybe that's what love is, wonderful pain. Kosan—Relomar, what kind of names were these? They had to have come from some arctic land, Norway or Iceland. Or beyond even that?

The spirits you prayed to, Mother, never came to feed us.

Choe felt the uncomfortable silence and gave Cathy an arch look. "We're listening, Cathy. It's not a good time to embarrass your teacher."

"Okay." Cathy stared down at the mat and made her face serious. "I have powers. I am being taught to use my powers. Powers are blessings and they are curses. If I want to use my powers, I must first understand this; then I must learn how to control them, how *not* to use them."

Kosan nodded appreciatively at Choe. Rel smiled at his brother and nodded. Sherwood sat taking this all in, his face gentle, but alert.

"To have powers and to use them is good; to flaunt them is evil," Cathy went on, talking to the mat. "You have to learn that true power can never be used to make people like you or respect you; that is false power. And only as a last resort can you use true power to make people fear you."

Choe felt a shudder. She was repeating him word for word, like a tape recorder. He hadn't realized how corny and Hollywood his teaching had become.

"If having power makes you vain and arrogant, it puts you in a miserable cage. You can only have freedom and true power when you embrace humility."

"That is very good, Cathy," Kosan spoke up. He smiled at Choe.

182   The Blue River Valley

Choe watched her, the beautiful being not of this world: She repeats the lesson word for word, as Sherwood said she does in the History class when the teacher tries to catch her not listening: a fool-proof way of mocking the teacher. She is not saying what she's learned, she's saying my own cliches'. Is she mocking me?

Choe could see no sign in her beautiful face of the malice that Sherwood absolutely assured him she was capable of. The beautiful face was serious. These things make you believe craziness, old man. It doesn't matter, I can live with mockery. Only: is she learning or is she reciting? It worried him, because this one has more than the ability to gain powers, she already has them, strange powers beyond understanding. And so too, he believed, do the uncle and grandfather.

"Humility is the only force that can control power," Cathy said to the mat. "They are the balancing forces, power and humility. Power is like fire, humility like water. But they are equal. Power without humility will burn your life away in pride and arrogance. Humility without power will get your ass kicked by those with false power—"

"Yes, excellent!" Choe spoke up.

Kosan gave him a surprised look.

"I paraphrased that one," Choe smiled. But so uncomfortable had this recital of his words become that when she started up again, he suddenly clapped his hands, startling them all. "That's very good, Cathy," he said. "Now, this part of the lesson is over."

She grinned up at him. "I know all the rest of it."

"Another day," Choe said, giving her a troubled look—(do I sound so David Carradine?): "Now for a physical demonstration. You must pretend that Sherwood is an enemy—"

"That won't be hard."

"And without interrupting your teacher again when he is talking, you must now show how you are learning to fight an enemy who means to attack you."

She leaped off the mat like a tight spring, her black ponytail whipping the air. The two spirits smiled fondly, almost amazedy at her. Sherwood gave Choe a cautious look. The boy had been letting her pound him to a pulp for the last hour, and Choe saw the grim exhaustion on his face, how skinned-up his knuckles were from holding the pad.

You didn't invent the disease, my young friend.

"Do you plan to attack her?" Kosan asked Sherwood.

"Not really, Sir, I'll only pretend to. I'm strictly on the defense," Sherwood said. He looked over at Choe; then he smiled at Cathy. "I'm the enemy she gets to ATTACK, the enemy who can't fight BACK. So, we have to keep that in mind."

Cathy gave him a red-faced grin and motioned him to bring it on. She couldn't wait to show off for her grandpa and Uncle Rel—at his expense, of course. She was so tickled that they had shown up here she couldn't keep the red out of her face. These tall, reserved men were her only family, besides her dad.

She worships them, Sherwood thought. How can you ever compete with that?

You can only try. He launched himself off the mat and pretended to go after her, a villain's sneer on his face. She giggled at him and assumed her stance, and Sherwood quickly held up the punching pad. She launched a furious attack, pummeling him with a tornado of kicks and jabs that actually sent him spilling to the floor.

"Oh, Sherwood!" she cried. "I'm sorry! I didn't mean to knock you down. I'm sorry!"

He gave her a narrow look; then launched himself off the mat. "I accept your apology, Miss Holmes. However, I still wish to rape you."

He surprised her by charging, then at the last moment ducking down in between her punches and kicks. His strategy was to grab her around the waist and gently fling her to the mat, to humiliate her in return—he had her, but—Jesus!-- he bounced off her suddenly. He fell awkwardly backwards and found his legs just in time to ward off a staccato attack from her fists. They were like steel pistons, and he backed away. Her foot shot out like a bullet, he felt it smash into the pad. Cathy's face was a red little monster.

Choe looked at Uncle Rel, who nodded at him. He then looked at the grandfather, Kosan, who was studying him. They saw what had happened. He nodded to the spirit grandfather. To know a secret is to have power, he said to the golden eyes. And you can only have true power by not using it: the strange paradox of it all. Humility is the key to all power, because humility is the beginning of rightness. David Carradine would say that one better than me, of course.

"All right!" Choe called out, feeling pity for Sherwood at last. "Very good! Very good, Cathy! You can stop now." He began applauding her, knowing that would make her stop attacking Sherwood. Everybody applauded her, and she stood, scarlet in the face, grinning down. Sherwood dropped the punching pad and clapped his chewed-up hands the loudest, then suddenly yelled out—"Sixteen in two weeks!"

They all clapped, Cathy red and giggling. Choe studied the spirits, their strange and reserved love and delight. Just a gathering of relatives for a sixteenth birthday, old man; if only he had not seen *it*. These were the men

184   The Blue River Valley

she had grown up with—he knew that Cathy had never had women in her life, only these two wealthy men and a father, who all spoiled her.

Were these even men though? Choe had met her father, Dr. Holmes, and found him distantly thoughtful and a worrier, but perfectly ordinary.

"I'll be sixteen!" Cathy cried out. She bit her lip looking at Sherwood, and the boy's Adams apple clearly lodged in his throat.

Choe stiffened as the tall grandfather came to him and bent to his ear. "Teacher," Kosan whispered to him. "Why is her sixteenth birthday so important?"

Choe felt the strange blue electricity sting and spatter around him. "Sixteen is the beginning of the world," he managed to say.

"Ah."

Choe looked at Cathy, hugging her Uncle Rel, Sherwood smiling at her. He felt the grandfather spirit near him, a ghost. I pleased the spirits this day, was all he could think. I pleased the spirits, Mama.

"I want her to be happy," Kosan whispered to him. "I don't want her to be different. I want her to be the same and happy."

Choe ventured a look at this imposing form. He could see with his eyes the diamonds of blue in the air, like sparkles in your eyes when you've stared at the sun too long. "She *is* different," he said.

"That's why Relomar sent her to you, to teach her Not to be different."

"No. She can't be taught not to be different when she is. And she knows it, of course."

This spirit paused. Choe felt modulations in the blue sparkliness. Is this *it*? Am I feeling *it*?

Finally the man surprised him with a heavy sigh. "I don't want her to be lonely," he said. "I want her to be happy."

"She can be happy with her powers," Choe said. "She seems happy at the moment."

"Does Sherwood know?" Kosan whispered urgently.

Choe felt a chill. He glanced into the golden eyes. "No, I don't think so."

"Good; it's best he not."

The grandfather spirit patted Choe lightly on the back, then went to his grand daughter and hugged her and told her how well she had done with the beating up of Sherwood. Choe shivered; then looked at the boy, who was watching him, sensing that he was being kept out of something.

Sherwood smiled politely and played his pleasant and ignorant role, but he wasn't the idiot they all hoped he was; he knew that there was energy of some kind around Cathy, and probably Uncle Rel and Grandpa. Not the figurative 'life energy', but some kind of real energy field, some reverse magnetic or gravity field or other. He couldn't explain it, but he knew the night he had kissed her upside down face in her miraculous bedroom; he had felt the bluish tingles raise the hairs on his neck.

A poet, he at first thought it was overwhelming true love and intense emotion and all that--but no, he had seen and felt too many things since then to know it was not anything imaginary. He had even studied electro-magnetism to see if it were possible for certain people to have unusually strong electro-magnetic fields around them, whether such a thing was hereditary. It was something for the whacko side of the History Channel.

He looked over to see Uncle Rel smiling fondly at him. "Do you like eating pizza, Sherwood?" he asked.

"Everybody likes eating pizza, Sir."

"Then when Cathy's lesson is over," Uncle Rel said with a flourish. "We are all going to the Valentino's pizza shop and feast! My treat."

"A good idea," Kosan agreed. "We should celebrate. But Cathy should get back to her lessons."

"I think it's a good time to end class," Choe said, hearing the words *Valentino's pizza.* "A good time now to celebrate." He traded eyes with Cathy. Mock me all you want—but learn!

"All right!" Relomar said. "To the pizza shop, all of us. Sherwood, what is your favorite pizza from the Valentino's?"

"I like their vegetarian," he said.

Cathy snorted at him. "Vegetarian. You are such a goob, Sherwood."

"I'll try a slice," Relomar said. "And you must let me taste your favorite pizza from the Valentino's, Mr. Kwang-su."

"I warn you, it involves pineapple." Choe smiled at them all. "Now! Class over. A gentleman has agreed to treat us to a free feast of pizza, and that's enough to celebrate."

"Let us be off!" Kosan said merrily.

Cathy was a giggling maniac, and Sherwood grinned at her. *They came for her sixteenth birthday party—and I'm invited too. But how to compete with this? She's already a damn ninja warrior.*

Sherwood, as well as everyone else, had seen her do things at football games, Super-Cheerleader things that bordered on the impossible: handsprings and spins and unbelievable flips that went far beyond normal. *How do you get Supergirl to fall in love with you?*

You can only try.

186   The Blue River Valley

As they left Choe's school, stepping into the cold evening, Rel whispered to Kosan, "We abandon reality and enter the dream, my old friend."

"Let us hope so," Kosan whispered back. "We go from Galactic Ambassadors to strange primitive explorers."

"Well, the only certain thing," Relomar said, "is uncertainty."

"I hope the uncertainty favors us in this dream."

"What do you mean?"

Kosan looked around him at the village, the wooden stores, the County Courthouse, the stone temple on its hill of brown grass and shaken trees: a stone temple on a primitive world, so beautiful and sad and distant from the truth.

"Word from my sources: Gota might be searching for Cathy."

TWENTY-EIGHT...

▼

A new Cult of Arrogance, the Bhutaran Gota thought, looking at the machine: The ultimate arrogance, which is no arrogance at all, only electric calculations. He understood that these things would be the masters now; Bhutar had only faced the facts.

52341, the Ty-cee Evaluator, analyzed him. "Your purpose," the flat plane of face made a mouth of waving modulations, "was to form comprehensive data concerning the Maran ambassador Kosan."

"Yes," Gota said. "I have managed to gather very disturbing data concerning Ambassador Kosan, and also Ambassador Relomar."

"Explain how that benefits circumstances as they now are," the machine said to him.

"A hybrid may exist," Gota said. "A Maran/human combination. It is possible that a hybrid created by Ambassador Kosan's own son is alive on Planet Earth."

"Explain how this information benefits the circumstances as they now are."

"It may be a danger, this thing unleashed onto a world."

"Explain how a danger to this world is important," 52341 said.

It was a voice that was not even a voice, only a sonic transmission of data.

"The laws against Hybridism protect the entire galaxy," Gota said, "from possible contagion—from randomness." He thought that would work: the Ty-cee, if they had the ability to fear, would fear randomness.

"The power of Mara is neutralized," 52341 said. "The ambassadors of Mara no longer concern the circumstances as they now are. You no longer have a purpose, Clerk Gota."

188   The Blue River Valley

Gota imagined a cruelty there, with the word *clerk,* but he realized that he was actually that, a clerk, sitting at a brain screen, studying for years that which had come to mean nothing. The Ty-cee, here to see if he was necessary, would not comprehend a cruel slight. There was no cruelty in the statement; only worse, a fact.

"It is possible," he said carefully. "That a hybrid could spread and mutate. A mutation can alter the Foam and make it impossible to predict."

"There is a nearly 100% probability that you are wrong," the Evaluator said. "You have failed, Clerk Gota, to justify your purpose according to circumstances as they now are."

Gota bowed his wrinkled head. New masters, you must submit to the truth and try to survive it: to be a slave at a brain screen or a slave in the mines. It was always true that organics would be slaves one day to these creatures, who were more powerful and terrible than any forgotten gods. We were only smarter slaves than the Marans, who were destined to be herded like livestock into the Celomese plexium mines; the dreamy, intellectual race, so smug in their warm glow of justice and affection and soft philosophy. Soon to be creatures of bone and skin marching under machines into the plexium mines of blasted Celome.

"Still, there is a possibility that I am right," Gota said. "A combination of inter-galactic species could disrupt the Foam in ways that cannot be predicted."

"Do you wish to maintain your relevance?" the machine asked.

"Yes," Gota admitted. "That is what I wish to do."

"In what way?"

"I would go to Planet Earth, and if there is a hybrid there, capture or destroy it."

"That would require the allocation of funds. Statistics indicate that this is a waste of funds according to circumstances as they are. It is probable that as many as 1,800,000,000 hybrids are alive in the galaxy at any one moment."

"A single virus can spread," Gota argued. "It is impossible to say what kind of Flux might arise--"

"State a condition by which you would remain relevant in your present position," the machine cut him off.

Gota bowed to his new master. One can only hope to survive circumstances as they are, by bowing to them, although deference itself had no meaning to these beings. It was always meant to be: that creatures of impossible power, products of accelerated metallic evolution, would one day rule. And that they would be gods beyond any notion of mercy.

"I would capture the Maran/human combination, show it before the Gathered as proof of the Maran Kosan's long treachery, and there would be no danger of an unpredictable disturbance in the Foam..." But Gota heard only death trailing his words.

"The funds you require are not justified."

"Funds can be adjusted," Gota said. "There may be a virus on Planet Earth. I will destroy it, and there will be no danger to the Foam."

His dwarf face looked at the flat crystal visage of the Ty-cee. We now enter the new age, when organics become extinct and Metallics rule. Live a slave, or die, that is truth. We dominated our world because we were the superior ones. No wispy Maran philosophy can change that. The Marans had come to dominate their own world by killing off or enslaving creatures that either challenged them or would benefit them. The Bhutaran and the Maran had evolved to rule their worlds by becoming superior to other things, and few ever thought that superior things would one day come to conquer and dominate *them*, to turn scholars and philosophers into plexium mules.

It is only now to avoid the Flux, to try and hold onto duty, relevance.

"I request only to ascertain if a Maran/human hybrid lives on Planet Earth," he said to the machine. "If a hybrid exists that could possibly alter the Foam in an unpredictable way, I will remove that danger for the Ty-cee."

"There is little probability that funding such a mission would yield a benefit," the machine said to him. "Analyses indicate that you have almost no relevance."

"I ask for minimal funding to prove my relevance," Gota said.

A pragmatic child of Bhutar, Gota was coldly aware of the circumstances as they now stood: We serve and obey machines now. The Maran had been insane to believe that they could unite against things like these, Gods of impenetrable metal and super-thought.

But we knew long ago, and we prepared. We understood duty and made it our religion; the Bhutaran worshipped duty because we knew that the machines would come one day and call us to duty. Mara rebelled against the truth; then beheld it, and now they will march to the plexium mines. It was at present not to bemoan or regret, only to prove relevance to the new masters and avoid the plexium mines.

Diplomats such as Autha had made noises of reassurance about the intentions of the Ty-cee, but no being of reason had believed them. Machines of such pure power had no obligation to reject deception or honor alliances. No matter, it was always meant to be: the Flux makes reality beyond any being's desires or philosophies or fables or delusions. The dragon eats the princess not because it is evil but because it is hungry.

52341 said nothing, only waited, its face a crystal mirror.

I am not yet dismissed to the mines, Gota thought. Survival might yet be possible.

"To remove a potentially dangerous hybrid," Gota went on. "That is my relevance. I require only minimal funds to achieve this goal. My life becomes one duty."

The flat plane of face showed no modulations, the Ty-cee Evaluator said nothing.

"I need only to spend time to investigate on Planet Earth; to find and capture a hybrid. Surely the Gathered --"

"The Gathered are not concerned with hybrids," 52341's mouth said at last. "It is understood that hybrids exist throughout the galaxy. The Spiral Arms are of no concern to the circumstances as they now stand. No worlds in the Spiral Arms contain production grade plexium. These planets are irrelevant."

Gota bowed to the machine.

As I obviously am as well.

Having studied Kosan for so many years, it had surprised Gota when the Ambassador, a disciple of duty, had given away his power and position in order to escape into obscurity; to willingly accept irrelevance. Yet there is one thing beyond duty, and that is survival.

Gota shifted his eyes out the plexium bubble and studied Planet Bhutar. For the first time in his life he had the very mad and un-Bhutaran thought that it might be time to escape.

TWENTY-NINE ...

▼

April finally softened Nebraska; the bitter wind spun round to the south and turned suddenly sweet and warm. The last stubborn patches of snow and desperate ice crumbled and melted into the black soil. Dawn saw frost sparkling on the brown prairie, but the green days of spring were creeping into the plains and for some, high school graduation was only a breath away.

Kyle Kuzma and Randy Lynch got out of Kyle's black pickup and were walking across the school parking lot when a crowd of students staring and pointing down the gravel road south of Mars City got their attention. They stared at the glittering yellow-and-black Hummer H-3 that rose over the hill a half mile away and roared down toward the high school like a chrome-framed tank.

"Check that thing out!" Kyle said. "That's like a Hum-vee."

"Sweet," Lynch said. "Who the hell bought that?"

"It's coming here," Kyle said. "My guess is Mr. Becker. His old man like stroked out, remember, and he inherited some money."

"So why's he still teaching at this crap hole?"

They stood with the other students and watched the gleaming monster turn into the parking lot. Kyle heard her name suddenly, muttered and whispered in disbelief:

"Cathy Holmes!"

He stared at the Hummer approaching. His face collapsed in stunned despair. My God, My God...no.

"It's the little bitch, Kyle!" Randy gawked. "The little bitch is like driving that thing! A Hummer!"

Kyle stared at her behind the steering wheel, a raven-haired ant inside a tarantula, the steering wheel barely letting her see out the windshield. It was Cathy. What the hell is this all about?

192   The Blue River Valley

"That can't be hers," Randy said. "It's her old man's."

She spun the monster round and parked next to the used Chevys and Fords. The brand new Hummer glistened in the morning sun, bumble-bee yellow and black and sparkling chrome. Kyle felt his heart ache, and at the same time he could feel himself getting mad. Spoiled rotten little show off. I don't believe it..

Randy Lynch dropped a spit to the parking lot. "What the hell is she driving that for?"

"It belongs to her grandpa," Kyle said. "Or her uncle. They're like rich businessmen? It ain't hers, she's just showing off."

Cathy climbed down out of the giant machine. She looked like a child next to it.

Ignoring the crowd of students, she hefted her backpack and started walking across the parking lot as if nothing were out of the ordinary. She hadn't gotten on the bus this morning, they all figured she was sick or something, although Cathy Holmes never got sick—but...

Kyle felt sick. I get my ass kicked by a soph pussy because of her, now Cee comes tooling up in a Hum-vee...

He could feel the crowd of students looking at him, wondering how he could be so stupid to dump her for a whore like Kirsten. Their eyes called him a loser.

He stared at Cathy, but she didn't even look his way.

Her face was completely reserved and humble--Mr. Kwang-su would approve—though her eyes were bright green and malicious. She nodded at some of the students who were gawking at her, and gawking back at the black-and-yellow Hummer.

"I don't friggin believe it," Randy Lynch said, watching her march calmly toward the school building. "A friggin Hummer, Kyle! That's a friggin Hummer!"

"I know what the hell it is." Kyle stared at her, the little princess mincing away without a word, without a look at him. All those times she said she loved him, what's the deal now? He stared at the old high school building. He would be leaving it soon, go off to Memphis State. Cee would stay here. She loves me and now she won't even look at me. What a mess you made of my life, Baby.

He looked back at the new Hum-vee. Her grandpa's, or her uncle's. Not hers, not Cathy's.

"Screw her, Kyle," Lynch said. "She's like a stupid little soph. She's a cheerleader. Next year we're going to be doing like college chicks, so why do you give a crap about Super Bitch?"

"Don't call her that."

"What? Come on, man. Did you even do her? Be straight with me, man."

"Hell yes," Kyle lied. "She wasn't even good."

Kyle watched her elf body twitch up the concrete steps and disappear into Mars High.

He had never loved her so intensely, he wanted her more now than ever; Cathy was suddenly a lost dream. He had never even gotten to first base with little Cee-cee, and he had nailed Kirsten on the first date. But after screwing Kirsten a few times he got bored, he started fantasizing. He didn't feel like he was cheating on his girlfriend, because Cee wouldn't put out. What are you supposed to do if your girlfriend won't give you sex?

Cee's dad was too strict, Cathy was too prudy; she didn't even want him feeling her up. Anyway, she was always the cute girl you took to the movies anyway, and then you got her home and went out to nail Kirsten or Crystal or Amy. But….what? She's a stupid chick. Randy nailed her down; she's a weird dink from hell, no doubt about it. She'll still be here in the middle of nowhere and I'll be in the big city…

Kyle stared at the high school building. A strange and terrible longing came over him. He looked back at the Hummer H-3. He wanted her because everything about her was—what? What was it? There's something—she won't put out, is that it?—I love her because she won't put out?

"The little bitch is dissing the crap out of you," Lynch warned him.

"Don't call her a bitch."

"Get over it, man. She's making you look like you can't screw anymore or something."

"Hey! Man, I'm not going to let her disrespect me. I did her, I nailed Cee, she put on my ring and I gave it to her blue in the face!"

"So? She's a bitch, man. She's a weird freakin' show off bitch. You nailed her, so? Get over it."

"She wasn't even a good piece of tail," Kyle said. He stared at the high school building, where she had vanished after making her spectacular appearance. No piece of tail at all, not even a feel of her little tits. A thing he would never admit to the team, but it was true: she didn't put out at all. He had never screwed her, or even close.

She said she loved me and then she wouldn't let me do anything. Now she's hooking up with the sophomore Karate Boy and driving a new Hummer to school. She don't even look at me.

194   The Blue River Valley

After Third Period Kyle finally corralled her as she was marching down the hall, the Princess of Mars High.

"Cee-cee, I need to talk to you," he said.

She stared at him, cradling her books. "How are you, Kyle?"

"Not good," he said. "I'm not good. Why are you ignoring me?"

"I'm not ignoring anyone. I'm on my way to class."

"Okay." Kyle frowned down the hall. Several students were witnessing this, his pussy desperation, the senior king of Mars High crying over a sophomore chick. "I just wanted to say happy birthday to you, that's all."

"Thank you."

"I wish I could have been at your party—but you didn't like even invite me."

"No." She gave him a sad look.

"Did you have a good birthday party?"

"It was wonderful," she said. "Grandpa and Uncle Rel were there, and Miss Mason and all the guys from the Astronomy Club, and Mr. Kwang-su. It was the best day of my life."

"Without me." Kyle sighed and shook his head. "I suppose you got your share of presents."

"I did," she said. "I got Hubble posters from the guys in the club, I got flying lessons from Daddy—"

"Flying lessons. What for?"

"You'll find out. And Miss Mason got me a year's membership to the Y in Mars. Mr. Kwang-su gave me a real Korean robe."

"What's that?" Kyle was looking at the pendant she wore, a tiny silver figurine hanging above her chest. "Another present?"

She reddened slightly. "Yes. It's a necklace, solid silver."

"Who gave you that, Karate Boy?"

"It's not even your business," she said. "Yes. It's a gift from Sherwood North, my friend. He carved it himself."

"The punk who broke my jaw. What, is it like supposed to be you?" Kyle stared at the pendant.

"No, it's a sprite."

"A what?"

"A mythological—Kyle, what do you want?"

He ground his teeth, feeling such strange anger and despair. "I wanted to get you something," he said. "But you're like blowing me off, ignoring me. You didn't even invite me to your birthday party."

"You dumped me for Kirsten," she said. "You broke up with me, Kyle. You don't want me jamming up your life, remember? So why would I invite you to my birthday party?"

"I don't know, I don't know. I don't know anything. All I know is that I like miss you. I just screwed up, Cee! What you want me to do, what I'm supposed to do to make it up to you?"

"Go off to college, Kyle. I can tell from your vocabulary that you're college material."

"What's that suppose to mean?"

"You're going to be graduating. What we had was a fantasy. Move on and forget about me."

"I don't think I can. I keep thinking about you, how stupid I was to break up with you, and--"

"No, you were smart," she said. "Go back to Kirsten. You were made for each other."

"No--why you doing this!—I wanted to get you a birthday present and all that—I never like Wanted to really break up with you."

"But you did," Cathy said. "I'm sorry, but I have to get to class."

"So now you're wearing the Karate Boy's necklace," he said. "The—"

"Sprite." She looked at him. "It's a sprite, and he made it for me by hand."

"And the Hummer—what's with that?"

"The Hum-vee H-3 is a gift from my grandfather," she said.

"That Hum-vee you drove in--it belongs to you."

"Yes, it does. Grandpa wanted me to have a car when I got my license."

"That ain't a car, it's a brand new Hum-vee."

"I know what it is. And *ain't* isn't a word," she said. "Just to let you know before you go to college."

"And it's bullshit. That Hummer don't belong to you."

"Yes, it does. It's my birthday present from my grandpa. And Uncle Rel got me a two-seat ultralite Maxair Drifter XP airplane. It was a very good birthday party, and we all had chocolate cake that Miss Mason made, and pistachio ice cream, and we ended up watching the Planet Saturn in Daddy's big telescope."

"Okay, okay!" Kyle said. "So what you're saying is, like there's no hope for me?"

She stared at him with those eerie green eyes. "Please go off and play football at Memphis State. Do your best at quarterback and remember me back here in Nebraska. You'll be there, I'll be here."

He frowned at the silver figurine dangling on her chest. "I would have gone to like Jerrod's or something, I would have got you a necklace of solid gold," he said.

"I don't want a necklace of solid gold."

196   The Blue River Valley

"But you want some cheap home-made silver elf thing that Karate Boy--"

"It's not an elf, it's a sprite."

"Okay, play your game, Cee-cee. Have it your way, that's always the way it is, right? You're always the princess. You want the Karate Boy because he like blind-sided me and made me look bad. The Karate Boy couldn't play football to save his ass, could he? Karate Boy never had the pressure of leading the whole team—"

"No, he didn't," Cathy said.

"So wear his necklace, go on out with the soph."

"I will if I want," Cathy said. "I'm going to be late to class."

"You're in love with this soph—or what?"

"I'm in love with none of your business. Please have a good life out there in the world. Graduate and follow your scholarship and be happy and all that."

"And you're going to stay back here and forget all about me."

"I don't know what's going to happen," Cathy said. "I'm sorry, but I don't want to be your girlfriend. That was a game we both played."

"A game? You were like crawling all over me and telling me how much you love me—"

"Yes, I was," she said. "Then you tried to slap me, and that woke me up."

"Because I screwed up, that's all! Jesus, can't you give me another chance, Cee?"

"No. And my name's not Jesus—and it's not *Cee*. Please Kyle. Graduate and go out there and—so on."

"You were begging and crawling all over me a few months ago."

"Well, I'm not begging and crawling anymore."

"No. Now you're tooling around in a brand new Hummer and doing the Karate Boy."

She blasted him with her wicked green eyes, and Kyle felt a shudder of fear. "I loved you, Kyle," she said calmly. "I even used to pretend we were married. But I'm sorry, you're a prick."

"And you're a prick-tease," he said. "Why do you think I got frustrated and broke up with you? You don't wear a guy's class ring and tell him you love him, then not have sex with him. What I was s'pose to do? You lead me on like we're going to finally have sex, then you turn into a nun. Jesus! You said you loved me, but you never damn did show it."

"Yes, I did," she said. "Only you were too stupid to see it."

"I'm stupid. That's why I'm going to Memphis State University next year."

"So you're going to be a stupid college football player, until you have to drop out. Don't worry, there will be plenty of girls there who'll give you sex."

He stared at her. "Why are you being like this? Just because Daddy doesn't like me?"

"No, because *I* don't like you. So go have a gay time with Randy Lynch, and leave me alone."

"You are a bitch," he said. "Here I'm trying to apologize, make it up with you, and—Cath, why are you like making me so pissed off?"

"Marry Kirsten," she said. "Marry her and be happy, you were made for each other."

"Kirsten Pavelka's a whore," Kyle said.

"Right. And so are you. Goodbye, Kyle."

"Okay. I gave you a chance. I'm going to be in college, and you're going to be out here in this small town doing your small town things, getting bored with the pussy Karate Poetry Boy. Okay. Have a good life, Cee."

"Okay," she said. "I will. Kyle, I don't want to be mean; but I'm so glad to be rid of you that I could puke."

"Screw you, Prude. You don't even have a set of tits. I'm going to be going to college in Memphis. What you think you're going to be doing back here?"

"I know exactly what I'm going to be doing," Cathy said. She smiled at him. "I'm going to be flying."

T H I R T Y ...

▼

Their sophomore year was over, summer bloomed gold and green over the Nebraska plains. Summer brought the warm south wind and the scent of new grass. Summer brought the rare perfect days to Nebraska. Summer brought a wonderful madness.

Sherwood North stared down out of the sky at the distant prairie and tried not to panic. They were flying—no, Cathy was flying--the two-seat Maxair Drifter XP ultralite above Harrison County, the green-black fields and creek bottoms flowing many many many many feet below them. Cathy steered the craft like a drunken sailor, spinning down, then soaring up, gunning the engine into the terrifying blue and white sky, trying to alarm Sherwood and wildly succeeding. She giggled back at him like a lunatic, her black hair flowing in wind-webs across his face.

Her dad lets her fly this thing without even wearing a helmet? Jesus! Don't think about dying and disaster, grab this perfect sensation and love the view, the earthy squares of Nebraska, the farms below, the prairie—even if it costs your life. This will make the poem of a lifetime. If you are crazy, Cathy, and decide to kill us both, that's okay. I will enjoy what few seconds of life I might have, and not even think of helmets and parachutes and air bags.

Despite knowing that she would test his 'chicken-ness', Sherwood had expected some preliminary instructions, at least a helmet, although what good would that do crashing out of the sky? He had not expected to just strap himself into the backseat of the thing and have Cathy send it wildly into the blue like this. She obviously knew what she was doing and had flown it before, but that didn't make the event seem any less suicidal.

"There's Mars!" she shouted back at him. "We're flying over Mars High, Sherwood!"

"I see it," he said.

- 198 -

This is a dream, this flying over the land.

He could not believe that he was soaring over the county with *her*; he was flying across the sky with Cathy Holmes. The reassuring cha-cha-cha-cha of the engine and her alarming skill made him finally bold enough to hug her around the waist. "This is insane!" he cried, grinning at the silver sprite necklace bouncing off her chest. "Unbelievable!"

"It is!" Cathy gunned the ultralite's engine. "Stop feeling me up, Sherwood."

"I'm not feeling you up, I'm holding on in pure terror."

"Stop touching my breasts! You're a pervert."

"Jeez, I bumped them by accident."

"There's Mr. Kwang-su's school," Cathy said. "But I better turn around; I promised Daddy I wouldn't attract attention. I'm not supposed to fly over Mars or stray too far from the farm."

"So, naturally that's what you're doing—ohhhh, Holy Shit!"

The ultralite swept away from Mars City, and Cathy zoomed eastward, the perfect squares of farmland flowing below the buzzing engine. The plane banked over the Blue River Valley, and they followed the river southward. Sherwood felt the sky in his face and knew that, death or not, he would rather be here with her than anywhere on earth.

He did wonder why her father and grandfather allowed her to do this, to just plop her little butt into a miniature airplane and go sailing off into the sky, a sixteen year old girl who never displayed a lot of caution. Did she rule them so completely?

She allowed him to hug her around the waist, and he could smell the minty gum she was chewing. Her black hair swept wonderfully into his face, and he said into her ear, "If we live through this, are you going to let me drive your new Hummer?"

She grinned back against his face, her cheek cold and red. "First you have to let me drive your motorcycle."

"Oh, no. I'll give you a ride, but I'm not going to be responsible—"

"You can teach me how. Then I'll ask Grandpa for one next Christmas."

"You'd wreck it and die in the flames," he said over the noise of the ultralite's engine. "Then your dad would kill me."

"Sherwood, I'm flying a plane. Don't you think I can learn to ride a wimpy little motorcycle?"

Good question.

"We'll see," he said. "If your dad says it's okay, and if we survive-- I'll show you how to ride."

"Then if your dad says it's okay, I might let you drive my car."

Sherwood pressed his face against her cold hair.

200 The Blue River Valley

Car. Okay, just a car.…

"Anyway, you can't push me around and get your way like you do your dad and your uncle and your grandpa."

She slid her cheek across his face and kissed him. "Why not?"

Another good question. He kissed her, his hands around her waist, her warm back against his chest. "Because I won't let you. I'm older and wiser than you and I know better."

"I'm sixteen and you're sixteen and a half." She swiped her tongue over his lips and turned her head back around giggling. "You're about as wise as a cow."

Sherwood stared out at the yawning blue-and-white sky. I'm sixteen and I'm flying over Harrison County and I love her so much it aches all over, and she is everything in the world. Can this be real? It must be; I can feel the silk-black hair sweeping my face; I can feel her little waist in my hands.

Even so, there was the strange worry of dream in all this: a sense that some impossible force ruled the day. Sherwood had never believed in anything supernatural, yet he *knew* there was something supernatural going on here; this was all so out-of -body and unbelievable…

Cathy finally banked the little craft away from the river and they soared northward toward her farm. "Better get back," she said. "Daddy's probably going to ground me for life; I promised him I'd stay close to the farm. I'm going to have to tell him that you made me disobey him."

"I'm sure he's going to buy that."

"It doesn't matter,' she said. "I'm always grounded anyway. All my life I've been grounded."

Sherwood's stomach dropped as she put the little plane into a suicide dive and the farmhouse soared up at them. He saw Dr. Holmes out in the farmyard standing with Woodrow, the great Saint Bernard barking at the thing chattering out of the sky. Sherwood reminded himself that it's not the flying that kills you, it's the landing.

He kissed the back of her neck, making her giggle. "Well, you're not grounded now," he said.

"Sherwood—"

"I'm not feeling you up! Just don't kills us, okay?"

THIRTY-ONE ...

▼

"Go on back to her, Kyle," Kirsten Pavelka said. "She's like got you ga-ga, you obviously can't get her out of your system. But I can tell you what she is: She's a witch. Go ahead and laugh. That girl is a witch."

"You're just jealous of her," Kyle said.

"And I don't mean witch like bitch—I mean like she really *is* a witch. She can cast spells. She can stop things from happening around her just by using her mind. Go ahead and laugh, but I've seen it happen."

"Come on. She acts weird sometimes. That crap might have been fun to tell like in middle school, but we're too old for ghost stories."

"She can like cast spells over people—she has magic powers."

"Oogie-boogie!"

"You weren't on the cheerleading squad with her—I've seen her do things, things like only a witch could do."

"Hello? Witches ain't real. Duh-uh-uh-uh."

"Screw you, Kyle. They are real, and she is one."

"You're serious, ain't you? That's crazy, Kirst."

"You've seen her do those flips and spins. I'm telling you, like she is a genuine witch."

"And you believe old man Hacker's ghost still hangs around the school gym."

"Go on back to her. She's making you crazy, everybody knows that. Give her your ring again. And when you're away at college, she's going to be putting a spell on somebody else, and you're like going to be miserable."

"I ain't giving any chick my ring. As usual, you got the school gossip wrong. It's her that wants to get back with me. Like ain't no way I'm going to be playing college ball and have some high school soph little chick pin me down. She wants to get back with me."

202 The Blue River Valley

"Oh, give me a break. I can see what she did to you," Kirsten said. "A love potion or something. Some Cathy Holmes spell."

"Yeah, right. Or she waved her magic wand."

"I've seen things—she is not normal, you know that, everybody knows that. She is a true witch. And her dad's probably a warlock or a sorcerer."

"You believe all those stupid stories, don't you? All the oogie boogie stories about the Holmes farm."

"Well, there's like a million folks scared crapless of her. You keep saying how weird she is, you know there's something very weird about her."

"Yeah, but not that weird. You need to get some therapy. I don't give a rat's ass anyway," Kyle said. "A month from now I'm out of this small town. She can tool around this piss-ant county in her Hummer all she wants. I'll be in the city of Blues, Booze and Barbeques, and she's going to be a high school junior out here in boring Craphole, Nebraska."

Kirsten gave him a bitch stare, shaking her head. "I see how you look at her. Like she worked some kind of witchcraft over you."

Kyle laughed, but it fell flat. The dread idea had in fact bounced around his brain, why he would be so obsessed with her that he couldn't get her out. It maybe *was* a spell of some kind. And the more Cathy ignored him, the more intense it seemed to get. This was his time, playing college football and doing college chicks—not little undeveloped girls with a crush like Cee-cee, who wouldn't put out because Daddy—

My God! She was more beautiful and mysterious because she *didn't* put out. Why the other cheerleaders made fun of her, and feared her. Cathy didn't give it out. She didn't put out. She didn't give herself away, her body, even when he told her he loved her...she didn't put out, even to me.

"Have you seen her flying all over the county?" Kirsten asked. "She like flies a little mini airplane—"

"I know. I've seen. So what, a lot of people have ultralites. She's like a science geek, so what?"

"She's like evil," Kirsten said. "I don't know what it is, but there's something evil about her. She's some like kind of evil witch. I know that."

He ground his teeth thinking of her, Cathy's clean pixie grin. Those green eyes. The haunting untapped image. "She ain't evil," he muttered. "She's good, that's why you're jealous of her."

"I'm scared of her. She's not right, Kyle, she never has been."

"She's better than you sluts," Kyle said. "She's better than all the sluts of Mars High. You hate her, you call her a witch—because you're sluts and she's not—that's what scares you. You put out and she don't, that's what scares you."

"We're scared of her 'cause she's scary," Kirsten said. "Every chick on the cheerleading squad knows that. She's only a soph, and she intimidates everybody. There's something really wrong with her. The only reason I'm saying this--I don't want you to get hurt."

"You hate her because she don't give herself away, and you do."

"I don't want her to hurt you, that's all."

"I'm going to like get hurt by a little 90 pound girl?"

"Like, don't bet against it."

Susan Mason also knew that something wasn't right. She took some of Cathy's writings to her father, a professor of Psychology at the university in Lincoln, and asked his opinion:

"Precocious, very talented," he said, after reading several samples of Cathy's writing. "Quite a bit beyond the normal 16 year old girl; but I don't really see much more. She's precise, proud of her intellect. She obviously has a powerful imagination."

"Nothing disturbing? Troubling?"

Dr. Mason looked at his daughter. "No. Her thoughts aren't confused or disarranged. I would imagine her to be a little vain, a bit of an intellectual show off."

"A bit," Susan said. "Dad, these are hardly the writings of a sixteen year old high school sophomore. Besides that, there are other things about her."

"Maybe she didn't write them."

"I'm sure she did. Dad, I've never seen anything like her. She does such brilliant things it scares me."

He lifted his eyebrows. "So you've got a genius on your hands. Why does that scare you?"

"I might become her step mother," Susan said.

He stared at her for a long moment. "Ahhh." He smiled. "This is the daughter of the Physics professor, your future husband."

"I think it's going that way. I know that Eric is in love with me and wants to get married. I don't know, though. I'm just a little scared. No, a lot scared."

"Maybe what scares you is the thought of becoming an instant mother. Whether this girl will feel intimidated and jealous and not accept you. She has a very strong mind, according to her writings."

"I've worried about that. But I don't think so. Cathy actually wants us to get married. She's never really had a woman figure in her life, and she's come

204   The Blue River Valley

to me a lot of times for girl talk. I love her to death, and she loves me. As for feeling intimidated, I don't think she's ever had that problem."

"She obviously has a dominant personality. Are you intimidated by her?"

"To tell you the truth, I'm not sure. She's fascinating," Susan said. "But there's something very strange about her; I can't explain why, but it's something I sense."

"Will I get to see a picture of my future grand daughter?"

Susan smiled, handed over the yearbook. "I wanted you to read her before you saw what she looks like. Cathy Holmes, in the sophomore section."

He gave her a bemused smile, opened the yearbook, turning to the H's. The face immediately got his attention, a beautiful grinning elf face, her hair long and raven black, her eyes a very unsettling light aqua, a face you could only fall in love with. She looked like she was thinking of a very funny joke.

"My God, she's beautiful," Dr. Mason said, blinking his eyes at the photo.

"She is. But beautiful in what way?"

He gave Susan a questioning look, restudied the girl's picture. Strangely childlike, but the eyes burned with intelligence and supreme energy.

"Was her mother oriental?"

"No, Caucasian. She was killed in a car wreck when Cathy was just a baby."

"Dr. Holmes?"

"Welsh and Scotch. He has light brown hair and brown eyes."

"So?"

"She has a grandfather and uncle who retired recently and bought a farmhouse near Eric's." Susan sighed and shook her head. "They're very strange. When you meet them all you'll know."

"Maybe it's them you're scared of?"

"No, not scared. They're nice, and they love Cathy to death. But whenever I'm around her family, I have this feeling that they have big secrets, and I'm being carefully kept out."

Dr. Mason frowned. "Well, every family has secrets, I suppose."

"There's something not right, I sense it. And I'm afraid I don't know what I'm getting myself into."

"You never do when you fall in love and consider marriage. But remember, if you do, it's Eric Holmes you're marrying. The daughter will be gone in a few years to college and her own life."

Dr. Mason stared at the photograph, the mischievous grin glowing out of the black frame of hair. Eyes that did seem to hold secrets.

"Beauty, brilliance, a doting father, now suddenly competition—no wonder you're scared."

"He's more than a doting father, I'm afraid," Susan said. "He's almost obsessively over-protective. Cathy could be winning science and writing awards, she could be the top girl gymnast in the state. She probably should be in college by now. She composes music and plays four different instruments, piano, guitar, violin and saxophone. She is off the charts, Dad. And instead of encouraging her, Eric tries almost desperately to hold her back."

"Odd, but not unheard of. For whatever reason, he's had no one in his life, you say, but his daughter. He's probably terrified of losing her. I know a little of the feeling."

"How so?"

"Oh, seeing your little girl grow up and having the sense that you're losing her to womanhood, and she's beginning to not need you—not in the old familiar way."

Susan smiled. "You always need your dad. It's so strange, whenever I try to talk to Eric about her he gets very nervous and uncomfortable. Whenever Cathy does something remarkable, he acts like it's a crime he has to cover up."

"Well, it's normal that you'd have second thoughts about changing your life so drastically, and it's probably good. But there will come a time when the calculations are over, and you'll have to follow your heart."

"Dad, this is going to sound very weird," Susan said. "But her uncle and grandfather—sometimes they don't seem like real people. And sometimes I get this strange thought that Cathy doesn't seem like a real person."

"Hmmm." Dr. Mason's eyes went back to the face in the yearbook. He did detect it, a certain 'otherworld' quality. Green penetrating eyes that did seem to hold secrets.

Dr. Mason looked at his daughter: "I don't think I've ever seen a more beautiful face in my life."

THIRTY-TWO...

▼

"You wrote in your book, Teacher," Kosan said. "That Planet Earth is located in an undistinguished corner of the galaxy, the *forgotten Spiral Arms*. I wonder where you heard that term."

Eric smiled. "You read my book?"

"Yes. You leaned heavily on the theory that this galaxy is probably teeming with organic life. You, of course, had to draw attention to yourself."

"Well, it's more than a theory now, isn't it?"

Such smugness these humans have. How they must risk their lives to show off. Kosan stared out the window of the farmhouse. Cathy was out there in the green yard, playing with the dog Woodrow, throwing a ball that it would lumber to retrieve.

"There, toward the center of the galaxy, toward the black hole, the Drain," Eric said. "That's where the majority of life is. The key is energy, isn't it?"

Kosan gave him a surprised look. "Yes, a special form of energy."

"Where there is energy, there's life."

"No, of course not." Kosan watched his grand daughter playing with the dog on the lawn of this place on Planet Earth. His eyes grew thoughtful. "Energy doesn't equal life. Life—even like the Ty-cee--needs very special conditions. Energy is only one. Life needs energy, it needs matter, and it needs a very subtle Flux in the Foam."

"Life needs very rare conditions in order to come about," Eric said.

"Of course. It constitutes a tiny atom of the galaxy. Almost nothing is what you would call 'alive'."

"So, as the stars gather more densely toward the center, the black hole—the Drain—chemicals are more energetic, life is more likely to be abundant and intense."

- 206 -

Kosan studied him. "Something like that. But nothing is ever what it seems to be. Life is a Flux in the Foam. You believe life is special, but it is not. You believe that you are alive because elements inside your form convey this message to your brain. Electric messages convince you that you are alive and independent. That is an illusion. You are utterly dependent on billions of other tiny machines that operate their tasks and thus operate you. All life is symbiotic. And all life is unaware."

"I feel alive," Eric said. "I feel other living things around me."

"That is why creatures like us grasp onto beauty and emotion, why we have the power to do things that are not coldly rational." Kosan stared at his grand-daughter out the window, wrestling with the big dog, hugging him, scratching his rump. "This is a very sensual world; a garden to some, a swamp to others. Many primitive races waste their time, and thus their lives, in fruitless play and sensuality."

"Maybe to reconcile us to mortality; to celebrate life before we face death."

"There is no such thing as death—not until the end of the universe anyway. There is only what you call atoms rearranging themselves."

"The Second Law of Thermodynamics," Eric said. "What did you think of that chapter?"

"Well written but primitive. I should say presumptuous."

Eric scowled. "In what way?"

"Rules, Laws, Axioms, Truths, Imperatives, Equations, these are the words of those who reside on a miniscule dot of reality. Only the Uncertainty Theory touches about the edges of truth: that the Flux is beyond prediction: that the Foam is everything, and so behaves as it will—but reality knows no rules or laws. Reality in fact does not exist, not as you would believe it does."

"All right," Eric said. "A good critique, I suppose. I didn't write it for super-advanced aliens."

"Sarcasm noted." Kosan stared out at his grand-daughter, the hybrid of Donis and Cynthia romping in the yard with the giant dog, her black hair flying in the wind.

"So even reality doesn't exist. That's crazy."

"No one knows the pure truth," Kosan said. "At least no race we have ever encountered. But it is said that when we, as organized living creatures move the Foam, we are constantly creating reality."

Eric stared off thoughtfully. "But we share reality with other organisms."

"Do we? Or are we unconsciously creating *that* reality as we go along? When you see something, it is real to you; when you don't see it—is it real?"

208   The Blue River Valley

"So the theory is that living things are constantly—in real time—creating their own existence?"

"Without control, of course," Kosan said. "Without consciousness."

Eric stared out the window at Cathy and Woodrow. "Good to know you advanced folks have crazy theories too. That somehow reassures me."

"Well, I've found that there is something beyond reality," Kosan said. "Something better."

Eric stared at his daughter romping in the sunlit yard. "You know, I've often wondered if I went into a coma, as if this were some science fiction dream or other. If Cathy isn't real, if all this is—if you're actually here, or if this is some madness my mind has created."

"Nothing is here for very long," Kosan said. "Even madness."

"So how does God fit into this?" Eric questioned. "I know you will say that God isn't real. But how can you actually know?"

"You take two steps forward," Kosan said. "Unfortunately, you often take two steps back. Sometimes more."

"Even you can't say there is no God."

"I never tried to say that. It might surprise you to know that I believe in God, as all Marans do—only a very different God than most humans believe in. But God and religion are not the same thing—they are in most ways exactly opposite."

"I tried to expose Cathy to religion," Eric said. "But it made me feel like a hypocrite."

"I don't think any religion of Earth would affect Cathy." Kosan smiled at this science teacher. "It is one thing to believe in God—quite another to believe in religion. All religions are lies if they tell you that only *they* know the truth of God. No religion knows the truth of God. Religion has done great work on your world, I know this. Religion has civilized you, protected the poor and sick and weak, and given you a moral framework from which you can flourish and create—write your book of science and so forth. Religion is a necessary step in any primate's evolution; that is why it is so similar and predictable. Religion is also the most dangerous enemy of mankind."

"I won't argue with you on that one," Eric said.

Kosan stared away. His gold eyes studied the farmhouse window. "If you destroy in the name of political ideology, or even for your tribe and clan, then you will only destroy so much. If you destroy for God, there is no limit, you will destroy everything. This is where humans are, on the cusp of the great battle between religion and science."

"As others have been?"

Kosan looked at him. "Trillions of others. The road to death is religion. The road to God is science. All living things must choose which."

"I'm one who believes they're both important," Eric said. "I believe they can co-exist."

"For awhile," Kosan said. "But sadly, not for long; science will unlock too many secrets."

The Maran looked at him strangely; his eyes slowly closed. "I hesitated to kill you all those years ago, Eric, because you told me that you were a teacher of science."

"So tell me," Eric said. "Other worlds have gone through what we're now going through, this great assembling war between science and religion. How did it come out?"

Kosan smiled at him. "On some worlds, science and reason prevailed. These worlds entered the Galaxy and the Spaceway. On others religion prevailed, one wrong religion or another, one idiotic belief or another—these worlds became extinct. On these worlds, beings exterminated themselves in the name of some absurd religion. Who is to say which world made the better choice?"

"What, you couldn't intervene?" Eric said. "The Marans couldn't save—"

"No, we couldn't. The absolute law of the Galaxy is to not interfere with the Flux. That is the law my son and Cynthia broke when they made Cathy."

"Religion and science shouldn't fear one another," Eric said.

Kosan grunted. "Truth either lives in revelation or dies in denial. Why is it that in all of your primitive religions a particular God finally destroys the earth?"

Eric stared at him. "Is that our fate?"

"No one can say," Kosan replied. "Many water worlds are going through the test that Earth is going through, as it builds up for the great battle."

"Great battle? What, between good and evil?"

"Between religion and science." Kosan smiled at him. "Only God can say which is good and which is evil."

THIRTY-THREE ...

Sixteen years ago it had been difficult enough to locate the ambassador's son, Donis. This search, Gota realized, would be much more daunting.

He had been part of a team then, now he was alone. Kosan and Relomar could have planned and prepared for this many years ago—if indeed they were even here on Earth.

Gota's pink eyes studied the brain screen. Is this truly duty, or is it madness?

Alone and now a criminal himself, a hunted being, he had very little time before they came for him.

Here over the humid atmosphere of Earth his ship's brain was scanning every 16 year old female who lived at present in this nation. Special attention was paid to high school records, academic or athletic achievements out of the ordinary, strange appearance, remarkable intellect. Gota had at first considered the Main Brain of this planet—the Internet—to be his best tool. Internet chat room talk and My Space gossip was plundered at the speed of light to try and detect any rumors of Mist or unusual powers, any girl whispered to be very different. All immediate candidates began appearing on another screen in such profusion that Gota soon realized this would be a poor tool at best.

He was astonished at how many candidates were detected: 16 year old females accused of being witches, vampires, zombies, space aliens—and he soon realized that most, if not all, were made up stories. A gullible, superstitious race anyway, this weakness must be especially acute in human females of this age. Gota soon realized that he would have to program filters into the search, to try and rinse away the vast majority of untruth in order to pluck that which could be true. Still, it was likely that dominant Maran genes would have transmitted to it notable differences in appearance or

- 210 -

ability that would almost certainly be suspected by other humans. Gota had not expected the deluge of rumors and gossip, stories, tales, innuendo that spewed out of the Internet. A severe setback. Bhutar had probably already dispatched hunters, and Gota would be racing against time.

The high school records, he decided, would be more promising. He searched for 16 year old students with exceptionally high academic achievements, greater skills and intellect than most. What was called 'photographic memory'; the ability to split attention, to perform different tasks effortlessly at once, even superior physical ability, a phenomenon who might have shot ahead through grades and was maybe now attending a university. No one could predict what Maran traits might be passed to a hybrid, possibly even Mist.

The human mother, Cynthia, had been light-skinned, what was called Caucasian, and of course Donis was Maran. The hybrid would be somewhat Caucasian looking, presumably. So he began steadily narrowing the search. He began screening over-achieving white females, cutting out those considered extraordinary, but not unusual. It was most important to try and pick up clues that this female had powers beyond human.

If we had indeed failed to kill the child that night 16 years ago, it could be that it generates Mist. That would make it vastly more powerful than other humans. How could such a thing remain unnoticed?

I hunt Kosan as a criminal and now they hunt me as a criminal.

Again his eyes squinted into uncertainty. There was no motive here— why would someone like Kosan, at the height of his power and prestige, let such a thing live, not knowing what it might become, how it could affect this planet? Why would he risk an abomination? A thousand disgraces against him and his dead son--for what possible purpose?

Yet I too have brought disgrace upon myself. And for what possible purpose?

Gota stared at the screen, the flowing pictures of 16 year old Caucasian females; he stopped the screen now and then to study a face or read biographical and academic information. There were many, many multi-talented candidates, but none that seemed anomalous--all fit into a rather predictable mold.

He aimed his pink eyes down at the surface of Earth. The dread thought did come to him that Kosan and Relomar might have dropped clues pointing to this world in order to escape to some other place and throw off any pursuers.

They have sources of information still, Kosan and Relomar. Surely they know that I would be the only pursuer: to laugh their Maran laugh thinking

212   The Blue River Valley

of Gota wasting his life scanning a primitive jungle. Gota soon to be hunted down by his own people.

No—doubtful. Kosan had made too many mysterious trips in the past, too many cloaked voyages that could not be explained.

You must assume that the hybrid still lives and is on this planet. Could it be that he didn't kill it simply because his son had made it?

Gota's eyes returned to the brain screen, the flowing pictures of brilliant females, none of which struck him as Maran in appearance. He fine-tuned the program to search for unusual facial appearance. If it lived, it would certainly have some Maran features.

Slowly the pool shrank, from a million to a thousand to a hundred. Gota read many promising biographies, studied a few interesting faces, but no one individual that didn't seem purely human.

They will come for me, to retrieve the ship and arrest me. Gota, the Traitor, the Betrayer of Duty. Or they will simply kill me.

The hybrid was unknown to the news media of this world, which seemed to be everywhere; so if it could generate Mist it was certainly hiding the fact. Such a thing would be an Earth-wide sensation. It could only be that Kosan and Relomar were taking pains to prevent this.

They will prepare themselves against me, and I am alone against them. I am alone against those in the galaxy who will hunt me down. They will probably not hesitate to destroy me, so I must not hesitate to destroy them: Kosan, Relomar, the Bhutaran hunters; but the hybrid has to be captured, I must have breathing proof to show to the Gathered. If that proves impossible, it must be destroyed.

He considered his situation, so far beyond what it had been for so long. He stared out at the wet atmosphere, white nebulae dominating the skies, and below, the planet so full of water. The hunter is the hunted. Why?

I have no other purpose, he thought. I have no where else to go.

THIRTY-FOUR ...

▼

Sherwood North pulled his 650 Kawasaki into the Nifty Drive Inn. He shook his head at the giant yellow-and-black Hummer H3 glittering on the gravel lot.

Inside the tiny and ancient fast food place Cathy stood behind the counter, wearing the Nifty uniform that had not changed in fifty years, the white dress and red-checkered apron, the white paper cap out of which her black ponytail flowed down her back.

He smiled and shook his head at her. "You Are teaching yourself humility."

She smiled back at him. "I'm working. I'm earning my own money. Are you ready to order, Sir?"

"Not quite yet, Ma'am." He scanned the menu on the wall behind her. "What's the special?"

"Everything we serve is special, Sir," she said sweetly.

"How about a vegetarian burger."

"I'm afraid that we don't make sissy food like that. I'm sorry for your lack of reading skills, Sir, but that item isn't on the menu."

"Okay, since you challenge my manhood—Ma'am--I'll take the double cheeseburger, fries and a Diet Pepsi. You have that sissy Diet Pepsi, I read."

"Yes, we do."

"That uniform looks very nice on you. Very cute."

"Thank you, Sir. But I'm not supposed to fraternize with the customers. Your total is $4.98."

He smiled at her. "Damn, you could have a future in this business."

"At least I'm working a true job. I'm not lying around the swimming pool with a foolish whistle around my neck."

- 213 -

"What else can a lean powerful studly champion swimmer like me do during the summer? The handsome chick-magnet always lifeguards in the summer. Don't you go to the movies?"

"Tonight. Or did you forget?" She grinned at the impossibility of That. "And I've decided we're going to take the 650."

"The 650. Oh, you decided that. You're already tired of your new Hummer?"

"I let you pick the movie."

"What's your dad say about that? Oh—wait—I'll bet he doesn't know!"

"He won't mind—all that much. He knows I won't be in any danger. Geez, Sherwood, on a date the guy's supposed to provide the transportation. Are you that dense?"

"Okay, but it's your idea, not mine. I want him to know that."

His order came and he gave her a smile. "Pick you up at seven, okay?"

"That's right," she said. "Now please, Sir, you have your order, and we don't allow any loitering around the premises."

A windy June evening; the hopelessly melodramatic thought that there was magic in the air. How profound, Sherwood Lord Tennyson.

He grinned into the rich wind. The gravel road bumpled under his bike tires, the sun painted the west. So many times he had fantasized this simple event, going on a movie date with Cathy Holmes. Good God Almighty.

Here it was. Not just teasing or hanging out or even kissing—a date. That event seemed to formulate, to solidify—what? Taking her out to a movie in Mars City, the pathetic small-town dream he had tortured himself with for so long, those nights when he sat in his room carving the sprite necklace out of silver

He rode his motorcycle down the long ragged rock drive. Susan Mason's car, of course, was parked beside Dr. Holmes' modest Honda and the outrageous Hummer. Sherwood rumbled his bike into the yard. The gossip was—(and gossip in Harrison County was always true)—that very soon Dr. Holmes and Miss Mason would marry. That would give Cathy another family member, she was gathering them quickly.

The porch light was on; Woodrow barked, growled and thundered down the porch, sniffing then lapping at him, and before Sherwood climbed the steps the door squeaked open. Dr. Holmes gave him a tight smile. "Sherwood, come on in. How's your summer vacation going?"

"Thank you, Sir. Great so far."

Sherwood stepped into the house, squatting to rub at Woodrow, who demanded a rub. He smiled round the corner at his English teacher. "Miss Mason."

"Hi, Sherwood."

The sound of her tennis shoes bouncing down the stairs. Cathy wore a purple sweater, blue jeans and her signature white tennis shoes. Her black hair fell glistening over her shoulders.

The dream. This is the dream…

"Hey, Cathy."

"Hi, Sherwood."

"You look great. You look wonderful."

She grinned. "Thank you. And you look slightly above average."

"Cathy, that's not a nice thing to say." Eric frowned at Sherwood. "Cathy informed me that you're going on the motorcycle?"

"Her idea, Sir."

"Yes, I'm sure it was. Well, drive carefully, and have a good time. Eleven o'clock, Sherwood, no later."

"Eleven o'clock, Sir." Sherwood blinked his eyes. It always astounded him how Dr. Holmes obsessively sheltered Cathy in some ways, and yet allowed her to go off in airplanes and military vehicles and on motorcycles without seeming concerned.

They walked to his 650 and he handed her the spare helmet. He got on the bike, and she climbed on behind, wrapping her arms around his waist.

The dream, the fantasy. My God, Cathy's arms around your waist… you've dreamed this moment how many times?

He fired up the bike, drove very carefully out of the Holmes farm, onto the gravel road and over the hill. Out of ear-shot, he goosed the bike and they roared into the wind.

Cathy laughed and hugged him and yelled out, "Yeah! Punch it, Sherwood! Punch it!"

They came to Highway 281, and Sherwood squealed onto the concrete and shot west toward Mars City. Cathy giggled into the wind, her face against his neck. He pushed the Kawasaki 650 to the limit and finally eased off. "That's all," he said.

"No—punch it!"

"I don't want a ticket."

"You're a chicken!"

"That's right. I'm a chicken and this is a dangerous machine. If you don't respect a motorcycle—"

"You chicken," she said. "I've studied motorcycles, and I know far more about them than you."

216   The Blue River Valley

"Well, you've never driven one—have you, Miss Holmes?"

"No, but I will."

"When?"

"After the movie, when you take me home, you're going to let me drive this."

"What? Ohhhh Noooo. After dark, are you crazy?"

"You're going to let me drive this motorcycle home, Sherwood."

"I am. How do you know this?"

"Because I demand it, that's why."

"Oh, you demand it."

"If you don't let me, that means you don't really love me."

"Ah. Well, as always, you know everything."

"I do." She kissed his neck, her body pressed against him, the warm summer wind in their faces. "So? Remember, I let you pick the movie."

"Beowulf." Sherwood said. "Come on, that's a no-brainer. I have the feeling that you've even read the damn poem."

"Of course. I've drawn pictures of Grendel."

"I'm sure you have."

"So I'm going to drive this machine home after the movie." She kissed his neck

"I suppose so, yes. You always get your way, don't you?"

"This time I want to."

Sherwood turned off 281 and obeyed the speed limit into Mars City. "You're not going to take this thing up to a hundred and kill us both."

"I promise."

"Your first time on a bike probably shouldn't be at night. Why don't we—"

"You just said I could drive it."

"All right!" He drove the 650 down Main Street and parked outside the Grand Theater.

This is the dream, he thought, staring at the marquee, the neon blinks and twists that played a carnival against the dark and dead town, the courthouse, the maple trees, Choe's dark and empty school. All of the dark buildings that made the night: Bernard's Hardware, Walgreens, Pat's Arts and Crafts, the Save-mart grocery store...

Sherwood tasted the evening wind, the sweet night. He was with Cathy Holmes on a date.

He did his best to follow the dream script: they shared buttered popcorn and sizzling cokes. Sherwood had his arm around her the whole movie, his face struggling against a triumphant grin. And when the movie was over they held hands going into the warm night.

"Excellent!" Cathy said. "A great movie; finally Grendel was understood."

They walked into the night, Mars City asleep, the prairie wind blowing across the courthouse lawn. Sherwood held onto his heart, knowing that this would soon be gone.

"How so?"

"Grendel was different, and hated," Cathy said. "Grendel wanted to belong, and they feared him as a monster."

"Well, he kind of fit the bill."

"It was sad how Grendel kept crying 'Ow!' almost like a child caught in a temper tantrum and being punished for it."

"So, a monster not necessarily evil..."

"A monster not evil, but different and tormented."

"--and really pissed off."

He smiled into her elf face, then kissed her here on the sidewalk outside the Grand Theater, as his dream had predicted. "Did you have a good time?" he asked her.

"Yes. Did you?"

He held Cathy in the warm summer night. "It was the greatest date in history," he said. "I had the best time of my life."

She grinned into his face. "Because you like me a lot."

"I like you a very lot—even though you're by nature unlikeable."

"Of course you like me. And now it's time to let me drive your Kawasaki 650."

"Yes, it's time, Miss Holmes."

She climbed onto his beloved bike and fired her up without a worry. Obviously Cathy had memorized everything he had done to start and drive it. Cathy Holmes, the human computer. Sherwood secured his helmet. He settled back behind her on the passenger seat and wrapped his arms round her tiny waist and prepared himself for probable death.

"Okay, elf-girl, let's see you drive this. But slow and easy. Take it slow and easy at first."

No.

Cathy rolled the hand-accelerator, gunned the engine and sped the 650 out of Mars City toward 281. On the highway she took the bike to the limit, racketing the engine so that Sherwood cringed against her, feeling death and destruction in the hundred-mile-an- hour hurricane. You are going to die now, he said to himself, holding onto this crazy girl.

"Jesus—slow down!" he finally yelled. "Do you want to kill us?"

"I don't know!"

What?

218   The Blue River Valley

"Okay....well I vote no! It might be better if we survive! Please?"

Cathy rolled the accelerator forward, turned onto the road to her farm, and the engine slowed thankfully down. Sherwood's heart thundered against her back. The bike gave up speed and finally stood growling on the gravel road, in the Nebraska wind.

"Jesus, Cathy!"

"This is great!" she panted against his cheek.

"This is great," he said. "Why?"

"Why what?"

"This is the greatest night of my life, you know it as well as I do. Tell me."

"Tell you what?"

"Why this is great? Tell me."

The 650 stood grumbling on the gravel road. Cathy pouted her face against his, taking him in, taking him in...

"Because I somewhat like you?" she asked.

"I love you so much it hurts," he spilled out.

"I know you do, Sherwood. I love you too."

He shuddered in disbelief. Did his ears hear that?

"You love me?"

"Yes. Are you so stupid you never knew?"

"Yes," he said. "That's how I am with you. I've always loved you, and you always knew it. I never thought you—"

"That's only because you're butt stupid."

He grabbed her raven hair, turned her face to his and kissed her.

"You eat vegan pizza," she said around his lips. "That makes you a sissy."

"You ride a motorcycle like a girl."

She grinned at him. "I'm going to ask Grandpa for a motorcycle next Christmas. Only not a puss 650; I'll be needing a 1200."

"I'm sure you will." He lifted the veil of black hair and kissed her neck, making her giggle. She wore the silver sprite figurine he had spent most of the winter crafting out of a block of silver, in his demented, obsessed bedroom, with dental picks and exacto knives, seeing her face in his mind.

They sat on the rumbling bike and made out, Cathy gently pressing back against him. Her tongue shoved her chewing gum into his mouth and he chewed it, gave it back with his tongue. He heard the wind flowing around them. His tongue explored her spearmint mouth. The dark prairie went away toward the Blue River Valley. He felt the sky-blue blanket enfolding them, a sparkling cover from beyond the world.

"Tell me again," he said around her mouth.

"Tell you what?"

"You know."

"I love you, Sherwood. I love you. I love a goofy soph creep who eats vegetables and writes poetry and kisses like duct tape."

He pushed her black waterfall of hair into his face, bathing in the black webs. "Oh, thank you, God," he said. "I finally made it to duct tape."

She laughed. "I love you."

"I love you, Cathy," he said.

"And that means I can always get my way."

"No, it doesn't."

She kissed him and grinned around his mouth. "Can I punch it home?"

He squeezed her waist, planted his chin against her neck and felt a calm perfection. Now was probably the James Dean time, to die in eternal flames.

"Punch it, Cathy!" he yelled, closing tight his eyes.

THIRTY-FIVE ...

▼

"My God, Sherwood, I'm going to have a mom, I can't believe it! "Grandpa's here, Uncle Rel is here, and now I'm going to have a mom. This is all so unbelievable..."

"Our English teacher, no less."

She shuddered against him. He lifted her face and kissed her. They had parked the Hummer on Walnut Hill, the tallest point in all of Harrison County; they were lying on a blanket watching the night sky. The full moon shone so brightly you could see the Blue River Valley far to the west.

She was like a live wire against him, and Sherwood tried to calm her by kissing the nape of her neck, where the black mane of hair came to a soft down. "Kind of scary, eh?" he asked her.

"My God."

"Okay, okay, okay." He massaged her neck. "There's the old prize fighter, see him in all his glory?"

"The moon."

"Yeah, the old prize fighter. His face is beaten, and he still….what? Not very original?"

"I read your poem." Cathy turned her head and bit him on the neck.

"Ow! What, it didn't meet your Robert Frostian standards or something?"

"The work of a talented amateur who kisses somewhat like a tapeworm."

"That comparison is only valid if you've actually kissed a tapeworm."

They made out under the bright moon. He felt her calming down, falling into his lips. Kissing her. My God, kissing the elf.

"What's it like to have a mom?" she asked against his lips.

- 220 -

"They make you clean your room and take baths," Sherwood said. "They treat you like you're six when you're sixteen."

"No, really. What about your mom?"

"Well, it's hard to explain because every mom is different. Mine is the greatest mom in the world, of course, so it wouldn't be fair to compare her to other moms."

"Your mom is great."

"That's why she raised such a gifted son."

"Can you talk to her about personal stuff?"

"What? Oh no. Personal stuff, believe me my mom would be the last to hear about that."

"Huh. Well, Susan and I talk about personal stuff all the time."

"Like, involving me?"

"No. Why would we ever talk about you?"

"Oh, in a general discussion: about gallantry, heroism, good looks, vast genius, that kind of thing."

"She likes your writing. And she is an English teacher."

"A very good English teacher. So you do talk about me."

"But of course she likes my writing better," Cathy said, giving out a sigh and gazing at the night sky. "Oh, alas, I can do so many things better than you, Sherwood."

"You don't kiss better than me."

"Like the earth isn't round."

"It isn't. It's spherical. Now you owe me a kiss."

She grinned and kissed him. "The perverted poet tries to lure me into a kissing game. How stylishly demented."

"I'll make a deal with you: get it right and save yourself from the tapeworm. Get it wrong, and you must *kiss* the tapeworm."

"Get what?"

"The earth isn't round, it's spherical. You're wrong, I'm right, you owe the tapeworm a kiss."

"No." She stopped his lips. "The Earth is elliptical. You lose, Poet. Now it's my turn."

"Turn for what?"

"To deprive you of another kiss. You can't win this. And quit trying to feel me up!"

He moved his Lewis-and-Clark hand away. "Bring it on."

"Look up there," Cathy said. "To the left of the moon. Do you see the three stars lined up in a rough triangle?"

Sherwood squinted into the night sky. "Yeah, I see them," he lied.

"Okay, for a make-out French kiss: tell me what constellation that is."

He squinted with all his might. Three stars, what kind of constellation is that? What can you get with only 3 stars?

"Come on."

"It's—the three-headed dragon."

"No, it's Vulpecula, the Little Fox."

"That was my second answer," Sherwood said. "Okay, my turn. Why did you single out that constellation?"

"To show you how hopelessly ignorant you are compared to me."

Sherwood made a game-show blare out of his nose: "NAWWWW! Sorry, wrong answer. Now you owe me a kiss. You pointed it out because there's something special about it. Now, pay up."

She leaned into him and they made out. The summer wind flew chaotically against this hill that had centuries ago somehow burst dramatically up over the Blue River Valley. Up here the wind, flying off the prairie, attacked in jagged, erratic gusts. The trees swam left, right, forward, back; the moon bathed the world in pale light. The wind washed against this hill like sea waves.

Sherwood held her and their bodies fell together. He felt that strange blue electric bubble enfold them.

His knuckles brushing her chest, Sherwood took the sprite pendant in his hand and kissed it. "You wear my necklace and you won't wear my ring," he said.

"You don't have a ring."

"Oh, that's right, I forgot."

"I'm going to have a mom." She tingled against him; they were in an azure cocoon, the night was magnificent in this moment. "Grandpa's here, Uncle Rel's here, and I'm going to have a mom!"

"What about the handsome Sherwood North? He's here."

"Oh yes, him."

She smiled at him, her green eyes sparkling. "I'm going to have a Mom, I'm going to have a whole family."

"A few months ago you were telling me that terrible things are going to happen, and now only good things are happening. You're wrong again. Now you owe me two kisses."

"I don't know about that." Cathy stared into the sky, toward the constellation Vulpecula, the Little Fox. "For some reason my eyes are always drawn to Vulpecula, when she's visible. I keep having the weird thought that there's something there."

"Like what?"

"I don't know, monsters. Anyway, terrible things could happen…"

"Oh, no, I'm not going to let you cheat at the kissing game," Sherwood said. "You owe me two long kisses, and if you don't pay up, you lose the game."

Cathy stared up at the night sky. Her aqua eyes glowed in the moonlight. "The game…"

"That's right, the kissing game. I've obviously beaten you at it. Now you're trying to distract me, change the subject."

"I've been seeing them, Sherwood. In nightmares."

"Monsters."

"But when I wake up I have this horrible feeling that they're not truly nightmares."

"What else could they be?"

All at once Cathy got very shivery.

Sherwood touched her hair. "What's wrong?"

"It's just—I'm scared. I'm really scared."

"I know. You're getting a new mom, your uncle and Grandpa are here, you're excited and scared—that's normal."

The aqua eyes studied him. "It's not about any of that. And it's not only about the things in my dreams. It's about me."

"Okay."

She took his hand and kissed it. He rubbed his other hand over her back, at the white cotton folds of the Cornhusker sweatshirt that enveloped her. She cried, scared, against him."

"Cathy, tell me what's wrong."

"All right." She took his hand and kissed it. "I feel like I'm speeding up or something!"

"Speeding up? What do you mean?"

"I don't know what I mean," Cathy said. "Only that I'm speeding up somehow, accelerating in some weird way. I can't get rid of the feeling that I'm speeding up."

He held her, stroking the white sweatshirt. "You still owe me another kiss. Don't try and cheat me. I knew that was Vulpecula, I was just tricking you."

She hugged him and smiled. "Then kiss me."

T H I R T Y - S I X ...

Ghalla stood before the Ty-cee Evaluator, 52341. Ghalla's face was a stern set of wrinkles, his mind holding one chilling thought: the plexium mines.

"How did Clerk Gota manage to steal the ship?" the machine demanded.

"We are uncertain—"

"A ship fully charged with plexium."

"Uncertain at this time," Ghalla said. "Our main focus is to find Gota and return him for inquisition."

52341's quartz-like slice of face was silent for a moment. Ghalla was of the Cult of Arrogance, of course, so his own face betrayed no fear—but, under the face, what organic being could not fear these plexium and metal insects?

"Why were no precautions made to prevent this?"

"Gota planned it out somehow. It was not expected that he could commit such a crime—it goes beyond reason. It can only be that he suffered a mental breakdown and fell into irrationality. Such a thing is not unheard of, but it would have been impossible to predict."

"This crime is not acceptable," the machine said.

"That is why I am determined to bring him back to Bhutar for trial. This will be accomplished soon. I believe I know where he is. I believe Planet Earth."

"It is probable then that he seeks to capture or destroy a hybrid. He spoke to me of this, however I detected no madness."

"No one could have predicted this behavior," Ghalla said hopefully.

"Behavior that is unacceptable," 52341's glass face rippled.

"Bhutar will deal with Clerk Gota. The ship will be returned."

"The plexium?"

"Completely reimbursed, I assure you."

- 224 -

Ghalla had spent every favor to promise this; he was now grasping to hold onto his usefulness, and he vowed to see Gota burned at the stake.

"We are sending hunters to Earth; they will apprehend Gota and he will be returned and executed. Only if we interrogate him can we know how and why he did this."

"Errors cannot be made that lose plexium through theft."

"I understand."

The machine; so absolutely still, so stiffly immobile and inert until circuits came to life. The perfect being, storing its energy until needed. Ghalla wore a scowl that at least put a face on arrogance, not that this Evaluator knew or cared. These Ty-cee had no memory of ancient wars and epic struggle—only a forgotten swirling and squirming and eventual joining together of metal and electricity; a synthesis, not a being, Ghalla thought, watching the thing.

"If plexium can be stolen by a clerk," 52341 said at last. ""Precautions against theft are inadequate."

"Yes, correct," Ghalla admitted. "All measures are being taken to prevent anything like this from occurring again."

He did not say, of course, that Gota had stolen the ship quite easily, simply because such an action was considered beyond possible: that a Bhutaran would abandon his post and duty, would disobey orders and perform such an irrational act.

However, as Ghalla well knew, the Flux had rippled wildly, and patterns of behavior had been washed out of kilt. These machines, the new allies, those who made possible the defeat of Mara—were swiftly changing the nature of the galaxy, heralding a new order of domination. Soft tissue organisms were likely to become extinct very quickly in the same environment as these super things.

"I will redeem myself," Ghalla said to his new master. "I will bring Clerk Gota back to Bhutar, and he will be made a terrifying example of. That I promise you."

"You must redeem yourself," the machine said. "Or be evaluated as detrimental."

Ghalla stared at the Evaluator, the machine designed to allow some organic things to live, and others to be culled. Plexium wires, electric precision beyond any power of an organic being. No subtlety, no mystery or what the Marans call emotion. That which was so precious to Marans, emotion, almost a religion, and what proved to be their downfall.

"I will redeem myself," Ghalla repeated.

Emotion: the ability to feel, the great weakness: to feel; to care about something else more than you care about yourself—a fatal evolutionary disadvantage, as it turns out.

226   The Blue River Valley

Long ago the Bhutaran had conquered that weakness: to care so insanely about something else, the eggs, the offspring created. Ghalla had made many eggs, but he felt nothing for any of them—why should he? Caring for offspring was a waste of energy. The Bhutaran had long ago evolved to the creation of a great many offspring, few of which would survive. To risk survival in few offspring, as the Maran did, was the road to eventual extinction. The evolution of emotion, the Bhutaran realized, was a dead end: that which could not feel had the evolutionary advantage, as taken to its extreme by these, the Ty-cee.

To feel emotions—the ultimate evolutionary mistake; yet the Bhutaran had not yet gone completely beyond emotions: Ghalla thought of the Clerk Gota, and he felt anger, a great and terrible anger.

"Lenience will be granted to you," 52341's screen-face rippled. "Have the clerk arrested, return the stolen ship and return the stolen plexium."

"This will be done." Ghalla bowed to his new lord.

Three Bhutaran operatives were sent to hunt Gota. Their invisible ship fell slowly into Earth's atmosphere, the plexium energy of its thrusters countering the strong gravitational pull of the planet.

A blue world; so much water that the atmosphere choked on it.

The Bhutaran Hunters stared through white clouds and rippling heat waves. No easy task finding Gota in this foggy mess of a place, but they were professional hunters, with a much better ship and much better sensors than Gota had. And, unbeknownst to Commander Ghalla, the Bhutaran Council had secretly ordered that Gota not be returned for inquisition but was to be executed on contact. A bad turn for Ghalla, the sacrificed lamb, but it made the hunters' job easier.

They spoke little, each hunter concentrating on his duty, programming and fine-tuning the electric brain and sensors. Ghalla would be sacrificed to the Ty-cee and the Council would avoid the embarrassment of a live and captured Gota. It was not the hunters' business to question any of this, and they didn't. New days were upon the galaxy; worlds that had ruled now were destroyed or enslaved. The Flux dances wildly and whips up warfare.

The dominant race that lived down there below were so primitive they were not even yet allowed to make contact, and could not be allowed to detect this business. Ape things dressed in outlandish costumes, all of them strutting in self-important idiocy; apes content and happily stupid, as they were on a million other worlds. No plexium here, nothing here but a misty infestation. All three hunters on the team wondered why Gota would ever escape here, to such a terrible place, but none spoke of it. It was their business to find him and destroy him, nothing more.

They did not underestimate Gota. Belittled as 'Clerk', he had once been a hunter as they were, and knew how to hide. He would know what kind of equipment was being brought against him.

One strange event may have defined his motives, in what way was not certain: Curiously, Gota had come here to Earth long ago as part of a team to destroy a Maran/Human hybrid. Somehow that must have meaning.

The pilot leveled the ship and they floated above Earth, so bright and blue it hurt the eyes. A steaming yellow home-star sent waves of heat to the surface of the planet. Gota could not survive long on the surface of this world, he would have to hover. And he could not remain long in the air without the sensors detecting the burning plexium.

Scanners were aimed at the skies, and the ship's brain began cataloging all aspects of this world: many giant cities, many many humans; a world swarming with life; so much moisture here that life existed virtually everywhere. The skies were filled with aircraft, the oceans speckled with ships. Grey ribbons of stone indicated streets and highways, grids of houses and buildings and sprawling civilizations.

The hunters settled into their individual tasks, monitoring sensors, studying scanner information. It was possible that Gota, cornered and attacked, would as a last act of desperation go to the planet's surface. Or he could go there intermittently in order to avoid detection. That was all problematic. To contaminate a primitive world with knowledge was a galactic crime, and to commit it, even unintentionally, would incur punishment from the Gathered. The hunters all knew that these were the days of the Celomar mines. Best to cautiously locate Gota's ship and down it before he could act, the trick being to not damage the ship beyond repair. The pilot programmed the ship's brain to accomplish this.

The last programming completed, a powerful beam sprayed out of the ship and the brain began detecting and ruling out aircraft. Gota would be changing course often, so much of the atmosphere would have to be re-evaluated as the hunt progressed. But Gota could not avoid detection for long. He was doomed, and Ghalla was doomed; two unfortunate Fluxes in the Foam.

THIRTY-SEVEN ...

▼

"This is the place where Wild Bill Hickok killed his first man," Choe said to Relomar, on one of their many road trips. "I should say *murdered* his first man: Rock Creek Station, a Pony Express depot. This was the bunkhouse."

"The communication system using horses and riders," Rel said. "Wild Bill was a famous villain then."

"No. Sadly, a hero."

"I shouldn't be surprised," Relomar explored the crude shack, the wood-and-rope bunk beds. He read the plaque: "This was more than a hundred years ago. The building is primitive in the extreme, but in remarkable condition."

Choe blinked his eyes at the man. "Of course this isn't the original bunkhouse. They reproduced it to show how it was back then."

"Ah; of course."

On their frequent explorations, Choe had come to understand that Relomar, for all his sophistication and deep dazzling intellect, was incredibly naïve and ignorant of the world, a distinctly unsettling combination. The man had obviously amassed wealth, and just as obviously had lived abroad most of his life. In many ways he was brilliant in the extreme, yet would never come close to making it onto Jeopardy.

However, throughout their travels in the '68 Camaro they had learned to suspend their mutual suspicions in favor of comradeship; conversations generally involved local history (Rel was fascinated with Nebraska and her uneventful past), and local flora, fauna and geology, none of which Nebraska truly excelled in.

Usually the conversations ended up edging toward the metaphysical, and Rel had startled Choe a few times with his views on matter, energy, existence and reality.

Often the conversation was light, as now. Choe drove his '68 Camaro out of Rock Creek Station--Rel smiling happily at the scenery--and drove to the nearby town of Rose, where the Main Street Café served rich and delicious small town food.

Might as well gorge, Rel always paid for everything; gas food and lodging, waving Choe away with the familiar yet stunning statement: "Money is nothing."

Choe introduced Rel to the ecstasy of a hot beef sandwich, skillfully salted and peppered, and nestled under home-made mashed potatoes. Rel destroyed the dish, washing it down with Coke, and smiled pleasantly at the locals, all of whom, of course, were staring at them: their small town Nebraska café invaded by a short, stocky old Chink and a tall, yellow-haired wizard.

"You're teaching Cathy well," Relomar said, startling him. "She is learning maturity, restraint and modesty."

"I don't know about the last two," Choe said. "If you still have room, I recommend a slice of the homemade cherry pie with a dollop of vanilla ice cream."

"Pie by all means," Rel's eyes narrowed greedily. "But no ice cream; Kos loves the ice cream; too cold for me."

Choe ordered two slices of cherry pie. "Cathy behaves as anyone would who has her abilities. I'm afraid she will always have the tendency to show off. No teaching will completely solve that."

"Well, now Kosan and Uncle Rel are here to help."

"You know about such things because of course you have abilities yourself." Choe avoided his eyes.

Rel tasted the cherry pie and closed his eyes in ecstasy. "Everyone has abilities, my friend. But I don't need to tell you that there are things we can't talk about."

"Yes; well we have to give Sherwood credit. He's been a great help in regards to Cathy."

"Will they mate?"

Choe stared at him, a forkful of pie suspended. "I can't tell you that one. I only know that he keeps her from being lonely, and more important, he stands up to her.

"It's likely that her showing off comes from being lonely—crying out for attention, that sort of thing."

"She grew up very lonely. For much of her life, Cathy's friends were a dog and wooden and plastic toys and dolls. Stuffed dinosaurs, puppets and things like that."

230   The Blue River Valley

"Yes, I know. And I believe I know some of why." He looked at Rel's frown. "But, of course, there are things not to be discussed."

Rel chewed the heavenly tart and sweet cherry pie. "I should not tempt you with this topic, Choe. I only brought it up because you know certain secrets. For once I will talk a little to you about this. I won't ask you what you know; only that supernatural things seem to be occurring around you."

"Strange things." Choe gave him a direct stare. He could feel his stomach grow hollow. "But I don't know about supernatural. I've never believed in the supernatural; I believe if it's real, then it must be natural."

"True." Rel looked away out the window of the café and slowly chewed the pie, relishing every bite. "What is also true, is that you're no longer the main worry."

"The main worry is Sherwood."

"And the English teacher, Susan Mason. I have spoken to Eric Holmes and Kosan about this. We must try to avoid letting them know what you know."

Choe stared away thoughtfully. "Why?"

"There is danger in them knowing."

"I sensed as much. But you can only do that if you take Cathy away from them, otherwise they'll find out sooner or later. She can't live her life with toys and dolls. She won't." Choe studied his friend, who grew a worried face. "So to know is to be in danger."

"To even suspect." Relomar scowled, but did not forgo the mouthful of cherry pie, sighing as he crunched. "The danger is distant, don't worry. The most pressing danger, as I see it, is the attention she might draw upon herself if too many people know."

"I've seen her do impossible things," Choe said bluntly.

"Yes, I know you have. That alone puts you in danger."

Choe nodded and took another bite of the cherry pie. "You did say that it's a distant danger."

"Distant, yes," Rel said.

"Will we know if it gets near?"

"Yes. Now enough of this. I'm sorry. You are already in danger, along with Cathy, Eric Holmes and Kosan. How can we keep Sherwood North and Susan Mason out of this?"

Choe sighed. "I hate to have to tell you this, but I think Sherwood already knows—or deeply suspects."

Rel stared at him. "Are you sure of this?"

"He's my best student. I've taught Sherwood for six years now. I've told him nothing because I promised Cathy that it was a dead secret. I've said nothing to him about *it*, and he's said nothing to me."

"Then he may also be in danger."

Choe stared out the window of the Rose café, the evening shadows coming out slowly to enfold this small town in Nebraska. "I feared as much," he said.

"And Susan Mason: how much does she know?"

"No idea. You have to ask Eric about that one." Choe gave his friend a sad smile. "But Cathy already loves her and spends much time with her—and she is no fool."

Relomar stared out the window of the café. "All cords unravel," he said. "An old saying from my childhood: a warning to never predict victory over anything."

"You worry about the people she loves finding out the truth about her," Choe said. "But you worry about what you can no longer control."

"The truth seems to be slowly unraveling," Rel agreed. "I have tried to talk to Kosan about it. We must now see that the unraveling stops."

"If there's danger, shouldn't we know *more* of the truth?" Choe questioned.

"No; not yet." Rel frowned grimly at the last of the cherry pie, so sweet and tart and piercing to the tongue. "Truth is what we have fought for 16 years."

Choe nodded thoughtfully. "What you're saying is that even Cathy doesn't know the truth."

Rel blinked his strange blue eyes. "What makes you say that?"

"She's my student. If I don't know my students, how can I teach them?"

Relomar scraped the last of the cherry pie off his plate. "You're right. Cathy knows very little but, I'm afraid, suspects quite a bit."

"I can tell you with certainty that Cathy's no fool."

"No." Rel stared away.

"What is she?" Choe ventured.

"Cathy is a sixteen year old girl. This meal was beyond delicious. Now, on to other topics: where are we traveling next, my friend?"

Choe smiled at him. "Ever hear of Morrill Hall, in Lincoln?"

"No. It sounds fascinating, the Morrill Hall in Lincoln. What is it?"

"An old and beautiful museum; it tells the story of life on Earth. You'll love it."

"When?" Rel asked eagerly.

"We might as well drive up there tomorrow," Choe said. "It's Friday, and that's just one day short of Saturday, which is a day off. I can fudge a little."

"Then I'll tell you more," Rel promised.

232   The Blue River Valley

"About the danger, I hope. It disturbs me, of course, to think of being in danger. But it disturbs me more that Cathy and Sherwood are in danger. And don't *know* it."

"One obstacle at a time. Not yet is there any danger. Maybe it's time you spoke to the teacher, Eric Holmes. Our careful cords could be unraveling, and it is up to us to hold them together as best we can."

"All cords unravel," Choe reminded him.

THIRTY-EIGHT ...

Gota studied the photograph on the brain screen. His pink eyes narrowed. Even he was astonished that this suspicion was finally, in fact, true.

Catherine Ann Holmes, age sixteen, a sophomore at Mars High School in Mars City, the state of Nebraska, the steppes of central United States. He could see the Maran features in its face, and he knew that he had been right, and that this was the one.

A very limited biography: academically superior, but little more. No indication that it exhibited strange powers, no hint of Mist. But he knew it was a hybrid, no doubt the one made by the Maran Donis. He ordered the ship's brain to scan the photo and analyze it, and was not surprised to find a ninety-five percent certainty that it was not entirely human. He could plainly seen Maran in its face. The monster he had tried to kill so long ago?

I was right, Gota thought. Why ever the Maran Kosan let it live, I was right. This can only be the one. He stared at the girl's photo. A small, possibly vulnerable thing, although it was almost certain that the Marans, Kosan and Relomar, were protecting it.

This could be the dangerous part of the plan. So many connections they have; what do they know of what I have done? They may know already that I am here, that I have stolen a ship and am on the hunt, and that I am being hunted.

He immediately programmed the brain to guide the invisible ship to the state of Nebraska. Now it was to capture it and show the monster before the Gathered. No easy task, he knew. There would be protection around her.

But they will not deny the crime when they lay eyes on it; they will see that my quest was true.

234   The Blue River Valley

He stared away, calculating. I am more than the *Traitorous* Gota. I am more than a clerk. I am once again a hunter. They will understand when the hybrid is shown.

No word for happiness, beauty or imagination, the Bhutaran did have a word for pride: Mal-at, the Bhutaran equivalent of God. Having accomplished your Mal-at against hardships and disbelief, that is God.

That is what I will show the Gathered. Mal-at, Mal-at.

Duty.

Suddenly his ship's brain blared alarm, and Gota's pink eyes squinted in fear. He quickly scrambled a swing of the ship, an erratic movement that could evade Melt.

He read the sensors. They have found me—No! Not now!

The invisible ship twisted into the Earth atmosphere; the hunters—descending in, sensing the kill—only seconds to live…No!

He must spin down and go to the surface of the world, he would not live otherwise. Suddenly all plans changed with this swirl of the Foam.

Gota saw the blue beam shoot out of the wet atmosphere. He twisted his stolen ship violently down and felt blinding Melt scorch the left side of his ship.

The hunters have found me.

He smelled the acrid burnt plexium, he dove his craft to the surface of Planet Earth. My Duty, he thought.

Mal-at—Mal-at—Mal-at…

Hunters try to kill me, for the good of the Galaxy, for the Ty-cee. My own people come to kill me, Gota the Traitor—Gota the Clerk…

His roasted ship stumbled wounded toward Earth. They have failed to kill me, his first thought. Find the place Nebraska and *kill* the hybrid, that which should never have been.

I can no longer capture it, that Flux is gone.

Blast me, hunters, if you can. I have found a hybrid, a crime against the galaxy. I have found it, and my duty is now to destroy it. I was right. The Maran/human exists. You can destroy me, murder my existence, but what I said is true: There is a hybrid alive on Planet Earth. There is a thing of Maran and human blood alive on this planet, and it is a crime against the galaxy.

Gota made a suicide dive at the green empty steppes. He knew the Bhutaran hunters would not risk death following, they would show patience in the hunt, hope to let the deadly humid Flux of this world do their job for them.

But Gota the Clerk was being underestimated, he had planned.

At the last instant Gota ignited the ship's plexium coils, hoping they had not been damaged. The invisible ship wrenched and tore against the powerful

Flux of this world, wobbled crazily down to rest on the plowed ground. Gota stared out the plexium hull at the neon-blue beam that shot from the sky and blasted a crater out of this farm field beyond him.

A last wild desperate shot. They will do nothing rash, I have time.

He gathered the cooling and dehumidity suit that would enable him, temporarily, to escape the dense poison of this world, the equipment and nutrients he would need to survive; then he ejected from the ship.

The ship belongs to the hunters, and I am stranded in this place. But I was a hunter once, they will know.

He found himself in a vast field of moist soil and early green growth. He quickly made his way toward a stand of shade, and soon found himself panting and sweating under the cruel wet-hot star overhead. Bhutaran sweat pores were not designed for such liquid compression, and he knew he would not last long in this environment. Only now to go into that cover, he thought, panting against the hot wetness overwhelming him, broiling him, filling his lungs. Only now to escape and remain alive.

Behind him was the swimming vision of a green-black field and blue sky. But he knew, of course, that the hunters were even now sailing down and would soon commandeer the stolen ship. They would take their time, aware that he was trapped and they would easily find him. He had none of their sensors, no way to escape. But he did have a tal, and a hand brain. Plans would have to be desperately re-thought.

Gasping at the dense air, Gota stumbled into the cover, the tall flora called trees, and the soft green masses of grass. He climbed into the survival suit and lay under these tree things, gasping until his body cooled.

The survival suit saved him; he felt himself recover, his mind cleared. Gota's pink eyes squinted at the world beyond this vegetation. The hunters were already converging on his dead ship; but slowly, with caution.

There is time to escape, Gota thought; and I will escape. They hunt the *Clerk* Gota and find the *Hunter* Gota.

He read his palm scanner—the growth in this field was called alfalfa, a nutrient-rich legume. He was gratified to find himself in the area called Nebraska, although more than 50 Earth miles from the hybrid.

Now it is to perform my last duty, or be no more. No ship, no escape, I cannot capture it now; it is now to destroy the monster, to perform my last duty as a Bhutaran, to kill a hybrid before the hunters kill me: To destroy this thing, once Ariel now Catherine Ann Holmes…

Gota programmed the hand brain to scramble signals around him. The hunters would know his general area, but not precisely where he was in that area. The best he could do. He was only buying time, but time was all he

236   The Blue River Valley

needed. He stumbled out of the cover of trees and waddled away across the mud-green fields of alfalfa.

Sleep in the suit when the star blazes, go toward the hybrid when there is darkness and less heat. What is behind me is nothing, what is ahead of me is duty, Mal-at. His palm brain, triangulating, pointed the way to the hybrid…

The Bhutaran hunters surveyed the crippled ship. They sprayed scanners across this region, a grain-rich portion of North America, Earth. Clerk Gota was not found dead in the ship, he had escaped, but why?

And where?

They programmed the ship's brain and found his signal, a hulking form trying to escape southwestward across this prairie. They stared out of the invisibility.

He could not possibly elude them. He was now mad, and he had no escape from this melted world. The prey would soon be trapped in webs of warm wet denseness. This planet must have seductions beyond control; though who could live in such a teeming mess of a place? Gota was a dead thing, they knew. The hunters knew that he had been seduced, had given his life to this blue-white stone in space. Why?

No matter. Only that Gota was doomed. No hurry now.

"He strikes out southwestward," a hunter said.

"Yes," the leader of the team said. "Our brain now indicates that Gota seeks to capture or destroy a hybrid."

THIRTY-NINE...

▼

Commander Zarya had saved a good portion of the Maran Spaceforce by moving quickly and unexpectedly. Long ago the Marans had prepared these plans against metal races like the Ty-cee, and Zarya was gratified to see that the great undertaking had in most respects succeeded. He had managed to move much of the fleet and an immense store of plexium into the Ferro-Magnetic Belt, right under the noses of the Ty-cee.

Zarya smiled grimly out of his ship's command center. Wrong words; the Ty-cee hadn't any noses.

Here in the vast ring of metal asteroids that orbited a spectacular giant blue star, the Magnetic field wreaked havoc on machines; the Flux writhed wildly as if insane, and no metal beings could survive here. So the Maran fleet was safe for now.

The downside being that all but the least sensitive (and therefore least complex), electric brains had to be shut down, causing two great problems: he would have no communications beyond the Belt, and the ships would have to be steered the ancient way.

For now, Zarya could not ask for more. He had escaped the Ty-cee by cutting all red tape and ordering the plans carried out without any hesitation, thus proving two important points: secrets *could* be kept from the Ty-cee, and they could be fooled by sudden and drastic action. They were not invulnerable gods as the Bhutaran believed.

Their powers can't reach me here.

But neither could the fleet stay here forever, washing around the Belt Flux like the dead asteroids that surrounded them, sealed away from rays and energy waves. Zarya had been so focused on carrying out this vital mission that he hadn't bothered himself with anything beyond saving the fleet and what plexium he could.

- 237 -

238   The Blue River Valley

Now…

He turned to his First Lieutenant, who was recording navigational information on a primitive palm brain.

"Now what?" he asked with a fatal grunt.

The lieutenant smiled up at him. "I was about to ask you the same thing, Sir."

"Well, we can't know what's happening out there, and we can't float here like so many coffins, not forever."

"Maybe if you got some sleep, Sir."

"Sleep? I've forgotten that. What is it?"

The lieutenant laughed. "You ask me what next, Sir, but I take that as a rhetorical question. I'm sure you know what's next."

"There can be only one next," Zarya said. "We have to sit here awhile and devise a strategy of attacking and defeating the Ty-cee. We can't know the fate of Mara, or even the progress of the war. So we must become mercenaries, if you will. Any offensive maneuvers against the Ty-cee will have to be conducted as we see fit, without any—shall we say, 'political' advisement."

The lieutenant smiled. "You always complained of politicians getting in the way."

"Yes. However, we will be undertaking offensive actions without knowledge of any treaties Mara might have signed with the Ty-cee. It could be that we become outlaws to our own people." Zarya seemed to find a dark amusement in the thought.

"What can be done about that, Sir?"

"Nothing. Now we must assume that we are at war with Ty-cee, and plan accordingly. They attacked us, and so they are the enemy. I didn't sneak this fleet into the Belt to let it sit and orbit. We have plenty of ships and enough plexium. I don't see why we can't engage the enemy. Our first order of business: Forget the usual models and teaching and begin to think in terms of the irrational and illogical."

Zarya turned his attention to the Ferro-magnetic Belt, the iron and zinc and lead and uranium clods that flowed mindlessly in the Flux of the great blue star. The lieutenant turned back to his calculations. The command center was strangely dark, only two brain screens operating.

Steering the ancient way.

Zarya stared out at space. That may be the key to defeating the Ty-cee, by waging war the ancient and primitive way. Try to use the unexpected and incalculable. He had already proven that they could be taken by surprise. And again, he stood where they could not.

Zarya smiled. If they are, as said, metallic gods, then so be it. A true Commander always wants to take on the gods.

F O R T Y ...

▼

Susan Mason sat on Cathy's bed wearing the headphones. She was listening to one of Cathy's compositions, a dense piano melody that reminded her of Chopin.

She looked over at her soon-to-be step-daughter, cross-legged on the bed next to her and shook her head in amazement: strange how she looked so like a little girl. She was shockingly brilliant, Susan knew, but also a little girl who wanted love and attention. Who grew up but never grew up.

The piano piece over, Susan lifted off the headphones and gave Cathy a hug. "That was sensational! My God, that's utterly beautiful!"

Cathy turned red. "I composed it for you; that's why I wanted you to listen to it."

Susan held her, felt her heart ache. This was no little girl, she was an effortless genius. So why did she seem like a little girl?

"Thank you, Cathy, it's beautiful!" Susan stroked her new daughter's long black hair. "You wrote that for me?"

"Because I'm glad you're going to be my mom," Cathy surprised her by saying.

Now Susan went red. "You want me to be your mom."

"Yes, more than anything. I've never had a mom. Not who I remember."

"What if I turn out to be a mean evil mom from Hell?"

Cathy giggled. "You read too much Shakespeare to be from Hell."

Susan smiled, shaking her head at this strange girl. Most girls of this age would feel frightened and threatened at the thought of a step mom, but Cathy almost seemed to plead for it.

"I love you."

- 240 -

"I love you too!" Cathy hugged her. "I warn you, though, Daddy's the distracted type, and sometimes when you're talking to him he'll be thinking about pulsars."

Susan laughed. "So I've noticed."

"But he loves you. He's never been this goo-goo and gaw-gaw before. I hope you love him."

"I do," Susan said. "What's not to love?"

"So I have your solemn promise that you won't be sorry?"

"I promise. After all, I'm getting a husband and a daughter in one. I'm a lonely old English teacher, and I'm going to pass this up?"

"When you marry my dad, can I call you Mom?"

Susan Mason smiled, feeling the blood in her face. "That would make me very happy. But on one condition: You have to let me call you Daughter."

"Agreed." Cathy grinned at her. "You can teach me about boys."

"Ah, boys." Susan stroked her hair. "Nobody can teach you about them."

"What is it about Daddy that you love?" Cathy asked.

Susan stared off for a moment. This was so exquisitely wonderful on Cathy's bed, the great Saint Bernard snoring against them.

"I can't really say. I like to be with him, I guess."

"What do you mean, Mom?"

Susan smiled. "I guess—well, you have friends, people you want to be with because you like them. But there's one person you always want to be with. Like you and Sherwood North. I've seen how you look at him. And everybody's seen how he looks at you."

"He's always trying to cop a feel then act like Dr. Innocent," Cathy said.

Susan smiled. "What do you expect? Sherwood's in love with you, he wants to—well, what all boys want to do."

Cathy smiled. "He's a very good kisser."

"That's because he loves you." Susan sighed, rubbing her daughter's long black hair. "Sixteen and in love—that goes beyond Shakespeare."

"We've held hands and French kissed and hugged," Cathy said. "But I'm not going past that. I've seen too many girls in sophomore class brag about what they do with boys, and I've seen how the boys treat them afterwards."

"My new daughter is very wise," Susan said. "But don't you want Sherwood to touch you?"

"Yes, it feels good. I'd never tell him that, though."

"I don't think you have to."

"How do you know you're in love?" Cathy asked.

"Well, at your age, it's an easy test. The older you get, the more complicated it gets."

242   The Blue River Valley

"So, what's the test?"

"The test at your age, is this: if you think you're in love with a boy, and he tells you he loves you—as they all will—then *don't* have sex with him. Tell him that you love him but you won't sleep with him. If the boy agrees, then you're on first base. If he walks away with a disgusted sigh—well..."

"Like Kyle did."

"I don't know about Kyle, but probably yes. You know that girls have a power over boys. You're very pretty, Cathy, and you know that you have power over boys, I've seen them staring at you during the football games. All of them want to touch you—you know that."

"That's because all boys are butts."

"All except Sherwood," Susan said. "You haven't slept with him."

"With Sherwood? No. I told him that it'd be like sleeping with the Worm God."

Susan grinned. "You've made it clear to him that you're not going to give him sex."

"I'm not going to have Sherwood North bragging--"

"Did that drive him away?" Susan interrupted. "Knowing you wouldn't sleep with him, did that drive him away, or did that draw him nearer? That's the test."

"I know it's drawing Kyle nearer," Cathy said. "Mom, he's almost stalking me, and I don't know why. The most we ever did was kiss and hold hands. He's obsessed with me, I think."

Susan thought of that word, 'Mom'. She sensed that Cathy was disturbed about many things. Tormented thoughts of a genius? Or a lonely girl finally getting to talk.

She patted the long black hair. "At your age, it's the girl who doesn't put out who finds *real* love."

"Was it like that when you were sixteen?"

"It's always been like that." Susan put her head against Cathy's, rubbing her back. "You go out with a boy you like, all at once he's telling you how much he loves you, and you go all the way with him. Next day, he's telling his buddies about it, and it's laughing and hand-slaps all over the locker room."

"That's what Sherwood wants," Cathy said. "He's no better than Kyle."

"No, he's different, and I think you know it. Sherwood wants that, because he's crazy about you. Of course Sherwood wants to touch you and make love to you—but there's a difference, and I think you know it."

"I know I like being with him," Cathy said. "He's wry and witty, he has a good sense of humor. I even told him that I love him."

Susan smiled, hugged her daughter. "That's the first step."

F O R T Y - O N E ...

▼

Cathy Holmes never came to the Mars City Municipal swimming pool to sun tan or socialize. Unlike most of the crowd, she actually came here to swim. She would hang with friends for only a few moments before diving into the pool and streaking through the water, her black hair trailing down her back.

Sherwood sat on his steel crow's nest, eight feet above the water. His sunglasses swept the pool area, but would always venture down to the figure in the water. She swam like an otter, wriggling and spinning, her long hair swirling round her. She wore a bright yellow bikini, and her skin was tanned so dark the suit seemed to glow against it.

Two young boys came sprinting out of the shower room, and Sherwood blew his whistle. "Hey! No running!" he yelled at them.

A sun-baked day; Sherwood felt the sweat dribbling down out of his lifeguard cap, soaking his hair. He watched Cathy swim across the pool and slide out; so tiny, like a little girl. She twitched over to the high board and climbed the ladder. Now every eye at the Mars City Municipal was on her, including--Sherwood noted--Kyle Kuzma, who sat by the pool flexing his muscles. It did torment Sherwood that the guy was a body builder, and movie star handsome. Star athlete, senior, he could be a little less muscled and chiseled. Is there any ugly quarterback in the world?

Kyle stared at Cathy as she climbed the ladder and stood on the high board. Her face was impassive, as if she were unaware of her silent audience. Then she trotted to the end of the board and launched into a perfect two-and-a-

- 243 -

244   The Blue River Valley

half flip, the yellow bikini spinning like a gyroscope, the water barely parting when she knifed into it.

Sherwood heard the usual gasps and claps erupt around the pool, but Cathy didn't hear them; she had dived down to the bottom of the deep end, and was doing her underwater gymnastics, hoping to freak out the lifeguards. Sherwood looked over at Kyle, who was staring at the deep end, face handsomely grim behind his shades.

Relax, Terminator. She always plays this trick, Sherwood thought. She can stay underwater forever. Besides, you can't even swim.

Cathy shot up and burst out of the water just as they called the ten minute safety check. Sherwood blew his whistle and watched until everyone had cleared out of the pool. He climbed gratefully down from his perch, took off his cap and toweled his face.

He looked up at the cloudless, sun-blistered sky.

Kyle stood up and wandered round the pool toward Cathy, all the girls admiring his god-like abs and pecs. Sherwood watched him and chewed his teeth. Won't be long you'll be gone--off to college--poof!

For good?

Or will you realize that college will expect you to read and write and learn things? Will you flunk out and show up back here? Depends on how good a player you are, what degree of dim-wittedness they tolerate.

Sherwood stared across the pool at Kyle approaching Cathy. She had wrapped a towel round her waist and stood squeezing the water out of her hair. What are they talking about?

Why are you even at the pool, Jerk? You can't even swim. Oh, that's right, you get to take your shirt off and show the rippling muscles, the Brad Pitt smile that had made her fall in love with you.

They stood for a long time talking. Sherwood got a bottled water and sat on a plastic lounger. A screeching hot day this was, no clouds to soothe the hateful sun. Across the pool he watched them, Thor and Circe. Mixed mythologies. He breaks up with her, now this. Why? He's almost developed a stalker mentality toward Cathy.

Sherwood had many fantasies about rescuing her from a berserk, steroid-whacked Kyle, how he would split that handsome face apart at the seams. How it would be like mythology: a warrior, an elf princess and a villain...

No, if Kyle got violent with her, Kyle would be the one needing rescuing. Sherwood watched them talking. He smiled grimly. How the worm turns. Not so long ago it was Kyle wanting *me* to leave his girlfriend alone. Ha ha, that's a good one. Yeah...

"Cee, I'll be off to Memphis in like three weeks!" Kyle pleaded. "Just let me take you out a couple of times. I won't try and push you for anything—"

"Kyle, I don't want to start this over again. What is wrong with you? Why on Earth would you want to take me out on a date?"

"I can't get you out of my brain. I'm like really super in love with you. I know I said some things, got mad—"

"Super in love?" Cathy tried to keep from laughing.

"I don't get why you're ignoring me this summer. I only got three weeks. I want to spend time with you, make it up to you."

"You don't have to make up anything. People think they're in love, they get together, people fall out of love and break up. You're going to be in college, I'll be here."

'Wasting your summer working at the Nifty."

"I like my job. I don't think I'm wasting my summer."

"I know you been going out with Karate Boy." Kyle tossed a glare across the pool at Sherwood lounging with his bottled water. "The Lifeguard Boy."

"Kyle, do not keep stalking me like this."

"Are you like going steady with him or something?"

"I'm not—like-- going with anybody."

"Jesus, Cee! Don't be doing this to me. I'm asking you for another chance."

"I understand that. But I don't want to give you another chance. I want you to leave me alone. When I said I loved you I didn't know what love meant."

"I don't think I can leave you alone." Kyle gave her an unsettling look.

Cathy wondered if this was the other side of the magnet, the Mist. "What's wrong with you?" she said, her voice catching. "Did Sherwood give you brain damage when he hit you?"

"Don't be a bitch. Come on."

"No! If you say *come on* again, I'll puke all over this swimming pool."

Suddenly the lifeguards blew their whistles, and Cathy shed her towel, turned and dove into the pool, streaking away like a striped water creature.

Kyle watched her, the water sparkling over her bikini. He looked around Mars City Municipal and felt suddenly embarrassed. What the hell was he doing, letting her make a joke of him? This should be his prime time; he should be a god around here.

Jesus Christ, I worked so hard to have this, a scholarship at a major university, everybody should be proud of me, what I like accomplished and all that—but she had to steal it.

He realized that he was wrong, and feeling sorry for himself; but the poison thoughts helped to fight this strange panic he felt losing her.

246   The Blue River Valley

He looked across the pool at Lifeguard Boy, Sherwood North, who was staring at Cathy.

He was the one who did it, spoiled everything; turned me into a school joke. He blind-sides me with karate crap; then Cathy goes running peeing her pants to him. The little dick who writes poems! Too much of a puss to play ball, and he's the one that did all this...

No, admit it, Kyle said to himself. You're the one to blame. He's the hero of this story. And he's no puss.

Cathy slid out of the water and twitched her cute little butt to the diving board, every eye immediately focusing on her. She climbed the steel ladder, ran to the end of the board and sprang into the sky, throwing herself into a one-and-a-half with a full spin. Her body neatly stabbed the water, and she swirled and flew mermaid-like down to the deep aqua-colored pool floor.

Sherwood North was watching her, the sunglasses blanking out his eyes. But Kyle knew what was in the eyes—some kind of demon dust or something.

She'll dump you before summer's over, Soph. Then she'll laugh in your face and forget all about you.

Cathy's raven head appeared out of the water, and she rolled onto her back, floating lazily, enjoying the attention she was getting, a satisfied cat-smile on her face as she stared into the hot blue sky.

Kyle heard a buzzing in his ears. Something close to madness seemed to burn his mind, the crazy thought came to him again that Kirsten might not be such a weirdo. Is Cee a witch or something? Is this some kind of wicked spell? She's just a little soph girl, no body, only a cute face. There's nothing special about her.

But his mind burned all of that away.

Sherwood climbed his crow's nest and pretended to ignore her, although out of the corner of his sunglasses he could see that she was walking around this side of the pool. He made a point of looking away. Cathy purposely sat down at the edge of the pool under the lifeguard tower, letting her brown legs dangle in the water: right underneath his perch, where of course Sherwood could look down at her in the yellow bikini.

The beauty of wearing very dark sunglasses: you can pretend to scan the pool as your eyes secretly stare down at her in the yellow bikini.

He grabbed his jaws in anger: always the little princess. You flirt with Kyle, now you want to flirt with me, just so that we might beat the crap out of each other.

Sherwood spotted a couple of kids pushing a friend into the pool, and he blew angrily at his whistle. "Knock off the horseplay!" he yelled at them.

"Jeez," her voice said below him. "You're a pretty mean lifeguard."

He looked down. Her face lay back and she was giving him a sardonic smile: the upside down face, just like in American History class, only now in a yellow bikini.

"Ah, Miss Holmes. I didn't see you. How are you today?"

"Hot."

"That's a very pretty swimming suit."

The upside down face studied him. "Thank you."

Sherwood glanced across the pool where Kyle was glaring at them. He was damned if he was going to let her play her little 'make the boys jealous' game. He scanned the pool, fiddled with his silver whistle. No fraternizing, you're at work. Your job is to keep the eyes on the kids, keep them safe.

Finally he glanced down. Cathy was now studying the pool water, splashing her legs lazily, sighing at the sun.

Sherwood scanned the pool. Kyle was again strutting his bod around the edge of the water, that hunky jock-walk. The stud was glaring at the lifeguard stand and Sherwood smiled and shook his head at the ridiculous feisty-rooster dance, the flexing of the muscles. Still, it would be better if Kyle were less impressive looking.

"Tonight, remember?" Sherwood muttered; then he bit his tongue.

Cathy's head flopped upside down again, the wet-black hair slapping her back. "Did you say something?"

His throat felt thick. His eyes studied the yellow bikini top against her brown shoulders. "Yeah, Friday night. That's tonight." He tried to keep his face neutral. "Remember, you got to pick the movie?"

"Oh yes, Friday night," she said thoughtfully. "Tonight. I'd forgotten. Thank you for reminding me."

"You're welcome. Remember, I get to drive the Hummer."

"Oh, yes, I remember now. But lifeguards aren't supposed to be talking to people, are they? They shouldn't get distracted."

"What makes you think I'm distracted?"

"Oh, I don't know." She stood up, gave him a sweet smile, then dove neatly into the water and swam away from him.

He watched her rear end bobbing out of the aqua blue as she breast-stroked toward the deep end. Not surprising, Cathy Holmes was a very fluid

248   The Blue River Valley

and graceful swimmer. She didn't come here to tan or "lay out"; she came to swim and of course dive off the high board and of course show off.

"You're going to find out about her," Kyle's voice startled him.

Sherwood looked down from the lifeguard tower. The quarterback stood below, his arms crossed, which only made his biceps bulge out more.

"Excuse me?" Sherwood said.

"Cee Holmes. You're going to find out about her."

"About what?"

"She'll like tease your ass to hell and then get bored and forget you ever lived."

"Like she did you?"

Kyle glanced up at him. "That's right, K-boy. She's too good for me, that makes it damn straight she's too good for you."

"That makes it damn straight—hmmm. Kyle, I'm on duty, I don't understand Pro-wrestler Speak, and I'm not supposed to be having conversations with the pool-goers. Kids might be drowning, stuff like that?"

"Don't say I didn't warn you."

Sherwood looked across the pool, at Cathy swooping out of the water and mincing back toward the diving board. His eyes took in every inch of her bare skin they could.

Is the warning valid if it comes from a caveman?

The sun-yellow bikini against her brown legs and arms and tummy: Kyle is probably right, Sherwood thought in despair. Every eye on her—did they all worship her as he did? Cathy Holmes blinks her eyes and a boy appears, crying for her love.

"You're smart, Sherwood," Kyle stunned him by saying. "And you got some pretty wicked fighting skills. I give you creds, soph. I never pretended to be Mr. Intellect, but I know there's something bigger than having brains, and that's having like instincts."

Like instincts, Sherwood thought. Hmmm, never heard of them before.

"I respect you, Soph," Kyle said. "Believe it or not."

"I respect you too, Kyle, believe it or not," Sherwood said. "And I'm sorry we ever got into that fight. I'm truly sorry."

"There's nothing to be sorry about, I was going to kick your ass."

"What about instincts?"

"Cee Holmes." Kyle stared at her, climbing the high board ladder like a monkey. "She's got powers, she can cast spells. She has a spell on me, and she has a spell on you, brother."

He said it so softly that Sherwood didn't think he'd heard correctly.

"What?"

"You'll find out soon enough. She has a spell on you, and pretty soon you'll be crazy. You'll try to touch her some time, and brother you won't be able to."

Sherwood swallowed down a sudden fear. He shook it away. "Well, anyway, I hope you do well at Memphis. Everybody back here's going to be rooting for you, and all that. I really do wish you luck, Kyle."

Kuzma gave him a strange stare. "You'll find out," he said.

FORTY-TWO ...

Boiling alive inside his survival suit, Gota crouched and panted and waited for the darkness. He was in deep trees, and he made no movement, knowing the invisible hunters were there in the darkening sky. The trees would give some amount of interference to their tracking signals.

Watching the merciless sun blast the horizon, pinking and yellowing the clouds, Gota understood the situation he was in: he must try and move more quickly (his hand brain told him that he had traveled less than 20 American miles across the plains), but even in the suit this climate was rapidly draining his strength, overpowering his weak Bhutaran sweat glands.

This was also, of course, a very bad terrain in which to try and evade sensors: no mountains, forests or caves; mostly open fields, and at every mile was a road of pebbles and hardened dirt. Between the scant stands of trees were vast flattish fields, far too symmetrical to aid in concealment.

Endure obstacles and consider advantages: an old Bhutaran saying. While mountains, especially metal-rich ones, would render the sensors useless, they would also have destroyed him.

He felt the relief of darkness as the last violent colors brushed the west. Cool shadows were easing over the land. Gota took nutrition and hydration strips, letting them dissolve on his tongue, and waited for them to restore him. He lay in the gathering darkness, trying to summon his energies, and prepared to move ever westward toward the Marans Kosan and Relomar; and the hybrid, once Ariel now Catherine Ann Holmes.

"He is moving," the navigator in the invisible ship said. "I will program the coordinates—no, we lost him again."

"He is timing his movement against the sensors," the pilot said. "Also, I am sure, to rest. His suit was hardly designed to withstand conditions on the surface of That place."

"With two ships hunting him, his time will have to be short."

"Best now to be careful, though." The Bhutaran pilot looked into the infra red screen at the planet's surface.

"He may be completely mad by now."

"If not, he soon will be. The pressure and heat and humidity will wreck his brain and his body."

"Only a little patience and soon must be the death of Gota. There, he is moving again." The navigator programmed the new coordinates, and both ships streaked to the area, hoping to form a hammer and anvil. Scanners searched the Nebraska cornfields for their wretched and doomed kinsman who crept ever deeper into the grain-rich plains.

"Lost again," said the navigator.

FORTY-THREE ...

▼

Cathy stood in the quiet summer night. Stars sparkled around the blade of moon. She felt her eyes see beyond this—not quite see, but sense: a strange swirling of the universe, and signals in her brain that she couldn't understand. She saw not only movement out there in the night, she *felt* it. She felt life, an inconceivable boiling of life that called out from the stars.

Oh God, she thought.

It was like falling upward into a silver and black river. The sensation frightened and captivated her; she couldn't look away from the stars that formed the Little Fox, Vulpecula. She felt a strange sense of being spoken to, by the stars.

Something is there, she thought. Something calls.

She felt her stomach empty, as when you're plummeting. She seemed to dive into the sparkling infinity of space and time. She saw the impossibility of its size, and how it was not points of light and matter after all, but an *essence*, swirling and flowing in infinite directions.

Then her mind saw again the gargoyles, the monsters.

She blinked her eyes in fear and willed herself to retreat out of the undulating universe. She took deep breaths and stared into the dark of the cottonwood trees. Her mind swept out of space and returned.

Woodrow whined at her side.

"Oh, Baby!" Cathy bent down and hugged her giant dog, rubbing him and pressing her face against his. "Big fat baby. It scares you when I get like this, I know."

The huge Saint Bernard lapped her face and whined, relieved.

"But I can't help it, Woodrow, I can't...I see things out there—oh, Woodrow, it doesn't matter." She hugged the dog, rubbing his massive head and pug face, kissing the top of him. "I'm okay again, stop whimpering. You don't know and you don't care. You love me and I love you. That's all." Cathy stared at the night sky.

Danger.

"It doesn't matter," she said, rubbing Woodrow about the ears, trying to convince herself, to erase the horror.

Danger.

"Is she okay?" Susan asked, staring out the farmhouse window.

"Yes. Cathy likes to meditate sometimes," Eric explained. "She's okay."

"She looks so strange standing out there."

"Well," he took Susan in his arms. "We're a strange family; I won't lie to you about that. But you agreed to marry me, and I'm not going to let you back out. You made a verbal contract, My Love."

"I did." She smiled and kissed him. "She's already starting to call me Mom."

Eric reddened in joy. "Cathy is—she's a sweetheart."

"Yes, she is." Susan looked at her out the window, now playing with the great shadow of the dog there in the night. "She's also lonely, Eric."

"I know," he said with a frown.

"For some reason, I think she's very afraid."

"I know," Eric said.

Sherwood danced away, panting and sweating, from the kicking bag. Choe Kwang-su tossed him a towel and they sat down on the mat. They were quiet for a long while, only Sherwood's labored breathing.

Finally Choe sighed: "You brood too much for a 16 year old."

"What makes you think I'm brooding?"

"I can tell when you work on the heavy bag. When you go after the poor thing with that special pissed-off look on your face, then I know you're troubled by something."

Sherwood looked at him. "I'm only wondering if it might be time to talk about things."

"What things?"

"Secret things."

"Ah."

The Blue River Valley

Choe's face grew sad. He stared a long time out the windows of the school, at Mars City in green summer. The strange 1950's look of the town square: the slow, windblown life in a small town in Nebraska. Maple trees around the courthouse.

Maybe spirits haunt places like this because there are few people, with their noise and rush-around, to drive them away.

"What if one who knows secrets has promised not to tell them?"

"Then he can't," Sherwood said. "But I know them, and I never promised anybody."

"Secrets about what, Sherwood?"

"Cathy."

The name sent a chill across Choe's back, although he already knew. He took a long breath, letting it out in a melodic whistle. "Then you speak and I'll listen," he said.

Sherwood didn't waste any time: "Cathy has some sort of force field around her! She is surrounded—sometimes—by some—force!"

"I see. And?"

"And—?" Sherwood stared at him. "What do you mean AND? Choe, she has a force field around her, some electro-magnetic—something! Uncle Rel, Grandpa Kosan—they have it too, and you know it!"

Choe frowned at him. "It is not up to the student to tell the teacher what he knows or not. Go on, I'm listening."

"Choe--? God, I can't believe I'm even talking about something so weird. But I know it's true. I don't know how."

"Do you love her less believing this?"

"No. I mean I always told you she was strange; there was something very different about her. But this goes into the supernatural. I mean, this is..."

"Unearthly?"

Choe stared out at Main Street, slow and peaceful and dull. So quiet that even indoors you could hear wind in the trees. Maybe the beings beyond explanation gather here in order to get a word in edgewise. Maybe it is the quiet and boring places of the world that they choose to haunt.

"Yes, that's exactly the word—*unearthly*!" Sherwood said. "You've seen me try and attack her in our exercises. I bounce off her, Choe! You had to know that I'd find out."

"I invited you to help with her practice partly because I knew you wanted to spend time with her. I see your eyes when you rag and complain about her, and I wanted to help you out."

"Before you knew what you were getting me into, I hope."

Choe sighed. "Yes. It was in my mind to give her a good boyfriend, she's so lonely; and I wanted to be your wingman, so to speak. I had no idea that any secrets might come up at that time."

"Well they did come up," Sherwood said. "And they're humongous."

"And so," Choe said. "I don't understand what this conversation is about, unless maybe to give you some mental relief."

"Can't you tell me what this is all about?"

"No. I thought I was the listener and you were the talker."

"She stares at the stars sometimes," Sherwood said. "It's like she's in a trance, like she's seeing and feeling things out there."

"Many young girls look at the stars."

"Not like this. It's like she's *talking* to the stars; in her mind she's talking to space. And there's more than that. There's some weird danger about all this—I can feel it. Somehow I can sense a danger."

Choe ground his dentures and stared at the wall. "I only wanted for you and Cathy to spend time together. I thought you could help me teach her, and she could help teach you as well. That much is working. I never knew anything else."

"I'm on edge lately." Sherwood stared out at Mars City. "I feel this odd sense of doom hanging in the air. And it's not exactly about Cathy, it's something else."

"When you came to me so many years ago, Sherwood--a skinny, picked-on kid--you said you wanted to be a warrior. Well, here's the last lesson I can teach you: doom hangs over every warrior."

Gota lay in the deep shadows of the trees, amazed that he was still alive. Overcast skies heralded an approaching thunderstorm from the west, his direction; the air was extremely dense and muggy, only the wind gave some weak relief.

He had to fiercely blink his eyes in order to clear them so that he could read his palm brain: Three nights from the hybrid, if his body held up; three nights of crawling through fields and over crop-covered hills. This painfully slow movement helped keep him out of the sensors, but it required time, and his time was running out.

He gobbled nutrition and hydration strips. His pink eyes studied the great dark boil of clouds that formed the storm front. His mind would drift in and out, sometimes swirling with disbelief. Marans could live easily in a climate and environment like this, so like humans they were.

256   The Blue River Valley

But not me.

The storm and heavy clouds would screen him from the hunters, but could he survive moving through such a disaster? Lightening zagged out of the great black nebula that dominated the western skies. Yellow wires stabbed the ground, and seconds later he cringed at the sonic explosion bellowing over the plains. How would a heavy rainfall affect him? His suit was not meant to go to limits like this. Yet he had to move, there was no other way to accomplish his goal. He could not wait or time itself would destroy him.

Crawling out of the trees, Gota steeled himself and began moving with agonizing slowness toward the great black thunderstorm: eighteen miles. He shut his mind to the madness and tried to focus it into a narrow beam: survive until it is seventeen miles; then survive until sixteen. He made himself believe that--madness or not--this was all that mattered.

On the drive back from Lewis and Clark Reservoir Relomar was unusually silent. He stared at the approaching stormclouds and would often nod thoughtfully to himself.

"Something tells me," Choe said at last, "that this will be our last road trip for awhile."

Rel smiled over at him. "You're too perceptive for your own good." He looked back out of the car window and seemed to be addressing the countryside, the dark wet skies: "Kosan and I have been having some rather warm conversations about events. We have consulted Dr. Holmes. Events seem to be pushing their way toward us, and things we vowed never to be spoken of must at last be spoken of."

"Secrets like yours can probably not be controlled," Choe said. "At least not here. The future has a way of outwitting even the most careful plans."

"What my people call the Flux in the Foam."

Choe glanced over at him. "Your people."

"The most difficult will be Cathy. She knows so little of the truth."

"She knows more than you think. Maybe we all do."

"What do you know?"

Choe hesitated for a moment, staring out at the stormy afternoon. He decided to dodge the question. "Sherwood senses danger. He doesn't know why, but he senses danger coming. I've sensed it for some time."

"Yes. Maybe we waited too long, avoided the inevitable. But we have long protected Cathy and her secrets. This was never meant to be."

"What you call the Flux in the Foam." Choe stared away. "Well, if you waited too long or not, what is important now is that we prepare for this danger."

"We agreed that you must be the first to know the truth," Rel said. "That you have a special relationship with both Cathy and Sherwood North; that you might…"

"Sweeten the medicine?"

"Yes, exactly that." Relomar took a deep breath. "This may seem an impossible tale, my friend, and you may not believe it. But it must be told. If the cords unravel, then Cathy will be told; then Sherwood and Susan Mason."

Choe felt a shiver.

Relomar stared out at the thunderstorm. "We fear that danger is very close now, and we must scramble to protect Cathy and those near her. I will tell you about Cathy, and things about her you may already suspect."

"Cathy isn't entirely human," Choe said to him.

"We will begin with that, my friend."

FORTY-FOUR ...

▼

"If you rub up against my butt again, Sherwood, I'm going to pound you into the ground."

"Geez! I brushed up against you. So sorry, Miss Holmes."

Cathy stood up from the telescope. She squinted at Sherwood, who tried to look innocent. Then she looked at her grandfather. He stood with Uncle Rel, and they would both watch her father who was standing away in the tree shadows speaking to Mr. Kwang-su. Cathy knew they were talking about the Mist, the force field.

Things were changing, she knew. Something had happened that had brought Grandpa and Uncle Rel here to live. Something was making her dad very nervous. In the middle of the best time of her life Cathy felt danger and terror all around her, even from Sherwood, who would sometimes study her, his eyes disturbed.

Different—different; Not the Same—Beyond the Same! The secrets they had kept from her, the strange secrets of her life— she could hear them clawing out of the grave at last. The great terror of it all was that she knew the secrets went beyond Earth.

She remembered a night, years ago, talking to her dad about the things that made her different from the other kids. She remembered that she was sitting on his lap, and he was stroking her hair, his face suddenly distant and troubled.

"Daddy, am I human?" she asked him.

Her father had shuddered suddenly. His eyes grew wide at her—then he covered the expression quickly and made the usual sounds: "Of course you are, Cathy. You're just special, that's all. What would make you ask something like that?"

- 258 -

The look on his face, though. The instant that had haunted her all these years. The awful question would jump into her mind sometimes, confusing and terrifying her. She never asked it out loud again, she was afraid to know, she didn't want to know, they didn't want her to know...

Sherwood's voice startled her: "Your dad and Choe seem to be in a deep conversation. They're probably talking about the magnetic field."

Cathy stared at him. "What did you say?"

"The magnetic field. I've been reading up on magnetism. Magnetism and electricity are the same force, did you know that?"

"Electro-magnetism." Cathy frowned. "The key to the Unified Field Theory: Michael Faraday, James Clerk Maxwell—"

"Yeah, those guys," Sherwood said. "Everybody believes that a magnet only attracts, that's the power of magnetism. But it has an equal power nobody ever seems to talk about."

"It also repels." Cathy studied him like a cat. "Why ever on Earth would you be curious about that, Sherwood?"

"I want to know if it's an electro-magnetic field. It's not purely magnetic, otherwise you couldn't turn it on and off."

"What!"

Sherwood shrugged. "The field that surrounds you sometimes. You have to be able to turn it on and off, otherwise I couldn't innocently brush against your precious butt and freak you stupidly out."

"What?"

"If you don't want to be touched, nobody can touch you. If you *want* to be touched—as when I might brush against you..."

His voice trailed off. Cathy Holmes was giving him a very disturbing stare. Those neon eyes...

"So, you must want me to brush against you—by accident—or you wouldn't let me."

"Sherwood, you're saying very insane things," she said. "Have you been smoking pot?"

"I'm only curious to know if I'm on the right track. It's a kind of electro-magnetism, isn't it?"

"I don't know what you're talking about."

"The force field that sometimes surrounds you. It's around Uncle Rel too—and your grandpa."

Sherwood had the lame thought that at least she was finally paying complete attention to him. He had shocked her back, whatever she was.

"Force field. You are a nut, Sherwood. You need to stop reading or something."

"Don't worry, Miss Holmes, I won't tell anyone. That is if you stop being *mean* to me."

"You're being very weird."

"And you're being mean to me." Sherwood made a Cathy Holmes pout at her, sticking out his bottom lip and crinkling his face.

She laughed. "I don't look like that."

"What's the big deal?" he asked. "I only want to know if it's something like electro-magnetism, that's all."

"I don't know—"

"Sure you do."

She startled him by taking his hand and leading him away into the cottonwood trees. They walked into the darkness all the way to the creek before she finally dropped his hand and gave him a very cautious look. "You don't need to know anything about me, Sherwood. Why should I tell you anything?"

"Because I'm deeply in like a lot with you. I know this thing is some kind of secret. If you don't want to tell me, that's fine. But I want to know about you because—God help me—I'm a nosey butt. You said so yourself."

"Mixed anatomy." She gave him a red smile. Her black hair waved in the night wind. "Wimpy poets are always falling in like a lot."

Sherwood took her in his arms and kissed her. "Not always," he said to her lips. "But sometimes."

She hugged him, pressing her face into his chest. "They call it Mist," she whispered against him.

"What?"

"Mist."

She stood with her face against his chest. He stroked her hair. He thought of the desk in American History class and the black magic spilling backwards, swimming over his hands.

"I think it has something to do with electro-magnetism," she said.

Sherwood stared into the trees. It is true.

"I didn't mean to upset you, Cathy."

"No. I should have known you suspected—something. I didn't think you'd go into some scientific study about it."

"Well, hooray, Sherwood isn't the stumbling idiot you always thought."

She smiled up from his chest and kissed him. "Now you know how weird I really am."

"Well, to be honest, what matters to me is that if it bothered you having me brush up—accidentally—against you, you wouldn't let it happen."

"You have to turn into a pervert, don't you?"

He shrugged. "Well…yeah."

"Sherwood, you can't know anything about this. You cannot use that word around Daddy or Grandpa, or anybody. You can never say that word."

"Okay. That'll be our own secret word--Mist," Sherwood said. "I know nothing! Like Sergeant Schultz."

"What?"

"Sergeant—never mind. It's our secret and our secret word. I will never betray you, no matter what it is." He stared away, trying to wrap his mind around this, trying to pull himself out of the supernatural.

"I'm scared, Sherwood!" she said into his chest.

He took a deep breath. "I know you are. I—don't understand, Cathy. But I want to. Whatever you're scared of, I want to share it; I don't care what it is. I want to share your fear."

She pulled away from him and stared into the night sky, at Vulpecula. "Sometimes I have the strange thought that I'm not human."

Sherwood looked up at the stars. The hairs on the back of his neck prickled.

He tilted her face back and kissed her. "You're close enough for me," he said.

Against his lips, she whispered, "I think the monsters are coming."

F O R T Y - F I V E ...

▼

A sudden noise on the front porch. Woodrow bellowed out and thundered angrily down the stairs.

"Jesus!"

Eric Holmes jumped awake, swung out of bed and bounded half asleep down the stairs in his pajamas. What the hell time in the morning? The Marans seemed to obey no rule of time; they thought nothing of getting him out of a deep sleep in order to terrorize him.

"Jesus Christ!" he growled.

If--pray to God--it was the Marans. Of course it was; the Bhutaran wouldn't be softly and politely tapping at the front door. Woodrow was roaring now, and growling in the living room. To be sure, Eric automatically slid the .38 caliber pistol out of his desk, the *Gota killer*.

"Woodrow, be quiet!"

He glanced out the window at the porch, where Relomar and Kosan stood, unperturbed, as if two in the morning were any normal time.

Eric opened the front door and grouchily welcomed them in, Woodrow sniffing at them and wiggling excitedly at the surprise company.

"Did we wake Cathy?" Kosan whispered.

"I—I don't know." Eric gave them a cold look. "It's—like two o'clock in the morning?"

"Yes, we wanted Cathy to be in bed," Relomar said. "Asleep."

Eric gave him a look of dread. "Why? What—"

"Take a moment to wake up, Teacher," Kosan said. "All apologies for disturbing you, but Relomar and I have been discussing certain things, and we feel that now is the time for you to learn more."

Eric stared at him. "Learn more."

"That's what you've always wanted, Teacher, isn't it? To learn more?"

- 262 -

"I—I'm not sure."

"You already know more than any human ever has," Relomar said. He was idly rubbing Woodrow on the back. "You have had to know things."

"Things a mad-man believes," Eric said. "What is this? Is Cathy in danger? Is my daughter in danger?"

"Possibly," Kosan said.

"Oh, Jesus Christ! Oh, Jesus!"

"I always told you that this day might come, Teacher."

"Oh, Christ! Okay—what? What now?"

"Gota may be near," Relomar said gently. "We think it unlikely, but we're not sure."

"Oh, God…" Eric Holmes stared out the window of the farmhouse, at the dark two o'clock Blue River Valley. Two o'clock courage, his mind said. Some quote from an old history class.

"That Bhutaran. All those years ago. My God!"

"The Bhutaran hold long grudges," Relomar said.

"Okay, okay." Eric stared out the window. "So what now?"

Kosan let out a heavy sigh. "Now, you bring out the tal."

"The—okay, the diamond; the tal."

Eric went to his office safe and scrambled the combination. He nervously took out the jewel. Composed of the element called plexium. It had powers…

"Hand me the tal," Kosan said. He traded looks with Relomar. "We had a warm conversation regarding this," he said to Eric. "Whether you should understand anything about the tal."

"You Marans have a real problem with trust, don't you?"

"Don't be insolent, Teacher."

"Then don't get me out of bed at two in the morning and scare the living crap out of me!"

"Eric, calm down," Relomar said. "We have discussed the matter, and we agree that you should know what the tal is, and how it can be used."

Eric stared at him. "It's a weapon, of course."

"More than that," Relomar said. "We speak of this to you, but Cathy can know nothing yet. She can only have the tal if—if something happens."

"Something—what's going to happen?"

"Rel, show him and let's get this over with," Kosan said grumpily.

"Take this." Rel handed the diamond to Eric. "Can you do anything with it?"

"No, I don't think so."

"But Cathy can—maybe. Each facet of this crystal is a power," Relomar explained. "Each face controls energy waves; each face can create a Flux. It is controlled radiation, just that."

"The Mist is too." Eric stared at them.

"Yes," Kosan said. "Everything is controlled radiation."

"So why can't I control the radiation in this—tal?"

"You haven't developed the ability," Kosan said.

"But Cathy—"

"We believe she can," Relomar said.

Eric turned the diamond in his hand. Helpless in his hand; and in Cathy's--?

"Each face of this diamond is a power." He stared at Relomar.

"Yes. The power of invisibility; the power to communicate through the Spaceway; the power to create and the power to destroy."

"Melt?" Eric asked.

"Yes: this face here."

Eric turned the diamond until blue flashed in his eyes. "This is melt. What I saw back then."

"Yes, this can make Melt."

"Focused gamma rays."

"Something like that," Relomar said. "This face here: invisiblity to optical light. Here, immediate communication with the Spaceway. This one, the yellow--"

"No," Kosan interrupted. "I think that's enough for now, we don't want to overwhelm him. We tell you this, Teacher, as a precaution, nothing more. We tell you this so that if Cathy has to have the tal—"

"Will she!" Eric demanded.

Uncle Rel and Grandpa Kosan exchanged looks, which didn't help at 2:30 in the morning.

"We think no," Relomar said.

"This is all we will tell you," Kosan said.

"So…" Eric looked at them. "I'm supposed to try and teach her how to use this thing if Gota—what!!!"

"Calm yourself, Teacher," Kosan commanded. "I was against telling you this, and Rel convinced me. He convinced me that you have earned the right to know more."

Eric stared out the window at 2:30 in the morning. He rolled the plexium diamond in his hand, gazed at its glittering colors. He didn't want to know more, but he had to. "This whole thing is coming unraveled. My God, every day of my life I wondered when she would find out."

"She has found out nothing," Kosan said. "And it is vital that Cathy know nothing of this. Cathy must know nothing about what she is—she must live a happy life here on Earth. She cannot know about the Bhutaran. She cannot know what she is."

"And out of the dark past comes Gota," Eric said. "If I can't use this thing..." He tried to hand the tal to Relomar, but the man refused it—"Then how can I teach her to use it?"

The Marans exchanged looks. Kosan spoke at last: "We think Cathy will know how to use it—if ever she has to."

"She'll already know?"

"Possibly," Relomar said. "We can't be sure. But for now, she can't know about the Bhutaran or any of that."

"Only," Kosan warned: "If Cathy is in danger, give this to her."

"And she'll know..."

"Nothing is certain," Rel said.

"If something happens, Teacher," Kosan said to him. "Give Cathy the tal. Otherwise not—forget about it."

"Take a breath, Eric," Relomar said. "We are only trying to prepare you. Gota will not succeed. We will first establish a neutralizing field around this farm that interferes with Mist waves. If Gota discovers us and enters this field he will have no Mist to protect him."

"Nor will Cathy?"

"That's correct. But the Mist is no protection against Melt anyway."

"Other precautions have been taken," Kosan added. "Gota is alone, we believe. He has no support, he is essentially killing himself. Signals we received from our scanners lead us to believe that Bhutaran hunters are after Gota. If they kill him, then that will be a wonderful end of the danger."

"Why is he after Cathy?"

"Because she was never meant to be."

The Marans bade their farewell and left the night. Eric Holmes stared a long time out the window at the darkness.

Quiet now. Horror quiet.

Woodrow came up to him, rubbed his leg. Eric absently scratched the dog. No going back to sleep now.

Marans—not human—leaving the night; leaving the name—Gota: some grotesquesness that wants to kill my little girl.

A sound startled him.

266   The Blue River Valley

What!

He turned around and looked at his daughter, who stood before him in her Albert Einstein pajamas.

"God!" he grabbed at his chest. "Cathy! What are you doing up?"

"Woodrow was barking." She stared at him. "Daddy, what's wrong?"

"Nothing," he said. "Go on back to bed."

"No. What's wrong?"

"Nothing! It was just Uncle Rel and—"

"Grandpa. I know who it was. What did they mean?"

"Mean by what?"

"Daddy—what are the Bhutaran?"

He stared at her. Sixteen years of fear and the dragon suddenly jumped awake. "Cathy…"

"The Bhutaran. Tell me what they are."

He couldn't hide his bloodless face: "You're not supposed to listen in on private conversations. What your grandfather and your uncle and I talked about is—"

"About me," she interrupted. "And *is* my business. What are the Bhutaran?"

Eric was grey with fear. That the end of the coma would come so quickly and horribly out of the night. "Cathy, you were listening in on a conversation that you never should have been—"

"Daddy, what are the Bhutaran? What is Gota? What is the tal?"

"You shouldn't even be up at this hour."

"They kept saying the Bhutaran. What are they?"

"They're nothing," Eric said. "Your damned grandpa and his brother— Uncle Rel—woke me up—actually, it was Woodrow who woke me up—at two in the morning…"

"I know," Cathy said. "Woodrow woke me up too."

"And there was your grandpa and your uncle. Now it's almost three a.m., Catherine, and I don't feel I have any explaining to do."

"Yes, you do." Cathy gave him a sad stare.

Eric's heart dropped. If it had been an angry stare he could have dealt with it.

"Oh God!" he broke down. "I love you, Cathy. You are, you'll always be my little girl, my precious. Nothing else matters. I love you more than anything in the world."

"What are the Bhutaran?" she asked him.

He looked into her jade eyes. He swallowed hard at his throat.

"What *am* I, Daddy!" She stared at him. "For God's sake, tell me what I am!"

He tried to hold himself together. He stared for a long time at the wall.

"You're right," he said at last. "I'd better call in sick tomorrow. And I think I'd better get Kosan and Relomar on their cell phone, bring them back. It's time. God give us strength, it's time."

Her dad suddenly cringed and cried into his hands, and Cathy hugged him, scared. "Bring my uncle and grandpa back, Daddy—I need to know."

"Yes," Eric sobbed in his daughter's arms. "My God! I told them they couldn't keep it from you. I always knew this day would come. Ah, Jesus!"

Cathy let out a great sigh. "It doesn't matter. I'll always love you," she said.

"I'm sorry, Cathy!"

"It's okay, Daddy. You tried to protect me, Uncle Rel and Grandpa tried to protect me. But I already know."

Eric stared at her. "Know what?"

"I'm not human," she said. "I've known that for a long time."

"Your mother was human."

Cathy gave him a sad smile. "And my father?"

F O R T Y - S I X ...

▼

Sherwood North rumbled his 650 into the Holmes yard. Cathy had invited him over for a quiet game of chess, but her voice on the cell phone was otherwise, and he sensed that this was not to be, and something was incredibly wrong.

Grandpa Kosan stood in the yard, staring at him in the headlight. Sherwood parked his bike, ripped off his helmet, traded stares with the man. He smelled the unmistakable smoky odor of doom.

Okay, whatever is happening here, I'm going to find out. Sherwood is not the dull fellow you all thought. Now I need to know what is going on.

Grandfather Kosan, so stately and menacing, like a wizard in a video game, even more menacing than Woodrow, who barked mightily at the night. And there's good old Uncle Rel, smiling in the background. Now, at last Dr. Holmes appears on the porch, with a ghastly white and shell-shocked Miss Mason.

Sherwood approached the farmhouse porch, a bizarre thought jumping into his brain that the porch was yellow with blue trim and looked so rustic with the swing hanging from chains; that a mourning dove cooed out of the calm prairie evening; that it was a Nebraska farm, lost in its quiet beauty.

He stared at them all, knowing something was going to happen, something was really wrong.

"Hello," he said cautiously to them. "Cathy invited me over..."

"Yes, Sherwood, I asked her to." Dr. Holmes' face was ill, almost drained of blood.

Sherwood stared round at the other haunted faces. "Where's Cathy?"

"She's in her room," Eric said.

"Is she all right?"

"No," Grandpa Kosan said to him. "I'm afraid not, Sherwood."

- 268 -

"Not?" Sherwood looked at Grandpa, then Dr. Holmes. "What's wrong here?"

"Sherwood," Dr. Holmes said gently. "Sherwood, we need to tell you things before you see Cathy. This is all going to sound insane to you, but we might not have time to let it sink in. What we have to tell you will seem unbelievable."

Sherwood felt a terror in his gut, tried not to show it. He looked at Susan Mason, who wore that stunned and devastated mask. He stared over at Kosan. "There's some kind of danger, isn't there?"

"Yes," said the grandfather. "We are all in danger, but Cathy most of all."

Eric Holmes let out a long, mournful note. His voice quavered in the dark: "Come inside, Sherwood, we have to tell you things and we have to do it quickly."

"They told you, Sherwood," she said.

He stepped carefully into her bedroom, leaving the door open, the rule whenever he was here. He stared around at the nest of science and knowledge and fascination she had built in this sanctuary. Can it be true? How can it be true?

He looked at her. "Well, they—they told me—some very crazy things..."

"Do you believe them?"

"I—I don't know...not really....that's some—"

"It's true," she said almost matter-of-factly. "I've suspected it for awhile."

"Suspected—Cathy that you're this alien/human Planet Mara thing?"

"I've always wondered if I was somehow adopted," she said to the window. "But lately I've sensed things happening out there, beyond Earth."

She began crying into her hands, and he immediately went over and lay on the bed with her, holding her, letting her cry against him.

"Cathy." He stroked her hair and tried to shake off the out-of-body disbelief. Can this be some sick and elaborate practical joke?

Not unless everybody involved was an Academy Award winner.

He swallowed at fear and took a deep breath. Choe had taught him all about fear, how it has ways to creep into you, like rootlings, slow and treacherous; and then how it sometimes leaps out of the dark at you, a panther.

270   The Blue River Valley

This was obviously the panther, and Sherwood tried to stop blinking his eyes. To wake up. He struggled to yank his brain out of the whitenoise.

They traded stares for a long moment.

"Whatever this is," he finally said. "I'm with you to the end. I'll see this through with you, whatever it is."

"No!" she cried. "Don't you get it, Sherwood? You need to stay *away* from me. You can't be around me anymore."

"What? Like hell. Why?"

"What you've seen and heard here is never going to be believed anyway, so you shouldn't be talking about it."

"Cathy, they tried to tell me that your dad was an alien from outer space! Some place called Mara? Come on, tell me the truth. What the hell is really going on here? I deserve to know."

She took his face gently into her hands and gave him a sad smile. "You don't understand, you don't think any of this is true. You don't understand what I am."

"Don't give me that. You're half space alien? Come on..."

"Well, never mind!" Cathy looked away. "You need to go now anyway. Go now, Sherwood, and never come back."

He stared at her for a long time. Neither of them seemed able to speak. At last he took a deep breath. A deep breath reminds you that you're still alive, Choe had advised. A deep breath is the enemy of fear.

Let's hope.

"What if the thing goes after me because I know about this? I wouldn't have anybody to watch my back," he played along.

"You're acting brave, Sherwood, because you don't believe any of this is true. Don't make me scare you away by showing you that it *is*."

He chewed his jaws and stared into her eyes. "I'll make a deal with you, Miss Holmes: if you can scare me away—without doing me any physical damage or pain—I'll run like Forrest Gump. If you *fail* to scare me away, then I get to stay the night."

"Stay the night."

"I'll call my folks and tell them I'll be home tomorrow some time, and not to worry."

"They trust you that much?"

"No, but I'll think of something."

"No, Sherwood. When you find out that all of this is true, you'll get out of here and never come back."

He tried to fight the dread with bravado: "Hey, bring it on, Missy. But remember, no physical abuse."

"I won't touch you," she said. "See this?" Cathy opened her palm, revealing a slender crystal.

"Cubic Zirconium?" He tried to sound cool, but his voice came out squeaky. Can this be--? No, this is one strange and kick-ass dream, that's what it has to be, one strange dream.

"It's called a tal," Cathy said. "Watch this, Sherwood."

Holding the diamond in her fist, she slid off the bed and stood before him. She wore a plain pink Nebraska sweatshirt and faded blue jeans, but never before had she looked so witchlike, her eyes glittering green. Sherwood took a deep breath, steeling himself, and tried to keep the shivers off his face.

"Now you see me," Cathy said.

Suddenly she vanished before his eyes.

Sherwood went into shock: "Oh God! Oh God! Oh Jesus God!"

"Now you don't," said her voice. "I'm still here, Sherwood, but not in visible light."

"Oh God...Cathy, come back! Ah...Jesus!"

Suddenly she reappeared and Sherwood jumped back, banging the back of his skull on the headboard of her bed. He gawked at her, not believing, not believing this.

"I was never gone," she said with a sad look. "I was only out of the visible light spectrum."

"Visible—Oh, my God!"

That familiar look, telling her she was a terrifying freak.

"Now you see that it's true, all of it. If you say this to anyone, they'll think you're insane," Cathy said, trying to sound cold; but then pouting suddenly, her eyes making tears. "Goodbye, Sherwood," she cried. "And thank you."

He stared at her as if she were not real. "Thank—what!"

"For wanting to be my boyfriend."

He stared into the frightening green eyes. "Cathy, I—My God, I can't believe—No, don't cry."

She sobbed miserably into her hands and he immediately slid off the bed and took her into his arms. He could feel his heart pounding against her, and he fought his scrambling brain.

Finally she pushed him away from her. "Now go, Sherwood. Go away and never come back here. Please!"

He took a long breath. Don't be a puss, was all his shocked brain could come up with.

His hands were shaking, and he had a mega-caffeine moment. He stared around at the science and art museum that was her bedroom: nothing ordinary but the bed.

272   The Blue River Valley

Can this be true?

He traded dumb faces with a purple stuffed pterodactyl in the corner. He couldn't stop blinking his eyes, although he knew it upset Cathy. He looked over and traded eyes with the giant dog Woodrow, who was watching, worried, out of his own big watery eyes.

Finally Sherwood could stare up at her. She stood crying, her face set in that familiar pout. He saw how scared she was, and he summoned a peaked smile. Don't wake up from this, he told himself. Not just yet.

"Is that the best you can do?"

"Sherwood, you have to go! This is not some—"

"Cathy, you lost, I won. I won the bet, so live with it. If there's some *thing* coming after us, then why waste time trying to weasel out of a lost bet?"

"I see the fear in you," she said. "I see how scared you are."

"Well—Duh! Yeah, you just scared the ever loving crap out of me. But the bet was to scare me AWAY. I'm still here. That means you lost the Scare-off Sherwood Game. Ha! You can't do it with your mini plane and you can't do it with—that thing, that tal. This is my dream."

"This is no dream! You have to get out of here now."

"Hey, back to the point: What if the damn thing is after me too?"

"Sherwood's right."

They both jumped and stared around. Uncle Rel stood in her bedroom doorway, the yellow-maned wizard. Uncle Rel smiled at them: "Sherwood has seen too much and knows too much, and he could very well be in danger."

Sherwood felt a chill. He knew well and good that he was dreaming this; that this was some beautiful twisted Cathy Holmes dream. He tried to keep his mind from going into a panic, as you do sometimes in dreams, when they get too intense. This is what Choe called 'The Fall', the time of terror, when you're falling and you either let yourself die or you find a way to stop falling. But I won't fall, I'll wake up. But do I want to? No, I want to go along. This dream must mean something. I don't want to wake up from it.

"The—alien thing, guy," he heard his voice say to Uncle Rel: "That—thing…"

"The Bhutaran Gota," Uncle Rel said. "He will have no Mist if he enters the perimeter of this farm, and we will know immediately if he does. But he could be watching the place, hoping to catch Cathy or one of us in the open, so to speak."

"So to speak," Sherwood's voice said. He traded looks with Cathy. This is a dream, so I might as well flirt; anything can happen in a dream:

"I always fantasized about spending the night with you," he said boldly to her, making Cathy's face go red. "It wasn't this detailed, of course."

"One advantage," Uncle Rel said. "Gota himself is being hunted under a death paj; so he will have to make his move very soon."

"Like—tonight?" Sherwood asked.

Uncle Rel looked at Cathy, giving her a comforting smile. "Probably. If he is even still alive. Bhutaran cannot tolerate a planet like this. Earth herself might destroy Gota for us. But no one can leave the perimeter. We have decided, just to be on the safe side, that Miss Mason stay here this night, as well as Sherwood."

Sherwood felt a crazy fear-joy. He took a long breath. Keep this dream going, for God's sake! "So you see, Miss Holmes," his voice said. "Once again I have out-witted you."

Now that he was convinced this was a Superdream, he tried to keep from waking up from it: "I hope you have micro-wave popcorn, the mega butter kind," he made his voice say.

"You're not dreaming, Sherwood." Cathy stared out her bedroom window. "Oh God, you better call your folks."

They stayed up in her room while the grownups fretted downstairs, monitoring the Ultra-computer Uncle Rel had set up in the living room, the sensors and alarms. The house was so quiet that Sherwood could hear them pacing down there, and speaking in hushed voices. He finally got control of his blinking eyes. They didn't seem to be able to blink this away.

This isn't a dream.

Susan Mason brought up sandwiches and Cheetos and cokes. She managed a smile, but her face was bone white, and she seemed close to a breakdown.

"I thought—I—that maybe you might—that..."

"Thank you, Miss Mason," Sherwood said.

Her eyes avoided Cathy. Her voice was tight, jittery: "Do you—Eric was asking—do you want to come down—downstairs?"

"We will in a little while," Sherwood said. "I think we're just going to hang out up here a bit. Thanks for the sandwiches."

He smiled her out the door, took Cathy by the hand. She couldn't keep her strange eyes from the window, the murky night.

They stared together at the dark glittering prairie.

"Well," Sherwood finally said. "At least we don't have school tomorrow."

274   The Blue River Valley

She put her arm around him. They sat on the bed and stared out at the night, Sherwood stroking her long black hair. It was very quiet, only the sounds of crickets and the pacing of the adults below, and the crying wind.

Finally he said into her ear: "I suppose it's not a good time to demand a kiss, is it?"

She smiled and kissed him. He tried to get it out of his mind, what she had done, how she had vanished before his eyes. He held onto all that Choe had taught him about fear, and how to use it: To not let fear trick you into thinking that what is happening is not happening, to not let fear...Oh, God.

Not a good time to lose it, he told himself, taking in a deep breath.

"You said before that you thought you could feel yourself speeding up," he said.

"Yes." She began crying, and Sherwood took her to the bed and lay with her, stroking the long black hair.

"Whatever this is, I'm with you to the bitter end. I'll see this through with you. That's only because I like you—better than most people."

Cathy stared out her bedroom window. "I've been researching cross-breed hybrids," she said coldly. "The general rule is that when two radically different species manage to procreate, their offspring is almost always mutated, and unlikely to survive for long."

"What? Don't say that! Come on..."

"So it could be that my metabolism is speeding up and will eventually stop my heart."

"Cathy—"

"Or other organs; and I will die—unless that thing out there gets to me first." She cried at the night.

"What do your grandpa and Uncle Rel say?"

"They tell me it's Maran Puberty. But they don't know, and I saw they were worried and they didn't know. No one can say what will happen with me, or even what I am!"

"I know that one." Sherwood smiled at her. "You are, my love, and always have been, a hopeless gwerk."

She studied the night. "You and that stupid word."

"I'm going to coin it," Sherwood said. "Every poet worth his stuff has to coin a word. That's mine, GWERK!"

"I'm sorry, Sherwood." She took his hand. "I didn't mean to drag you into this, put you in danger."

"I don't see how any of this is your fault. Besides, these aren't problems, just—really bizarre obstacles."

"It's my fault that Gota wants to kill us all."

"How can this be your fault?"

"He needs to kill me because I'm something that never should have been."

"Well, you *are*."

Cathy cried into his chest. "Just when I got a life; and everything was perfect. A real life, with a mom and family here and I was feeling normal— but I'm not normal, I'm something that never should have been."

"You also have a boyfriend," he reminded her.

She looked up and stared out the window. "I tried to do as I was told. I tried to be the same. Now it's all some tragedy or something."

"No, no, let me correct you. I can tell you about a *real* tragedy. My cousin John was two years older than me; a great athlete and a great guy. He treated me as an equal, even though I wasn't even close. In fact, I was a skinny little loser. But he didn't treat me that way; he let me hang out with him, he taught me how to throw a football, a baseball—he never looked down on me or made fun of me. I worshipped him; I loved him to death."

Cathy looked at him. "And then he died."

"Yeah, he did, three years ago, you remember. He found out on his 15th birthday that he had inoperable brain cancer. He didn't get bitter or self-pitying. I'm sure he was scared, but he never showed it around me, and I never saw him cry, not even after they had cut open his head."

"I remember him."

"So, my cousin John was dying of cancer, what did he do? He went out for track, the high hurdles and the 100 meter dash. Then six months later he died."

Cathy sat silent for a few moments, rubbing Sherwood on the back. "Are you telling me to quit sniveling and feeling sorry for myself?"

"I'm telling you that I liked it better when you were snotty and mean and not a wuss. To be honest, it kind of scares me when you're sad and vulnerable. I'm Sherwood the Creep, remember?"

She laughed. "I'll quit being a baby."

"That thing," Sherwood said. "The diamond, the—"

"The tal," she said.

"Can I check it out?"

She put the diamond into his hand. Sherwood stared at it, held it up to the light.

"Okay, how do I make myself invisible?"

"It won't work with you," Cathy said. "You're not a freak."

"There are a lot of girls who would disagree with you. My take is that everybody's a freak."

"You have to be a Real freak to make that work."

276   The Blue River Valley

He handed the tal back to her. "Well, so much for my girl's locker room scheme. This thing might also be a weapon?"

"Yes."

"Okay, then don't let it go off by accident." He kissed her. Cathy was trembling, and he tried distracting her: "Now that we're camping out together and I'm finding out your deep dark secrets, I guess it's my turn to tell you one of mine."

"You're still a virgin."

"Hey, I didn't mean that dark."

He tickled her ribs and finally got the familiar giggle.

"Sherwood! Don't even think of feeling me up, I'll use my powers against you," she warned.

"No you won't. You like me a lot too much."

"That's not very literary."

"My secret is—I'm a cross-dressing female. Just kidding. No, my terrible secret is, I'm extremely double-jointed. Ever see the movie Deliverance?"

"I read the book."

"Yeah, no surprise. Now watch this."

Humming the opening strains of *Dueling Banjos*, Sherwood popped his shoulder out of joint and contorted his arm, forcing it back at a crazy angle over his head. "Help!" he cried. "I've just gone down the rapids after Ned Beatty's been raped by the hillbilly and Burt Reynolds arrows the redneck, and my arm—Owwwww! Pretty cool, eh?" he said under his contorted frame.

"God, Sherwood, that's gross."

"Yeah," he grinned. "You see, I'm a freak. And I'm proud of it. You don't hear me bawling like a baby."

"Up your butt."

"Bawwwww!" he howled at her. "The gross monster Sherwaloid terrorizes the innocent little cheerleader, forcing her to kiss his ugly, misshapen form! Baww-ha-ha-ha-ha! Now you must kiss the ugly freakish monster SHERWALOID—!"

"Sherwood…" Cathy said.

He glanced up to see Dr. Holmes standing in the bedroom doorway, staring at him.

He immediately popped his shoulder back and retracted his arm. "Dr. Holmes," he said. "Hello, Sir."

"Hello."

Eric gave Cathy a grim, guilty face. He quickly looked away from her eyes. "No signal," he said. "From—well, no signal from their sensors—the detection things they have." His eyes ventured to Cathy's. He let out a tragic sigh. "Are you—are you all right?"

"I'm okay, Daddy."

"Do you want some time alone?" Sherwood said, looking from father to daughter.

"No, no. I just—I—wanted to check up on you, that's all."

A truly uncomfortable silence.

At last Dr. Holmes gave another painful sigh to the floor. "Well, anyway…Sherwood, I made up the couch for you, the one in the den, I hope it's comfortable enough."

"It'll be fine, Sir." Sherwood gave him a dry smile. He should have known that one wasn't coming true.

"Cathy." Eric couldn't quite meet his daughter's eyes. "Susan would like to share your room tonight, if you—well…"

"That would be great, Daddy," Cathy said. "I'd like that."

Eric brightened some, put on a hopeful face. "She would too. She called it a girl's sleepover."

"I'd like that." Cathy smiled at him. "Don't worry, it'll be okay."

Eric gave her a desperate look. "Susan is kind of—well, afraid is putting it—I'm sure-I'm sure—mildly—and that all of us are—afraid…"

"It'll be okay, Sir," Sherwood said.

"Okay!" Eric avoided their eyes. He stared at the bedroom wall and seemed to go comatose for a moment. His face made a tortured scowl, and Sherwood saw the wretched guilt scour his face. He seemed almost insane with remorse.

"You're not to blame, Sir," Sherwood said to him.

Dr. Holmes' eyes flickered over, the paralysis broken. He stumbled backward into the hallway. Sixteen years of dreading this time, and knowing it would come.

"You two seem to be—to—I'll leave you alone."

His steps were halfway down the hall when Cathy called out, "I love you, Daddy!"

A pause. A sobbing reply: "I love you too, Cathy!"

FORTY-SEVEN ...

▼

The alarm on the brain screen sang out. They all stared at the device.

"Is that Gota?" Eric cried. "Him, the thing?"

Relomar studied the screen. "No, it's Choe Kwang-su."

"What? Why—"

"I called him over," Relomar said.

They watched the vintage 1968 Chevy Camaro roll up the drive. It parked, forming a strange group: Kawasaki 650, vintage Camaro, Honda Civic, Toyota Camry and the giant bully Hummer H3.

Eric looked at Relomar. "You invited him here, at this time."

"Yes."

"Why?"

"I promised him," Rel said. "I promised to tell him when the enemy was near."

"He has the right to know this," Kosan said.

Susan was clinging to him, and Eric stroked her hair. "Are you all right?" he whispered to her.

"Eric, I'm—I—"

"I know. God, I'm sorry—God! I'm so sorry, Susan! Forgive me!"

"Remember, we agreed to quit saying that?"

"I only dragged you into this because I love you. I love you so much I couldn't--"

Woodrow set up a terrible HOWL-and-BARK that scared everyone half to death. They watched Choe exit the Camaro and wander cautiously up to the house. Before he could even knock several voices yelled, "Come in!"

Choe stepped into a very nervous nest of people. He looked at Rel and said, "So, the enemy is at hand."

"We think so," Rel answered. "We'll know if he approaches, and he will have no protection when he enters the perimeter."

"He will not have *it*," Choe said, glancing at Eric Holmes. "This Mist."

"Correct," Kosan said. "He will have no Mist if he ventures into this zone."

Choe nodded thoughtfully at the golden eyes. "Will any of you?"

"No," Kosan said. "This is the chance we take. None of us have protection here."

"All right." Choe blinked his eyes at the floor.

Then he betrayed a very inappropriate smile. You lay back like a puddle of nothing in the comfort of old age, you become a soft old nothing—then suddenly you have enemies to fight once again, and the juices stir from their sleep. Now, strangely, you are something. The spirits have come for me at last, Mother. He performed the old reverent bow of childhood.

Thank you, Gods or spirits, or whatever you are. You have given me the chance to fight once more for my life. You have given me another chance to be a warrior. He hid the joy behind his hopefully inscrutable Asian face.

"Where is Cathy?" he asked.

"She's up in her bedroom," Dr. Holmes said, holding Susan Mason in his arms, a woman clearly in a state of shock.

"And Sherwood—I saw his bike in the yard."

"He knows, but he doesn't truly believe," Relomar said. "Sherwood's upstairs, with Cathy."

"Ah, of course," Choe said.

"We can only hope this doesn't traumatize him."

Choe gazed up the dark wooden stairway. "Don't underestimate Sherwood," he said. "May I visit them?"

"Yes," Eric Holmes said. "I think they'll be relieved to see you."

"I'll visit them briefly," Choe said. "Whatever this all means, they won't want an old man hanging around." He smiled at Rel. "You will let me know, I hope, when it is time to fight the enemy."

"Gota must attack soon," the Grandfather Kosan said. "He is being pursued by enemies himself."

"That can only be good news—I hope," Choe said. "I'll go on up and visit briefly with my students."

280   The Blue River Valley

"Oh, My God, Mr. Kwang-su!"

Choe came into the room, was stunned at the things he saw around him: her fortress of knowledge, her libraries and laboratories, her hidden and lonely chamber. Cathy embarrassed him by jumping off her bed and giving him a frantic hug. "Oh, God— Oh, My God! You came!"

He hugged her and blinked his eyes against tears. "Hello, Cathy. Hello, Sherwood. Yes, of course I came."

Sherwood was staring at him. "Choe! What the hell?"

"I won't bother you two for long," Choe said. "It seems an enemy is near." He patted Cathy's black waterfall of hair. "I don't know as much about him as I'd like to, but Eric says he resembles—a gargoyle?"

"He's a Bhutaran," Cathy said, pulling away from him. "The monster in my dreams. Mr. Kwang-su, I'm sorry! I never wanted to drag anybody into this—I didn't know!"

"Cathy, stop crying and sniveling," Choe lectured. "Have you forgotten my first and best lesson—Stop being a bawl baby. The world as it is does not tolerate bawl-babies."

"I'm sorry!" she cried against him.

Choe traded looks with Sherwood. A hopeless cause. He smiled at the boy. He sensed the spirits; he sensed that he would be given a last wonderful fight. Old age and stiff joints be damned, Choe smiled in eternal gratitude. Out of the dull puddle of old age life comes suddenly and savagely at you again.

"Your uncle invited me here," he said to Cathy. "They have explained things to me, of course."

"They think the—gargoyle thing, Gota—they believe," Sherwood said. "That he might try and strike tonight."

"All right." Choe stared out the bedroom window and felt joy and gratitude. "Then let him strike."

"He won't be able to generate the Mist," Cathy said.

"A good thing, that," Choe said. "But he will have the tal."

He looked at Sherwood, who was, of course, gazing at Cathy. He clapped his hands ceremoniously. "All right! I'll leave my two student warriors alone and go down and mingle with the other *old* people downstairs. Cathy, tell me you made some of your chicken wings."

She hugged him. Choe's moon face went red.

"There's a few in the refrigerator," she said. "You'll have to microwave them."

"No problem. So long as I don't have to fight Uncle Rel for them."

Cathy cried against his chest. "I love you, Mr. Kwang-su! I love you so much!"

"I love you too, Cathy." Choe hugged her and smiled at Sherwood. "One enemy and all of us," he reminded his student. He patted Cathy's black hair. "I think that together we might beat one small gargoyle."

"I'm sorry, Mr. Kwang-su!" Cathy cried against him.

"No need to be sorry," Choe said. He grinned at Sherwood. "At this moment I am happier than I've ever been in my life."

"What did he mean by that, Sherwood?" Cathy asked when Choe was gone.

"He meant that he's been allowed to fight for his life one last time."

"He's grateful for that?"

"Yes, a thousand times. I asked him once when I would have the right to call myself a warrior. He told me you can never be a warrior until you've fought for your life. Unless you have been in a fight for absolute life or death, you can never truly know. I think that's what he meant. Choe's fought a few times for his very life, and so I naturally asked him how that felt, to fight for your life and the death of your enemy. He said for him—and it made him ashamed to say it--it was an intensity that nothing else can measure up to."

Cathy rubbed nervously at the tal. "When Gota comes, I'm going to be the first to fight him. It's me he's after, all this is because of me."

Sherwood interrupted her with a loud, game-show blare. "Wrong as always, Miss Holmes. The thing is after all of us. I have longer legs than you; I can run faster than you."

"No. He'll have one of these. You will not—"

Again the loud nose-blare: "Where do you get off trying to give Me orders? You're sixteen, I'm sixteen and a half; I don't have to take orders from you."

"Sherwood, please. This is no joke. Don't you believe this is real? This is really happening!"

"I've been in love with you from the first second I laid eyes on you, Cathy. Just in case something goes wrong, I wanted you to know that."

Cathy smiled at him and stroked his hand. "But you were so far below me on the social and intellectual and athletic and good looks scale that it was out of the question. But just because I became very insane, and you're my boyfriend, doesn't mean you go charging out like some sort of poet hero trying to impress me. I want you to let me and Grandpa and Uncle Rel handle this—just in case. Please, Sherwood, promise me. Gota has a weapon that we all have. You're human, you can't use this weapon."

He stroked the long black hair. I'm her boyfriend. God, please don't let me wake up from this dream.

"I'm not going to let you—Miss Catherine Ann Holmes--deprive me of the chance to be a warrior. Squinch your face up at me all you want, if I get my chance, Baby, I'm taking it."

"I allow you to call me Miss Holmes," Cathy said. "But if you call me *Baby* again, I'll punch you into oblivion. If you're going to be my boyfriend, don't ever call me Baby."

Sherwood smiled at her in amazement. He didn't believe any of this was real, of course. This was some kick-ass dream that he would wake up from and literally cry because it was over, the dream he would carry the rest of his life. His mind actually told him to make sure and remember this when he woke up, because this was one bases-loaded bottom of the ninth homerun.

"You don't think this is real." Cathy shook her head at him. "I can see it in your eyes."

"Well, give me a break. It's not like your everyday—"

"Sherwood! This is real!" Cathy's eyes turned witchlike again, green, supernatural, intense. "This is truly happening!"

Sherwood smiled into her eyes. His heart bubbled pleasantly in his chest. "I like that when you make your eyes green and scary. But you're not going to scare off a warrior poet with your eyes, or by turning invisible, or sparkling your blue—sparkles—around him."

"God." Cathy looked out her bedroom window. She rubbed the tal nervously in her palm. "God, Oh God Oh God…"

He stroked the long black hair. They were quiet for some time. They listened to the crickets, the wind.

"So." Sherwood tried to keep a violent grin off his face. "You've admitted that I'm your boyfriend. That you're my girlfriend."

"We're sitting on my bed together," Cathy said.

"That's right, we are."

"And you don't understand what we're dealing with."

"You do?"

"Yes, I do."

"Like how?"

Cathy looked away out the window. "I don't know how. I feel danger close, that's all. Real danger." She looked at Sherwood. "And it's close."

He fought the chills: "You're not the only one. Okay, so—being boyfriend and girlfriend and all that, maybe we should spend the time waiting for it—instead of worrying and fretting—maybe, I don't know, making out or something."

Cathy gave him a smile. "My brave hero warrior poet."

Sherwood smiled back. "Who kisses like the soft, delicious winds of Heaven."

"No. I truly feel like purging after I kiss you, Sherwood. I kiss you because I feel sorry for you, but you kiss worse than barf."

"You kiss so bad," Sherwood said. "That I want to wash myself with gasoline afterward."

"Then why do you desperately want to make out with me?"

She gave him a deep smile, her eyes dark emeralds now.

"Because, if we're waiting for danger and death to show up, I'd rather be doing that than arguing with you. If you're my girlfriend, then I should be making out with you. That makes sense, doesn't it?"

He stared at her. That loving face, the long cascade of black hair. My God, at last I've crashed on the rocks.

"My advice, Cathy, is that we make out until this thing attacks. Okay, we're sitting here waiting anyway. We're sitting here *waiting*: we don't have enough time to watch Lord of the Rings. Why don't we just relax and…"

"Make out," Cathy said.

"I want to make out with my girlfriend—Jeez, is that some terrible crime?"

"Only if you don't follow through with your threat." Cathy leaned into him and they kissed and lay on the bed holding one another.

When they came up for air Sherwood bit her ear, knowing it would cause Cathy to giggle. "So—I'm your boyfriend—and you're my girlfriend," he said. "This is true, I'm not dreaming?"

"Sherwood." She kissed him quickly. "You're not dreaming—this is really happening. The tal, the Mist, the Bhutaran, the monsters—this is really happening."

He smiled and kissed her. "I sure as hell hope so."

FORTY-EIGHT ...

The black pickup truck sat on the hill overlooking the Holmes farmhouse. Kyle sipped at the pint of whiskey and stared at the place.

Cathy down there, the Bewitcher. The house was strangely lit up, and there were several cars parked in the yard.

Must be one of their comet nights or something, but he didn't see anybody out looking at comets. He saw Sherwood North's Kawasaki standing down there. They must be having another nerd party. The parties I never got invited to.

Like what I'm doing, what I'm doing? I'm supposed to be in Memphis—Jesus, I could lose my scholarship. What the hell I'm doing?

He took a fierce guzzle from the bottle, falling into the self-pity that had only grown and become more bitter.

I'm a star athlete, I lead the team! God damn you, Cee, you made me believe you loved me. I give a little sophomore chick my ring and she winds up making a fool out of me, a joke. I make one screw-up and you can't forgive me? You did something to me; you put some spell—why can't I get you out of my damn brain?

Cathy, why can't you—why you driving me crazy?

He heard a noise outside his truck, he stared over. His drunken brain recoiled. A monster stared into the truck, a grotesque thing, panting and shaking.

Not real! He thought. Oh, God, oh God!

No! Not real! Not real!

"What!"

Kyle stared at the thing.

- 284 -

Its pink eyes squinted at him. It seemed sick, its breath hoarse and croaky: "Who are you--why are you here?" it demanded in a gruff, exhausted accent.

"Why—My God, what are you?"

"Is that the house where Catherine Ann Holmes lives?"

Kyle stared at the thing. "Cathy—why—"

The creature held up a strange jewel. A sharp spat of blue struck Kyle, and he felt pain so intense he screamed. The thing reached into the pickup and clamped a wrinkled paw over his mouth, choking him still.

"Silence! Or you'll get more," it said.

Kyle whimpered and moaned as the fire-pain subsided. He recoiled in horror, shuddering in the truck cab. The claw released his mouth.

"Oh, God! Mister—please! Don't taze me again!"

"Does Catherine Ann Holmes live in that house?"

"Yes!"

"Why are you here staring at the hybrid's house?"

"She—she used to be my girlfriend." Kyle stared at this thing. He felt his bowels go loose and he wet his pants. This wasn't human, it was some god-ugly demon. This can't be real, I'm having a nightmare...Oh Jesus, that terrible pain...

"So you have entered this property before," the thing gasped at him.

"Yes."

"And if you enter it again, you will not cause alarm."

"I—I don't know—"

"Human, do you want to feel the pain of this again?"

Kyle stared in horror at the jewel in its paw. "No! Please, please! No, I won't cause alarm."

"Good. You have saved yourself from much agony. I ask you again, human, do you want to feel the pain again?"

"No, please! I'll do anything! Please!"

"If you do not want the pain again, then you must do exactly what I tell you to do. Do you understand this?"

"Yes! I will, I will." Kyle stared at the terrible jewel and whimpered. "Please! I'll do anything!"

"You will help me climb into the back of this vehicle," the monster said. "You will drive down there. If you do this simple thing you will escape pain beyond anything you can imagine."

"Oh, God!" Kyle pleaded. "No, please! I just want to get out of here."

"Perform this simple duty, human, and you will have your wish."

"I will. Just drive down there, then I can leave?"

286   The Blue River Valley

The creature's pink eyes squinted at him. "Yes. It will take some time for me to crawl out of that bin. After that, you are to leave immediately and not look back."

The alarm went off and they all studied the scanners.

"What is this, Eric?" Relomar asked. "This black pickup truck?"

Eric glanced out the window. "Oh, Christ, it's that damned quarterback. It's—oh man, it's Cathy's ex-boyfriend; that quarterback. What in God's name is he doing here?"

"The boy in the black truck," Kosan said, staring out the window. "The boy who said he no longer wanted to be her friend, and made her cry."

"Does he come here often?" Relomar asked.

"Too often," Eric said.

"Why does he come here this night?"

"I don't know. He loves Cathy, I don't know."

Choe Kwang-su watched the black truck drive in and park in the yard. He blinked his eyes at it. "This Gota is a cunning thing?" he asked Uncle Rel.

Relomar studied him. "Very cunning."

"Then I believe I'll take a walk," Choe said. "Get a little fresh air."

Relomar watched him exit down the hallway and out the back door. Rel stared at the black truck parking in the yard. "What do we tell this quarterback?" he asked Eric.

"God, I don't know. I don't know!"

"Get rid of him," Kosan said to Eric. "We need no more distractions, Teacher."

"He sits there waiting for Cathy," Eric said. "He—he comes around—I don't know what he wants. He always wants to talk to Cathy."

"We need no more distractions," Kosan said. "Gota will attack soon, I can feel this."

"I can as well," Relomar said.

Eric stared at them. "What do you mean?"

"Choe Kwang-su senses it," Rel said. "Why does this boy come here?"

"He's got some kind of obsession," Eric said. He looked fearfully at Susan. "I don't know, I don't know!"

Kosan and Relomar traded stares. "Why does he just sit there?"

"I told you before," Eric said. "He knows I don't like him, he sits there in that truck until Cathy comes out to talk to him. Woodrow doesn't like him, I don't like him—he sits there like that. I'll tell Cathy to get rid of him."

"No, wait," Relomar said.

Cathy looked out her bedroom window. "It's Kyle," she said. "What in God's name is he doing here?"

Sherwood stared down at the black pickup. "He's supposed to be gone—to Memphis."

"There's something wrong," she said.

"Why is he showing up tonight?"

"I don't know. But something's wrong."

Sherwood felt a flutter of fear. "Maybe we should go down and see."

"Yes, we should."

He touched her hair as they scampered down the stairs. A sting of jealousy. She's my girlfriend, Bluto. Go away and play football, for God's sake.

The adults in the living room gave them stunned looks as they appeared. Sherwood smiled at a very pale Miss Mason.

"Cathy, get rid of him," Eric said. "It's not a good time to have this—"

"No, wait," Relomar said. He studied the black truck, Kyle sitting there looking scared at the house. He looked at Kosan.

"We'd better not take any chances," Kosan said.

"I'll go out and see what he wants," Cathy said. "I promise, I'll get rid of him."

"No, wait," Kosan said. "Relomar is right. I feel something."

"So do I, Grandpa," Cathy said. "I feel something."

Sherwood looked around. "Where's Choe?"

"Out there," Relomar said.

Sherwood stared out the window at the black truck. Kyle looked sick. His face was a Greek mask.

"I'm going to take a walk," Sherwood said.

"A walk?" Cathy looked at him.

"Yeah, a walk. A walk in the trees."

She stared at him; then she glanced out at Kyle's truck. "I'll go with you."

"No, you don't have to, Cathy."

"Yes, I do."

288   The Blue River Valley

"Why?"

"Because I'm your girlfriend. Daddy, I'm going to take a walk with Sherwood," she said.

"Cathy, no! You will not leave this house!"

"Daddy, I have to. I'm sorry, I have to. Let's go for a walk, Sherwood."

"Sherwood your boyfriend," he grinned at her.

"No!" Eric cried. "You're not—"

"The boy has a strange expression," Kosan said, staring out the window. "That boy is very afraid."

"We must be careful." Uncle Rel looked at them. "Something is wrong."

"He's out there," Cathy said. "I know that Gota is out there."

"Sherwood! Cathy, no. Stay here!" Eric cried.

It was too late. She left the room and went bounding out the back door behind Sherwood.

"Cathy!"

"We must follow them," Kosan said. He studied the brain screen. "Turn off all lights to the house, Eric. Get down to your basement and take Miss Mason with you."

"What's wrong?" Eric said. "Is Cathy in danger?"

"We must go out there," Kosan said. "Gota is here."

Choe watched the squat shadow crawl slowly and tediously out of the pickup bed and waddle into the shadows of the trees. The pickup immediately spun round and roared away back out the drive.

Choe's throat caught in mid-breath. It's true, it's all true! That was the Bhutaran Gota. It's all true.

Suddenly he heard the back door of the farmhouse ease open, and saw Sherwood, then Cathy sprint madly across the yard and into the shadows. Moments later Rel and the grandfather spilled out of the door and ran crouching into the trees behind them.

Well, they must know. Choe moved from tree to tree toward where the thing had crept. He moved slow, and often stopped to listen, wishing he had the ears of his youth. He was angry at Sherwood and Cathy for dashing so recklessly into this danger.

Now I will have to move fast.

Gota crouched down behind a dense bush, panting, trying to get his senses back as his tiny sweat pores were crushed dry by the dense humidity. He was almost spent; he would soon drop from exhaustion and the awful toll this world was taking on his body.

Now at the end it was vital that he think clearly; yet he could feel his brain shutting down with his body. His eyes glowed crimson as the torture spread, and he blinked them at the darkness.

It was perhaps always destined, this Flux in the Foam. What he had done was coldly planned, but it was also mad. He understood now that the Ty-cee were right: the hybrid meant nothing. But the hunters would know that his hunch had been correct; when the sensors on their ship went out, indicating his death: they would know something had killed him, and it could not have been an Earth human.

He would still try to destroy the Maran Kosan, if he could, the one who had rendered his duty and his life meaningless, the Maran who had long covered up this crime and created Gota the Thief, the Betrayer, the Shamed.

Destroy the Maran Kosan if you can, his foggy mind thought, and at least have some purpose, some dignity in death.

He took gulps of the poison air and managed to stand. But his mind was swimming and he knew he would have to act fast. He was getting irrational; the cloudy air was interfering with his very reason.

He tried his legs, but they soon buckled, and he crept back behind the bush. No strength to attack, he would have to stay here and let them come to him.

He lay in the watery night, summoning all his remaining faculties and energies, for he knew he would only get one opportunity. He listened to the darkness, swarming with insects and night birds: this world a sickish miasma of life. He knew that he could not generate Mist. But it didn't matter, nothing could save him. He must kill whatever enemies he could until his body dropped into shock.

At last he heard movement. Grasping his tal, he crawled to the edge of the bush and peered out. He saw the tall figure sprint from behind one tree to another. It was the ex-ambassador Relomar. Gota had never understood his part in this story, but no matter. All stories end, none can be explained.

There is no time left, Gota's brain said, clawing against a steamy lethargy. He aimed the tal, squinting at the figure running out from behind the tree. The blue tube of Melt blistered the air, a wild shot blasting one of the cottonwood trees and setting it to blaze.

Now comes the end.

He had missed the Maran Relomar, and he rolled quickly away as a blast shot out at him from another direction. The night lit up fiercely blue, the bush exploded in flames. Gota saw the Maran Kosan out there. Tapping the last of his strength and sanity, Gota crawled to his feet. He aimed the tal at Kosan.

As he sprinted out of the trees, Choe Kwang-su tried to get the flashbulbs out of his eyes, the sparkles from that blinding blue light. The creature was about to shoot his weapon again when Choe launched himself into a flying kick. His foot burst into the gargoyle and it collapsed. One last blast of melt shot recklessly skyward, scorching the air and temporarily blinding Choe. He smelled the queer odor of fried air.

Sherwood went after the thing at a dead sprint. It turned its shattered face to him only to feel the explosion of another flying kick.

Sherwood went into a rage, pounding this ugly thing with his fists until he heard her voice:

"Sherwood, stand back!"

He froze: Cathy's voice. He looked around at her, then down at the battered thing.

"Sherwood—Stand Back!" Cathy yelled at him.

He obeyed, drew away from it. He saw the beam of blue shoot out of Cathy's palm and the monster burst into blue rags and was gone, the ground spattering in flames.

The Bhutaran hunters in the main ship saw the Melt blast upward into the night. Gota's life-signal blinked out. They stared at one another in wonder; then each felt a relief.

"Look, Gota is dead," the pilot of the commandeered ship radioed them.

"Yes we see. Very good for us, we will not have to go to the surface."

"He must have taken his own life."

"Or they sent another team and they got to him first."

The Hunters peered down at the dark surface of Earth. There was no way to fool the life signal, Gota was certainly dead. The pilot steered the main ship upward and the Bhutaran crafts shot into space. Once outside the atmosphere they sent a message through the Spaceway for instructions, although they knew they would be ordered back to Bhutar. They had the stolen and repaired ship, Gota was dead, the Melt had erased all evidence of his existence. Why risk remaining here?

"This mission is over," the pilot said. "Good for us."

"Bad for Gota."

The hunters prepared to escape back into the Spaceway and away from this miserable world.

FORTY-NINE ... .

The Ty-cee representative stood before the Gathered and requested Death Paj for all Marans involved in the conspiracy.

There is no conspiracy, the Maran Directorate argued. The Maran fleet is on maneuvers, nothing more.

A violation of the treaty Mara signed. A theft of great amounts of plexium.

No. The fleet was dispatched before any treaty was signed.

Why has it not been recalled? The Gathered asked.

Mara is unable to contact Commander Zarya, or any ships of the fleet.

They have entered the Ferro Belt. We request that the Bhutaran Fleet be permitted to engage them there and neutralize Commander Zarya and all others who engaged in this deception and violation of treaty.

The Ferro Belt is not in Bhutar's proximity, said the Gathered.

Ty-cee claims the Rights of Conflict.

There is no conflict, said the Maran Directorate. We are no longer at war.

It is apparent that Maran commander Zarya remains at war, said the Ty-cee.

What of the plexium?

The fleet is supplied with plexium, of course.

Zarya took millions of ingots of plexium, far beyond what any fleet would need.

Ty-cee requests a Bhutaran expedition—

Mara is no longer at war with Bhutar, said the Maran Directorate.

It must be an organic force if it is to enter the Ferro Belt, said the Ty-cee. Commander Zarya is now an outlaw, beyond the command of Mara. Therefore, he is beyond the normal rules of warfare. Commander Zarya

- 292 -

conceived and executed a secret and illegal plan. He has commandeered much of the fleet of Planet Mara without authorization. Others conceived this plan with him, Ambassador Kosan included.

Kosan is no longer an ambassador of Mara, the Directorate said.

Ty-cee requests Death Paj for all Marans involved in this action.

The Gathered, political creatures, were torn. To appease the Ty-cee would set a dangerous precedent. Powerful they were becoming, but they could not be allowed to dictate: that would upset the tenuous balance of the Foam. Organics could not be allowed to rule, nor could machines, regardless of their abilities.

Political creatures, the Gathered (most of them organic, a few metallic), decided on compromise, which is another word for balance: They ruled that Death Paj against Zarya and Kosan and any others accused was premature and should be suspended but not dismissed. Further developments were in order before any violation of proximity could be permitted.

No living things exist in the Ferro Belt, the Ty-cee argued. Proximity should not be an issue.

The ruling stands, said the Gathered, with trepidation. The Ty-cee suit against the Maran commander Zarya is suspended but not declined.

The Gathered had ruled. Now it was to see if mechanical beings would obey. If not, a very great galactic war could erupt and possibly envelope the galaxy. How strange that a mere fleet commander could in his defiance trigger such a possibility. A ripple in the pond disturbs the Foam exponentially.

The ex-ambassador, Maran Kosan, was instrumental in this piratical endeavor, the Ty-cee continued. Other Marans were involved, ex-ambassador Relomar for one.

Death Paj is suspended, for the time being. Suspended but not declined.

Such is compromise, such is politics: the shrewd and practical balancing of the powers of the universe—or lessons in futility?

The Gathered had ruled, yet even the Gathered were in the dark. The Flux shifts, the Foam sends ripples or tidal waves, no being can say which.

Metallics were moving to rule. The wise could see that. Forms present themselves and power shifts toward or away. The organic beings in the Gathered understood that survival depends on control.

But how to control that which can understand at the speed of light?

They all saw, in the flat plane of the Ty-cee representative's *face*, that the balance was upset, and maybe had been long ago. The organic beings in the Gathered began to understand that this might not be a war for plexium, but a war for survival.

294 The Blue River Valley

The power of these metal beings, and their calculating computer minds... things that could not feel or taste or love or regret—insects of metal, with only the need to conquer and spread.

It was said that the Foam only favors the most powerful things. And power taken to the limit is power that has no weakness. Organic beings, soft and able to feel, are the weaker by far. Pure electricity and super-evolved alloys--the Ty-cee--beings that, as they spread and conquered, might become gods...

F I F T Y ...

"You kiss like what pops out of the Devil's zits," Cathy said to him.

They took a break from the martial arts exercises, the pummeling she always delivered to him. Mars City lay quiet and tired and bored out the school window.

"All right!" Sherwood panted, toweling his face. "Satanic zit juice--that's what I was going for."

Cathy stunned him by giving him a hug and putting her spearmint lips against his. "What do I kiss like?" she asked with her tongue.

"Like—changing gum?" He grinned against her lips.

That was their big sensual thing now, kissing and trading gum. Sherwood's tongue pushed a wad of wintergreen into her mouth and Cathy's tongue pushed a wad of spearmint into his, and they chewed each other's gum as they kissed.

Strange, impossible events throbbed between them now, but the sharing of the chewing gum seemed to blot them out. It didn't matter.

This was beyond all the universe. What matters...the chewing gum.

"Ah!" Choe called out, entering the gym. "My students are *understanding* one another, that's good."

They unlocked their lips and looked at him, embarrased. They stopped hugging and sat down respectfully on the mat.

Choe sat down cross-legged. He stared for a time out of the school, at the small Nebraska town. Then he looked at them.

"So, we have all gone through an interesting experience, haven't we?"

The silence grew as they both stared at him and he refused to speak. He read their faces.

Finally Cathy, of course, spoke: "Mr. Kwang-su, this is all bigger than—"

"Nothing is bigger than you imagine it to be," Choe cut her off suddenly. "Unless the Rocky Mountains, which your uncle nagged me into taking him to look at, next week. You see, Cathy, I know how to interrupt too." He smiled and looked over at Sherwood. "Secrets are known—so?" He looked over at Cathy. "We can either let these secrets turn us into cowards, or not. You have fear in your eyes, both of you; and I don't like seeing fear in the eyes of my students. The Honorable Tran Lee would be angry at me, looking out from those long dead years, if I were to allow my beloved to choose fear over courage. He would have slammed my skull into a post in his shame and disappointment.

"So I ask you, my warrior students, to choose: Will we go on stewing in fear and worry, or will we not? Will we control these things we have seen and get on with it, or will we decide to be pussies: Sherwood?"

"I vote against pussies," Sherwood said.

Cathy giggled. "I vote against pussies."

"I second the motion." Choe smiled at Sherwood. "So, my best and favorite students: do we press on with courage, or not?"

"Yes, by all means, Choe, we press on with courage," Sherwood smiled.

"Cathy?"

She chewed the wintergreen gum of Sherwood. She looked at them: "We can't go back," she said.

"That's a brilliant statement, Miss Holmes," Sherwood said. "How perceptive."

"Up your *rear end*, Sherwood. I'm more perceptive than you'll ever hope to be."

"And more modest and humble. Yeah, I can see that, Cathy."

"You kiss like worms, Gwerk."

He smiled at her.

They stuck their tongues out at one another.

"It seems," Choe smiled at them. "That we, in some very immature way, agree."

Cathy grinned at Sherwood. "We agree," she said.

THE END